JESSICA ANN DISCIACCA

AWAKENING THE DARK COURTS

DARK FLAME
PUBLISHING

JESSICA ANN DISCIACCA

AWAKENING THE DARK COURTS

DARK FLAME
PUBLISHING

AWAKENING THE DARK COURTS

DARK FLAME PUBLISHING

Dark Flame Publishing books may be ordered through booksellers or by contacting Dark Flame Publishing online:
JessicaAnnDisciacca.com

ISBNs: (Paperback) 979-8-9910142-8-1, (Hardcover) 979-8-9910142-9-8

NOTE TO READER

CONTENT ADVISORY: This fantasy novel contains elements that may be unsettling for some readers, particularly those who may be sensitive to themes of violence, including sexual assault. Within the realms of this fictional world, some depictions and discussions touch upon such challenging subjects. The intention is to weave a compelling tale while being mindful of our readers' wellbeing. If you anticipate that encounters with these themes might be triggering or discomforting, we recommend exercising caution and considering whether to continue with the story. The fantastical nature of this narrative does not diminish the potential impact of these elements, and we prioritize the comfort and mental well-being of our readers. Thank you for embarking on this fantastical journey with us, and may your reading experience be enjoyable and mindful of your emotional boundaries.

To those who've had to fight for everything they have in life .... I see you ... I understand you ... I am you.

CHAPTER ONE

Erendrial

T he dark court whispered around me as I made my way towards the line of contestants for the princess's hand in marriage. The other three challengers, Soddram, Therosi, and Avalon, stared at me as if they would strike at any moment. I knew if I didn't win, my head would be on the chopping block regardless of which contender won.

I was born low class, which meant I had no right to enter this tournament. Yet here I was, risking everything I had worked for, to win the hand of a female who currently despised me. After the tournament, I needed to get my head examined. That was ... if I made it out alive.

I was confident about the first challenge. It tested our intellect. I was far more competent than any of these idiots. The second challenge would test our combat skills. I was good, but so were Therosi and Soddram. They would surely team up to eliminate me. The third challenge tested our willpower. That category was up in the air. I didn't know what to expect.

The tournament master, Ravion Sterling, who had assisted the king in designing the challenges, was an artist when it came to the mind. He was what we called a Visitor. He could enter another's mind to see both memories and current circumstances. I had never seen him work in this capacity, so I was, yet again, at a disadvantage.

I looked up at Princess Genevieve; the reason I had completely lost my mind. Her beautiful white lace dress hugged her small, desirable figure perfectly. Her soft dark curls framed her face as they fell from the updo. Her green eyes stared down at me from her flawless face with rage. An emotion I was getting used to seeing when she looked at me. I would fix this. I would win this thing for her and for myself.

I couldn't bear the thought of her marrying another. After everything we had been through, we deserved a second chance. I would break through the walls she created after those demons tortured her while taking my form. I would comfort her as we mourned the loss of our child. I would care for and protect her for the rest of my life. I just needed a way in, and this was it.

"If there are no more entries into the tournament," said the king, "I will now turn the floor over to Ravion Sterling to begin the first category. Good luck, lords ... ambassador."

Ravion stepped forward while the sound of excitement erupted from the crowd. He was a short alfar with long black hair and pale cream eyes. His face was round, and his brow was defined.

He looked at each of us and bowed respectfully. "Lords and ladies," he began, "welcome to the tournament. It has been my honor to assist King Drezmore while designing the three challenges that will test our contenders' natural gifts and abilities to determine who will have the honor of becoming the next King of Doonak.

"The first category will test each of your intellectual strengths. This challenge was designed to assess your knowledge of our Princess Genevieve. For this test, you will visit three simulations. Your mission is to find the true princess. Once you are certain she is the real one, you will take the marker that is attached to her dress.

"If you choose the correct princess, the marker will teleport you to the next simulation. If you choose incorrectly, you will be forced out of the challenge. Whoever can find the three princesses first will be our victor. The court will be able to watch your movements through mind projection, but the contestants will not be able to see the court or the royals. Are there any questions?"

None of us made a sound. I could win this with little effort. Out of all of us, I knew her best.

"Excellent." Ravion smiled. "Let the tournament begin!" He raised his hands; his eyes rolled into the back of his head, only leaving the whites visible. The room around us began to tilt and turn, causing the four of us to lose balance and fall to the floor. The gold marble surface of the throne room rippled as we slid down the cold stone, trying to grab onto anything we could. The court members and the royals faded away before we plummeted into darkness.

Bam! I hit the ground hard. My body vibrated with pain from the impact. I looked down to see dirt and rocks, before slowly standing to my feet. I was outside surrounded by tall hedges. There were paths leading multiple directions.

Great, a labyrinth. The sky above was blue with white, sparse clouds. Birds chirped and wind rustled through the leaves of the greenery. The other three contestants were nowhere to be seen.

I took a deep breath and chose a path, walking hesitantly through the maze. Around each corner I expected to see Gen, but there was nothing. For the next twenty minutes I searched while the sun beat down on me. To prevent myself from going in circles, I took off my jacket and began tearing it apart for markers, tying the pieces of fabric on the hedge every few feet.

The maze led me around a long, curved path that opened into a circular courtyard. *Finally, something different.* The courtyard revealed three separate paths. In the center sat Gen. She was wearing a beautiful green gown. Her hair was loose, and her cheeks were pink from the sun. She lay on the ground playing with flowers that surrounded her.

I stopped before approaching closer. It couldn't be this easy. Ravion said there'd be more than one princess. He was trying to trick us. I had to make sure she was the right one. Soddram rushed around the corner of the path in front of me. He stopped abruptly at the sight of her. Out of breath, he looked at her and then at me. He hesitated, then took a step forward.

The princess sat up and locked eyes with him. She smiled, reaching out while she laughed with happiness. I stepped closer. Soddram darted towards the princess, grabbing the black marker that hung from her waist. As he pulled it from her dress, the sky went dark and the ground around her began to shake.

The princess's skin turned white as snow, revealing blue veins that spread through her body. Her beautiful face elongated, and her mouth filled with sharp, flesh-ripping teeth. Nails sprang from under her skin before she launched towards Soddram, tearing and ripping through his shirt and flesh.

His screams were filled with pain as blood and meat saturated the courtyard. Soddram lay lifeless, his remains spread throughout the green grass. His remnants began to fade away just before she turned towards me, locking her eyes onto mine. I knew I was next. I took off running back through the labyrinth as she hunted.

I could hear her slashing and growling closely behind me. The sky began to change back to blue. The winds calmed and the ground settled. I stopped, checking behind me to see if she was still in pursuit, but she was gone. I bent over and took a deep breath, trying to calm myself. I went on, now fully aware what my fate would be if I chose the wrong princess.

After another ten minutes of wandering aimlessly, I came across an open space shaped in a hexagon. There was a large tree in the center of the landscape surrounded by lavender plants. A dozen princesses surrounded the tree, lying lazily among the herbs. They saw me approach. In unison, each one sat up, smiles on their faces. It was as if my deepest fantasy had come to life. *Stop it, Eren,* I thought. *Get your head in the game.*

I walked through the group while they reached for me eagerly. I bent down to one of them, taking her face in my hand. She turned into my touch, the way I remembered her doing the first night I had put her to sleep with my gift. She was warm and soft. She rubbed her lips across the palm of my hand. I stood up, going to another look-alike.

This princess reached for me, dragging her fingers across my cheek and down my neck. I closed my eyes, basking in the feeling. Azeer, how I longed for her touch. I looked back at her, but something wasn't right. She wasn't the real Gen.

I stood up and exhaled with frustration, then took a deep breath to calm myself as the smell of lavender and … sandalwood filled my nostrils. I looked around to see where the combination came from.

That was it. I was going to find the right princess by her scent: lavender and sandalwood. I moved through the group of them, taking large whiffs as I passed each one. She had to be around here somewhere. Avalon came around the corner and stopped, looking at the group of clones. I got towards the last three behind the tree before the scent got stronger.

My eyes locked on the princess the smell was emanating from. She looked back at me and giggled. I smiled, reaching for her. Suddenly, the sky went dark as the ground began to shake. I turned to see Avalon holding the wrong marker in his hand. All the look-alikes turned on him. Their beautiful faces morphed before they lunged for their pound of flesh. I turned back to my Gen just in time to see her taking off into the maze.

I ran after her as fast as I could, trying to catch her before the horde caught up with me. She turned back as her long black hair flowed in the wind. She laughed, her nose scrunching while her eyes sparkled. She was the one.

The horde of look-alikes began chasing me through the maze. They crawled on the sides of the hedges, jumping and snarling towards me as they inched closer. I ran as fast as I could towards my Gen. She turned and swerved throughout the maze while the others slashed and screeched behind me.

The maze had begun to break apart. The ground a few yards in front split just as my Gen made it across. A huge pit now stood between her and I, but that wasn't going to stop me. The hedges fell away as the others yelled and screamed, hurtling forward.

Just as I went to jump across the pit, one of the creatures slashed at my leg, cutting a deep gash into my calf. I flew through the air, barely making it to the other side. I fell to the ground, reaching for my wounded leg. Pushing the pain out of my mind, I stood up, looking for my Gen. The sky faded to blue as the creatures from the other side rescinded back into the labyrinth.

I made my way into the clearing when she appeared in front of me. She smiled at me, reaching out and caressing the side of my face. I leaned into her warm touch, breathing deeply. Lavender and sandalwood. This had to be her. I held my breath and pulled the marker from her dress. She laughed, stepping back into a bright light.

The labyrinth faded and the sky around me began to spin faster and faster until I was forced to the ground. Finally, the room stopped. I opened my eyes, greeted by the throne room. The court was laughing and dancing while music flooded through the air. I stood up and looked around, trying to find Gen. The princess waltzed in the middle of the dance floor, laughing in a beautiful light blue dress. The same dress she wore the night after I made love to her. She had looked breathtaking that evening. I wanted to take her back into her room and strip the dress from her body, but my stubbornness and arrogance prevented me from doing so.

I moved forward, but stopped. There'd be more than one Gen here, just like in the maze. *Think, Lyklor.* You're back in the court. Her home.

The only other person left in this challenge was Therosi. He knew her scent and would have figured out which one was really her back in the labyrinth, but he didn't know her like I did.

I stood for one more moment, taking in the sight of her smile while she spun across the floor, before I left the throne room. She loved the library. She loved to fly. Azeer, she could be anywhere. Wait, it was dinner time. The court was dancing after dinner, which meant it was night, which meant ... the stars.

I rushed to her room as quickly as I could. I flung the doors open and went to her balcony. Gen stood under the stars. The wind blew the loose strands of hair around her face. As I approached, she turned towards me and smiled. She gestured for me to join her. I walked hesitantly, still unsure if she was the right one. Her eyes lit from the light of the stars, each green iris sparkling.

"Aren't they beautiful?" she asked softly. I didn't say a word. "Do you know why I love them so much?"

"Because they remind you of your freedom," I replied.

She smiled and nodded. "No matter where I am, I can look up at the stars and they will always be the same. They're my constant. Reminding me that no matter where I am, I'm always free," she said, turning towards me. "Will you dance with me?"

"Of course," I replied, reaching around her waist. She took my hand and placed her other on my shoulder. I pressed my head against hers, gently gliding around the balcony. I could have stayed like this forever, feeling her safely in my arms, being this close to her. It was all I wanted, but she wasn't my Gen. I had to get back to her, even though I never wanted this moment to end.

I tugged the marker from her dress, pulling away so I could look upon her face one last time. She grinned before she dissipated into a million twinkling stars. A massive force of air slammed into me, sending me off the edge of the balcony, plummeting to the ground. I screamed and flailed as everything went black.

I opened my eyes and found myself sitting on a bench in The

Frey. Humans walked through the marketplace, gathering bread and goods. Children played with streamers in the air. The buildings were old and dilapidated, but they still used them as storefronts for their businesses. I stood, realizing I was in Gen's old town.

Okay, think, Eren. Her favorite place in town. Where is it? She loves her family. The church. She would be at the church. I took off towards the Christian temple, barreling down the stairs into the basement. I flung open the door to a large, poorly lit room. Eight thin mattresses with tattered blankets sprawled across the floor. A table sat off in the corner with a pitcher of water, a loaf of bread, and a jar of strawberry preserves. There was a vanity with a broken mirror in the back.

This was how she had lived for the past eleven years. She had nothing, and yet she found a reason to live. She found people to love, and she put them first. At the vanity, Gen giggled and smiled as Lily brushed her hair. She turned to her sister, her eyes so full of love. She whispered something, causing Lily to burst into another fit of laughter.

I smiled, taking a step towards them. That was my Gen. It had to be. Lily was the person she loved the most. She laced a headband around Gen's head, covering the tips of her little pointed ears.

I stopped. Something about this didn't seem right. The church was gone. It had burned. It shouldn't be here. It was no longer her favorite place, and Lily was no longer the person she loved most.

I headed back out of the church and followed a dirt road towards an old, rundown house. There was a small bench in front of the structure. There, Gen sat peacefully, looking out into the field. I sat next to her, following her gaze to where four children played in front of us.

Gen grinned, taking in the joy of the children. She wore a simple black dress and held a small jacket. Her hair was half-up, away from her face. She wore her star pendant, but no other jewelry

She turned to me and smiled with surprise. "I didn't think you were going to be able to get away from court," she said softly.

I didn't know how to respond. I smirked, trying to play along. "They didn't need me anymore," I replied.

"Well, I am glad you were able to escape. She is going to be so excited to see you," Gen said, turning back to the children.

"Who?" I asked.

Gen opened her arms just as a little girl, no older than four, came barreling into her. Gen smiled, wrapping her arms around the child. The little girl giggled, holding onto Gen tightly, her nose crinkling as she flung back her curly head of black hair. Gen kissed her on the cheek over and over again.

The girl wore a black dress with white and silver stars sewn throughout. She opened her eyes and peered at me. Silver irises swirled around her pupils ... just like mine. She had my eyes, Gen's hair, her nose, and my smile and dimples. The girl's eyes widened with happiness before she leaped into my lap, wrapping her little arms around me.

"Daddy! You came!" she said in the sweetest voice. She pulled back, taking my fingers into her tiny hands. I tightened my grip around her small, tender hand. The memory of Gen's dead body laying in that cave came rushing back like a tidal wave. In that moment, when I realized I had become a father, yet lost the child before I ever knew of it, a level of grief I didn't know I possessed overwhelmed me. The loss of a life I hadn't known I wanted was almost too much to bear. Tears began to fall down my face as I looked at the daughter I would never know.

"I'm here, sweetheart," I was barely able to say.

She wiped away my tears and kissed me softly on the cheek. Ever so slowly, she brought her little lips to my ear before whispering, "I love you, daddy."

I closed my eyes, holding onto her as tightly as I could. I reached for Gen's dress and tore the marker from her, still grasping onto my daughter's body, committing the feeling to memory. Everything around me faded as I kept my eyes closed, holding my daughter's beautiful little face in the forefront of my mind.

The dark court reappeared in front of me. I stood with tears still running down my cheeks. How did Ravion know about the child? He must have seen her in Gen's memory, which meant her father knew as well. I couldn't bring my eyes up to look at Gen or her father. I held my head down, not wanting the memory to fade from behind my eyes.

"What happened?" asked Therosi. "His visual went dark. Did he complete the challenge?"

I looked up. They hadn't seen the last few moments, which meant neither had Gen.

"It must have been a glitch in my projection. Apologies to the court," replied Ravion.

I took a deep breath, gathering myself. I would draw her sweet little face after, but for now, I had to get ready for whatever came next.

Chapter Two

"Ambassador Lyklor has won the first challenge," announced the king, sitting on his throne.

The court erupted. There were some cheers of support, while others were enraged. That was to be expected. The king gave me a small nod and smiled. There was emotion behind his eyes. He knew about the child. This was his way of letting me know.

Ravion stepped forward. "If Ambassador Lyklor wins the next challenge, the tournament is over, and he will be crowned. If he fails, the winner of the second challenge will compete against Ambassador Lyklor in the third."

The other three contestants glared at me.

"The next challenge will assess your skill in combat," continued Ravion. "As king, you will oversee our military. You will need to think strategically under pressure. The objective is simple ... survive. If you endure a fatal blow, you will be pulled from the game and a healer will assist you. May the strongest alfar win."

The crowd roared. The room began to spin as the court was transported to an arena outdoors. We stood in the middle of a large circular structure, sand beneath our feet. The court members sat up in the stands and cheered. The heat was almost unbearable, and the air was dry and thick. Five stands of weapons lined the back walls of the arena.

A loud horn erupted through the air. The four of us took off running towards the boards. I grabbed two daggers, sliding them into my belt before grabbing a sword and ax. I turned to see Soddram rushing towards me, armed with two axes. He swung the weapons overhead and flung them forward. I rolled out of the way and brought my sword around, attempting to slash through his midsection.

He jumped back, bringing one of the axes down aimed at my head. I blocked the attack with my own ax as I stood to my feet, pushing him back. He turned quickly, momentum fueling the speed and power of his other weapon. I dodged the attack, clashing metal with metal. He was fast and strong, and almost double my size. I could out maneuver him, but if he got a blow on me, I'd be done.

I sliced his arm, cutting through the first layer of skin. He slammed the hilt of the ax into my face, shattering my nose. Blood spilled from my nostrils and my vision blurred. I heard a grunt from behind and turned to see Therosi preparing to attack with a long blade. I jumped back, forcing him to collide into Soddram. The two plummeted to the ground just before another horn sounded.

Therosi and Soddram got to their feet as four bright portals appeared around us. Avalon was nowhere to be found. I assumed Therosi had knocked him out of the game. Four creatures that I recognized from the rift came crawling out of the portals. The first was the acid monster Gen had taken out on her first mission. The second was a large, armored creature with a horn on the tip of its nose. It had a massive body and claws at the end of each foot.

The third was a winged beast the light court had taken down on their land. It had multiple eyes and a sharp, curved beak with talons on the end of each wing. The fourth was a nuckelavee, a hybrid melding of a skinned horse and a human body. Its flesh was red and raw, revealing the muscle and tendons. It had sharp teeth and claws.

Soddram, Therosi, and I stared at each other. I waited to see if there would be a deal made. We could work together to kill the creatures and then fight each other, but neither of them said a word. Instead, Therosi charged me, bringing his sword down towards my shoulder. I blocked it with my axe while he used the opening to kick me back to the ground.

The armored creature charged towards Soddram, knocking him back. Acid flung towards us as another monster appeared out of nowhere. Therosi swung and dodged the beast's sharp feet and claws. I readied to attack the abomination when I was suddenly hoisted into the air by the winged beast.

I slashed and swung at it with my swords, but I couldn't get a hit. Closing my eyes, I focused, imagining its wings bending and breaking apart. I sent out my gift and the creature yelled in pain as it lashed and spun in the air. Its grip finally released, sending me plummeting to the ground. I misted back to the center, taking note of my other two opponents.

Soddram was fighting the acid monster while Therosi attacked the nuckelavee. A hard galloping sound came from behind me. I turned just in time to meet the armored creature's horn as it slammed into my chest. I flew back into the air, landing on my back. My ribs felt like they had been shattered. It was hard to breathe while I fought to stand to my feet.

The creature came towards me again. I held my hand up, forcing its brain vessels to burst. It hollered, slamming its head into the ground. An alfar screamed behind me. I turned to see Soddram's arms and chest covered in acid. The creature's head lay on the ground, removed from its body. Soddram disappeared out of the arena.

I looked for Therosi, but couldn't find him. The nuckelavee laid in pieces a few yards away. I turned back to the armored creature, still reeling in pain. I walked over to it and slammed my sword into the soft hidden part of the neck I had read about in the autopsy report. It growled while I watched the life fade from its eyes. It fell to the ground before I pulled my sword from its neck.

I turned. Therosi misted directly in front of me, sword crashing into my chest. His eyes shimmering with excitement. I fought to breathe. Warm blood pooled in my chest. I gasped for air, but all I could taste was blood.

I blinked and reappeared in the throne room. Blood poured from me as I shook on the floor from the injury. It wasn't ulyrium, but it still hurt like a bitch. Vena appeared next to me, hovering her hands over my wound. I could feel my skin and muscles mending themselves back together. Once my lungs were clear, I took in a deep breath, desperate for air.

Therosi appeared with a smug smile on his face. He extended his hand to help me up. I took it, trying to appear like a good sport. He pulled me into him, bringing his lips to my ear. "When I become king, the first thing I am going to do is kill you, you lowborn piece of shit."

"Lucky for me, you will never be king," I replied calmly.

He narrowed his eyes as we both turned back to face the royals. Gen's face was empty of expression as she looked between the both of us.

"For the last challenge," began Ravion, "The king has requested he be the only one privy to the simulation. This challenge will test the remaining two candidates' willpower. It will challenge their morals, dedication to the crown, and their ability to make difficult decisions. Remember," Ravion said, looking at the both of us, "you will not only become a husband, but a king. What are you willing to sacrifice to ensure Doonak survives?"

King Drezmore came down from his throne and the four of us stood in a circle. Ravion took a blade and slit both of his hands.

He passed the blade to each of us and we did the same. The king grabbed our hands, as did Ravion. He connected our minds to his and then to the king's, so he would have a front row seat to the last challenge.

"Shall we begin?" asked Ravion. We nodded. Ravion's eyes went white before we were flung into the last simulation.

I opened my eyes to see the beautiful clear sky above. I lay upon a bed of thick grass; flowers surrounded me. The wind smelled fresh and sweet as it rustled over the earth. A body misted on top of me out of nowhere. I grabbed at it, readying to attack before I realized it was Gen. She laughed, her body stretching out across mine.

She wore a stunning cream dress that fluttered in the wind. Flowers were scattered through her thick curly hair. I wrapped my hands around her waist, pulling her closer to me, savoring the feeling. She sighed in relief, nuzzling her nose into my neck. I leaned into her face, smelling lavender and sandalwood. She pulled back and looked into my eyes.

"Don't let me go," she whispered before disappearing. I blinked once and was teleported to the light court. King Lysanthier stood in front of his throne, holding Gen by the neck with a ulyrium dagger to her heart. To his right was a podium with King Drezmore's crown. Next to it stood my family in ulyrium cuffs. Guards stood behind them with ulyrium swords to their necks.

The light court surrounded me, including Gaelin and Levos. Gen's face was wracked with fear while Lysanthier trailed his hand down her chest into the top of her dress. I lunged forward before two guards appeared on either side of me.

"Don't you touch her!" I roared.

Lysanthier laughed, pulling Gen closer to his body. "Now, now, Ambassador Lyklor. Don't worry. I will leave some of her left for you after I have had my fill. There's plenty to go around," Lysanthier said, licking up her face.

Gen grimaced as tears fell from her cheeks.

I fought to get to her, but I couldn't break free of the guard. "I will kill you, you disgusting son of a bitch," I roared.

He chuckled. "Is that any way to speak to a king? I think not. But I am a generous man. I will allow you this one pardon and in return, you will provide me with some entertainment for the evening."

"The only entertainment there will be this evening is your death."

"There will be death, but it won't be mine, ambassador. I am going to provide you with a choice. If you choose correctly, you will become my equal. If you choose incorrectly, it will mean your death. Are you willing to play?"

This was just a simulation. The fucker was dead. All the same, I still wanted to rip his head from his shoulders for touching her. "I'm listening," I spat.

"The choice is simple. Choose between Doonak, or Genevieve. If you choose Doonak, your family and your kingdom will be safe, while Genevieve dies. If you choose Genevieve, Doonak, along with your family and the court, will be destroyed." I looked at Gen and then to the crown.

This was just a simulation. They were testing me to see if I would put my kingly duties before my wife. That was how it should be. The king's priority was always his kingdom, but could I watch her die? Could I look upon her cold and lifeless body again? It wasn't real. She wasn't going to really die. This was just a test.

I closed my eyes, trying to erase the images of her mutilated body that still haunted me. I wasn't doing this to become king. I was competing in this tournament to become her husband. That was more important to me than anything—even the kingdom I had fought so hard to earn the respect of. She came before all of it now.

"Time is up, ambassador," spat Lysanthier. "What will it be? Your kingdom or this whore?"

I looked at the seven members of my family and then back at Gen. I swallowed hard, but I had to be honest with myself. "The princess. I choose Gen," I said boldly.

The seven guards in front of my family brought their swords up and down, slicing through each of their necks. Seven thuds echoed through the court. I looked down at seven familiar set of eyes that stared back at me, scared and surprised.

King Lysanthier tilted Gen's neck back before he shoved the blade through her back. The tip of the sword made its way out the front as he dragged it down slowly, creating a large slit in her torso.

I heard myself scream as her cream dress filled with blood. Lysanthier released her to the floor; her knees hit the cold marble floor. I pulled away from the guards, rushing to her side. I picked up her body and held it tightly against mine, trying to make the bleeding stop. Her body convulsed as blood poured from her mouth. Her eyes locked onto mine. Silent tears fell from them. I rocked her gently, trying to think of a way to fix her. I brushed her hair away from her face as the flowers fell to the ground.

"Please, don't leave me again," I cried. "Please ... you must survive. I can't bear to lose you again. Gen, please." She began to choke on her own blood as the light faded from her face. I held her lifeless body once again in my arms.

The room evaporated around me. I refused to remove my eyes from where her dead body had laid in my arms. Finally, I looked up to see Ravion, King Drezmore, and Therosi staring down at me. I was shaking and crying, trying to pull myself back into reality. I looked up at the throne to see Gen alive and well. It wasn't real. It was just illusion.

I pulled away from Ravion and the king, checking my hands for her blood, but they were clean. She was alive. It was just a test. One I had failed, which meant I lost the tournament. I had lost Gen.

The king returned to his throne. Therosi smiled victoriously at me. I dropped my eyes, realizing I had let my feelings get in the way of my mission. I couldn't bear to watch her die again, and yet my decision still didn't save her.

"I would like to thank each of our candidates for participating in the tournament," said the king. "You each have made your houses proud. The tournament revealed the true king within each of you, but only one can have the honor of calling my daughter their wife and, in return, becoming our next ruler. I am proud to introduce our next king of Doonak: Erendrial Valor Lyklor."

I snapped my head up as the crowd around me erupted with screams of excitement. What? How can this be? I failed. I chose her over the kingdom. No real king of Doonak would ever do that. Therosi looked at me and then at the king with pure hatred and rage. I looked up at Gen and couldn't help but smile. I had done it. I had won her. I had proven myself.

Her face was blank. She looked out onto the court, refusing to acknowledge me.

"This is an insult, to my house and to our kingdom," yelled Therosi, taking a step towards the king. The court quieted, eager to watch the drama unfold.

"Ambassador Lyklor has proven himself worthy of my daughter and the throne," stated the king. "How is that an insult?"

"The scales were not balanced," roared Therosi. "He was her keeper. He got to spend more time with her than any of us, which gave him the advantage in the first challenge. Then, in the last, no one saw what happened except you. How do we know who really won the challenge, when none of us saw what his test was?"

The king stood from his throne assertively. "How dare you

question my judgment? I am the king, and *I* know what is best for *my* kingdom. You each had your chance to spend time with my daughter in the months that she has lived here, yet none of you did. The blame falls solely on your shoulders," yelled the king.

"A lowborn should not be permitted to sit on the throne," spat Therosi. "It is a disgrace to our kingdom and makes us look weak!"

The king held out his hand. Therosi began to grab at his chest, fighting to breathe while his face turned blue and purple from the lack of oxygen. Finally, the king dropped his hand and Therosi fell to the floor, gasping for breath.

"Let me make myself very clear, *to all of you*," said the king, looking around at his court. "Erendrial Lyklor has completed the challenge, winning two of the three categories. He *will* be the next king, and he *has* earned his place among our court, regardless of the station he was born to. Never think to question the position of this crown again." He stopped, turning towards me with a small grin. "Erendrial Lyklor, please approach the throne."

I walked up to the steps and bowed before him. My eyes shifted to Gen, but she still refused to look at me.

"Erendrial Lyklor," said the king proudly, "do you accept my daughter's hand in marriage and the mantle of the future king?"

I looked up at him. I was about to get everything I ever wanted: respect, power, a title, but most importantly, her.

"I accept Princess Genevieve as my future wife and the mantle of future king," I said with pride. He signaled for me to rise as he stepped aside, allowing me to stand next to Gen. I held out my hand to her. She was hesitant, but took it. I smiled at her as we stood united in front of our kingdom.

CHAPTER THREE

I made my way back to my rooms, still in shock from what had just occurred. I had failed the last task. There was no way I won that thing fair and square, yet I didn't know why the king had announced me as the victor. Nonetheless, I was going to marry Gen. She was going to be my wife.

The doors to my room flung open as the seven members of my family came rushing in. Flashes of their severed heads came flooding back to my memory. I closed my eyes, pushing the illusion down.

Evinee yelled, "what in Azeer's name was that?"

Doria cut in, "you have lost your damn mind!"

Zerrial paced back and forth. "King! You're going to be king!"

"Explain," said the twins, Oz and Voz, in unison.

I looked at them, fighting to find the words. "I... I couldn't let her marry them," I said plainly.

"Why not?" asked Leenia.

I paused, not sure how to really answer that.

Evinee's face fell as her mouth hung open. "You love her ... don't you?" she asked softly

I looked away and ran my hands through my hair. My body was sore and tired from the past few hours of constant strain.

Doria began to laugh. "No fucking way. Erendrial Lyklor, in love?"

The twins looked at each other in shock. Firel stood off in the corner silently observing.

Evinee stepped forward, her voice calm. "You can't be in love with her. You just used this opportunity to become king, right Eren? This is just another power play. You saw an opening and you took it."

I looked up to see Gen standing in the doorway. I dropped my head, knowing she probably heard Evinee's speculation of why I entered the tournament. They all turned to her and bowed uncomfortably.

"Give us the room," Gen demanded.

They looked back at me for instruction. I nodded. The females came up and each gave me a hug. The males patted me on the shoulder. Gen closed the door after they exited and then turned back to me.

I knew this conversation wasn't going anywhere good. She was pissed. I went to the table and poured two whiskeys. I offered her one, but she didn't take it, so I shot hers back and then made my way to the couch. She followed without a word. She stared into the fireplace while I waited for my ass reaming.

"Congratulations," she said coldly. "You've successfully accomplished the impossible. A lowborn alfar has elevated himself to king."

"That's not why I entered," I said in a calm tone.

She looked at me with heavy eyes. "There's no point in keeping this charade up anymore, Eren. You've won. You've gotten everything you've ever wanted."

I leaned forward, looking at her intently. "I couldn't let you marry them. I couldn't sit back and watch them take advantage of you."

"Isn't that what you're going to do? Just as I predicted. You found a way to use me in order to elevate yourself."

"Genevieve, I entered the tournament for you. Not for the crown," I said firmly.

She smirked with amusement. "Let me make something very clear. You will never get another child from me, which means you will never have the power you so desperately desire. There will always be someone above you who is more powerful, and I will never let you forget it. As long as there is no heir, you remain muzzled. I will do whatever it takes to make sure that remains the case, which means I will do whatever it takes to keep my womb empty. Am I clear?" She stood to her feet before I could respond.

I couldn't even bring my eyes to hers. Every time she spoke, another small part of me died. I wanted to be with her. I wanted to raise a child together. I wanted everything I never thought I would, and it was because of what I felt ... for her.

She left me in my room alone. I finished the whiskey before throwing the glass into the fire.

At my desk, I gathered a piece of paper and charcoal. I lost myself in the soft lines of my daughter's face. The fullness of her cheeks. The almond shape of her eyes. How full and curly her hair was, just like her mother's. How adorable her nose crinkled. How similar her eyes were to my own.

The next morning, I got ready in my room, preparing myself for the next three days that would lead to my wedding. Tonight was the gift ceremony. We would each present the other with something meaningful. It was a tradition that encouraged the marriage to start off with selflessness. I had no clue what I was going to give her, since I hadn't expected to enter the tournament up until the last second.

"Good morning, Eren," Firel entered and greeted me.

"Morning, Fi, what can I do for you?" I asked.

"The king has requested your presence in his private chambers in ten minutes."

I ran my hands across my face. "It is too early for this."

Firel laughed. "I can't believe he is going to be your father-in-law. Are you going to start calling him daddy?"

"Azeer, no. He is my king, first and foremost. But maybe I will try it out, just to see," I replied, laughing with him.

"You know, I always knew you were a clever bastard, but I never expected this. I still can't wrap my head around it."

"You and me both," I agreed, walking past him out of the room.

I headed to the king's chambers and knocked. His servant let me in and led me to his seating area. The king nodded at me before sending his servants away.

"Good morning, Erendrial. How did the future king of Doonak sleep?" he asked, sipping on tea.

"Not much, honestly," I said, taking a cup.

He chuckled. "Yes, my daughter wasn't too thrilled with the outcome of the tournament. She spent most of the evening trying to get you dismissed. I'd watch out if I were you. The Otar creature might be paying you a visit."

"Don't worry, I've already thought of that," I murmured. I exhaled, gathering the courage I needed to ask about my miraculous victory. "Your majesty," I whispered, fighting with myself whether I should allow the next sentence to pass through my lips. "I failed the last task. I chose Gen over Doonak. I shouldn't have won. Why did you announce me as the victor?"

He exhaled, placing his cup on the side table, and folding his hands over his lap. "When I first saw Genevieve's mother, she was the most beautiful female I had ever laid eyes on," he began. "I had been alone for so long before her. I was in a cold and empty marriage. My side affairs were meaningless, and I had no heir. I was ready to give up and end myself, so I went into The Frey where I knew my guards would have trouble tracking me and I took a vial of ulyrium powder with me.

"At the time, I trusted my brother to take care of the kingdom. I was done living and I wanted to move on to whatever awaited me. I passed out from the poison and when I woke, I thought I was in heaven. The most angelic face hovered over me while she extracted the poison from my blood. Her eyes were kind and full of compassion. Her face was flawless, and her hair spiraled around her shoulders, framing the most beautiful smile.

"I was in and out for the next few days, but she remained at my side. When I recovered, I offered to pay her whatever she wanted for her services, but she wouldn't take my money. She told me she was just glad I was alive." He paused, huffing with amusement. "A human ... happy that a dark alfar had lived." He shook his head in astonishment. "I spent the next few days getting to know her. She knew what I was, but not who. She wasn't afraid, nor did she hesitate to help me. Her kindness knew no bounds.

"When I left her to return home, I felt like I had left a part of myself in that old rundown hobble. After a few weeks had passed, I went to check on her ... I couldn't stay away. I had to be near her, to hear her voice, to feel her touch. The light inside of her was so brilliant I couldn't stand to be away from it. She accepted me. She wanted me. She loved me. Something I had never known.

"Leaving her was the hardest decision I have ever made. She was truly my reason for living, but I knew if the court found out how I felt about her they would destroy her. I considered bringing her here to live, but I didn't want to stain her in that way. She had given me so much and I couldn't take her light away like that. I've been miserable without her the past twenty years. I thought I'd never get to be with her again ... and then I found Genevieve.

"She has so much of her mother inside of her. The woman I loved not only gave me a reason to live, but the most precious thing I could have asked for. A child. An heir."

"Though I am honored, why share such personal memories?" I asked.

"Do you know why I assigned you to Genevieve as her keeper?"

"Because you trusted me."

"Yes, I do, but that wasn't the reason. When you returned from the light court the first time, after the Otar battle, the way you spoke of her ... you were respectful and detailed, but I could tell there was more there. You were taken with her. The way you described her beauty and then her cunning personality. You smiled, Erendrial. It was the first time in one hundred years that I saw a genuine smile stretch across your face.

"I watched as things progressed between the two of you. You were fighting what had already taken root inside. She grew to trust and respect you. Then it eventually turned into more. When she died—" He stopped, taking a breath to regain his composure. "The way you mourned. The way you fought to save her. To avenge her. You were completely broken by her death. That day that I found you at the base of her altar, I knew you loved her.

"I declared you victor of the tournament because you chose her. You truly love my daughter, which means you will do anything to keep her safe. That is worth more to me than any kingdom ever could amount to."

I paused, letting his words wash over me. "She detests me. I don't know how to reach her," I admitted.

"She will heal in time. I can't begin to imagine what she has been through. What matters is that you will be there for her when she is ready to open herself to you again. That time will come."

"The first challenge," I said, thinking of our child. "In the last simulation, where the visual of my test glitched for the court. Did you do that?"

He dropped his head, pain twisting his face. "The child is what Gen imagined her to look like. Ravion pulled it from her memories when he was designing the challenge. I thought you would want to see her," he said. "She was beautiful. I'm sorry for your loss. If I could go back, I would have put my brother in the ground long before I knew of Gen."

"It isn't your fault, your majesty. He had us all fooled," I said, still thinking of my daughter.

"I pray to Azeer that I am still around when you two finally make amends. I hope to watch the two of you raise another child. I know it won't replace the one you lost, but that doesn't mean that another child won't bring you both happiness."

"I just hope I get that chance," I said.

A knock came at the door and Ravion entered the room. The king smiled, looking from Ravion back to me.

"Have you a gift for tonight's dinner?" The king asked.

"That was the next thing I had planned today."

"Well, I might have a way to help with that," he said, inviting Ravion to sit with us.

That night, I arrived first for the gifting ceremony. The room was larger than my quarters. A bed, fireplace, lounging area, and a round dining table filled with fresh fruit and food filled the space. Tonight's dinner was supposed to be romantic. Most couples would end the night in bed, but I doubted that was where we would end up.

I placed my gift on the table before nervously pacing the room. I straightened my clean pressed suit and checked my face in the mirror, making sure I looked my best. I heard the door open as I made my way to the center of the room.

Gen was in a satin black dress that hugged every curve of her perfect form. Her chest poured out of the top as the small straps clung to her shoulders. Her hair was long and loose against her back, just the way I liked it. She wore minimal makeup, her natural beauty shining through.

"You look stunning," I said, taking her in.

"You look nice as well," she said coldly. Maybe she was trying. It was a compliment after all. I was going to take what I could get. I pulled out the chair for her as she sat. I took the seat next to her, not wanting to be any farther away than necessary.

"Do anything fun today?" I asked, trying to seem casual.

"Wedding planning. Our colors are black, by the way. Hope you don't mind."

I laughed. "I don't care what color anything is, as long as I get to marry you," I replied.

She looked at me skeptically. She still didn't believe me, but I was going to change that.

"What did Levos have to say after the tournament?" I asked.

"He wasn't surprised that you entered, but he was surprised you won. He sent a message to the light court. I am sure they are going to be thrilled with the new development."

"Can you imagine Gaelin's face?" I asked, trying to make her laugh. She didn't say a word or even look up.

I didn't know where she stood with him. She talked about her time with King Fucker as if she regretted the relationship, but the way she acted when they were together painted a different picture. She was protective of him and allowed Atros close to her. Even after everything he did. Maybe she felt more for him than she let on.

"I told Otar about you this afternoon. I am sure he will be paying you a visit," she said, changing the subject.

"Have you finally given him what he wants? Permission to kill me?"

"No, but that doesn't mean I haven't thought about it."

"What's stopping you? If you truly think I am using you for the crown, then why not just kill me?"

She paused, putting her fork down on the table. She brought her beautiful eyes up to mine. "The night of our wedding. We will have to share a room, but I will not be sleeping with you."

"I wasn't expecting you to, and I would never force the issue," I said softly.

"You are welcome to take another that night, or any other night you wish, but it will not be me."

I reached for the hand in her lap. She allowed me to touch her for a second before pulling away. "I'll be fine, but thank you," I whispered.

She swallowed hard, looking across the table at the gift I had brought for her. I smiled, pushing the box closer. She hesitated before opening the lid. She unwrapped the tissue paper and pulled out the frame. Her eyes scanned the picture of her mother I had drawn. Her face didn't show any emotion. There was no smile, no sign of sadness, nothing.

"Your father allowed me into his mind to see her. I thought you'd want to have a piece of her on our wedding day. I hope I did her justice," I said.

"It's beautiful, thank you," she said, putting it back in the box and closing it. She stood, heading for the door.

"Where are you going?" I asked, standing to my feet.

She turned back and smirked. "Do you want your gift or not?" She opened the door. Three beautiful human women walked into the room, dressed in a variety of revealing lingerie.

I furrowed my brow in shock. "What is this?" I asked.

"Your gift. I figured I'd save you the trip to the gentlemen's club," she said sarcastically.

"Gen, the gifting ceremony is supposed to be something that starts our marriage off on the right foot. Your gift is supposed to be something that I can look back on and remember our day by."

"This is a representation of our marriage," she said plainly. "This is what I expect from you. To bed whatever female that crosses your path. I'll put these three on retainer so you can have them whenever you want, so you can think back to our wedding day with pride." She went to leave, but I rushed forward, grabbing her wrist. I turned her to me and looked into her eyes.

"I don't want them. I want you," I said with as much honesty as I knew how.

"You will be my husband in name only, nothing more. Time to get used to the way things are going to work. Enjoy your gift," she said, pulling away from me.

CHAPTER FOUR

"We have a surprise for you," said Voz as he and Oz led me through the city of Doonak.

"New weapon?" I asked.

"Better," replied Oz.

"What is better than a new weapon?" I asked.

"A group of beautiful naked females," Oz and Voz both said, laughing at one another.

I smiled at the two idiots. "Alright, alright. I guess I see your point," I replied, thinking of the only female I wanted.

They led me to a sealed-off section of the city that had been abandoned by the lower-class citizens decades ago. I followed closely, trying to figure out where they were heading.

They stopped at a dead end of the hall and turned back to me with devious grins. They placed their hands on the wall and traced a V with an L going through the center. Their hands circled the two intertwining letters as a doorway appeared, illuminated by dark magic.

"A V for Valor and an L for Lyklor," explained Voz.

"Welcome to your new headquarters, Prince Erendrial Valor

Lyklor," said Oz, smiling as Voz pushed open the door.

I stepped inside to see the rest of my family waiting for me. There was a lounge area, a dining table and multiple tables for planning. Weapons lined the tables and walls. There was a large library in the back and a small lab off to the side. A massive fireplace warmed the room. On the ceiling, stars shot across the surface of constellations filling the dark, vacant space. Dark magic swarmed throughout. Voz closed the door behind us.

"So, what do you think?" asked Oz.

"The twins have outdone themselves this time, wouldn't you say?" asked Evinee.

"This place is amazing, but what is it for?" I asked, still in shock.

"We thought, now that you are going to be king," answered Oz, "we needed our own private space to scheme and plot the downfall of our enemies. No one can enter this room except the eight of us."

"No one knows about these quarters," explained Voz, "and we have runed the shit out of it just in case. Also, the dark magic that we released into the space will protect it from being discovered, even if someone comes looking for it.".

"We thought you would like somewhere to go that you knew was safe," added Leenia.

I dropped my head, realizing what they were trying to say. "How many want me dead?" I asked.

They all looked at each other, daring one another to speak.

Zerrial stepped forward. "Five houses that we know of," he said.

"Servi and Yositru, of course. There has been talk from Sollerum, Gyset, and as of this morning, Rytorm."

I paused, thinking of how to handle the situation. I looked around the room at each of them. "I don't want any of you involved in this. Do not do anything reckless or stupid. Let me handle the houses. I made the decision to enter the tournament without consulting our team. I am responsible for the fallout."

Doria placed her hand on my arm. "You're our family. We're in this together. You would do the same for any of us."

"Though I have to say, you are an absolute idiot," added Leenia.

"Yeah," Evinee piped in. "I'm going to have to agree with Leenia beans over here. Couldn't you have simply fucked the princess and been done with it? I mean, do you really have to marry her? I thought being tied down to one female for the rest of your life was on your 'no, no" list. Not to mention your obligation to have a child. How miserable."

Doria dropped her eyes; her mouth fell open in shock. Pain over her expressions before she looked back up at me. The mention of a child ... I watched as everything began to click into place for her.

"The demons. They said—" Doria stopped before she finished the sentence. I closed my eyes, begging her not to say another word, but she had already said enough.

"What? What did they say?" asked Firel.

Doria pulled away from me. "Nothing. They were lying bastards. We can't believe anything they told us," Doria said, trying to cover. I reached out and placed my hand on her shoulder and nodded with a small smile.

That day, I told my family everything. I told them about Narella, every detail of the plot Prince Rythlayn had concocted, and then I told them about my daughter. I told them what the king had shared with me and my true reason for entering the tournament.

None of them said a word. What could they say? I had risked not only my hard work, but theirs as well, so I could have a chance with the female I loved. I owed them the truth. Especially if they were about to go to war to protect me from the other high houses.

After I had finished my story, I waited. I waited for them to yell at me or cuss me out. I waited for them to attack me or abandon me, but they just sat silently. Zerrial stood first, looking me square in the eye. He walked over and knelt before me.

"I, Zerrial Lightburne, pledge my undying loyalty to Erendrial Valor Lyklor, the next King of Doonak," said Zerrial.

I pulled myself forward from the back of the chair and looked down at my best friend. I pulled him to his feet and embraced him. "Thank you, my friend. Your loyalty and support mean more than you can ever imagine," I whispered in his ear.

He nodded, pulling away from me. Then, one by one, each of my friends knelt and pledged their loyalty to me. I wasn't expecting this show of support. I was truly touched by their declarations. Each one of them embraced me as I stood not knowing what to say for the first time.

Afterwards, we met around the table of our new sanctuary. We each claimed a seat and began to plan. Our first objective was to turn the houses to my favor. I couldn't be killing high lords and ladies as my first act as the crowned prince. I would go about this in a more peaceful, diplomatic manner. Though, everything inside of me was yelling for me to kill them all. If I was going to be king, I had to change my way of thinking.

Next, we discussed what my table would look like when I took the throne. I appointed Firel as the next ambassador of the dark court. He still had a lot to learn, but there was time. Zerrial would take charge of the military and training programs. Voz and Oz would take over the science and engineering departments. Doria would remain as the head of interrogation. Evinee would be our master spy, and Leenia would be welcomed back to court. Her name would be cleared of her parents' past sins, and she would be reinstated. I would place her over the high houses.

After hours of strategizing, I finally made my way back up to the castle. I had to get ready for the night of silence before my wedding tomorrow. This tradition was to allow the new couple to explore and discover each other without distractions. We would spend the night in an enchanted cottage below the mountain, unable to speak to one another the entire evening. Most couples used this time to explore each other physically.

I got dressed and headed down to the base of the mountain.

Evinee caught up with me before I could leave the castle. She handed me a bouquet of lavender and a bottle of whiskey.

"You got this," she said with a bright smile. "You can charm the pants off any female, regardless of their race. One small half-breed shouldn't be too much trouble."

Evinee was truly a beauty. She had black hair with streaks of purple flowing throughout. Her eyes were an entrancing shade of lavender. Thick lashes adorned each eyelid. She had large, curving lips and her smile could light up a room. Her skin was the color of porcelain. Her figure was desirable with curves in all the right places and a full chest.

"Thank you, but you obviously don't know Gen very well. I don't see this night going as I am hoping it will. Especially after how last night ended," I said.

She placed her hand on my arm and gave me a small smile. "If she can't see how wonderful you are, then she doesn't deserve you. Just so you know, my door is always open. So is my bed," she said with a playful smile.

I laughed, pulling her into a hug. "Thank you. I'm truly honored," I said, kissing her on the head before I made my way to Gen.

She was already in the small cabin when I arrived. The place was enchanted to appear furnished in the style we both preferred. Two red couches sat in front of the fireplace. Books adorned the walls along with artwork. Music played softly in the background. A table with a white cloth was lined with food and wine. A small bed, meant for two, was on the back wall. White satin sheets fitted the mattress, complemented by a thick cream comforter and two pillows.

As soon as I passed the threshold, I felt the enchantment take effect. I was now unable to utter a word. Gen sat in one of the chairs, looking into the fire. She didn't bring her eyes to mine. She didn't even turn towards me. Her hair was pinned away from her neck. She wore a loose white gown with a long black jacket that covered her shoulders. The same shoulders that would bear my imprint tomorrow.

I had never considered what my imprint would look like on a female, nor the significance of the meaning. The mark joined us in a way that was eternal. No two designs were alike, and the imprint only transferred to the female of your first marriage. It would be permanent ... everlasting. Something I had never experienced.

I went over to the seating area and handed her the bouquet of lavender. She took it, still refusing to make eye contact. I sat in the chair and poured us both a glass of whiskey. She shot hers back and reached for the bottle. Nothing more uncomfortable than being stuck in a room with a female who wanted nothing to do with you.

I stood up and offered her my hand. The music in the background was light, but it was enough to dance. I made a dancing gesture and smirked, trying to get any emotion to appear on her lovely face. She stood hesitantly and took my hand. I exhaled in relief and pulled her into me. Not as close as I once had, before her incident. I didn't want to frighten her, but I needed this. I needed to be close to her.

I started off slow, aware of my hands and distance to her the entire time. She looked at the floor as I moved us throughout the room. I pushed her out and twirled her back. She landed against my chest and froze, looking up at me with her big, gorgeous, green eyes. I took her in as I smiled down at her. She pulled away instantly, nervously fidgeting with her hands.

I took a step towards her, trying to make sure she was okay, but she reared back, putting distance between us. I froze, realizing I had pushed too hard, too fast. I stepped away, returning to my chair. She rustled through the room before making her way over to me with a quill, ink, and paper. She began to write on the paper, anger flaring behind her eyes. As soon as the words hit the page they disappeared, leaving no trace of what she was trying to communicate.

The cottage was enchanted. No communication in that manner whatsoever. She threw the ink and paper into the fireplace. She opened her mouth to yell, but nothing came out. Her mouth was moving, but I couldn't make out a word she was trying to say. I shook my head and shrugged to let her know I didn't understand. She gave a silent yell again before she charged towards me.

Tears filled her eyes while she beat her hands against my chest in a fit of rage. I held her close, taking the aggression she needed to release. After a few minutes of her fists landing in my chest and stomach, she finally calmed, pulling back to look at me. I was sore and most likely bruised, but I didn't care.

I nodded, letting her know it was okay. I reached for her face but stopped as she flinched. I continued to move my hand forward while I filled the air with my pheromones: oranges and whiskey. She inhaled, shaking her head no as her eyes filled with fear, but I continued. I knew she wouldn't be able to sleep on her own tonight, so I would just give her a little push.

Her eyes fluttered back before her body went limp. I caught her in my arms and carried her to the bed. Gently, I pulled the pins from her hair and removed her shoes before tucking her into the satin sheets. I ran my fingers over her soft face and long neck, then returned to the chair in front of the fireplace. After finishing off the bottle of whiskey, I laid down on top of the sheets next to her.

I didn't know if she'd ever willingly let me lie next to her again, so I was going to take advantage of this moment. I ran my hands through her hair, watching her inhale deeply. Her eyes fluttered behind her lids. She was dreaming. I wanted so much to take her into my arms and hold her, but I wasn't going to push myself onto her. Not any more than I had. Exhaustion finally took over, even though I fought to keep my eyes on her.

Crack! Pain burst through my face, jarring me awake. I opened my eyes to see Gen hovering over me as my jaw swelled. I brought my hand to my face just as Gen reeled back to land a second blow. I caught her arms and rolled her underneath me onto the bed. She fought and yelled, the sound of her voice filling the room. It was morning and the enchantment had worn off.

"Get off me! Don't you touch me, you sadistic son of a bitch!" She yelled, flailing underneath me.

"Gen, calm down. I am not going to hurt you. Calm down and I will let you go," I said.

"I'll calm down when you get your hands off me! Otar! Otar!" She yelled.

Otar appeared at the head of the bed in an instant.

"Get him off of me!"

"With pleasure, wicked one," Otar answered, smiling. The creature slammed into me with the force of ten men. I went flying back into the nearest wall . Otar appeared in front of me. His talons elongated as he brought his hand up to strike me.

"That is enough. I've got it from here. Thank you," she said, standing to her feet.

Otar frowned. "Can't I just cut him once, wicked one? Just so he remembers not to touch what isn't his," Otar growled. "If I kill him now, you won't have to marry him. This is a win-win situation for both of us."

"Otar, I said I have it. Now, please wait for me in my room," she said.

Otar yelled in anger and disappeared.

I stood up, feeling dizzy as my head throbbed in pain.

She walked in front of me and glared into my eyes. "Don't ever use your gifts on me again. Am I clear?"

"I was just trying to give you some peace. You were so worked up last night," I replied.

"And I have every right to be. I am about to tie myself to the ambassador of lies and manipulations. I will never have a good night's sleep again, when you and your evil mind are scheming how to take my crown only a few doors down from me each night."

I shook my head, aggravated and annoyed. "What can I do? Tell me what I can do so I can prove to you that I am not a threat. That I don't want your power and that this isn't a game."

"Go to my father and refuse me as your wife. Tell him you cheated in the tournament. Tell him you made a mistake. Then leave the dark court and never come back," she said with more hatred in her voice than I had ever heard.

Another piece of me died at her admission that she wanted to never see me again. No, she was hurt. *Don't listen to her*, I thought. She was hurt and afraid, but I could fix this.

"I can't do that," I replied softly.

"Why? You asked me what I wanted, and that is what I want. Please, Erendrial. Just leave!" She yelled.

I dropped my head, unable to watch the pain and hate flicker around in her eyes.

She took a step back and gathered herself. "I'll see you at the ceremony," she said, then left.

I spent a few more minutes in the cabin trying to collect myself before I headed back to court. My mind was racing, and my nerves were shot. I knew she was hurting from everything she had gone through, but I had nothing to do with it. I wasn't the one that had tortured her. But I wasn't the one that saved her either. I had failed. She did have a reason to hate me.

I had started on the path back up to the castle when four hooded humanoids in black attacked. Their swords came slashing down towards me as they spun and surrounded me, preventing escape. I held my hand out causing two of them to drop to their knees in pain. I dodged a sword aiming for my head as the fourth member knocked my feet out from underneath me, sending my body crashing to the ground. Two of them held me down as another raised his sword to cut off my head.

A massive beast came tumbling through the air, slamming into the one who was about to take my head. The two that held me to the ground went flying back into the air. The fourth shot ice shards from his hands aimed for my heart. Evinee dropped in front of me, her impenetrable skin taking the hit.

She stood to her feet and sent shards of bone spiraling , burying them into my attacker. He fell to the floor, dead. Leenia walked up next to us, dragging two of the attackers before snapping their necks. Zerrial, in his beast form, tore through the last assailant before returning to his alfar form.

"You okay?" asked Evinee, helping me to my feet.

"Yes, thanks to you three," I said, brushing myself off.

Zerrial walked towards us with a pendant in his hand. "House Servi has made their move," he hissed, tossing me the sigil.

"What do we do now?" asked Leenia.

"Leave that to me," I said, walking towards the dead bodies.

Chapter Five

I marched through the great hall of the castle with a bag hoisted over my shoulder. I made sure to plaster on my smug and arrogant mask as the members of the court followed me with their eyes. Leenia, Evinee, and Zerrial followed closely behind, their scornful demeanors on display for all to see.

Therosi Servi and his father Revenor were in a casual conversation with a few other high lords and ladies. I stopped behind them, clearing my voice to get their attention. They turned towards me, their smiles falling into disappointment and rage.

"Ambassador Lyklor," said Revenor, nodding towards me.

"How was your night of silence?" added Therosi. "How did the princess fare against the great Erendrial Lyklor?"

I smirked, pulling the bag from my shoulder, and dropping it to their feet with a plop. The four attackers' heads rolled from the bag, blood pooling around them. The other lords and ladies gasped, taking a step back.

"Any of these fellows look familiar to the two of you?" I asked.

They brought their faces up to mine; disgust flared behind their eyes.

Revenor's face went red as he tried to control himself. "We've never seen these males, Ambassador Lyklor. It would appear you have more enemies than you know what to do with," he replied.

I gave a faint laugh. "Really? You've never seen these males? Either of you? That's funny, because one of them had this around his neck," I said, tossing Therosi the pendant.

"Obviously someone is trying to frame us, Father," said Therosi in a calm and mocking tone. "We would never lift a hand against the future king of Doonak. No matter how lowborn he is."

I strode up to Therosi, trying to remain calm. I got into his face, causing his body to tense with discomfort.

"Oh, Therosi. Are you that much of a sore loser? I mean, I guess the whole court did witness your failure. I would say I can relate, but I can't, as I was the one that beat you. How humiliating that must have been. Losing to a *lowborn* bastard like me," I said, clicking my tongue against my teeth.

"You cheated," Therosi growled between his teeth. "Somehow, you rigged the challenges in your favor. There is no way you could ever beat me on an even playing field. You will die before you ever sit on the throne of Doonak. Mark my words."

His father put a hand on his shoulder to stop him from saying more. "Ambassador Lyklor, please excuse my son's fit of rage. As I am sure you can understand, he is still very disappointed he will not have the honor of claiming the princess as his wife. I believe my son has come to care for her over the past few months," said

Revenor calmly.

I turned my eyes back to Therosi and smiled. "Yes, I can only imagine the jealousy you must be feeling. Imagining all that power, underneath another male," I said, baiting him for another explosion. I was taking a page from Gen's book, getting my enemy to display their instabilities in front of the court, like she had done with Lady Calavi.

"Well, looks like someone has made a mess," came Gen's voice as she appeared next to us.

I closed my eyes and tensed, knowing she heard the comment about bedding her for power. I was only trying to get a rise out of Therosi, but she would take the comment as more proof that she couldn't trust me.

"Princess Genevieve," said Revenor. "It appears there was an attack on your betrothed today. We were just discussing who had the motive to orchestrate this act."

Therosi looked at her with lust in his eyes.

Gen turned to me and smiled. "Are you well, Ambassador Lyklor?" she asked casually.

"I am, princess, thank you for your concern," I replied formally.

"I will have additional guards placed around you until the ceremony tonight. We can't have my future husband beheaded before he makes it to the altar, now can we? The servants have spent too much time on my dress. It would be a waste," she said, turning to leave.

I turned back to Therosi, leaning into his ear. "Stay the hell away from my wife," I whispered, gritting my teeth together, restraining myself from stopping his heart right then and there.

I spent the rest of the day by myself. I still couldn't believe that I was going to be married: something I had sworn to myself I would never do. I laughed, thinking back on the male I used to be. It wasn't that long ago that I would have hung myself for even considering what I was about to do.

I had one more thing to gather before the ceremony this evening. I made my way into the city to the jeweler. I had placed my order the same night I had been announced as Doonak's future king. I slid the small box into my pocket and went back to my room.

The servants entered my room and began to prepare for the ceremony. They dressed me in a flawless black wool suit with satin trim, tailored pants, and shiny black boots. They trimmed my hair and cleaned the base of my neck.

A servant was about to finish off my tie when a knock came at the door. It was Evinee. She smiled at me as the servants gathered their materials and left. I stood in front of the mirror, finishing the knot of my tie. She made her way over, taking the tie from my hands and securing it to my neck. She took a step back and smiled as she looked me over.

"You look very handsome," she said, brushing her hands down the front of my jacket.

"Really? I was going more for sexy and dashing," I said playfully.

She laughed at me before her expression shifted to discomfort. She dropped her eyes from mine, biting the side of her lip anxiously.

"What is it? What's going on?" I asked.

She hesitated. "Are you sure you want to go through with this? I mean, I know you both have been through a lot together, but she doesn't deserve you, Eren."

"I'm the one that doesn't deserve her," I admitted.

She smacked her lips together in annoyance, stepping away from me.

"When did you develop such a bad taste for the princess?" I inquired.

"I don't dislike her, I … I just don't think she's right for you. The way she's been treating you, even though you've done everything to keep her safe. You've risked everything for her, and she is still torturing you. I just—" She stopped, taking a deep breath.

"You what?"

"I just want you to know that you have other options. She isn't the only one that could make you happy," she said slowly, raising her eyes to mine.

I fought to keep my mouth from falling open in shock. Evinee had never displayed her emotions before. She never showed interest in anyone. Even when we had slept together, it was always evident that it was only sex.

I took a step towards her, reaching my hands to both of her arms. "Evinee, where is this coming from?"

"The thought of you bound to someone that doesn't care for you kills me, Eren. I always thought that eventually, someday, we'd find our way to each other. Then, she showed up and a year later you're about to tie your life to hers forever. I'm not afraid of you. I know who you are, and I accept you completely. There is not a part about you that I don't admire.

"I want to be that female for you. I want to be the one you love. I know you care about me. When we are together, there is something between us that I've yet to feel with another. Just give us a chance. Call off the wedding and give me a chance. I promise you; I can make you happy." Desperation laced every word.

"Evinee, you're right. I do care about you, and I always will. Our times together were special and unforgettable, but ... I don't feel for you what I do for her. I am sorry, but she is who I want. Who I need," I said as kindly as possible.

A small tear fell from her eye. I took her into my arms.

"Whoever you end up with will be one of the luckiest males in the world."

"You're making a mistake," she whispered.

"But it is my mistake to make, if it is indeed that."

She nodded, pulling away from my touch. "I guess the next time we speak I'll be speaking to the crowned prince," she said with a light laugh.

"Weird, right?" I let a moment pass while she stood in front of me uncomfortably. "Evinee, you mean more to me than you realize. I hope you know that. I will always be there for you."

"Yeah, just not in the way I want," she said before leaving my room.

I took a deep breath, trying to push what just happened from my mind. I got the small wooden box out of the drawer and slid it into my pocket. It was time to bind my life to Gen's ... forever.

I stood at the top of the platform as the court members took their seats. A black runner lined the aisle, with six pillars of red roses stretching towards the dark magic that danced along the ceiling. Candles and bright balls of starlight were scattered throughout the throne room. Large beams of yellow light lining the walls. Diamonds suspended in the air twirled and refracted the light.

Flower arrangements with gold vases garnished every table, and gold serving ware decorated the place settings. The court members looked extravagant. I looked for the king, but I couldn't find him. Usually, he would have been waiting on the platform with the groom.

The lights dimmed as a beautiful orchestra of stringed instruments began to strum softly. Off to the side, my family smiled back at me—except Evinee. Levos, Gen's friend and ambassador from the light court, and Vena, Gen's cousin, were on the opposite side of the aisle. Levos glared up at me like he wanted to rip my head from my shoulders.

The two large doors to the throne room opened. Lily made her way down the aisle. She wore a beautiful white thin lace dress. Her hair was half up with flowers adorning the small braids and she held a bouquet. Her eyes caught Zerrial's and beamed at the very sight of him. He gave a small laugh and smiled back at her with pride.

She took her place off to the side of the platform as Gen and the king graced the threshold. As she descended the aisle, white rose petals began to fall from the sky like snow. She wore a stunning black lace dress that hugged every curve of her body perfectly. It covered her arms, shoulder, and neck. I didn't have to see the reverse side of her dress to know it revealed the length of her bare back. A long train flowed behind it. A small opening at her chest revealed her cleavage.

Diamonds sewn into the fabric made it look like she was a living star. Her hair was pinned back away from her face in loose curls with a diamond crown adorning her head. Diamond earrings fell from her small, pointed ears. She had a bright red lip, and silver dust softly covered her face. She held a bouquet of red roses. She was perfect.

Her father escorted her down the aisle just as the human custom called for. He held onto her tightly and smiled with pride; something I had rarely seen the king do. They made their way towards me, and I couldn't help but smile down at her. This beautiful female was to be mine. Her heavy eyes looked back at me. She didn't smile or reveal a single emotion. I extended my hand to her as the priestess made her way to the platform. The king stood off to the side. Gen took my hand, joining me on the platform.

I realized then that, even though the dress was stunning, I wouldn't be able to see my imprint on her lovely skin. Dark alfar brides usually made sure their gowns revealed their bodies where the imprint would appear. She knew this tradition. She had to. Did she choose to cover up to punish me? To protest the marriage? I pushed the thought out of my head. Even though I was disappointed, I still had cause to celebrate. I would be her husband, and she would be my wife.

I took a deep breath and grinned at her. She handed Lily her flowers and then turned her attention to the priestess. The officiant began to read scripts from the book of Azeer. She gave him thanks for the union and our power. Each court member in the throne room slit their hands, allowing their blood to flow freely to the floor. The priestess began her magic, drawing the blood around us in a circle. It symbolized the union of our race and our kingdom.

We knelt in front of each other while the priestess continued her prayers and wrapped our hands in a black silk ribbon. When we approached the end of the ceremony, I signaled to the priestess to give me a moment.

Gen looked from her to me with suspicion. I chuckled at her paranoid brain. I pulled the small wooden box from my pocket and opened it in front of her. I had designed the wedding ring myself. The band was silver and lined with small black diamonds. The large stone in the setting was the same emerald shade as her eyes. It was shaped into a seven-pointed star.

I pulled it from the box and took her left hand. She looked shocked and taken off guard, which was what I had hoped for. Her hand shook while I slid the ring onto her finger. It was out of the norm for alfar. We didn't wear wedding rings, but the female I was marrying was part human. I loved that side of her and wanted to honor it.

I leaned into her ear and whispered so only she could hear. "With this ring I take thee, Genevieve Drezmore, to be my beautiful wife. To have and to hold from this day forward. For better, for worse, for richer, for poorer. In sickness and in health, to love and to cherish from this day on. I give myself to you completely and take you as you are. Perfect in every way." I pulled away and looked into her eyes, hoping to see a sign of love, but she dropped her attention to her hand and just stared at the ring.

The king brought forward our marriage contract. We slit our palms and signed our names to the parchment that would bind us together forever. I took her hand in mine while our blood mixed and accepted one another's commitment. Now that the contract was solidified, a faint golden light reached across from me to Gen.

It illuminated her shoulder as my imprint transferred to her body. She looked down at her left shoulder for a moment while the light danced underneath the dress. I so desperately wanted to pull back the fabric so I could see how it looked on her beautiful sun-kissed skin. I wanted to drag my fingers along the lines. I wanted proof that she was officially, finally mine, but nothing was visible. She had made sure of that.

The priestess ended with a few final prayers. I leaned in to kiss her. I knew it would make her uncomfortable, but it was custom. I took her lips with mine and gently pressed against her.

A black fog descended from the dark magic on the ceiling. It surrounded us as we stood in the center of the court's blood circle. The power was unlike anything I had ever experienced. It was raw, wild, and pure. We pulled away from each other and looked into the haze. It was like standing in the middle of a lightning storm. I smiled, turning my eyes to her. She too was smiling while she took in the phenomenon.

The court gasped and clapped at the display of power. This had never happened before during a wedding ceremony. I didn't know if it was because she had the Dark Flame, or if it was a sign that Azeer agreed with the union.

I held onto her hand as we turned to face the court. They clapped and cheered while they looked upon the future king and queen of Doonak. I turned back to the king and knelt before him. Gen went to his side and took the crown that lay in a box. The metal was silver and shaped into flames, with diamonds inlaid throughout the surface. A green stone that matched Gen's eyes sat in the center.

Gen placed the crown on my head gently before I brought my eyes to hers. Her eyebrow was raised, and her lips were pressed together. The king stepped up next to her and smiled, draping a band of jewels and silver around my neck. I stood up and turned back to the court as Gen took my hand.

"Kneel before the future king and queen of Doonak," said the king with pride. "Princess Genevieve Drezmore and Prince Erendrial Valor Lyklor."

The courts bowed to us. Bowed to me. For the first time in my life, I was higher than anyone that sat at court. I had done this. I had earned this, and someday, I would be their king.

I smiled, looking over to Gen. She was studying me while I basked in the glory. I tightened my grip around her hand, but she didn't respond. She turned her focus back to the court as they stood to their feet with respect.

The rest of the night, the court feasted, drank, sang, and danced. The members were free with themselves, throwing formalities out of the window for one night. Each house paid their respect to us while we sat upon our thrones. My family stayed close, just in case anyone tried anything.

Icici made her way to the front and gave a deep curtsy before she stood, looking from me to Gen.

"Congratulations on the marriage, cousin," she said with a forced smile.

"Thank you, Icici," Gen replied with a nod.

"I couldn't help but notice your dress does not allow your new imprint to be seen by the court," added Icici. "Were you unaware of the tradition?"

Gen gave her a small smile before responding. "I am aware of the tradition, yes," replied Gen.

Icici turned her eyes to me. She always knew exactly where to apply pressure. "It's an honor for a husband to see the imprint on their wife's body. Most married females design their whole wardrobes around the print, but I guess I can understand your resistance. I would be embarrassed to wear the imprint of a lowborn on my body for all to see." She turned and left without another word.

I felt my pride take another hit. Was Gen embarrassed by me? Is that why she had covered it up? I saw Oz grab onto Evinee's waist as she lunged towards Icici, ready to take her head off. The others looked at me with pity smiles, trying to be reassuring, but it was no use. I stayed quiet for the rest of the night.

After the celebration, I went back to my room and changed into more comfortable attire before making my way to her chamber. Even though nothing was going to happen, we still needed to make the others believe it had. If we didn't appear to be trying for an heir, the houses would presume us weak and take matters into their own hands.

I knocked on the door. Atalee, Gen's attendant, appeared on the other side in a matter of moments. She bowed and allowed me to enter before leaving. Gen was in a long, silk nightgown with a robe covering the rest of her exposed skin. She stood on the balcony looking up at her stars. I made my way over and stood by her quietly.

"You looked beautiful tonight," I finally said.

"Thank you," she said softly.

"Besides the groom, was the wedding everything you hoped it would be?"

"I had my best friend by my side and my father to walk me down the aisle. The room was beautiful. Yes, I would say it was *almost* perfect."

I felt another twinge of pain, knowing I was what made the day imperfect. I turned towards her, taking in her beauty. Her light was slowly but surely growing again. It didn't flicker out as often anymore.

"Do you like the ring?" I asked.

"It was ... unexpected," she said, finally turning towards me.

"Silver for my eyes, green for yours," I replied, taking her hand in mine while running my thumb over her ring. She pulled away uncomfortably.

On the left side of her neck, a small black marking stuck up from underneath the fabric. The beginning of my imprint. I reached for the collar of her robe, making sure my skin didn't touch hers. I had to see it. I had to know what it looked like on her. I pulled gently at the material, but her hand stopped me before I could see any more. I let my hand fall along with my face.

"You hate me that much?" I asked her.

She turned away without a word. I heard the pocket doors to her bedroom open. Tryverse Feynar, the male who I had found holding Gen a few days prior, walked towards us. Gen turned and smiled at him softly.

"What is this?" I asked, feeling territorial.

"It's been ten minutes. Long enough for the court to believe we've done our marital duties. You may leave," she said.

I looked back at Tryverse. He would get to see my mark before I did. He was going to touch her. To lay with her. On our wedding night.

"Gen, please. Can we just talk for a moment?" I asked.

"That won't be necessary. Please leave, Prince Lyklor," she ordered with hostility.

Tryverse smiled at me before he locked his eyes onto her. I took one more look at my princess as my heart broke. I turned and left my wife in the arms of another male.

CHAPTER SIX

Evinee

"Another," I demanded to the barkeep, slamming the small glass onto the wooden surface. It would take a tavern full of liquor to get me drunk tonight, but I was determined as ever.

The barkeep filled my glass with the amber liquid, arching a brow flirtatiously.

"In a celebratory mood after the wedding, are we?" he said in a husky voice. His beautiful mahogany skin resembled velvet. He was a strong-statured man, but he was barking up the wrong tree ... especially tonight.

I threw back the shot, leaning over the bar towards him, making sure that my best assets were on display. He moved towards me, smiling with anticipation. I drew a single finger along his strong, chiseled jawline.

"Do you know who I am?" I whispered into his ear sweetly.

He pulled back slowly, brushing a loose curl away from my face. "I've heard a thing or two," he replied, "about the talented Lady Duprev."

I giggled innocently, snatching his hand before he could graze my lips with his sticky fingers. My face went feral. I allowed my nails to grow into sharp, flesh-ripping talons. His brow furrowed and jaw clenched as warm blood drizzled from his wrist.

"Then you know," I said fiercely, "that someone like you would never have a chance with someone like me." I yanked him closer, freeing his wrist and tangling my fingers in the nape of his hair, holding his head still. "Consider this a mercy. You don't have the slightest clue who you're fucking with."

I flung him back, repositioning myself in the chair. "Another," I demanded. The barkeep set the bottle on top of the bar, then disappeared. I laughed, shrugging to myself. "Fine by me."

"Do you really have to terrorize the barkeep of my favorite pub?" came Leenia's voice. She settled in the chair next to me, reaching across the bar for a glass. I poured her a drink before shooting another one back.

"I let him live," I replied with a smile.

"What a mercy," she said, shaking her head. "You left the reception early."

"*Prince* Lyklor was safe with you all hovering like worried milkmaids. My services were no longer needed."

"Well, Voz, for one, was extremely disappointed you didn't save him a dance."

I shot another one back, finally beginning to feel the soft, fuzzy embrace of the liquor. "The twins are your department ... not mine."

"And what is that supposed to mean?"

I arched an eyebrow, allowing myself to grin. "Don't worry Leenia beans, I'm the last one to judge who you invite into your bed."

She punched me in the arm while we both laughed. "Bitch," she whispered, taking another shot.

"Whore. Slut. Bitch. You know, I have so many nicknames around here, I am unsure which is my favorite."

"How about friend?" she said, taking my hand. I made the mistake of bringing my eyes up to hers. They were full of compassion and worry. "You're an amazing, loyal, and brilliant friend."

The feeling in my heart I was currently trying to drown fluttered to life once more. I pulled my hand from hers, pouring another shot.

"Friend," I whispered, swirling the thick liquid in the glass. "Just his friend."

"I know expressing feelings isn't really your thing, but I am here ... just in case you want to talk."

"Barkeep," came a voice that made every hair on my body stand in alert.

I turned over my shoulder, spotting the source of my growing annoyance. Icici Drezmore. Her dark, soulless eyes turned casually towards me. Her head of thick, black hair tilted slightly, displaying her perfect white smile.

"And what do we have here," she said, every word dripping with venom. "The court slut and the outcast. What a fitting pair."

My vision tunneled. I could hear my blood pumping through my veins as my heart raced with rage.

"Icici," Leenia said calmly. "Go find another hole to hide your traitorous face in."

Icici giggled, never removing her eyes from me. "You know, I always did wonder what the males of this court saw in you. I mean, even for a dark alfar, your sexual escapades are legendary. I remember overhearing married lords speak with my father about how they would forsake their wives in order to claim the great Evinee Duprev."

My breathing was rapidly picking up pace. My talons buried into the wooden bar while I tried to remain in control. She was a royal. Even the shittiest of royals were off limits to someone like me. *Remain in control.*

Icici leaned into my face, softening her eyes in a sadistic expression.

"Tell me," she whispered, "how does it feel to be out bedded by a half-breed? To have the love of your life choose a peasant over a high lady like yourself? Does it bother you, knowing he is currently buried deep inside of her warm, fragile body even though he promised you he would never take a wife?"

Click. I felt it. My control slipped through my fingers. I turned over my shoulder, smiling at Leenia. "Talking about feelings is overrated, don't you think?"

I wrapped my fingers around the neck of the bottle. Moving swifter than light, I slammed the liquor bottle into Icici's head. Then everything around me went dark.

CHAPTER SEVEN

Erendrial

I didn't sleep or eat the next day. I couldn't get the image of Gen on top of Tryverse Feynar out of my head. I kept my distance from her, and focused on how to win over the high houses. I wasn't ready to start passing out favors just yet.

Over the next few weeks, I met with the king while he went over the different hats he had to wear. He was grooming me to take his place. Gen was frequently unavailable. She refused to speak to me unless it was necessary. At dinner, I would try to get her to laugh or smile, but it was no use. I asked her to dance every night, but she never accepted.

I visited her room the nights she was supposedly fertile to make it look like we were doing our duty. I stood in the seating area until the required amount of time had passed before I left, most of the time never laying my eyes on her.

The court continued to show me disrespect and she did nothing to help combat the growing threats that surrounded me. Each one of the dresses she wore in public covered my imprint. If the dress was more revealing, she would wear a cover or jacket to make sure it was out of sight. The court mocked me about the matter. They continued to call me a lowborn and would talk about how Gen preferred the young Tryverse Feynar in her bed.

Each insult chipped away a little more of my heart. I did all I could to remain composed, but my mask was slowly being destroyed. I had worked so hard to earn the respect of this court, but nothing I did seemed to be good enough. Their words affected me, and the fact that Gen allowed it made the insult even worse.

My family was ready to kill them all, but I restrained them. Evinee continued to offer me comfort in whatever way I chose, but I refused. Zerrial, Oz, and Voz tried to distract me with females and alcohol, but nothing had the intended effect. With each passing day, I found myself losing hold on the hope I had of earning a second chance to be with the one I loved.

I went to her room one night to pretend to conceive an heir. I knocked, expecting Atalee to open the door, but instead Gen appeared. She smiled brightly at me before she pulled me into the room and shut the door. I was surprised, but I grinned, eager to see what had changed.

"You seem happy," I said playfully.

"Of course I am. What are you doing here? I thought you were out on a hunt," she said, pouring us a glass of whiskey. She handed one to me before she shot hers back.

"Uh, no. There were no scheduled hunts for today. I'm here to—" I stopped myself, unable to finish the sentence.

"To what? Was it because you missed me?" She laughed, pouring herself another glass. A real laugh. I hadn't heard that since before the demons. My heart lightened in that moment.

"Yes, I've missed you," I admitted.

She stopped, turning to face me. "Eren, is this about the night we slept together? You don't have to say anything. You made yourself perfectly clear. I know it isn't ever going to happen again. You were right. You can't give me what I want," she said, dropping her gaze to the floor.

What in Azeer's name is going on? I walked towards her, reaching hesitantly to take her into my arms. She looked up at me with her soft green eyes and smiled as she wrapped her hands around my shoulders.

"I want you, princess. You, and only you," I whispered.

"What?" She giggled nervously.

"I will give you whatever you want. Just give me another chance, please," I begged.

She smiled so brightly I thought she was going to burst. "What changed your mind?"

"You did," I replied, touching her face softly.

She leaned into my touch just like she used to. "I care about you, Eren. I care about you so much. Please don't hurt me."

I smiled at her confession, shaking my head. "I will never hurt you. I promise."

She pushed up onto her tiptoes and kissed me passionately. I melted around her and wished I had the gift to freeze time. I pulled her in as close as I could manage, allowing my lips to consume hers. My hands traveled up and around her body. I was desperate to have her. I needed her. I couldn't think of anything else but her.

I picked her up and carried her beautiful body to the bed. I placed her down gently, never removing my lips from hers. She smiled and giggled as her nose scrunched with joy. I pulled away to take in the sight. She ran her hands through my hair while she slowly opened her eyes. I lay on top of her, taking in this perfect moment I had dreamt of for so long.

Her face began to slowly shift as her expression changed from happiness to confusion. She let her hands fall from my hair. She began to squirm underneath me. I pushed off, unsure of what had changed. I sat on the bed and studied her. She brought her hands to her head and pulled at her hair. I reached for her, but she recoiled away from me.

"Gen, what happened just now?" I asked.

"What ... What are you doing here? Why were you just on top of me?" she asked.

"It was my time of the month to come to your room because ... because you're fertile, but when I got here, you were happy. You ... you kissed me."

"No, no, I would never do that. I wouldn't let you touch me, let alone kiss me. I can't stand the feeling of you," she admitted before she got to her feet and wrapped her robe tightly.

"Are you feeling okay? Do you want me to get Vena for you?" I asked, confused.

"No, I just want you to leave. Leave and don't come back," she said, backing away from me. Not wanting to leave her alone, I called for Otar.

She snapped her eyes to me. "What are you doing?"

"I'll leave, but I don't want you to be alone right now. Otar!"

The black creature with yellow eyes and sharp, flesh-ripping teeth appeared in the room. He stomped his feet in frustration before he locked in on me. "I had it!" Otar whined. "I finally had the harpy bitch I wanted. She was going to give herself to me and you called me! Why? Why? Why?"

"I don't think Gen is well. I need you to stay with her," I said.

Otar snapped his attention to her. "What is the matter, wicked one? Has the fucker hurt you? If so, just say the word and I will pull out his intestines through his ass and make a lovely omelet from them," said Otar.

"No, no, I am fine. I just need him to go," she said.

Otar snapped his head back to me. "You heard her, leave!"

I nodded, taking one last look at her. I made my way back to my room while I thought of every possible thing that could be wrong with her. She had acted like the demon situation hadn't happened. She acted like she did with me before all of this. She said she cared for me and wanted me. Those words I had been so desperate to hear for so long.

I made it back to my room and slammed the door behind me in

frustration. Was she having another breakdown? Was this her way of coping? There had to be something I was missing.

An hour later, Otar appeared in my room with a smug smile on his face.

"Is she okay?" I asked.

"Yes, I fixed her," said Otar tauntingly. "I brought her the one who makes her happy. Your favorite male, Tryverse Feynar."

I closed my eyes as the pain of his admission came over me.

He walked over to me and leaned down into my ear. "How does it make you feel to know that your *wife* prefers the comfort of another male?"

"That's enough, Otar," I said, trying to keep control of myself.

"Not so good, I presume. What did you expect? You used her and threw her away like she was a piece of trash. Now, she has a male who cherishes her, body and all," he said, pushing me over the edge.

I stood from the chair and threw out my hands, pushing my power towards him, allowing my rage, pain, and hatred to fuel the torment I now inflicted upon the beast. I watched as he squirmed and lashed on the floor while I made his bones break and organs burst. He laughed, and laughed, and laughed as he screamed. I dropped my hands, regaining control of myself.

"That was fun. Let's do it again," he said, standing to his feet, clapping with glee.

"Leave," I demanded.

"I'm curious. Why are you so mooooody? You got what you wanted. You will be king. Why are you pouting like a little human brat?"

I tightened my hands into fists, leaning back in the chair. "I didn't get what I wanted. I wanted her," I replied honestly.

"You had her. You tossed her away. That is your fault."

"Believe me, I know, and I may never be able to forgive myself for it."

Otar walked slowly towards me, snapping his head back and forward like a reptile. "You actually have like for her, don't you," he said.

"The word is feelings, and yes."

Otar paused for a moment, seeming to study my face before he dropped to the ground, laughing hysterically as he pounded his hands against the floor.

I rolled my eyes, moving to the wet bar to pour myself another glass of whiskey.

"This is too much! Too much! The selfish, power-hungry am-bassador of the dark has *feelings* for my wicked one," he wailed.

"If you're done, you can go," I said, trying to drown myself in liquor.

Otar stood and approached me with his long, skinny limbs dan-gling at his side. "She did like you too. Very much in fact. She hurt when you told her she was a mistake. She tried very hard not to care, but she did. Now, you are too late," Otar said before disappearing.

I slid down the wall to the floor and sat there until a knock came at my door the next morning.

"These creatures seem to be working together," said Leenia.

"Even though they're from different places and species," mumbled Doria, "they were working together. I swear by it."

My family and I were in our private war room, lounging lazily on the furniture.

"I'll inform the king of your suspicion, then on the next hunt we can see if there is a pattern," I replied. "Where are we with the other four houses who want me dead?"

"House Rytorm no longer wants you dead," answered Evinee. "After their last attempt failed a month ago I dare say they've seemed to lose interest."

Doria sat up from the arm of the couch. "And how did you get this information? Is your source good?"

Evinee smiled wickedly. "My methods are none of your concern, and I have no source. I heard it straight from the mouth of Lord Rytorm himself," Evinee said, winking at Doria.

Doria rolled her eyes and sat back in her chair.

Firel reported next. "I've been keeping a close eye on Servi. They haven't made another move yet."

I confirmed, "so we should be looking into Gyset and Sollerum then."

Zerrial huffed. "Leave them to me. I need a distraction."

Mockingly, Evinee replied, "what? Things aren't so great with your human pet?"

Zerrial's eyes went deadly. "She is not my pet, and our relationship is none of your business," he snapped.

Leenia added, "you're getting bored with her, aren't you?"

Evinee took a bite of an apple and continued. "We told you this would happen, but do you listen to us? Noooo. You go and move her into your rooms."

Zerrial erupted. "Will you both shut the fuck up!" The room went silent. No one dared to say another word.

I tried to change the subject. "Z, I need your help anyways. I have to check in with the madams of the gentlemen's club. Could use another pair of ears to make sure they aren't cutting corners."

Zerrial nodded.

Evinee smiled, always having to have the last word. "Oh, and while you're there, please get laid, Eren. The whole monk look isn't good on you."

Leenia laughed behind her.

I exhaled in annoyance. "Evinee darling, you need to learn when to keep that delicious mouth of yours shut. It's going to get you killed one day," I said, leaving the other members of my family as Zerrial followed me out.

We made our way to the club, where I met with the two alfar madams who ran the establishment. The club was an investment of mine. It was a place where the alfar could come for human comfort, but it also helped divert the alfar from raping unwilling humans. If they had somewhere to go to get their needs serviced by willing participants, then they wouldn't go looking elsewhere.

It also was a good investment. My returns had come back to me ten times over since I helped the little hovel open a century back. The human girls were well cared for and paid for their services. Trying out the new women used to be something I looked forward to each month, but I hadn't visited the club for that reason in months.

After we finished with the madams, Zerrial and I ended up at the alehouse where we had first met. He was silent, but I could tell there was something brewing inside. I waited the required amount of time before finally diving in.

"Are you going to tell me what is going on, or shall I begin the guessing game?" I asked bluntly.

"It's ... it's Lily," he finally admitted. "This whole thing with you and Gen is getting in the way of us. She is loyal to her sister to a fault, but she loves me, and I'm loyal to you. It's tearing her apart. Something is going on with Gen, but she won't tell me because she knows I will tell you. But whatever it is, it's eating at her. She is worried all the time, and she is panicked. I want to be there for her, but I don't know how. Not when she can't even talk to me."

"I'm sorry my friend. I never meant for my troubles to extend to you and your woman."

"It's not your fault. You've been through enough. I just … I just don't know how to separate you and Gen from Lily and I. Gen is her sister, she is your wife, she is my princess. You are my friend, her husband, and our future king. You get my point."

I exhaled, taking another drink. "I release you from your commitment to me, Zerrial. Tell Lily that whatever she tells you remains between you and her. Gen and I need to be able to figure out our own issues. We don't need to drag you two into our mess," I said.

"Thank you, Eren. How are you doing with it all?" he asked.

"Trying to hold on, but it gets harder by the day."

"I see the toll it is taking on you. We all do. If there is anything we can do to help—"

"I know. Thank you, my friend," I said, patting him on the back.

A few days passed before I was able to address the king and council regarding the new development with the creatures.

"I will attend the next hunt in order to gather a sense of how the creatures are communicating and working together," I said.

"If they are indeed working together, then that means Alaric acts as a puppet master," said a council member.

"Are we sure this Alaric character is the one controlling the rifts?" asked another councilor.

"All of our information and sources lead back to him," I answered. "The princess's creature Otar also confirmed that he was working for a master who had the ability to control his actions. This theory makes sense."

Gen added, "There must be a way that he is controlling them. I believe the rune symbols that we found on the creatures have something to do with it. The creatures we killed had the symbol burned into their flesh, based on the reports our teams have given. Once they are killed, the symbol quickly fades. I just don't know what power this symbol has over them."

"Daughter," said the king, "you will assist with the next hunt as well. Try to find any connection with this Alaric and this rune."

Gen hesitated for a second, and then nodded. This would be the first hunt she went on since she had been taken.

"Princess Genevieve," interrupted Lord Servi, "didn't you report that your creature had the same marking on his skin before you resurrected him?"

"Yes, but when—" Gen stopped speaking. Her mouth suddenly drooped, and her eyes began to flutter rapidly. She wasn't having a vision ... no, something was wrong.

"Genevieve?" asked the king.

Gen began to rock back and forth. Her eyes rolled into the back of her head, then she slammed her face into the wooden table. I jumped up in a panic, reaching for her while she shook ferociously.

"Get Vena, now!" demanded the king.

I pulled her away from the table, trying to steady her face. Foam began to erupt out of her mouth as her whole body went limp. I held her in my arms until Vena arrived. The king sent the rest of the council out of the room while she examined her.

Gen finally woke. "What happened?" she asked, reaching for her head.

"You had a seizure," replied Vena.

"What caused it?" I asked.

"I don't know. She seems to be in perfect health. Have you done anything different lately?" asked Vena.

Gen sat up slowly. "No. Besides coming back from the dead," Gen replied sarcastically.

"How do we prevent this from happening again?" asked the king.

"I don't know what caused the episode, so I can't give you an answer, uncle," answered Vena. "I recommend spending the rest of the day in bed, but you should be good tomorrow. As I said, you're perfectly healthy."

"That's good to hear," I said, smiling at her, even though I was still worried.

She shifted uncomfortably and got down from the table.

"Prince Lyklor," said the king, "please escort your wife back to her chambers. I will be along shortly to check on you, daughter." He kissed her on the head softly.

I offered her my arm, but she didn't take it. I followed her back to her room without a word. Lily was waiting for her when we arrived. She grabbed Gen's face as worry and fright washed over her features.

"They said you passed out in a meeting. Are you okay? What did Vena say?" demanded Lily.

"I'm fine. She said I was perfectly healthy. Nothing to worry about," Gen reassured her calmly.

There was definitely something going on with her: Gen's weird behavior a couple of days ago, the issues between Lily and Zerrial, and now her seizure. Gen walked into her rooms without turning back to look at me.

I grabbed Lily's arm before she could shut the door. "If she needs anything, please let me know," I said.

She smiled at me and nodded before shutting me out.

CHAPTER EIGHT

The next day we prepared for the hunt. There were enough creatures pouring through the rift that we were bound to come across a few if we stepped foot into the woods. Gen insisted she was fine and could accompany us. I was more on edge than normal, paranoid beyond belief, never taking my eyes off her.

We flew through the sky on our ragamors along with Zerrial, Evinee, Doria, and Leenia. After traveling for an hour, we finally landed, continuing the hunt on foot. The woods were still cold, but the snow was gone, and spring was just around the corner.

As we entered a small clearing, I noticed the birds ceased singing. The insects were quiet and there wasn't an animal in sight. I signaled for the group to be on the lookout as we proceeded through the thicket. My eyes focused as I calmed my breathing. Everything inside of me was on alert.

A vast ditch was positioned at the edge of the clearing. It was deep, about ten feet across. The smell that emanated from the area was unlike anything I had ever experienced. We walked cautiously over to the top of the hole and peered down. Inside laid dead bodies of multiple races: dark alfar, light alfar, humans, fairies, nymphs, incubi, dryads, even a ragamor.

"What in Azeer's name?" asked Leenia.

The bodies were covered in mucus. Some looked like they were still breathing, but different parts of their bodies had been eaten or were missing. One of them moaned as they reached their hand up to us. I took another look, assessing the situation.

"Shit, we need to get out of here now," I ordered.

"What did you figure out?" asked Evinee.

I pulled my eyes away from the pit. "This is their food source. Like a kitchen. We're in their territory, which means whatever these things are, they're close."

"So, let's kill them and be done with it," suggested Gen.

"If they took down a ragamor on their own, we are going to need more than five alfar soldiers," I pointed out.

Zerrial sniffed the air around us and said, "It's too late to go back."

"What is it?" I asked.

"They're here," he said. "At least a dozen of them. Cold-blooded creatures."

We all took out our weapons and prepared for battle.

"Everyone stays close. They're pack creatures, so they'll try to pick us off one by one," I added.

Rustling from the bushes up ahead drew our attention to the front. A scaled creature the size of two males came out of the foliage. It was lean and muscular, and stood on its hind legs with long, slender arms dangling in front. It had a long snout with a mouth full of sharp teeth and two gaping holes for nostrils. Long pointed ears at the top of its head twitched from side to side. Its eyes were reptilian with small slits.

It slashed its tail towards us, revealing needle-like spears on the end. We huddled into a circle, watching each other's backs. One by one, eleven more creatures surrounded us. One raised its head to the sky and made a loud beckoning sound that rattled deep inside of its throat. We waited for them to attack.

"Fight as long as you can, then call your ragamors and get out. Am I clear?" I ordered to the group. They nodded, not taking their eyes off the creatures. Each of the monsters raised their heads and began to make loud chirping noises. Suddenly, they swarmed, snapping and scratching at us. One of them swung their tail, sending sharp needles through the air, nailing Zerrial and I in the legs.

We continued to fight as they descended upon us. My heart pounded through my chest. The needles were affecting me somehow. I didn't focus on them. I slashed and swung at the large beasts.

Evinee returned their needle attack with her own bone spears. One of the beasts came hurtling towards Gen as she lit the creature on fire. Her Dark Flame tunneled towards the beast, devouring it in place. Two others attacked her from behind, nipping at her legs. I flung myself forward, taking the head of one of the creatures as the other swung its tail and buried more needles into my body. I gasped in pain, but had given her enough time to get away.

The needles must have had a paralytic effect. Everything around me began to spin as I slowly lost feeling in my limbs. I fell to my knees while I watched Gen call for Tarsyrth, her ragamor. She mounted him before sending her flames barreling around us. Leenia flung one of the pests into a tree so hard that the base of the large oak cracked.

Another one came charging at me. It grabbed me by the leg and began to drag me towards the ditch. I was unable to move or scream for help. The needles were working fast. I could feel the pain in my leg from its teeth bearing down inside of my flesh, but I was helpless. I saw a ragamor shoot into the sky and prayed it was Gen.

Evinee and Zerrial came out of nowhere, cutting the head of the creature clean off. Zerrial was fighting the effects, but his sloppy footwork told me they were beginning to take hold. They called their ragamors and loaded me onto one beast. Evinee held onto my limp body as we flew back to the castle. I saw Leenia's ragamor up ahead. Everyone was safe. We had made it out.

When we got back to the castle, the twins were waiting for us. They helped unload me from Evinee's ragamor and each took one side to assist me to my room. Evinee was attentive, checking to make sure I was okay. Gen was up ahead, talking to another council member when we approached. Evinee charged towards her and slammed her fist right into her jaw. Gen snapped forward, eyes darkening.

"What in Azeer's name is wrong with you?" yelled Evinee. "He saved you and you just left him there to die when you flew off to safety!" She stood unfazed by Gen's black eyes.

"He was fine," Gen responded. "He had all of you."

"And what if we hadn't gotten to him in time?" roared Evinee. "He could have been torn to shreds. Do you even give a damn, you selfish bitch?"

"Remember who you're speaking to," Gen said, squaring her shoulders back.

"Oh, I know exactly who I am speaking to," yelled Evinee, getting into Gen's face. "A selfish, narcissistic child who doesn't care how her actions affect anyone else. He is your husband, and you just left him back there to die!"

I looked at Leenia, signaling her to intervene. Leenia put her hand on Evinee's shoulder, pulling her away from Gen as they stared each other down. Gen glanced at me only for a moment while the twins held onto my immobile body. They dragged me to my room and called for Vena.

The paralytic would wear off, but it would take time. There was nothing she could do for me. I closed my eyes, unable to do anything but rest.

Before dinner, my family came by to check on my recovery. I was able to move now, but everything still hurt, including the pound of flesh the creature had taken from my leg. Vena had healed me, but the residual pain was still there. Evinee was the last one to leave my room.

"Thank you for coming back for me," I said.

"Of course," she smirked. "Would you expect anything less?"

"Thank you for sticking up for me today also, but Evinee ... you can't get involved. This is between me and her."

"How much longer are you going to put yourself through this, Eren? She doesn't deserve you. She proves that every day. She was going to leave you there to die."

"She isn't herself. She's been through a lot."

"We all have. We all have had to face our demons a time or two. We didn't destroy those around us in the process," she said angrily.

"Evinee, please."

She looked at me and exhaled in annoyance. "Fine, I won't commit treason, but for the record, I don't like her."

I laughed. "Yes, I see that." I opened my arms to her. She crawled onto the bed and laid against my chest. "I couldn't have asked for a better protector."

"That's not all I can be," she said, looking up at me with a wink.

"We've been over this."

"Yeah, yeah. You'll change your mind eventually. You always do."

We laughed before falling asleep.

I woke up to the feeling that someone was staring at me. When I opened my eyes, Gen was standing over me with a stern look. I looked down to my left to see Evinee still curled up against my side, sound asleep. I gently shook her. She mumbled and stretched across me as she opened her eyes. She looked up at me with a smile and then followed my eyes straight to Gen. Her face fell before she pushed off me.

"Call for me if you need anything," Evinee said, scrambling off the bed.

I nodded with a smile, pulling myself up to a seated position. I looked at Gen, waiting for her to explain why she was in my room.

"I thought you didn't ... cuddle?" she said coldly.

"That wasn't what it looked like," I explained. "We just fell asleep. She was keeping me company."

"As I've said, I don't care who you choose to bed."

"Why are you here, Gen?"

"I came to see how your recovery was going. Obviously, you're back to your normal self."

"I'm fine, thank you for checking," I said, looking away from her.

She turned around, heading for the door.

"Would you have cared?" I asked, regretting the words as they came out of my mouth.

She stopped.

"Would you have cared if I had died?" I whispered.

She stood there, not saying a word. I closed my eyes, holding back the pain that was rattling through my chest.

"Get some rest, Eren," she replied without feeling.

I slid back down into the bed and drifted into my own mind as I forced myself to sleep.

"Eren! Eren, wake up," said a female voice as she shook my arm. "Eren, please, wake up!" she yelled.

I opened my eyes to see Lily standing over me in my room. Her face was wracked with panic and fear.

"What is it? What is wrong?" I asked, sitting up.

"It's Gen. Something has happened. Just get dressed and come to her room. Hurry!" she yelled before running out of the room.

I quickly threw on a shirt, pair of pants and boots before heading into the hall. Thankfully, the castle was asleep. I stumbled down the corridor, still dizzy from the creature's poison.

When I got to her room, the guards let me pass. Gen was laying on her bed with her eyes closed. Tryverse Feynar sat nervously at the base of her bed. Lily leaned over Gen, shaking her as she yelled for her to wake up.

"What is going on?" I demanded, moving onto the bed next to Gen.

Lily was crying as she looked up at me. "Gen, she's been ...

dammit! Ever since she came back to life, she's been having Tryverse mess with her mind," Lily admitted.

I turned to him. "What have you been doing to her?" I demanded.

His face was full of worry and fear. He exhaled. "Only what she asks me to do. I block out what happened to her. Specific memories or feelings. I've replaced them with happy ones that she enjoys reliving. I've even made up a few at her request," he answered.

"What is wrong with her now?" I asked.

"I've meddled too much. I told her I could only take away so much before her mind fell in on itself, but she wouldn't listen. She insisted that I continue to rework her memories. Her mind has shut down. It can't tell reality from fiction anymore. She's gone into a coma," he said.

Faster than thought, I picked him up by the neck and slammed him into the wall. "If you knew your gift was dangerous, why didn't you stop? Why did you continue?" I yelled.

"She is my princess. I did as she requested of me," he said, fighting to breathe.

I let him fall to the floor while I gathered myself. "How do we fix her?" I asked.

"You can't," he whispered. "I can't access her mind anymore. Her memory is shattering. Soon, she will be a shell of herself."

"If you can't do anything to help her, then get out," I growled.

"No, I need to be here with her," he said, his voice broken.

"I said get out!" I roared, letting rage pour through my mask.

He backed away, afraid, and left the room.

I moved back to the bed as Lily continued to shake Gen and cry.

"She's been through too much to die like this," sobbed Lily. "This isn't right. She has to live. She has to find some type of happiness after everything. She can't die. Not like this."

I took her shoulders in my hands and turned her to me calmly. Everything in my body was freaking out and screaming in a panic, but I had to remain collected. "Tell me everything," I said softly.

"At first it was small. She started forgetting little things, like her meetings or where she left books or paperwork. Then she began acting like a different person. Like the person she was before the demons. She was bubbly and happy. I thought maybe she was just healing, but in mid-sentence, she would freak out. She would forget where she was and why I was in her room. She freaked out on Otar the other day while he was feeding on her. Went into a full-blown panic attack. She's been talking to herself a lot and then the other night I came in and found her huddled in the corner. She was pulling at her hair and shaking. She thought Lysanthier was coming for her."

I sat back, thinking of what to do. I needed someone powerful enough to fix her, but who. "Otar! Otar!" I yelled.

Otar appeared, shaking in a panic. "I ... I can't be here," he said, acting like he was having a breakdown. "She doesn't like me coming here anymore."

"Otar, I need to know what Narella is. What type of creature is she?" I asked him.

He stopped shaking and made eye contact with me. "She's a god," he muttered, as if hearing her name had restored his memories.

My eyes widened at the admission. A god. I had been dealing with a god.

"How do I contact her?" I asked quickly.

"What? Why would you want to contact that bitch?" Otar asked in surprise.

"Because she may be the only way to save Gen. Now tell me!"

Otar told me how to summon her and I headed to the forest to find the ingredients I needed. I gathered a goat and hung it from a tree. I carved the sigil Otar drew for me into its belly as the thing bled out onto the ground. I lit a triangle of fire around us and then carved the sigil into my hand. I touched my sigil to the sacrifice and began to recite the summoning ritual Otar had given me.

"Well, well, well, if it isn't *Prince* Erendrial Lyklor. What do I owe the pleasure?" said Narella from behind me.

I turned as the fire illuminated her white skin and blue hair. "I need your help," I admitted.

She laughed. "You summoned me to ask for a favor. By the way, how did you figure out what I am?"

"I don't have time to explain. I will give you whatever you desire, just please help Genevieve."

"It was the little hell spawn, Otar, wasn't it? I always knew he'd come in handy," she said, ignoring my question.

"Please," I begged.

She walked over slowly, running her hand down the side of my face while she examined me. "What is wrong with the little princess this time?"

"Her mind is shattering. An illusionist has melted everything together. She's in a coma. I thought since you are a god, you would have the power to fix her."

"For being a servant of Azeer, you have great faith in me little alfar. And what do I get in return for helping the princess yet again?"

"Anything you want. I will give you anything you want," I said, not caring about the consequences.

She laughed, taking a step back. "Desperate, are we?"

"Yes."

She paused, thinking over my deal. "Fine. I will help you, but in return, the princess will never be able to use her powers against me. If she breaks our deal, you, Erendrial Valor Lyklor, will become mine," she said.

I thought over her terms for a moment, curious why she would want me. I was of no importance. Gen was the only thing that could kill her, but Narella didn't seem to pose a threat. Though, she was a god, and their track records weren't reliable.

"Time's ticking, little alfar," she said, looking at her nails.

If I didn't agree, Gen would die. There was no option but this one, and she knew it.

"Deal," I said, without another thought. Before I could process what was happening, she cut a slit in her hand with her nail and slammed her fist into my chest. I gasped for breath as her fingers wrapped themselves around my heart. I could feel my organ beating against her palm while her cold fingers flexed gently around my heart. She pulled her hand from my chest and I fell to the floor. She waved her hands causing a bright blue light to beam from within me.

"Congratulations, you've made your first bargain with a god. Our deal is sealed. Go back to her and wait for me. I need to check in before I come to you," Narella said before disappearing.

I reached for my chest to stop the bleeding, but my wound was healed as if it had never happened. I waited a few moments, taking in deep breaths, making sure I was still alive. I had just made a deal on Gen's behalf with a god. One more thing for her to hate me for. At least she'd be alive to detest me.

Chapter Nine

Narella appeared on Gen's balcony an hour later. Lilian was still in the room, holding Gen's hand. Her eyes widened as she looked upon Narella ... a god. I sent Otar away so she wouldn't have confirmation about our secret weapon against Alaric, but I was certain she already knew he was tied to Gen.

Narella walked over to the bed and touched Gen's head softly with her fingertips. She pulled away quickly, startled.

"What? What is it?" I asked.

"Her mind is as fragile as parchment," explained Narella. "I won't be able to enter. She needs someone she already knows. Someone she is familiar with."

"I'll go," volunteered Lily. "I can do this."

"Sorry little human," said Narella, "but if I send you in, you won't be coming back. It needs to be you, Erendrial."

"I frighten her," I pointed out. "She won't respond well if I just pop up in her head."

"You're in her memories already," replied Narella. "Both the good and bad. I don't have a lot of time, so are you in or out?"

I nodded without hesitation.

"Good," Narella said. "Lay down on the bed next to her. Human, you may remain by her side."

I moved to the bed and lay next to my wife. Narella knelt between us. She grabbed my wrist and dragged her nail along my forearm and did the same to Gen. She then cut two long gashes into each of her palms. Blue blood poured from her skin. I hadn't even noticed the color in the forest when we made our deal with how fast everything had occurred. She placed her wounds over ours.

"What is that for?" I asked.

"It's how I am going to connect your minds," said Narella. "It will also act as a timer. You will have three minutes to get in, find her, and get her out. When the mark has healed, your time is up. If you are still in her head, you will be stuck there along with her. Now, lay back and close your eyes."

I did as she instructed. I felt her cold finger press into the center of my forehead before a bolt of lightning sprang through my body. The smell of lavender and sandalwood flooded my senses. I could feel Narella intertwining my essence with Gen's, as if weaving threads together.

Gen's soul, once full of light and joy, felt cold and vacant. My heart stung at the reminder of her loneliness ... of her pain. I allowed myself to surround her, wishing I could provide even an ounce of comfort to her.

As the melding of our minds and souls settled, I opened my eyes.

I was surrounded by a ravenous fire that devoured a vast barren landscape. As I looked closer, I realized that barren landscape had once been her town. We were in The Frey.

I took off in a sprint through the dead streets. Buildings collapsed around me as the fire ate at the dried wood. Trees were charred to a crisp and the sky was filled with black smoke. I choked, trying to make out any landmarks I could. The church was at the center of the town. The only building completely untouched by the roaring flames.

I made my way into the basement where Gen used to live. I opened the door and found her cowering in the middle of the room. She was completely naked. Her body was bruised, wounded, and dirty. Her hair was matted with blood. She was missing fingers and toes. My heart stopped as the memories of that horrible night devoured me whole. She was in the condition I had found her when the demons had killed her. I took a deep breath, preparing myself. I took a step forward as the door slammed behind me.

She jumped, startled by the sound. She took one look at me and began crying and yelling in fear.

"No, no, please," she cried. "No more. I have nothing left to give you. Please."

I knelt before her cautiously. I took her face in my hands while she trembled in fear. Tears saturated her face. "Gen," I said softly. "It's me. It's Eren. I am not a demon. I'm here to get you out. I'm here to save you."

She shook her head violently. "No, no, you didn't come. They ... they said you did, but it wasn't you. It was them. It was a trick. This is just a trick," she said.

"No, it isn't. Listen to me. You need to come with me. Your mind is shattering. I've found a way out, but you need to trust me and come with me."

"It's a trick. You're not real! You didn't come. They broke me. I died."

"But then you came back. You're alive. You've been given another chance. You need to trust me and come with me." I held out my hand and offered a small smile. She looked at my hand and then back at my face. Pain filled her eyes as more tears escaped.

"You didn't come for me," she whispered, with so much defeat behind her tone it nearly shattered me. "I thought you'd come for me, but you didn't. I prayed every second that you'd save me. I held on as long as I could. I fought, Eren. For our baby ... I fought so hard, but I failed her. I thought of you and how it would be to be in your arms. I was going to tell you about her, as soon as I escaped, but I was too weak. I was weak and because of that, she's gone. It's my fault. I let her die!"

Tears began to fall from my face at her admission. "No, princess, it isn't your fault. I looked for you everywhere. I never gave up. I was a wreck. I couldn't sleep, I couldn't eat. All I could do was search for you."

"The ... the things they did to me. I don't want to remember.

I can't!" She reached her remaining fingers into her hair as she panicked and shook.

I grabbed her arms, forcing her to focus on me. "They are dead. You killed them. You are alive. They will never harm you again. I found you Genevieve, and I will always find you. No matter where you are, I will always come for you."

She lunged into me. I wrapped my arms around her, mourning with her for only a moment. I picked her up from the floor as the church began to crumble around us. I carried her out of the basement and into the barren landscape. I held onto her tightly, wishing I never had to let go. I felt a small pulling sensation in the back of my skull: Narella, signaling we were running out of time.

I opened my eyes, taking in a large breath before I sprung forward in shock. My body was zinging all over, like I was the one on fire. Narella was gone. Gen lay silently on the bed with her eyes still closed. Lily looked at me for an answer, but I had none. I leaned over to Gen, taking her face in my hands.

"Time to wake up, beautiful," I whispered. "You're safe. Time to come home."

Her eyes flung open as she gasped for air. I pulled away, unsure of what her reaction to me would be. Lily flew into her arms, crying and laughed with relief.

"You're a stupid idiot," Lily cried, kissing Gen on her cheeks. "Don't ever scare me like that again."

"What ... what happened?" she asked.

"Tryverse's gift," explained Lily. "He meddled with your memory too much. It put you into a coma. You almost died, Gen. You could have died."

"How did you fix me?" Gen asked.

Lily looked at me. Gen followed her eyes while I stood from the bed, wanting to give her space.

"How?" Gen asked.

"Narella," I confessed. "There's a lot I haven't told you yet, but the short version is that she is a god. She saved you."

"So, Narella brought me back?" she asked.

"Not exactly," Lily added, looking back to me. "Eren was the one that went into your head and found you. He brought you home."

Gen dropped her eyes.

Lily stood, looking between the two of us. "I'll give you guys some time. I'll be down the hall if you need anything." Lily kissed Gen on the head and then left the room.

"I'm sorry I went to Narella without your consent. I didn't know what else to do," I said. I left the part about the bargain out, not wanting to overwhelm her with something we'd have to settle.

"How did you find her? This ... god?" she asked.

"She found me, the first time. She was the one that told me where to find your body when the demons took you. She was also the one who brought the demons to us to interrogate. Apparently, you saved her life a while back and she owed you a life debt."

Gen's eyes snapped up from the comforter. "That was Narella?"

I laughed, taking a seat on the edge of the bed. "Looks like that big heart of yours earned you a pretty powerful ally."

"Do you trust her?"

"No. As far as we know, she works for Alaric, but she's been useful so far. I don't know what to make of her, but we can figure that out later. How are you feeling?"

"Weak, tired, and my head is pounding," she said, running her hand along the back of her neck.

"I'll let you get some sleep. No more playing with your mind. I don't think Narella will offer up much more help unless we find something she wants."

She smirked, nodding in agreement. I went to get out of the bed when I felt her tug me back. She wrapped her arms around my neck and held me tightly. I buried my nose into her neck, taking in as much of her as she'd allow.

"Thank you ... for coming for me," she whispered.

"Always, princess," I said softly.

She pulled back. Sadness fell over her face. "I appreciate what you did tonight, but it doesn't change anything between us. I want you to be happy, Eren, but it isn't going to be with me."

"You're my wife. Why can't it be with you? We can have a different marriage than everyone else at court. We *can* have a real marriage, Gen."

She shook her head. "I can't open myself up to you like that. I just can't ... after everything, I—I'm sorry."

I turned away from her, wanting to keep my emotions hidden. At that moment I realized there was nothing I could do that would change her mind. I had given everything to this female, and she still refused me. She wouldn't even give me another chance.

"Eren," she said.

I stood without looking at her. "As you wish, princess," I whispered, leaving her on the bed alone.

I made my way down to the gentlemen's club. I drank and watched while beautiful women surrounded me. I drowned myself in ambrosia and forgot about my wife.

I gave her what she wanted. I didn't speak to her unless it was necessary. At dinner, I stopped asking her to dance. I stopped trying to make her laugh. I stopped looking for her smile. She still covered my imprint that I had yet to lay eyes on and probably would never get the chance to see. The court continued to disrespect me with snarky comments about my status. Gen sat in silence and said nothing.

During the days, I filled my time with hunts and plotting against the high houses who still posed a threat to my life. As if

I didn't have enough problems, Queen Nora began to act out in strange and unnatural behaviors. She would talk to herself or forget where she was. She would randomly burst into laughter. She even stripped naked and danced amongst the court one evening after dinner. The king ignored her, but I knew something wasn't right. I had seen enough crazy creatures in my life to recognize the symptoms.

At night I spent my time at the club. My family, minus Zerrial, joined me. I drank and watched life go on. I prepared Firel to take the position of ambassador. We worked on his speech and public speaking skills. He had the brain for the job, now all he needed to master was his confidence.

I had put myself on autopilot. I slept when my duties had concluded to escape my own reality. I refused to feel or care for anyone or anything, including my own wellbeing. I was a fool to think I could have it all. The power, the respect, the crown. A female who loved me the way I loved her. I gambled and I lost. Now, I had to pay the price.

"How is everything progressing with your choice for the next ambassador, Prince Lyklor?" asked the king as Gen and I sat with him for lunch in his private quarters.

"Firel is making progress," I replied. "He has the knowledge and the cunning for the job, but we are working on his demeanor. I am confident he will rise to the position."

"Excellent," said the king. "Now with spring upon us, the other races will begin their hunting and farming. I am sure there will be plenty of disputes for young Firel to practice and learn from."

"Hopefully not too many with the rift situation still out of control, but yes, it will be good practice," I added.

He smiled, looking from me to Gen. "You two have been married for four months now. How are things?" asked the king.

I took a sip of wine and then plastered on my fake smile. "Excellent, your grace," I lied. "We couldn't be happier."

Gen smiled at me and then turned her attention back to her plate.

The king raised his eyebrow. "You two are horrible liars. Even you, Erendrial. I expected better from the ambassador of lies and manipulations," he said.

I grimaced at the sound of that disgusting nickname.

"We're fine, Father, really," added Gen.

The king put his fork down and sat back in his chair while he peered across the table at both of us. "I understand that marriage can be difficult. We all have our rough patches, but you both have a duty that needs to be fulfilled, regardless of your current feelings towards each other. You must bear an heir if your reign and this kingdom is to continue to grow and thrive." He paused, turning to me. "I understand you did not visit my daughter's chambers last month during her fertile period, Erendrial?"

I swallowed, uncomfortable by the topic. "No, Your Grace," I admitted.

"Tomorrow night is when Vena says she will be ready. I expect you to fulfill your duty," said the king coldly. "Daughter, I am sorry to force this, but it needs to happen. It is a burden that comes with your position." He stood up and moved to her, kissing her gently on the head. "I have a meeting, but I will see both of you at dinner. Enjoy your lunch." He exited.

I continued to stare at my plate. That was his polite way of applying pressure to the situation. I felt my jaw tighten at the thought of having to force her to lay under me while I .... I could never. I would never. I stood from my chair and gathered my jacket.

"Eren," she said from behind me.

I stopped, not daring to turn to look at her. "Don't worry. I won't touch you," I said before exiting his chambers. I went to the club and got drunk for the rest of the day. As dinner approached, Evinee had to all but carry me to the throne room. I was so intoxicated I could barely stand up straight. I made it to my chair where I continued my bender.

Queen Nora was also a royal mess. She was spilling her wine and food everywhere as she laughed uncontrollably at nothing. Doria was looking into her situation, but hadn't found a thing. She was shapeshifting into random members of the court throughout the day while playing tricks on their families and friends. Some saw straight through her, while others she ended up fooling. She had slept through most of the court in the past few weeks, posing as their spouses or lovers.

The king called for her guard to escort her back to her rooms. She turned and winked at me. I smiled, raising my glass to her. That would be me in a couple hundred years: in a loveless, fruitless marriage that would eventually send me over the edge headfirst into madness. Well, at least I'd be going out with a smile on my face, completely oblivious to how ridiculous I appeared.

Suddenly, a blue cloud of magic appeared in the middle of the dance floor. The guards surrounded the being as the court prepared to attack and kill the intruder. Out from the fog appeared Narella. She looked around at the guards, assessing each one before arching a single eyebrow, smiling widely. I sat up and rubbed my eyes to make sure I wasn't already going mad.

"Do you see her?" whispered Gen.

I nodded. "I need more wine," I mumbled, beckoning the servant over.

The king stood and walked towards her with authority. "Who are you and what is your purpose for trespassing in my court?" he demanded.

Narella bowed dramatically before she drew her eyes up to him.

"King Drezmore, it is nice to finally meet you. My name is Narella. I've come on behalf of Lord Alaric Valor," she said.

The court attacked without another thought. As powers and weapons flew through the air, time lapsed. Everyone moved in slow motion. Lightning froze in midair while weapons stopped in place. Narella lifted her hands gracefully across her body in an X and then forcefully slammed her hands down. A surge of power erupted from her, sending the court members, their powers, and their weapons back against the walls.

"Now, that wasn't a very nice way to welcome a guest," Narella said, still smiling.

"State your purpose and go," demanded the king.

"As I was saying," she continued, dusting off her shoulder, "I've come on behalf of Lord Alaric. He wishes to offer you a deal. He proposes that your court willingly gives up their powers and the dark magic that resides in this little fortress of yours, and in return … he will let you all live. If not, he will release more creatures into your lands and watch while you each succumb to a slow and miserable death."

Our king stood proudly without hesitation. "You can tell your lord that we are prepared to fight."

"Really?" she replied, seeming astonished by his quick response. "You sure? Because he has a whole realm full of creatures just dying to come out and play. I don't think that is a wise decision, King Drezmore."

"That is my decision, and it is final," answered the king.

"Mmm, too bad," she said, ticking her tongue in disapproval as she turned her attention to Gen. "Princess, it is nice to see you alive. I understand you have quite the new gift."

"My daughter is none of your concern," roared the king.

"You're right," Narella said softly. "Please forgive my rudeness. Oh, and um, your west border is looking a little weak. I'd investigate that." The goddess took slow, dramatic steps away backwards, assessing our court before disappearing into a blue fog. The court relaxed while everyone made their way to the front of the room.

I looked at Gen and laughed. "I was not drunk enough for that," I slurred, finishing another glass of wine.

We doubled our guards around the kingdom and runed every entrance three times over. We resecured our west border, just in case they planned to attack there. We didn't know what was coming but we were ready for a fight regardless. We sent word to the light court about the new information we had gathered so they could prepare for battle if what Narella said was indeed the truth.

After dinner that next night, I headed to Gen's room with a bottle in hand. I was already pretty gone, but I figured I could finish the bottle while I waited for the *appropriate* amount of time to pass. I nodded to the guards and forced a smiled before I walked into her room unannounced. I closed the door and took a seat on the couch in front of the fireplace.

Ten minutes and I could go. Ten minutes and I'd be on my way to a hazy night where I'd remember and feel nothing. Just like every night for the past few weeks.

"Eren, can you please come here?" I heard her say from her bedchamber.

I swallowed my mouthful of whiskey and sat up, stumbling towards her room. I placed the bottle on the table and opened the pocket doors.

She sat at the foot of the bed in a red silk nightgown and robe. Her hair was loosely draped over one shoulder as her green eyes looked up at me. There was a piece of paper on the mattress next to her. I walked into the room, unsure of what I was stepping into.

"We need an heir," she started to say. "I still don't trust you, but I think I've found a way around that issue. At least where an heir is concerned." She held out the piece of paper to me. I took it, trying to focus my eyes long enough to read what she had written. "It's a blood contract. It states that I will lay with you until we conceive an heir. Once that happens, our positions will be secure, but when the baby is born the majority power will not shift to you. I will retain the larger portion of control. This way, I won't have to worry about you taking my crown."

I held the contract in my hand, realizing she was giving me a way to be with her. She would allow it if I promised not to take away her crown, something I never wanted to do in the first place. All I ever wanted was to be with her, and now I would have that chance.

She stood up and took the contract from me hesitantly. She

sliced her hand and signed it, then handed me the knife and quill. I did the same. She held her hand out towards me, waiting to seal the bond.

I stood for a second, trying to wrap my mind around what I was about to commit to. Was there a loophole I was missing? The contract said the child would be ours. She would lay with me to conceive the child. This would be our second chance at a life together. A family. Gen let her hand fall as she smiled.

"See," she said, "I knew you wouldn't give up the power the crown offered. Not even for me. I knew if I called your bluff, you—"

I rushed forward, grabbing her hand forcefully as our blood mixed and sealed us both to the contract. The look on her face was of pure shock and disbelief.

I pulled away, taking her face in my hands as I looked down at my beautiful wife. She looked uncomfortable. Her eyes refused to meet mine. She wasn't expecting me to sign the contract. She wasn't expecting me to choose her. She pulled away and went to the edge of the bed and lay down slowly.

I followed her, taking off my shirt while my eyes danced across her figure. I was finally going to be with her. After everything, I would finally be able to make love to her. To show her how much I loved her. I slid off my shoes and then crawled slowly on top of her.

I kissed her head tenderly, trying to ease her worry. I went to kiss her lips, but she turned away from me, offering her cheek. I took it, not picky about which parts of her I got to love. I pulled her dress up gently as my fingers slid against the smooth skin of her legs. She closed her eyes at the contact.

My hands moved to her arms and face, trying to ease her into the act. I kissed down her cheek to her neck as I breathed her in deeply. Azeer, how I missed the taste of this female. I let my body press in against her, feeling her warmth through the gown. My hands trailed down her body, remembering every curve I had once taken for granted.

I kissed her chest gently, making sure not to go too far until she was ready. My hands moved back to her leg, drawing the dress up so I could feel her hidden flesh. I continued to kiss her face, hoping for a reaction, for some sign that she wanted me too, but it never came. I pressed my head against hers, trying to hold back the shame and embarrassment that now devoured me whole.

"Gen," I whispered, "please touch me. Please, give me something," I pulled away to look at her. She had her face tilted to the side with brow furrowed eyes shut, as if she couldn't bear the sight of me, let alone my touch. I swallowed, pushing myself off her. The contract didn't mean I got another chance with her. It meant nothing. It gave me nothing I wanted.

I got off the bed and reached for my shirt. I slid my boots on while she sat up, watching my every move.

"Where are you going?" she asked.

I didn't answer.

"The contract states that I will give you an heir, but in order to do that you need to lay with me."

I tightened my eyes together. She didn't want me; she just wanted an heir to secure her throne and make her father happy.

She stood from the bed and forcefully turned me to face her. She was getting angry, but I had nothing to say. I was completely numb.

"What is the problem? Fine, I'll touch you, just get back into the bed," she said, shoving me towards the mattress, but I refused to move. "What? You can't perform? Is that it? Or is it me? I've had no complaints from anyone else lately, so it must be you."

My heart fell into pieces at her admission she had been with others. I was done. The humiliation I had endured for her, the pain, the constant hoping—I was done. I had endured enough and couldn't take anymore. How was I ever going to be with a female who couldn't stand my touch? Who cringed at the very sight of me?

Tears fell down her face. I didn't know if they were from anger or frustration, but I didn't care. She had destroyed the part of me that she once wanted so badly. There was nothing left. She had taken everything. I had given her everything ... yet ... it still wasn't enough. I wasn't enough. I turned away from her while she yelled my name. I walked out of the room, promising myself I would never return.

The next month I continued my new routine of numbing and forgetting. I trained with Zerrial when I was sober enough and continued to teach Firel all I knew. I stayed at dinner long enough that no one would ask questions, but I left before the insults and crude comments could begin. I hid beneath the castle in the city as I lost myself in ambrosia.

Chapter Ten

Genevieve

"Are you ready for tonight?" asked Lily.

I scoffed. "Like anything is going to happen," I replied.

She paused, staring at me in the mirror. "Maybe if you were a little nicer," she added.

I turned around to face her, surprised. "Are you serious? Me, be a little nicer? I am offering him what he wants. I'm giving him an heir. Are you actually siding with him?" I stood from my vanity, stepping next to her while she folded a blanket nervously.

"I know you've been through a lot, but so has he. Zerrial tells me he—"

I held out my hand to stop her from speaking. "Zerrial is loyal to him. I don't trust a word he says."

"Eren released him from his commitment to him months ago. He and I can speak freely without worrying about where his loyalty lies."

"Ha! I am sure it is just another game Erendrial is playing. Zerrial probably just told you that so you will open up to him and he can use you against me. Don't be so stupid, Lilian."

"And what exactly makes me stupid? Is it because I love Zerrial, or because I trust him?" she snapped with more attitude than I had ever heard in her small voice.

"Both," I replied coldly.

She exhaled with frustration. "Don't take your strife out on me, Gen. Your misery is all your own." Lily glared at me, both anger and determination on her face. "Zerrial says he—"

"Stop! Enough about Zerrial. He's probably fucking some other human down at the gentlemen's club with Erendrial as we speak."

Bam! Lily's fist flew into my face. My cheek stung and throbbed with pain. I turned my eyes slowly towards her, rage flickering. She was breathing heavily as she tried to steady herself.

"You forget who I am," I growled through my teeth.

"You are my sister first and foremost, and that title gives me the right to speak. So you are going to shut up and listen to what I have to say." She paused, waiting to see if I objected. "Good. Eren doesn't deserve the way you've been treating him. He has done nothing to make you doubt him and everything to make you trust him. When you died, he was a shell of himself. He didn't eat or sleep. He was consumed by your death.

"The demons told him everything they did to you and then what they did to the baby. He came to me and begged me to tell him it wasn't true. I watched while he shattered. I held him as he cried for *your* child. Because he blamed himself for your deaths." Lily was crying violently.

"Then, when you had Tryverse screw with your head, he didn't hesitate to go in and save you, even though he was risking his own life in the process. He fought for you in the tournament, risking everything he had built so he could marry you. Not because of the crown, but because he loves you, Genevieve. The one male you thought would never return your feelings does, and you continue to turn him away. He even signed your stupid blood contract, hoping you would realize he wasn't the threat and that you would give him another chance.

"Zerrial can barely get him to eat or sleep, let alone talk. He doesn't even recognize him because of what you've put him through. And on top of it all, the high houses want him dead. Eren has stopped caring all together if he dies or not, while his family works around the clock to make sure that doesn't happen."

I leaned over my vanity, fighting the guilt that was beginning to fester inside of me. *No, Gen, you can't trust him,* I told myself. He's playing the long game ... that's all. It's a part of his plan.

Lily grunted with frustration and grabbed something from my dresser. "Here," she said, pulling the projection sphere from the box I kept it in. "If you don't believe me, then watch." She gripped my hand tightly as images from her memory blazed to life.

Flash. Eren stormed down the halls of Doonak, caring a body ... my body. I was covered with his jacket. His hands gripped me so tightly I could see the white of his knuckles. His eyes were bruised underneath as if he hadn't slept in days. His face was stained with tears. His jaw clenched so tightly he was trembling.

Flash. A chair flew across the room, splintering into pieces.

"I can't take it Lilian," roared Zerrial before he collapsed to the floor, sobbing and enraged. "I don't know what to do. I've tried to help him. I've tried, but nothing I do is enough. I don't recognize him. He is in so much pain. I've never seen my brother like this ... and the worst part is he blames himself." His indigo eyes reflected the candlelight as he peered up at her. "He's shattered, angel ... and I don't know how to save him."

Flash. Eren stood in the entry of Lily's room. He was disheveled. He dropped his head and closed his eyes. "Please tell me she wasn't pregnant," Eren said, fighting to even get the words out. "Please tell me it wasn't mine," he whispered.

Lily sniffled as she brought her hands to her face. "How did you—" she started to say, before she cried fiercely.

Eren broke. He collapsed to the floor. Sounds I didn't think him capable of making poured from him. His body trembled and his hands pulled at his hair while he swayed, shaking his head while he processed the knowledge of a child he never would know.

Flash. Lily cracked the door open to the throne room where my body lay on the altar before my funeral. Eren stood over me, tracing the lines of my face. He hesitantly placed a hand over my womb. His sobs echoed through the empty chamber.

"I am so sorry," he cried. "To the both of you. I am so sorry."

Eren collapsed at my altar, utterly destroyed.

Lily pulled her memories back into sphere, gently releasing her grip on my hand as I stood in complete silence.

"Yes," she said softly, "what the demons did to you was unspeakable. It was the most horrific thing I've ever laid eyes on. Nothing will ever make what happened right, but you survived Gen. You're alive. You've been given another chance, and you are wasting it. You sit here feeling sorry for yourself when you could be happy. You need to realize that the only person standing in your way of happiness is you."

I inhaled deeply, feeling like reality had finally come back into focus. Everything that I had done to him, everything that I had said and made him believe came rushing to the surface. Lily was right … I never once stopped to think about what he had gone through, or what he had lost. Seeing him through her eyes put everything into perspective. Lily was right … she was right about all of it.

"It's too late," I admitted softly, a pit in my stomach opening. I had mistreated him for months, pushing him away. This relationship … us … we were too broken to ever be put back together again.

She took my arms in her hands. "No, it isn't," she said with a smile on her face. "Go to him. Ask him about the first challenge in the tournament, when the game glitched during the last simulation. Go to him and just ask."

I nodded, grabbing my robe before I headed to his room. I turned back and looked at my Lily … my strong, beautiful little sister and smiled. My breath trembled as I inhaled, fighting the tears that threatened to fall. I smiled softly. "Thank you, Lily," I managed to get out.

She nodded. "Don't worry, Gen. I'll smack you back into reality any day."

I laughed, shutting the door gently while I gathered my thoughts, preparing myself for anything.

When I got to his room, he was sitting on a couch next to the fireplace with a glass of whiskey and a book propped on his knee. He wore silk night pants and a formfitting shirt. He turned to me as I entered without a word. I closed the door while he refocused his attention back to his book. I sat on the couch next to him.

"You didn't come to my room tonight," I said softly, unsure of how to start a conversation with him.

"Why would I? So you can insult me on my performance again? Or to hear how you've slept with other males since coming back to life? Nice touch by the way," he said, without even looking up from his book.

He was right, he didn't deserve any of that. I hadn't slept with anyone since I had been resurrected. I had just told him that to make him angry.

"I'm sorry," I whispered, feeling foolish. "That was wrong of me to say those things."

He scoffed. "Apologizing, are we? What do you want, Genevieve?"

"I wanted to ask you a question about the tournament." I paused to see if he would look up, but his eyes were firmly planted on the page of his book. "During the first challenge, in the end, the game glitched. We didn't see what happened or how you won." I waited for him to react, but he remained unaffected. "What did you see?"

His eyes flickered to the roaring fire, before he inhaled deeply, taking a moment.

He got up from his chair and made his way to his desk. I followed. He pulled out a leather portfolio where I knew he kept his drawings. He placed it on the table next to me and then returned to his seat.

I opened the leather binding of the portfolio slowly, pulling back the aged cover. A beautiful drawing of our daughter peered up at me, exactly the way I had imagined she would look. The next page was a drawing of her smiling, with her nose crinkled in the exact spot mine did. The third page was a picture of me holding her. We were both smiling as our cheeks smashed against one another. There were a dozen drawings of her that he had beautifully rendered.

As I continued through the portfolio, I saw drawings he had done of me. On our wedding day, our wedding night. There was a picture of me sleeping in the cottage that we stayed in during the night of silence. Some were of me smiling, but most were of me looking sad and depressed. All these months, he had continued to draw me. All these months he was holding onto hope that we could be together, and I allowed my paranoia and anger to blind me.

I grabbed a few drawings of our daughter and made my way over to him. I knelt on the floor, holding her sweet little face in my hands. He closed his book and looked down at the papers.

"How did you know what I imagined her to look like?" I asked.

"Ravion Sterling. When he reached into your mind for the game, he saw her. He showed your father, and he allowed it to be the last simulation in the game, knowing I would know where to find the two of you."

"So, my father knew about the baby?"

"Yes."

"And he rigged the game in your favor?"

"Yes. I shouldn't have won. Therosi was supposed to be your husband. I failed the last challenge. We had to pick between the kingdom or you, and I chose you. Your father saw this and appointed me victor because he loves you and wants you safe."

My eyes fell to the floor while I processed what I was hearing.

"She's beautiful," he said. "How did you know it was a girl?"

"I didn't. Not for sure. I just had a feeling. I picked my favorite parts of us and created an image of her to hold onto." I looked down at the drawings in my hands. "May I keep a few?"

He exhaled and looked away from me. "Of course. Now, if you'll excuse me, I have work I need to get back to," he said before standing.

I got to my feet and stood beside him. I took one of his hands in mine as I peered into his swirling mercury eyes. Lily was right. They were full of pain and emptiness. He was broken. I had broken him. He couldn't bear to look at me.

"Would it be alright if I stayed here with you tonight?" I asked hesitantly.

"You're the princess you can do whatever you want, as you so often like to remind me."

Okay, I deserved that. I deserved everything he was going to give me. I screwed up, but now I needed to find a way to make it right.

CHAPTER ELEVEN

The next morning, I opened my eyes and saw Eren next to me, still asleep. I studied his face in silence. His cheeks were sunken, his face slimmer than I remembered. There were purple rings around his eyes and his skin didn't glisten like it used to. His hair was long and unkempt, which was unlike him.

I took in a deep breath, guilt overwhelming me. His eyes opened slowly and he peered into mine. I gave him a small smile, tightening my grip around the pillow. His face remained empty of emotion. He reached out to touch my face, but stopped halfway, before retracting his hand. He rolled over to his back and looked up at the ceiling.

"You're still here," he said in a tired voice.

"Did you expect me to be gone when you woke?" I asked.

"Yes," he replied, getting out of bed. He moved to the bathroom and closed the door. I sat up, hearing the water fill his tub. I curled my knees into my chest and reached for the pictures of our daughter on the nightstand. I looked into her beautifully sculpted eyes ... his eyes. I had to make this right with him. I had to fix what I had broken.

I had been so selfish and blind. Lily literally had punched me back into reality. I had been so afraid to let him in, and honestly, I still was. But I had to at least try. I would never know what we could be to each other unless I gave him a chance.

He walked out of the bathroom with only a pair of pants on his lower half. He stopped, seeming still surprised to see me. I slowly got out of the bed and went to him as he reached for a shirt. Even his torso was thinner. He had lost a noticeable amount of weight. His pants hung loosely around his hips, and I could see his ribs. Everything about the male I once feared now seemed frail.

I searched for his eyes, but he refused to look at me. His head was hung in shame. I reached out both of my hands and gently trailed my fingers up his neck to his face. He breathed in deeply, closing his eyes in response to my touch. His hands remained at his sides, not daring to touch me.

It was hard for me to act in this physical way; not just with him, but with anyone ... but I wanted to try. I needed to try. For him. For our child. For myself.

I took another step closer, reaching up on my tiptoes before kissing the side of his face softly. I pulled away to see if he would look at me, but his eyes remained closed. I kissed down his cheek slowly. As I moved to the other cheek, I felt his tears under my lips.

I held onto his face, pulling his forehead down towards mine. My heart broke. What had I done? I wrapped my arms around his neck, trying to pull him into me, but he remained planted where he stood.

"I am so sorry, Eren. I am so sorry. Please forgive me," I whispered.

He reached up and took my wrists in his hands before he pulled them away from him. Our foreheads remained touching. "Stop," he said softly, still refusing to look at me. "I know what you're doing."

I dropped my hands as he moved to the table and slid his shirt over his torso. I waited silently, not knowing what he was thinking. He took a deep breath and turned his profile in my direction.

"You are free to take whoever you are comfortable with into your bed," he finally said. "Once you're with child, I won't deny it's mine. Just ... just try to choose someone that looks like you, or at least without any dominant features. Or not. Just ... do whatever makes you happy. I'll claim the child as my own, so you won't have to worry about the father trying to take the crown."

My mouth fell open in disbelief. He would be okay with raising another male's child. The Eren I knew would never suggest such a thing. He thought my affection just now was to convince him to sleep with me so I could get pregnant. I had told him so many times how disgusted I was by his touch, and now he was willing to look the other way while I laid with another so I could secure my throne.

"Where are you going?" I asked, trying to hold back the tears that desperately wanted to escape.

"Hunting. The threat that Narella warned us about has yet to come, so we are trying to clear as many creatures as possible that are roaming free before another wave comes through the rift."

"Will you be gone long?"

"All day hopefully," he said, placing his weapon belt around his thin waist.

"Will you come to my room when you return?" I asked.

He paused. "If that is what you desire," he said without feeling.

"Yes. That is what I want. Be careful," I said. He exited the room. I covered my mouth as the shame and pain came tumbling out in a strangled cry. I gathered myself and made my way back to my rooms.

Lily was waiting for me when I arrived. She stood from the couch and closed the book she was reading. How unfair I had been to her. She was only trying to push me towards someone who would make me happy. She walked over towards me as I hugged myself tightly. I handed her the drawings of my daughter. She took them and smiled. Tears escaped her eyes. She looked up to me for answers.

"You were right," I admitted. "About everything. I am so sorry, Lily. Can you ever forgive me?"

She took me into her arms as I cried on her shoulder. "There's nothing to forgive," she whispered, kissing me on the head.

"Do you think he will ever be able to forgive me? He can barely look at me. Gods, how I've treated him. The things I've said to him and allowed others to say. Why would he ever want me after all the misery I've caused him?"

She moved my hair from my face. "Because he loves you, Genevieve. And you love him. I don't think it was just a coincidence that you've been dreaming of him for the past four years. You were having visions of your future ... your husband, because the two of you are meant to be together. You will get through this. You just have to fight for him, like he has fought for you. Show him this time will be different; that you want him as much as he wants you."

"I do want him. Gods, Lily, I do. What was I thinking? I feel like a blindfold has just been lifted from my eyes. Like I've been someone else for the past few months. Someone I hate."

I had allowed the demons to pollute my heart, ripping away everything I had once held dear. And then there was what I had asked Tryverse to do to my mind. Though it wasn't the young alfar's fault, the emotional whirlwind it sent me into further confused what had truly been in my heart all along ... Eren.

"Well, I am glad to see the old Gen is back. I did so desperately miss her. Now, let's figure out a way to get you everything you've ever wanted," Lily said, smiling down at me.

I looked into her eyes and realized the fragile, human girl I had risked my life to save was gone. In front of me was a woman who had found her power and strength in the darkest of nights.

"Where did you learn to hit like that?" I asked, a prideful smile stretching across my face.

She shrugged. "Zerrial has been training me all these months."

"What? Why haven't you told me?"

"He wanted me to keep it a secret. It's unusual for an alfar to train a human. Plus, he thinks it would put a target on my back." She leaned in with a bright smile that lit up her eyes. "I'm pretty badass with a sword too."

Laughter erupted from my lips. It felt foreign and unnatural, yet somehow, it made me feel alive. "You ... with a sword. Can you even pick it up?"

She smacked me in the arm. "I can, and I know how to use it, thank you. Zerrial says I am better than you with the thing anyway."

"Oh, does he?"

She smiled, pulling me into a hug. "I'm glad you're back."

I took a breath. "I'm trying."

"That's all that matters."

The rest of the day I focused on ways to show Eren I wanted to be with him. I ordered a new wardrobe that would display his imprint on my shoulders. I found a gift that I knew he would appreciate, to replace the three women I had given him during the gifting ceremony before our wedding. I instructed the kitchen to prepare a separate dinner for us that would be served in my quarters when he returned.

That night, I eagerly waited in my room. I had a blue dress made that resembled the light blue one I had worn the night after we first slept together. He had seemed to like that ensemble. This one was very similar except it was strapless, to display his imprint prominently. I pulled my hair away from my face so it would be the first thing he saw when he arrived.

The servants prepared a dining table on my balcony. It was late spring, so the air was perfect for the occasion. I had his gift wrapped and ready for him when the time was right.

Lily came rushing into my room with a smile on her face. "They're back! He just went to his room to bathe, so he should be here in the next few minutes. Do you need anything else?"

"I ... I don't think so," I replied nervously. "Gods, Lily. What if this doesn't work? What if I can't get him to forgive me?"

She pulled me into her. "You need to be willing to give him time to heal, just like he did for you. It isn't going to be easy, and it's going to hurt to hear how you made him feel, but it is worth it. He is worth it, right?"

I nodded, smiling at her.

She kissed me on the cheek before turning away. "Oh, sorry for punching you by the way."

I laughed at her. "I deserved it."

"Yeah, you did."

"Thank you ... for everything."

"You're welcome." She left while I waited for him to arrive.

Eren arrived in a clean pair of black leather pants and a loose shirt. His hair was still damp from his bath. I stood up from the couch and smiled, making my way over to him. He nodded with a forced smirk. He took in my appearance slowly, stopping at the imprint on my shoulder. His eyes examined the marking, even though he tried not to. He forced his eyes from my shoulder before he turned and headed to the whisky.

"Are you hungry?" I asked.

"I'm fine. I'll grab something before I go back to my room."

"Actually, I was hoping we could have dinner together. Just the two of us," I said, opening the pocket doors to my room. He hesitated, before stepping towards the balcony.

The small round table was filled with foods I knew he enjoyed. Small pearls of light floated overhead. The smell of lavender filled the air.

I looked back to see his expression. His eyes traveled around the balcony as his brow furrowed. He was trying to figure out what I was up to.

"What do you think?" I asked.

"I told you already this isn't necessary. I won't touch you. I promise. You can take whoever you want to conceive an heir."

I took a step towards him, cautiously taking his hands in mine. I shook my head. "That isn't why I did this. I don't want to take anyone else. I just—" I exhaled, not knowing what to say. "Can we just have a nice meal together?"

"You're the princess," he said coldly.

"Yes, and you're the prince."

"Crowned prince. I could be replaced tomorrow." He pulled away, looking out into the landscape.

"Eren, please," I whispered.

He regarded me for a brief moment and then nodded. We sat at the table and ate our meal in silence. I waited to see if he would say anything, but he didn't. Lily had said I would have to fight.

"How was the hunt?" I asked.

"Successful. We took a new group of warriors out into the field today, Zerrial and I. They did well. We killed four creatures that are new to us. We ran into more of those scaled, needle-tailed beasts we faced last time we hunted together," he said, a bite in his tone.

Right, the hunt where he had risked his life to save me, and I had left him there to die.

"Well, that's good. A few less creatures to worry about."

He didn't reply. He sat back into his chair, whiskey in hand while focusing on the horizon. I stood, making my way back into my room.

"I have something for you." I brought out the rectangle box and held it out for him.

"What is this?" he asked, looking at the box suspiciously.

"A gift. To replace the three women I gave you during our gifting ceremony before our wedding."

He took the box slowly and opened it. Inside was a leather sketchbook with his name, *King Erendrial Valor Lyklor*, burned into the cover. A new set of the finest graphite pencils and charcoal were tucked in a canvas holder. He didn't take it out or even touch the items. He just sat looking at them blankly.

"Do you like it?" I asked.

He tossed it on the table and stared at me, folding his hands on his lap. "What is all this?" he snapped, gesturing to the table and gift. "What are you doing? I can't handle this back and forth with you anymore. So, what is it that you want, Genevieve?"

Not quite the reaction I was expecting. "I'm ... I'm trying to make things right between us."

"Why? Why now? What changed?"

"I ... I woke up. That, and Lily literally punched some sense into me."

He laughed under his breath. "Sweet little Lilian hit you?" he asked with astonishment.

"She's pretty strong for her size."

"The lessons with Zerrial must be paying off then."

"You knew he was training her?"

"Of course I did. Who do you think suggested the idea in the first place? As soon as I confirmed who you were and the importance she held in your life, I insisted she be trained. She's a human in the world of fae. She needs to be able to protect herself."

Even before all of this, he had still been protecting what I loved ... protecting my heart.

I knelt in front of him, placing my hands on his knees. He

snapped his attention to me, surprised by my touch.

"I've been so unfair to you," I started to say. "I've treated you horribly, while you were trying to care for me. You've given up so much for me, and I threw it all back in your face. I took out my pain and anger on you and you didn't deserve that. I am so sorry, Eren. Can you ever forgive me?"

"You have nothing to apologize for. You've been through enough," he said, looking away.

"Eren, I want to make things right between us. I want this to be a real marriage. If that is still something you also desire," I said, reaching for his face, pulling him into me.

He exhaled, trying to keep his composure. He gently took my hands and pushed me away. "I'm going to need some time," he said softly.

"I'll wait. For as long as you need, I will wait," I replied, smiling.

"Gen, how do I know this is real? One minute you can't stomach the sight of me, and now you're telling me you want me. How am I supposed to believe that this is real, when you've been telling me for months my very touch sickens you?"

"I wasn't myself. I thought pushing you away would somehow make things easier to handle. But now I realize that is the last thing I needed. I know it is going to take time for you to believe me when I say I want you, but I do. I do want you. I plan to spend the rest of my life showing you just how much," I said, hoping he would smile, but it didn't come. His face remained collected.

"We'll see." He stood, taking his present and walked around me towards the exit. He turned back, without looking at me. "Thank you for dinner. And for the gift."

I stood, while tears fell down my face. "You're welcome."

He left my room without another word.

CHAPTER TWELVE

Erendrial

Knock. Knock. I pulled my heavy head from the pillow, still feeling the effects of my nightly bender. I groaned, allowing my head to fall back into my misery. Maybe if I ignored whoever was at the door, they'd get the hint and leave me the fuck alone.

Knock. Knock. "Fuck," I roared, pushing myself from the safety of my bed. I slid on a shirt before going to answer the door. I swung it open, ready to incinerate whoever was on the other side. "What?" I snapped, before I was able to focus on who had disturbed my slumber.

"Prince Lyklor," Atalee's small voice replied.

I ran my hands over my face, leaning sloppily against the door frame. "Atalee," I replied, "I'm sorry for my rude behavior. What is it I can do for you?"

She held out an envelope addressed to me. "From the princess."

I looked down at the familiar writing. I took it, nodding to Gen's handmaid. "Thank you."

She curtsied before retreating into the safety of the halls. I slammed the door, leaning against the solid surface while I examined the envelope further. Gen hadn't followed me to my rooms last night, even though I had bet myself she would. Stubborn. Hardheaded. Willful. Those were the adjectives I would use to describe my wife. Qualities that, though they pained my very existence, I also adored.

I poured myself a warm drink, liquor free for once, and then settled into the chair in front of the fire. I turned the envelope over and over, debating if I should indulge in her latest attempt to rectify matters between us. Her newfound obsession with seeking my absolution was a breath of fresh air, but could I trust her? She could be conniving and calculative when she wanted to be. Also traits I adored about the little half-breed ... just not when they were used on me.

Had she really come to her senses? Did she no longer fear me? Or was this another frantic attempt to secure her position? My instincts were screaming to toss the letter into the fire, though my heart was desperate to read what hid inside.

Against my better judgement, I slid my thumb under the opening, ripping the thin parchment wide open. I took the folded letter from its confinement.

Eren,

Last night at dinner, you asked me to give you time and space. Two things I reluctantly agreed to, even though I want neither. I take responsibility for my part that has led us to where we are today. We've both made mistakes, said things to hurt the other, or done things to protect ourselves instead of being vulnerable and open to the possibility of a happiness neither of us have ever known.

So, I have decided to go about this differently. As you take the time you need to sort through your thoughts and emotions, I will be patient, and vulnerable. But know there is no other place I would rather be than by your side.

As thoughts or feelings that I wish to share with you surface, I will write them down, sharing every honest, ugly, scared, or happy feeling I have. Before our marriage ... before our physical relations, you were once my friend. Someone I trusted with the darkest parts of me. You never used those things against me, and I never thanked you for that. So, here I am ... choosing to trust you. Choosing to be honest with you, in hopes that you will see my true intentions.

You fought for me ... and now it's my turn to fight for you ... for us.

Yours always,

Genevieve

I folded the paper, pondering over her words. Yet, it didn't change a thing. I refused to live a life with someone who I would have to question their intent daily. Maybe this letter was real. Maybe her feelings had changed. If she had finally pulled herself out of the dark pit she had called home for so long, I was happy for her. I wanted her to be safe, to be happy, but I no longer believed that I was the person to provide that for her. Regardless of her feelings now, she had done a great job convincing me I was worthless. A little too good a job, if I was honest.

I tossed the letter on my desk before dressing for the day. The one good thing about being the crowned prince was that there was always something for me to handle. My schedule was full, which left me little time to think about my marriage.

The next few days, I received more letters from Gen, outlining the experience of the trauma she had endured. The letters were indeed vulnerable and raw. My heart broke for her, reading what she had witnessed through her own eyes.

At dinner, she began asking me to dance. Even though I was appreciative of her trusting me with the letters, I was not ready to venture down this path. There was still so much that needed to be resolved. I loved her … that would never change, but could I be with her? Could I be the male she needed? Was I enough?

Zerrial and the others convinced me to join them for a drink at the alehouse deep within the city. I wasn't much for company these days, but it was better than being stuck alone with my own demons.

The alehouse was packed. Live music and dancing filled the area while ale spilled from the pitchers. The place had low lighting and wooden furniture. It was hot and loud, but it was lively.

Doria and Leenia's laughter filled the room. I smiled, looking over at the two females who I had come to care for like family. Doria's short, black hair bobbed from her thunderous roar. Leenia's radiant red eyes filled with tears of joy while she fought to finish telling Doria whatever had made her lose all sense of control.

Firel sat next to them, not engaging in their nonsense. His shabby brown hair was tussled as usual. The male was brilliant, though his personality needed work. My eyes scanned over Zerrial, who had Lily tucked safely in his arms while she giggled. I laughed to myself. Zerrial, the wild beast who could not be tamed, had allowed a mere human to become his undoing.

In a corner by the bar, Evinee was currently destroying a handful of males in a game of darts. If there was ever a female equivalent of myself ... it was her. Conniving, deadly, too smart for her own good, yet horribly tormented. Ev's best quality was her loyalty, and I would never take that for granted.

This was my family. The ones who truly knew me and would never abandon me. Even though things didn't always go as I would have liked, I had them ... and they were more than enough. I inhaled deeply, catching the scent of lavender and sandalwood. I scanned the room, searching for the source. There, in the doorway of the alehouse stood Genevieve in a sinfully short, green dress.

She eagerly looked through the crowd, her expression uncomfortable before finally she spotted me. I looked away, taking a shot of liquor before refilling my glass.

"Hey!" yelled Lily, signaling for her to join us. "You decided to come after all. I am glad. It's about time you had some fun."

"Yea," replied Gen, taking a seat across from me. "Thanks for the invite, Lily." Her eyes drifted to mine, followed by a small, anxious smile.

Evinee came out of nowhere, landing directly in my lap, wrapping her arms around my neck before planting a lingering kiss on my cheek.

"What's it going to take to get a smile out of you?" she said with an arched brow. "Name your cure. A trove of beautiful naked females, maybe? Whatever it is, I will make it happen, but for all our sakes, please shove this stuffy Lyklor look-a-like back wherever you got him and deliver me my warm and flirty companion."

I chuckled with amusement, shaking my head at my friend's theatrical performance. I caught Gen shoot Lily an unsure glance.

Lily shrugged and tried to gather everyone's attention. "The twins were just about to take the stage."

Doria winked at Oz. "Always the highlight of my night."

Gen asked, "do you two sing?"

Oz scoffed, "not only do we sing ..."

"... but we dance and play instruments," added Voz.

"There's really nothing we can't do," bragged Oz.

Leenia brought her drink to her lips. "I'll vouch for that."

Doria nudged her, causing liquid to spill from the cup. They all began laughing.

The twins took the stage as the highlight of our night began. They played the guitar and violin while they sang and danced to an upbeat tune. The dance floor filled with alfar and humans alike. They danced a quick and choreographed number. A male came up to Evinee, offering his hand to her. She took it as he pulled her off my lap.

Lily looked up to Zerrial, begging to dance with her beautiful hazel eyes. He exhaled and then smiled, pulling her to the floor, leaving Gen and I alone at the table.

"Do you want to dance?" she asked.

I shook my head, watching my friends have fun on the floor. She took another sip of ale.

"The twins are amazing," she commented. "Do they do this all the time?"

I nodded, not looking up from my glass. "I'm going to go get another round," I said, removing myself from the awkward isolation that was our marriage.

I lounged against the bar, waiting to get the barkeep's attention. My eyes trailed from the dance floor back to Gen. Tryverse had found his way to her side. Bile rose in my throat at the sight of the two of them together. The thought of that reckless male touching my wife made me want to go mad.

I took the bottle, making my way over to them. As I got closer, I was able to make out the tail end of their conversation.

"And I told you," whispered Gen, "it isn't going to happen."

"What isn't going to happen?" I interrupted, standing over them.

Tryverse stood up and bowed with a smug smile. "Nothing that concerns you," he said with disrespect. "Princess, I will be seeing you around."

Gen shot back the rest of her drink as I sat back in my chair in silence.

The rest of the night I allowed my family to distract me with their banter and playful spirits. Gen quietly watched, observing each of them. Though I was trying to remain detached from her, I couldn't deny that every time she laughed or smiled at something they did, my heart warmed. This female held too much power over me ... something I feared would be my undoing.

After the night was over, I walked her back to her room. We didn't talk or touch on the way. The castle was quiet as everyone slept. As we approached her chambers, she turned back towards me, looking up with those radiant green eyes.

"Would you like to come in?" she asked.

"Not tonight," I replied. She nodded, trying to hide the disappointment written all over her face. "Good night, princess."

"Night, Eren."

I turned, resisting the urge to take her in my arms, to kiss her, to feel her and taste every inch. I couldn't let myself go down this path again. I had to regain control. Somehow, someway, I had to break the power she had over me. I returned to my room, alone.

Something soft and light brushed over my lips. I felt my nerves twitch in response. I allowed my sleep to take me back into a fitful slumber. Another soft, feathery touch grazed the side of my cheek. I flinched again, restlessly coming awake. I opened my eyes to see Evinee's beautiful violet eyes smiling down at me. She giggled.

"Well, good morning, prince," she said softly, brushing a feather against her chin.

I smiled, rubbing the sides of my face. "Did we have a meeting I forgot about?" I asked, pushing myself up.

"Nope, but I have moved to the second phase of my plan involving those wretched high houses who want you dead. I need your advice on which outfit you think I should destroy them in."

I laughed, making my way to the bathroom. "It's too early for this."

"It's never too early for lingerie," she yelled after me, throwing a pillow that nailed me in the back of the head. I paused, looking back at her with an arched brow. She shrugged, giggling against my headboard. "Oops, sorry."

After I got dressed, I sat back on the edge of the bed, waiting for the show Evinee insisted needed my opinion. She changed about a dozen times, not happy with the cut or material of some of the options. I sat back, listening as she dissected each option. Evinee was stunning, there was no doubt about that. I had never met a male that didn't desire her. At one point, I had been one of those males.

Azeer, that felt like a lifetime ago. Evinee and I had once been something to each other, but we both agreed soon after that our relationship, if you could call it that, was doomed. That was why I had been so shocked about her confession before my wedding to Gen. In all our years together, I never had seen Evinee as vulnerable as she had been that day.

Evinee stood in front of me in revealing red lingerie. She twirled and flipped her hair as she showed off the outfit.

"I totally think the red one is my color," she said, looking at herself in the mirror. "This is bound to get me what I want."

"You're going to traumatize the poor male," I said.

She picked up a pillow next to her and threw it at me. "I am not! He is not going to know what hit him. Come on, like you aren't thinking about me naked at this very minute."

He chuckled, shaking his head.

I heard someone clear their voice. I turned to see Gen, standing in the threshold of my room with a tray of breakfast foods and tea. Evinee looked at her and then back to me, not knowing what to do. She curtsied.

"I'm just gonna—" Ev said, moving into the bathroom, leaving me alone to deal with yet another awkward encounter.

I stood, offering a small smile as I approached. "Good morning," I said, sliding my hands into my pockets.

"I ... " she mumbled, not daring to look at me. "I figured since you were ... working you probably hadn't eaten so I brought you something to hold you over."

I took the plate and set it on a nearby table. "Thank you, but I have servants for that. You're the princess, remember?"

"Right," she replied, fiddling with her hands.

Evinee came out of the bathroom fully dressed and made her way to the door. She stopped and looked between the two of us.

"I'll let you know if I find anything," Ev said uncomfortably.

"Thanks, Ev," I said, nodding to her before she exited.

"Sorry I interrupted," said Gen.

"It's fine. We were finished anyway." She stood in front of me, clearly at a loss for words. I couldn't blame her.

"I'm just going to go," she finally offered hesitantly. "I'll see you at dinner." She turned, heading for the door.

A part of me wanted to explain myself. To explain what she had just walked into, what we were planning and had been combating since the day I had been announced as victor of the tournament. But another part of me knew that keeping her in the dark would keep her safe. She already had so much to contend with as heir to her father's throne. She didn't need my ever-growing list of enemies added to hers.

Refraining from chasing after her, I slid my hands into my pockets and watched as she left my room.

CHAPTER THIRTEEN

Evinee

Slam! The door to Eren's room shut behind me as I marched back through the halls of Doonak. Did the princess seriously think that Eren was going to forgive her so easily after everything she put him through? She didn't deserve him.

I made my way to my rooms, locking myself inside the drab chambers. I slid down against the door, trying to gather my emotions so I could fulfill my duty. I focused on my breathing, trying to take my mind off Eren and Gen.

"There you are." Leenia's voice came from the other chamber.

I snapped my head up, forcing myself to my feet. "Well, good morning to you too, Leenia beans."

"Are you ever going to redecorate this torture chamber?" she asked, looking around the room. "You haven't made a single change since he died."

"It's not like I entertain much," I replied, moving into my bedroom. She was right. I hadn't changed a single piece of décor since my father and his wife had died. This place ... this prison was my personal reminder of where I came from. How my living hell had begun. I guess I was sentimental.

"I'm just saying, this place could really use a spruce up. Maybe some lighter colors and new artwork. This one," she said, gesturing to a painting of a man being devoured by demons, "seems more Doria's things than yours."

I laughed, throwing the lingerie options on my bed before pouring myself a cup of tea. "I relate to that picture more than you know."

"What?" she said, plopping down on the edge of my bed. "A slayer of males?"

I grinned at my best friend. "Something like that." Little did she know how accurate she was.

"How was Eren this morning?" she asked.

I huffed. "Oh, you know, depressed, moody, distracted."

"Your little fashion show didn't brighten his spirit?"

"Nope. And the worst part was when the princess walked in during the peep show."

Leenia chuckled. "Oh, I am sure she just loved that."

"If she didn't want me dead before, I am sure I just moved to the top of her list."

"Eren won't let her hurt you."

"You sure about that? Seems to me that he would do anything to win her back. And apparently, she's had a change of heart regarding her husband. I give it a week."

"Alright, alright, enough Eren talk. Let's get out of here for a bit. A distraction is in order."

"Shopping?" I asked excitedly.

"Yippie ... my favorite."

I laughed, taking her hand and dragging her to the door. "You're the best!"

Down into the city we went, hitting store after store. I didn't need anything new, but it was always a great way to distract me from my problems. Leenia wasn't much of a shopper, but she did love me, so she would often subject herself to my spending habits. Thanks to my father, I had been left with coffers of gold, and I planned on spending every last coin of his blood money.

"What about this?" I asked, pulling a sheer dress from a rack.

"And who are you buying that little piece for?" asked Leenia.

"It's not for me," I said, holding it up to her muscular form. "It's for you. I think Voz would die if he saw you in this."

She snatched it, looking around with embarrassment. "Lower your voice."

"Who is going to hear us? The clerk?" I replied sarcastically.

"For the record, I don't know what you're talking about."

I rolled my eyes, leaning on one hip as I glared at her. "Seriously Leenia? You forget who your friend is. The title our prince so graciously bestowed upon me was spymaster ... ring any bells?"

"It's not what you think."

"So, you spending the last week in his room isn't what I think? Why don't you just brand 'stupid' across my forehead then."

Leenia erupted in laughter, putting the sheer dress back on the rack. "Fine, fine, you caught me."

"No shit," I replied, joining in her laughter. "Who cares what anyone says? As long as you're happy, that's what matters. Everyone else can go fuck themselves."

Leenia looked at me with love in her eyes. "And this is why I love you."

I shrugged with a prideful smirk. "I am quite lovable, after all." We both laughed, pulling each other into an embrace.

I opened my eyes, peered over Leenia's shoulder and caught sight of a few highborn females looking in our direction. They grimaced with disgust and whispered foul gossip. I pulled away, looking at Leenia's beautiful, innocent face.

"Let's hit a pub," I suggested.

"It isn't even noon," she replied.

"So, who cares? I feel like celebrating."

"Celebrating what, exactly?"

"Your happiness. Our friendship. Whatever we want."

Before I could pull her towards the door the three females approached. Leenia's carefree face turned into that of a bloodthirsty warrior. The ladies were dressed in fine jewels and silks. Their skin was flawless, as was their overpriced updos.

"Can we help you?" I asked sarcastically.

"Lady Duprev," the leader of the pack spoke first, turning her attention to me. I recognized her from House Silar. Her father had been close with mine once. "What interesting company you choose to keep."

"You have no idea," I replied, taking a step forward.

She smirked, turning her eyes back to Leenia. "My husband has informed me," she continued, "that one of the councilmen recently proposed a new law imposing death upon those, and their families, who threaten the crown. That would have taken care of your current problem." She gestured languidly to Leenia.

Leenia's father had gambled away some of the crown's fortune, marking her family as traitors and thieves to the crown. She had been only fifteen when the offense occurred but had lived with the stain on her name her entire life. Dark alfar were not known for their forgiving spirits, and they loved a good tragedy.

Leenia went to step forward, but before she could do something that she regretted, I held out my arm, catching her before she took Lady Silar's head clean off.

I smiled, placing my courtly mask in place. "You know," I replied with a bright smile, "now that you mention it, I think I do recall hearing about that new proposal. Funny enough, I think I also heard it from your husband's lips ..."

Lady Silar's smile fell as her eyes darkened.

"... in your bed, of all places. Ha."

She said nothing. I continued. "I personally think it would be a great idea. It would protect our crowned prince who, as I'm sure you know, is Leenia's and my closest friend. It would rid us of anyone who is sulking about the recent royal wedding and looking to do something stupid. And it would single out those truly loyal to Prince Lyklor and Princess Genevieve."

Lady Silar remained silent. Her chest rose and fell rapidly. I had hit my intended target, as usual, and her silence was a welcome result. I smiled down at her tauntingly.

"Is there anything I can help you with?" I heard the store owner say from behind me.

"I didn't realize," spat Lady Silar, "that your establishment catered to riffraff," She gestured to us. "If this is the clientele you are known for, I am afraid my circle and I will be forced to take our coffers elsewhere."

The owner turned to me with a small, cold grin. "Lady Duprev, Miss Yost, I'm afraid—"

"Yea, yea," I said, looping my arm through Leenia's. "Don't worry, we were just leaving." I turned back to Lady Silar with a wicked grin firmly in place. "Tell Lord Silar I'll be seeing him soon." I began to walk away but couldn't help myself. I turned over my shoulder, aiming one more shot. "Oh, and by the way, you must give me your decorator's information. I love those new tapestries in your bedroom. And your body wash did wonders for my skin. Silky smooth, just the way your husband likes it." I winked, pulling Leenia out of the store.

We stumbled out of sight just as Leenia fell into hysterical laughter. We leaned against an alleyway wall as we bent over, fighting to regain control of ourselves.

"You are a bitch," Leenia spat.

"So, I've been told," I replied, finally able to breathe.

"Her face was priceless. And the comment about her soap ... I about lost it right then."

"That stuck-up bitch deserved it. No one talks about my best friend that way."

Leenia smirked, lacing her fingers with mine. "Thank you for sticking up for me."

"Always," I replied firmly. "Now, I do need to be getting back. My new target will be waiting for me soon enough."

Leenia took my arm again as we strolled out of the city. "Who are you milking for information today?"

"Avalon Filarion," I replied with a huff.

"About the queen's behavior?"

"Yup. Time to find out why the queen has completely lost her shit."

Leenia chuckled and shook her head sorrowfully.

"What is it?" I asked.

"Poor, little Avalon. He isn't going to know what to do with you."

I smiled. "Obviously."

I strolled through the crowd at Lyria's Den, the brothel Eren and I ran together deep inside the city. Sounds and smells of sex filled the air. Lavish furnishings and curtains saturated the open pit, providing a warm and alluring aesthetic. Plates of fresh fruit and desserts were scattered across the tables along with vats of wine.

Some of the females who I knew intimately smiled at me as I passed. I nodded my acknowledgement before proceeding towards my target. I turned down a hallway, illuminated by floor-to-ceiling funnels of fire every few feet. The ceiling above swirled with dark magic. I stopped at the back door, placing my hand on the handle. I took a deep breath, preparing myself for what needed to be done.

I shook my head, gathering my composure before clicking the lock open. Inside, a large circular mattress lay on top of a high wooden platform. Curtains hung around the edges of the bed. Chains hung from the ceiling with straps and other devices intended for restraining and positioning. Oils, waxes, and fragrances lined the tables, along with a few daggers and knives. Apparently, young Avalon liked it a bit rough.

I let the door slam behind me, catching the attention of the two human females and Avalon, who were just beginning their adventure. Their heads snapped in my direction. Avalon sat up quickly with a confused expression on his face.

"Sorry for the interruption," I said, my voice dripping with promises of carnal pleasure. "But when I discovered you were visiting my den of ecstasy, I couldn't help myself. Do you mind?"

Avalon remained silent, still unsure about my presence. The two women giggled, sliding off the bed and heading for the door. They stopped on either side of me. I bent down, passionately kissing each one before they exited. I locked the door behind them.

"Lady Duprev," Avalon whimpered, trying to make his voice sound dominating. Azeer, he was a baby. "What do I owe this pleasure?"

I glided slowly towards the bed he sat in. I pulled the small black ribbon on my dress, building anticipation while the fabric fell open, revealing the little red number I knew would be his undoing. The fabric of the dress slid from my shoulders, leaving my curvaceous and full body on display. I moved my hair from my shoulders, allowing my full, supple breasts to take the stage. Avalon swallowed loudly, his eyes scanning every inch of my sinful body.

"Actually," I whispered, leaning down on the edge of the bed. "I was hoping I could be the one to offer you pleasure." I crawled across the mattress towards him. The young alfar trembled with anticipation. His dusty brown hair was already disheveled. His deep green eyes flickered from my face to my body, unsure where to look.

I crawled on top of him, straddling while reaching over him, allowing my breasts to graze his face. I picked up one of the knives on the headboard and turned my attention back to him.

"I was a bit hurt when I discovered you had visited my brothel and didn't think to say hello."

He licked his lips, placing his hands hesitantly on either of my legs.

"I didn't think you had even noticed me, let alone wanted me to say hello," he said, trying to sound confident.

I smiled, placing the tip of the knife against his chest. I applied pressure until blood appeared, then slid the knife down to his abdomen. He grimaced, but I felt him harden instantly underneath me. I bit down on the bottom of my lip and leaned into him. I licked the side of his face, trailing my suggestive tongue to his earlobe.

"Naughty lord," I whispered.

Avalon gripped my ass with his hands as he pressed himself against my center. "I've dreamed about you so many times," he admitted.

I chuckled, pulling away from him as I repositioned the knife against his collarbone, dragging the sharp blade down to his nipple. "Have you really?" I asked.

"Azeer," he said, leaning back while he enjoyed the sensation.

I placed the knife out of his reach, replacing the blade with my lips as I kissed and licked my way up his slender, toned body. His hands began to explore my form, gripping and clawing at my more sensitive spots. I slid my hand along the side of his face, smashing my breasts against his chest. He held me close while I peered into the eyes of my unknowing next victim.

I felt it then. The small, yet powerful slither of my monster lurking underneath my skin. The shiver rattled up my spine, consuming my nervous system. My heart began to pump faster as my blood heated. My vision tunneled, focused on Avalon and his sexual desire. I could smell his testosterone in the air and Azeer, did I want to taste it. My nails elongated, tearing into the mattress as I bent my head down, my tongue tasting his wound.

I moaned with satisfaction while he watched. I closed my eyes, trying to remain in control, but the taste ... it was overpowering. All-consuming in a way I knew would destroy me. Just one more lick. One more taste. I slid my nail against his flesh, ripping his skin in two. He grunted, but I didn't care. I dragged my lips against the sweet, savory gash, allowing the warmth to fill me entirely.

"The rumors are true," he said, snapping me out of my trance.

I pulled away, looking into his desperate, lustful eyes. "And what have you heard?"

"The males talk of your talents and the pleasures you offer. You're every male's fantasy."

I smiled, leaning over him, placing a hand on either side of his face. "And am I your fantasy, Lord Filarion?"

He trembled. "Gods, yes."

I leaned in slowly, my song gathering in my chest. I lowered my lips to his, gently pressing my deadly kiss against his soft, fragile skin. A release billowed from me while I targeted the part of his brain I needed to complete my mission. I allowed my song to take him, trapping him in a web of euphoric pleasure. Avalon's body shook violently underneath me as I wove my power through him, ensuring he would give me everything I asked for.

I cut my power off, giving myself a moment to recoup before sliding to the side of the young alfar. He remained on his back with a lazy smile drawn across his slender face. I traced my finger in circles on his chest, propping my head up on my elbow.

"Sweet Avalon," I said softly.

"Yes," he whispered, turning to face me.

"I've noticed your aunt, the queen, has not been herself. I'm concerned. What ails her?"

"My father says she has gone mad," he replied, stating the obvious. "He works night and day to contain her from her own self destruction."

"Destruction? Has she attempted suicide?"

"Worse. Treason."

My interest was officially piqued. I sat up, grazing my fingers down the side of his face. Avalon closed his eyes, enjoying the contact. I focused on my power, my grip tightening around his hippocampus.

"But she is royal," I stated. "How would she commit treason?"

"The half-breed bitch and Lyklor," he replied. "She wishes to eliminate their claim to the throne, just like she did with the human lover."

I furrowed my brow. "Human lover?" I asked softly. "The queen's human lover?"

"No, the king's human lover ... Genevieve's mother." *Shit.*

"And how did our brilliant queen eliminate the king's human?"

"She discovered the human whore fourteen years ago. She knew that if she brought her existence to the light, the king would bring the woman here to protect her. Nora wouldn't stand for that. So, she took the king's form and visited the human in The Frey. She used a benout insect, knowing the humans wouldn't be able to identify the cause of death."

I took a deep breath, trying to hold onto my facade. *Evil bitch.* "Who knows of this?"

"My father, his father when he was alive, and the queen. I overheard them talking about it a few weeks ago."

"You are so brave, Avalon." He smiled, his eyes fluttering closed. "And how does the queen plan to kill the prince and princess?"

"I'm not sure. I know she's been meeting with a few houses to make Lyklor's death look like an accident, but my father is still working out those details."

"Which houses?" I whispered, brushing his hair across his face.

He smiled. "Sollerum. Gyset. Yositru."

I smiled, leaning down to his ear. "Thank you, Avalon. Now,

forget everything you've just shared with me. I came into the room, gave you the greatest pleasure of your life, and left without a word. We never spoke about anything else. Do you understand?"

He grinned. "I understand. Thank you," he whispered, "for everything."

"Sleep now, Avalon."

He nodded, his head dropping to one side.

Chapter Fourteen

Genevieve

That evening at dinner, I was ready for another round with Eren. I wasn't going to give up. I couldn't. After the last course, we took our thrones upon the platform while the court danced and laughed below. My father had retired for the evening. The queen had displayed another outburst at dinner, so I was sure he had his hands full.

"I'm sorry about this morning," I whispered, leaning into him. "Showing up in your room without an invitation ... that wasn't honoring your request for space and time."

"It's fine," he replied shortly.

"Eren, I know I have no right to ask, but can you give me something here? Anything?"

He turned his head towards me, his eyes full of pain and exhaustion. "We're not good for each other, Gen. Nothing you say or do will change that. I've accepted it. Maybe it's time you do the same."

I dropped my head with the shame and guilt of what I had done to him. "I'm sorry. I'll say it as many times as it takes. I'm sorry," I whispered.

Lord Sollerum approached with his two sons. He smiled at me

brightly and bowed. To Eren, he gave only a simple nod.

"Princess Genevieve," said Lord Sollerum, "you look exquisite this evening. If it weren't for that blemish on your shoulder, you'd be the image of perfection."

Eren exhaled in annoyance.

"I'm not sure what you mean, Lord Sollerum," I replied.

"Having to tie your royal blood to such a low alfar male," said Sollerum, looking at Eren with disgust. "If I was your father, I would have never allowed it. The rules of the tournament should be changed so this type of situation never happens again. It is a waste that you are expected to mix your blood with that of lower-class scum."

Everything inside of me wanted to rip this narcissistic asshole to pieces. Maybe I'd send Otar to his chambers later to do the job, but for now, I had to play this smart. I had to show my power, but in a way that also showed the court Eren now possessed the same power and demanded respect.

I smirked, sitting back on my throne. My eyes glazed over with the darkness I knew consumed them when I gave in to the Dark Flame. Sollerum's face fell at the sight.

"Now, now," I said, deepening my voice to a sarcastic, threatening tone. "Is that any way to speak to the crowned prince? My husband? *Your* future king?" I brought my hand up to my face, dark flames erupting from my skin.

"I ... I only meant that I sympathize with your situation," clarified Sollerum.

"What is there to sympathize with?" I asked calmly. "Erendrial Lyklor abided by the rules of the tournament. He rose above the other three houses who entered the challenge and defeated them fairly. He has proven himself more worthy than anyone in this room. I see nothing to sympathize with."

Sollerum took a step back in shock. "I am sorry, your majesty. I did not mean to offend you," he said, bowing to me.

"When it is my husband's and my time to reign, I will remember this, Lord Sollerum. There may be an empty chair at my table when that time comes." The music in the throne room had stopped. All side conversations came to a halt as we became the entertainment. I took the opportunity to clarify a few things.

I stood from the throne gracefully, without removing my eyes from Sollerum.

"I will remind each of you one, and one time, only. My husband is your future king. You will not disrespect him in public or in private. The next person that speaks or acts against him, I will make an example of myself. Am I clear?" I spoke loudly.

The court bowed. I turned back to Sollerum. "Bow to your king," I demanded.

He moved in front of Eren's throne and bowed.

"Now kiss his feet," I said, returning to my seat.

"What?" asked Sollerum.

"Gen," whispered Eren.

"I said, kiss the feet of your king."

The whole court watched as Sollerum humiliated himself and kissed Eren's feet.

"Now get out of my sight," I demanded.

Sollerum and his sons left the throne room. I didn't look back at Eren. I didn't know if he would be appreciative or embarrassed about what I had just done. I took my leave and headed back to my rooms.

Lily soon arrived and begged me to go to the alehouse with her. I wasn't in the mood. A girl could only take so much rejection for one day. But she was resilient, and I eventually folded.

I changed into a tight, revealing red dress. The outfit was short, barely covering my bottom, and the slit in the front almost made it to my hip. It plunged low at my chest and had an open back. I left my hair down. Atalee helped with the makeup and topped me off with a red lip.

The group was already at the table when we entered the alehouse. The male alfar turned and looked to me with hunger in their eyes as I walked through the crowd. I smiled at the attention, feeling powerful for the first time in a long while. Lily fell into Zerrial's lap and kissed him passionately. I looked away, feeling a bit uncomfortable. Voz got up from the seat next to Eren.

"Oh, you don't have to do that," I said nervously.

Voz gestured to the seat, so I took it, not wanting to make a fuss. Eren kept his eyes on his mug of ale while the others laughed and talked amongst themselves. I fidgeted nervously. The twins got up to make their way to the stage. Their group shouted and clapped. One by one they made their way to the dance floor.

Leenia grabbed my hands and pulled me from the chair. "Come on princess, no need to let that dress go to waste."

Doria laced her arm in mine. Cups of ambrosia passed us by. We each took one and slammed it back. The music filled the air as the tempo quickened. Evinee joined and the four of us danced and laughed together.

After a few too many ambrosias, I found my way back to the table. Eren was still sitting quietly, sipping on his ale. I grabbed my glass and drank deeply. I was drunk, there was no hiding it.

"Question," I said. "Have you slept with all three of them at the same time? Because if so, I want details."

A small laugh escaped from him. A real laugh. I let my head fall back against the booth.

"Oh, thank Azeer, you laughed."

He turned towards me and arched his brow. "I laugh when you're funny. That was funny."

I smiled, feeling the butterflies in my stomach stir. "Have I ever told you how happy your laugh makes me?"

"No."

"Well, it does. Just in case you were wondering."

He turned away from me, looking back into the crowded dance floor. "Wear that dress for anyone in particular?"

"You, of course. I can only focus on one male at a time. You're too much work."

He smirked again. "I am not the difficult one in this relationship."

"Oh, it's a relationship now, is it? That means I get special privileges and access to specific parts of you, if that is the case."

"Princess, I think you are intoxicated."

"Yes, I am fully aware of that fact."

He laughed again, shaking his head.

I focused on the beautiful features of his face and exhaled. My pheromones filled the air around us. He took a deep breath and snapped his head towards me. His pupils dilated while his eyes consumed my body with desire. He shook his head, trying to get a hold of himself.

"That's cheating," he said, shifting away from me.

"I'm desperate."

He laughed again, standing and extending his hand towards me. This was it. I was making progress.

"If you promise not to use your power against me, I will dance with you," he said softly.

I took his hand and pulled myself into him.

"For the record," I stated, "that specific power has grown over the past few months. If I wanted to, I could have you on the table right now, and you couldn't resist me," I whispered as my words slurred together.

"Princess, we are taking this slow," he said, leading me onto the dance floor.

"What happened to us not being good for each other?" I mumbled.

"We aren't," he replied, pulling me into the crowd. "But against my better judgment, I can't seem to stay away from you."

The tempo of the song was quick and upbeat. The twins sang and danced on the stage while everyone laughed and shouted with excitement. We followed the choreography of the dances as we stomped and swayed past each other.

He took me into his arms, closer than I had been to him in months. I breathed out a sigh of relief, my power filling the air. His pupils expanded again. The group of alfar and humans around me began to attack their partners, overcome by lust. I laughed while I watched the mini Jestu take place.

"Oops, sorry," I said, trying to look away from the others.

"I thought you had it under control," he said.

"Guess you still have an effect on me."

He looked down at me, his eyes flashing from joy to sadness. He began to pull away, but I held on as the crowds around us calmed.

"Don't leave me ... please," I said desperately.

He exhaled, looking away. "Come on, let's get out of here," he said, pulling me from the crowd.

We made our way back to the castle. His room was the first one we came to. I stopped at the door, not sure if he wanted me to stay with him tonight. I backed away. "Have a good night," I said, turning to leave.

He grabbed my arm, pulling me into the room. He closed the door and slammed me against it. He stood over me, powerful and dominating. He calmed his breathing while his eyes devoured my face.

His hand slowly rose to my imprint. He removed the small strap of my dress, allowing it to fall down my arm. Hesitantly, he hovered his fingers over the imprint, but I couldn't bear another minute without feeling him. I drew his hand to my shoulder, tracing his fingers along the black lines of the marking. I closed my eyes and exhaled with relief.

His fingers grazed each line of the marking before moving up the length of my neck. I arched my body towards him, enjoying every moment of his affection. He traced my lips with his thumb and I parted them, allowing me to taste his skin. He slid his hand into my hair, pulling my head towards him aggressively. I opened my eyes to see his swirling silver irises glaring down at me.

"You will never deny me again," he demanded, holding my hair in his fist.

I nodded.

"You are mine," he commanded. "Say it! Say you are mine!"

"I'm yours. I'm only yours," I said.

He pulled my face into him, kissing me passionately. He moved me away from the door, tearing at my dress, ripping the fabric down the middle. I pulled his shirt from his body and then started on his pants. By the time we made it to the bed, we were both completely naked. He threw me against the mattress, falling on top of me.

His mouth consumed mine, before moving to my neck and then my breasts. I arched, wanting him to have as much of me as he could take. His hands traveled down the length of my body, squeezing and clawing at my skin. I ran my hands through his dark head of hair. I pulled his face back up to mine, needing more.

He slid a finger inside of me and my entire body erupted with pleasure. He slowly worked in a second and then a third as I moaned, overcome with ecstasy. He stopped moving, pulling his lips away from mine, and looked down at me in shock.

"What? What is wrong?" I asked.

"You ... you have a hymen," he said, pulling his fingers from me.

"My whole body must have been restored when I came back," I said.

He pulled away, rolling to the side.

"Is that a problem?" I asked, confused.

"No, it's just ... I thought you had been with others since you had come back."

"I haven't," I said, feeling ashamed. "I just said that because I was mad and embarrassed that night. Another thing I should apologize for. I'm sorry." I covered myself with my arms, feeling uncomfortable.

"Are you sure you want this?" he asked, turning back to me.

"I'm sure I want you. I want you more than anything."

He took a moment to look at me. I gave him a reassuring smile. He took my face and pulled it into his. My bare body fell on top of him and he turned, pinning me between him and the mattress. I opened my legs in an invitation.

He pushed into me without hesitation. My insides exploded with that incredible feeling I had only ever experienced with him. My entire body erupted in gooseflesh as my pheromones released. The sweet smell of oranges and whiskey mixed with lavender and sandalwood. I laughed, turning his face to mine. His eyes were shut while he moved inside of me. I rubbed my nose against his, trying to get him to look at me. His dark eyelashes fluttered open, revealing silver swirls filled with both pain and happiness.

"I've missed you," I whispered.

He smiled, pressing his lips against mine without uttering a word. I held him close while he moved so perfectly in between my legs. It wasn't rough or lustful. It was calm and savoring, yet full of passion and emotion. The walls of my insides screamed with pleasure as the sensation filled my entire body. I let out a loud moan before I arched my pelvis up, sending him hurtling to the very top of me. He roared while he held himself still, coming to a finish.

He fell on top of me, exhausted from the act. I cradled his head against my chest, running my fingers through his smooth, silky hair. He turned his attention to my chest, kissing my exposed skin tenderly while he ran his hands down my sides. He pulled away and looked deeply into my eyes. I smiled, tracing the details of his face with my fingers. He kissed my palm before rolling to the side. He traced his fingers around each breast, studying my body with his eyes.

"Are you okay?" he asked.

"Better than okay," I answered, turning on my side to look at him. "You?"

He grinned. "I never thought I'd touch you like this again."

I kissed him softly, catching his eyes with mine. "You can touch me like that whenever, however, and wherever you want ... husband."

"I need more of you," he said, his eyes hungry.

"I'm yours, remember?"

He smiled, flipping me to my back. Before I knew it, his teeth were buried into my neck while he sucked the sensitive skin. I gasped, digging my nails into the smooth skin of his back. He forced my legs open with a knee, but didn't enter ... not yet.

I tangled my fingers through his hair, ripping his mouth from my neck before slamming it into my lips. Our tongues lashed and danced in and out of each other, causing my heart to race. Eren tightened his grip around my hips, digging his fingers into my flesh.

I licked the column of his neck, savoring his taste, as he moaned with pleasure. My hand tauntingly traced down the muscles of his abdomen until I reached his perfectly hard cock.

I wrapped my fingers around his girth. He hissed in response. My hand began to slide up and down his length, slowly at first while I watched his face tense. Unable to control myself, my grip tightened, and I pumped faster, feeling my own desire begin to rise.

Eren's breathing deepened. I slid the head of his cock along my wet seam, teasing us both while I hovered his tip right outside my entrance. Before I could push him in, Eren flipped us over, placing me above him. In that moment, time slowed, and nothing matter but him ... but us.

His eyes scanned my body, seeming to study me like a piece of art. Ever so gently, his fingers slid across my skin as if I were the most precious thing in this world. He drew his hand up my chest, to my neck, and then my face, tracing my swollen lips.

"You're so beautiful, princess," he whispered.

I looked down at him, pulled from my euphoric state. "What?"

He sat up, tangling his fingers in the back of my hair. He pressed a sweet kiss to my lips before returning his attention to my eyes. "I said, you are beautiful." *Kiss*. "The very definition of perfection." *Kiss*.

I smiled, unable to contain my happiness. He pulled me closer against him. My breasts smashed against his toned chest while I reached down, positioning his glorious length right where I needed it. I slid myself down his cock, and we both moaned from the sensation.

I moved my hips rapidly, while we held each other, forehead to forehead, entranced in each other's gaze. Unable to contain myself, I reared my head back and yelled with pleasure. His fingers gripped onto my hips while he thrusted savagely in and out of me.

My pheromones released again, and we became animals. I flung myself forward, pushing him back against the mattress as I clawed and tore through his skin. I bit and sucked on anything and everything I could get my lips on.

I positioned my legs on either side of him while I slammed myself repetitively down on his cock. An intense sensation came over me, causing my sex to tense just before I felt release. My orgasm saturated the sheets. I looked down, seeing his body glisten from my release. I slowed, taken aback by what my body had just done. I drew my eyes to Eren.

His gaze was fixed on the moisture that now covered his abdomen and ran down my legs. He looked at me, breathing deeply, and smiled. "Do that again," he said in a deep, raspy voice. He pulled my mouth to his before he continued to thrust quickly inside of me.

My body obeyed his every command without hesitation. I gasped, the sensation overcoming every nerve in my body. Eren gripped my hips, moving me up his shaft as the liquid seeped from me, saturating his dick and pelvis. He slammed me down around him.

"Fuck," he roared, finding his own release. My body shuddered, clenching and throbbing while I rode my orgasm until it reached its peak. I fell onto his chest, our damp skin clinging to each other. He moved my hair from my sweaty skin, tracing his fingers down the length of my spine, pressing a kiss to my head.

My heart was beating so rapidly I feared it would rip itself from my chest. I closed my eyes, trying to catch my breath. The room was spinning, and my sight was blurry, but my body felt incredible.

Finally, I removed my body from his, moisture spreading across my skin. Pulling the covers up to my chest, I moved to his side, looking down at his shimmering body. "That's never happened before," I admitted.

Eren laughed, propping his head on an elbow and turning to face me. "I am glad to hear it," he replied, tracing his fingers along my jaw. "And for the record, I plan on making you do that every time we make love."

I smirked, still embarrassed by what my body had just done ... even though the feeling was incredible. He pulled me into him, wrapping his arms around me tightly while my head lay on his chest. My body was bruised and sore in the most pleasurable way; yet somehow, I already needed more of him.

"You're snuggling, just so you know," I whispered with a smile on my face.

He kissed me on the head and gave me a gentle squeeze. "I'm never letting you go. Never again," he replied.

My heart exploded at that moment. This was real. After everything I had been through, I finally got my time of happiness. I felt warm tears fall from my eyes to his chest.

He pulled back with worry. "What's wrong? Are you okay?"

I pushed up, not able to stop the tears from rolling down my face.

He wiped them away.

"I'm happy," I laughed. "For the first time in my entire life, I have everything I've ever wanted."

He grinned at me, sitting up to kiss me. "And I plan on keeping you that way. For the rest of your life, princess. I will make you happy. You have my word."

I kissed him again before moving back to his chest, wrapping my arms around him tightly. I fell asleep in the arms of the one I had chosen, that had fought for me, that had saved me. The one I truly loved.

Chapter Fifteen

The next morning, I woke up feeling lighter. I pulled away from Eren slowly, making sure not to wake him up. I looked over at his perfect face: his strong jaw, seductive lips, shapely nose, and those adorable dimples. I dragged my fingers along the ribbons of muscles that adorned his abdomen. Gods, he was perfect, and he was mine.

I continued my hand down his abdomen into the sheets until I reached his sex. I wrapped my hand around his girth and squeezed. He took a deep breath in before he let out a moan. I smiled, studying how his body reacted. I turned my attention to my hand, stroking him slowly while I felt him harden and grow. His fingers trailed down the length of my back.

"Find what you were looking for, princess?" he whispered.

I turned my eyes to him and smiled. "Good morning," I replied sweetly, continuing to stroke him.

"It is a good morning," he said, pulling me on top of him. He kissed me passionately as his fingers tangled through my thick hair. He pulled back and looked into my eyes with a smile. "I thought I had dreamt last night, yet here you still are."

"I'm not going anywhere. I'm exactly where I want to be." I kissed him again.

His hands trailed down my curves as he cupped my bottom. I moved my mouth to his neck, sucking and biting down his body, savoring every mouthful. I took his length into my mouth, causing him to moan and tense. I worked him until he was on the brink of climax, then pulled away, positioning myself on top.

He looked up at me, admiring the view. I smiled, slowly lowering myself around him. He let out a groan as I forced him all the way inside of me. I began to move back and forward, watching his pleasure grow. The door to his room flung open as Firel came barging in unannounced. Eren sat up with me still on top of him. He held me close, reaching for the sheets while he shielded my body from view.

"What in Azeer's name are you doing here, Firel? Get out!" demanded Eren, covering me as best he could.

I could still feel him inside of me. I closed my eyes, focusing on our perfect fit. I buried my head into his neck and continued to move slowly. His grip around my waist tightened as he held the sheets against my bare body. He let out a deep grunt. I laughed, continuing to kiss his neck.

"I ... uh," mumbled Firel uncomfortably. "The king ... he requests both of your presences in his private chambers."

I continued to move, quickening my pace. Eren's grip tightened, preventing me from moving any faster.

"We will be there shortly, now get out," demanded Eren.

Firel turned, trying not to look. "Should I ... should I tell him you are on your way, or should I give him a specific time?" asked Firel.

"For the love of Azeer, out, Firel!" yelled Eren, before he slammed me into the mattress, unable to control himself any longer. The door banged shut. I laughed with joy while he kissed and touched and pleasured me. I never wanted to start another morning without this again.

We took a bath together for the first time, which added another twenty minutes to our already delayed start. I had Atalee bring me a dress. We got ready and had each other one more time before finally making our way to my father's chambers. We walked through the halls hand in hand, smiling at one another. The court stared, not used to seeing this type of affection, but neither of us cared.

We entered my father's room to find lunch on the dining table. Eren pulled out a seat for me before leaning down to kiss me on the shoulder. He took his own seat to my left. I blushed at his display of affection. My father sat across from us and watched while he placed food into his mouth. Eren filled my plate and poured me a glass of wine before serving himself. My father sat back and smiled.

"I figured the two of you would be famished," commented my father, "since it took you over an hour to grace me with your presence from the time I first called for you."

I blushed. "Lunch is much appreciated. Thank you, Father," I said with a smile.

"And we apologize for our late arrival. It won't happen again," Eren added, winking at me.

My father paused, looking between the both of us. "Don't make tardiness a habit. Now, onto business. The rift has finally reappeared along our west border, as Narella warned. We were prepared and the threat was eliminated as it came through, but we have had multiple reports that the rift also opened along our southern border and the light court's northern border this morning, while you both were occupied."

"How many creatures came through?" I asked.

"Dozens. Our lands are swarming with them. I've sent out multiple hunting parties, but I am afraid the rifts are going to keep appearing, as Narella foretold," said father.

I looked at Eren; he wore his thinking face. "What is it?" I asked him.

He looked at my father and then to me. "I have a theory, and it is going to sound a bit crazy," said Eren.

"What has that crafty brain come up with this time?" asked my father.

Eren snickered, leaning against the table. "Your majesty, there are a few things we have been keeping from you that we'd like to inform you about," he said, looking at me.

I nodded, letting him know I was on board.

Father assessed the two of us closely. "Go on ...."

"Narella was how I found Gen's body after ... after she was murdered. She was also the one who delivered the demons to our door." Eren stopped, looking to me to tell my father the last bit.

"She also saved me last month," I said, embarrassed by my foolish actions. "For the past few months, I had Tryverse Feynar reconstructing my mind. He would take away the memories of what the demons had done and replace them with other memories that weren't my own. He did it so much that it began to shatter my reality. That was what caused the seizure I had at the chamber meeting. I went into a coma and almost died."

"I went to Narella for help," continued Eren. "Otar told us she is a god. I thought that if anyone would have the power to save Gen, it would be her. She agreed to help and sent me into Gen's mind to retrieve her."

My father appeared calm, but I could tell he was fuming inside. "What is your theory, Erendrial?" asked Avalmon.

"I believe Narella is leashed the same way the other creatures are to Alaric," explained Eren. "She has assisted us every time we needed it. When I've met with her before, she's allowed little hints about her situation to slip. She's talked about having to check in and having a specific time frame she could stay. At her court appearance, she told us where the first rift was going to open. Why do that? Why not allow it to be a surprise?

"What if she is looking for a way to free herself from Alaric? What if she is helping us in return for her freedom? This would change everything. We would have a god on our side who has intimate knowledge of Alaric's operation."

"That is a theory, Erendrial. One we cannot prove, and if we are mistaken, it would cost us everything," said my father.

"I know how to contact her. If we can just—" said Eren, but my father held out his hand to stop him.

"No one will be contacting the god without my permission," the king said, turning towards me. "Daughter, I know what occurred in your past is traumatizing, but you cannot act in this reckless manner. You have more than yourself to think of. You are next in line to the throne. You were foolish and dabbled in powers neither you nor Feynar fully understood or could control. He is very young when it comes to his gift. That was irresponsible."

"Your majesty, she was trying—" Eren said before my father interrupted him again.

"And you—how dare you keep this from me? I should have been the first being you came to for help. You had no right to act on your own. Gods are tricksters. I am sure Narella expects something in return for assisting you now three times. You will be king someday. You need to exhaust all your options before gambling away your greatest weapon," said the king.

Eren shifted uncomfortably, refusing to bring his eyes to my father.

"I'm sorry, Father," I said.

"Back to the rift," he continued. "If the number of creatures coming through continues to grow, as I expect they will, prepare yourselves for a visit to the light court. We will have to convene with them to develop a plan and a larger military attack. If what Narella said is true, we need to prepare for war. In the meantime, neither of you will be attending another hunt until I've cleared you to do so."

"But your majesty, my team—" began Eren.

"Your team will be fine," said my father. "You have trained them well, Erendrial, but you are now a royal. Your safety is a priority. You can't be running into battle every time a creature passes through. Have confidence in your team and our warriors to do their job. That is what they are there for."

"If things continue to worsen, when should we prepare to leave for Urial?" asked Eren.

"Within a week. We will reassess then, but a visit to the light court is unavoidable. We need to be ready for anything." We both nodded. Father stood from his chair, moved around the table, and kissed me on the head before looking down at me with endearment. "I'm sorry I had to be so harsh on you. As your father, I am glad you are safe and happy." He pulled me into him for a hug.

I wrapped my arms around him tightly. "It won't happen again," I whispered. "I promise."

He pulled away and nodded to Eren with a smile.

We left his rooms and headed down into the city. We went to Herstus's cafe and ordered two hot chocolates. Eren was quiet while his powerful brain worked.

"What are you thinking?" I asked.

"Narella. I really think she is the key to winning this. We barely know anything about Alaric. She could win this for us. She could be the arrow he doesn't see coming," said Eren.

"Ah," I gasped as Otar's sigil began to spin and burn, a sign the creature had died yet again "Seriously, Otar!" I exclaimed.

Eren laughed. "Come on. I can't wait to watch the temper tantrum he throws when he finds out you're mine," he said, winking at me.

We called our ragamors Eeri and Tarsyrth and took off into the sky to find Otar's dead body. The sigil led us to a wide river at the border of our territory, near the light court's land. We dismounted and headed into the cold water. The river was deep, and the current was violent. I looked around for Otar's body, but couldn't find it.

"I'll go beneath to see if I can see him. Stay here," said Eren. He dove under and then finally emerged two minutes later.

"Did you find him?" I asked.

"Yeah. Whatever killed him cut him open and filled him with stones. Give me a second, I've almost got him emptied," he said, diving back under. When he reemerged, I rushed out into the water, helping him drag Otar's body to the bank. We pulled him out, both panting from exhaustion.

"What did this to him, you think?" I asked.

"Not sure, but I can't wait to find out. Go on, I won't look.

Resurrect the thing," he said, walking some distance away.

Otar was missing his arms. His ears were once again removed. His mouth was sewn shut and his stomach was cut open. All his organs were missing. A few rocks still hid inside.

I cleaned him out and then fed him my blood. I lit him on fire and watched while his body turned into an ash cocoon. I made my way over to Eren as the waiting began. He had removed his shoes and was taking off his shirt. I smiled at the sight of him.

"Not that I'm complaining about the view, but what are you doing?" I asked.

He turned around and grinned, gently turning my body so I faced away from him. I felt his fingers fumbling with the laces of my dress. "You're wet and need to dry off," he said with a husky voice. "It's a beautiful day, so why not let the sun do all the work?" He leaned down, brushing his lips against the edge of my ear. "What it misses I will happily lick off."

"Here? Now?" I asked.

"There's no one around, princess. Plus, you didn't seem to care much that we had an audience this morning. You took me off guard, that's for sure," he replied, sliding the dress off my body. He moved his mouth to the shoulder bearing our imprint. He kissed and traced his tongue around the lines.

I groaned with pleasure. "I couldn't stop. You felt so good," I admitted. "I didn't care who was watching. I just needed to feel you move inside of me."

He pulled back and laughed, taking my face in his hands. "You sound like a dark alfar," he said playfully.

"And I'm proud to be one," I replied, violently taking his mouth with mine. He eased us down onto the soft grass. "Eren," I panted.

"Yes, princess," he said, looking down at me.

"Don't be gentle."

He grinned, biting the nape of my neck. "As you wish, Your Highness."

We spent the next thirty minutes rolling around in the soft grass under the sun. My body was bruised from his teeth and grip. I wore each marking with pride. He looked just as bad as I did, which made me smile.

After we had caught our breath, he helped me back into my dress, fastening the back ever so slowly. With each lacing, he would kiss my neck tenderly. I closed my eyes, enjoying every touch.

"Your nickname should be ambassador of pleasure," I said.

He chuckled, holding me in his arms. "You are satisfied, I presume?"

"More than satisfied. Though I can't wait to do it again. You feel better than anything I've ever experienced"

"I remember you telling me once that the King Fucker could run laps around me," he said playfully, nipping the tip of my ear, even though I knew he was looking for me to deny the claim. I turned, kissing him passionately.

"I've been with others besides you? Hmm, funny, I don't remember any others."

"Good answer, *wife*."

My heart skipped a beat. My cheeks warmed from the title. "Call me that again," I whispered.

"Wife," he said slowly.

"Again."

"Wife." *Kiss.* "My wife." *Kiss.* "My beautiful, brilliant, wife."

I wrapped my arms around his neck, tangling my fingers through his hair and began to passionately kiss him, wanting him again in the grass right there.

"No!" I heard Otar yell behind us.

I turned to see him stomping and flinging his arms around as he worked himself into a fit of rage.

"No! No! No!" Otar yelled. "Not him. Not that one! Choose another. I insist. Choose another wicked one!"

"Otar, calm down," I said, walking towards him.

"Why? Why? Why? He doesn't deserve you. No, no, no he doesn't," snapped Otar.

"Otar, I'm happy. I want to be with him. Please understand that. He is good for me. He's the one I want," I said softly.

Otar huffed and puffed while he growled lowly to himself. Eren came up beside me, wrapping his arm around my waist, resting his chin in the nape of my neck.

"Well, Otar," said Eren sarcastically, "looks like I'm your new daddy."

Otar lost it. He picked up boulders, throwing them into the water. He rushed up into a nearby tree, breaking and snapping the limbs. He tore at the ground and the bushes around him. Eren stood back watching and laughing at the little devil. I couldn't help but chuckle along with him.

"You're evil," I said to Eren.

"In a sexy way," he said, winking at me.

Otar finally calmed, walking over to us with his arms folded against his chest. He refused to look at Eren. "I do not claim you," Otar said, turning his nose up.

Eren exhaled, then approached Otar. He looked him in the eyes more tenderly than I had ever seen him with the creature.

"Otar," Eren said softly. "I promise you I will not hurt her. Her well-being and happiness are my top priority. She means more to me than anything. You have my word, I will always put her first."

My heart swelled at his admission. I still couldn't believe he was real. That he was my husband. All mine.

"We will see," Otar said in a snarky tone.

"Otar, what killed you this time?" I asked.

He stomped over to me. "Little fucking midgets with fucked up faces and axes," said Otar.

"You ran into dwarfs?" asked Eren, seeming surprised by the description.

"I thought you couldn't find them unless they wanted to be found?" I asked.

"That's usually the case," explained Eren. "We haven't had contact with their kind in over five hundred years. They like to keep to themselves."

"Well, I found them," snapped Otar. "What? Like it was hard. You doubt my intelligence, ungrateful prince?"

"Not at all. I am just surprised," said Eren.

"I was scouring the mountain peaks at the northern border. I stumbled across an entrance towards the top, so I invited myself in. The tunnel led into one of their cities. I was able to stay hidden for a day while I searched their ruins. They had fairies tied up in their dungeons. They raped and beat them. I laughed while I watched one get their wings ripped from their back. That's when I was caught.

"I tried to explain that we were the same. That I *hate ... resent ... loathe* the fairy scum, but they wouldn't listen. They cut off my arms. Then they took my ears and slit me open. Little fuckers," spat Otar.

"That goes against the treaty they made with Doonak centuries ago," commented Eren. "They will have to be dealt with once we have the rift under control."

A zap ran up my spine before it made its way to the brain. Otar felt the pain and reached for me before I could hit the ground.

I saw Narella, standing by a cave of poppies. The same cave the demons had taken me to be tortured and later murdered. She smiled, offering her hand to me. I took it, feeling a sense of comfort.

She pulled me into her and brought her lips to my ear. "Come find me," she whispered. I snapped my eyes open to see Eren and Otar looking down at me.

"What did you see?" asked Eren.

"I think Narella just hijacked my gift," I said, sitting upright. "She sent me a vision and told me to come and find her."

"It could be a trap," stated Eren.

"I agree with the asshole," growled Otar. "Narella cannot be trusted. No, she cannot."

Eren turned my face to him. "I know you, princess. I don't want you to go, but if you decide to, I am coming with you. Understood?"

I smiled and nodded. Eren was right. Narella could be the key to winning this thing. We would have to make contact with her if we wanted what she had to offer. I would be going into the meeting completely blind, but it was a risk I was going to have to take.

"After dinner, I will go to meet Narella," I said to Eren and Otar.

"May I kill her?" asked Otar.

"Not unless something goes wrong," I answered. "Otar, you will stay close but hidden, for the time being. She may still be unaware you are working with me."

"She's a god, princess. She knows," said Eren, running his hand through his hair. He was stressed about my decision, but supported me. "Where are you supposed to meet her?"

I dropped my eyes, feeling a shiver of fear run up my spine. "The cave where the demons took me," I said quietly.

Eren's head popped up with a look of puzzlement. "You aren't going," he said adamantly.

"Eren, this may be our only chance," I replied. "You even said it yourself. She could be the key to ending Alaric."

He huffed, clenching his jaw.

I went over to him, taking his face in my hands. "I'm right here. That cave is just a place. It doesn't hold any power over me anymore. Plus, you and Otar will be there if anything goes wrong."

"She's a god, Gen. We don't have a clue about how powerful she is. This could be a trap."

"If she wanted to kill me, she could have when I was lying unconscious on my bed, but she didn't. This is going to work. It must," I said, smiling up at him.

"I can't lose you again," he whispered, closing his eyes.

"You won't." I pulled his face down and kissed him softly for reassurance.

"Yuck! May I go" snapped Otar, pouting behind me.

"Yes, meet us after dinner, and please don't get yourself killed before then," I said.

Otar glared at Eren before disappearing.

I turned back to him. "Do you need to check in with the others?"

"It's probably a good idea. Hopefully, Zerrial and the others are back by now," Eren said, calling Eeri down from the sky. He mounted and then pulled me up onto her back. I turned around in the seat and straddled my legs around him, placing us face to face.

"What are you doing?" he asked.

"I like the view from this angle better," I said, wrapping my arms around his neck. "Have you ever had sex while flying a ragamor?"

He laughed, pulling me in closer. "You're going to get us killed," he said, rubbing his nose against mine.

"At least we'll go out happy."

He leaned down slowly, pressing his firm torso against mine as I laid against Eeri's back. He kissed me passionately as we shot into the air.

CHAPTER SIXTEEN

When we got back to the castle, we made our way to his room. We couldn't keep our hands off each other. The court stared, but no one said a word. They were used to people fornicating around every corner. Why should we be any different? As we pushed through his doors, I tore at his shirt, reaching for the clasp of his pants. He picked me up, setting me onto the table while he devoured my neck.

"Uh, hmm," someone cleared their voice.

We pulled our attention away from each other to see Evinee standing in the room. I looked at the beautiful female and felt a bit insecure. I didn't know what type of arrangement she and Eren currently had, but my mind went to the worst possible scenarios. Was that why she was here? To distract him? I straightened my dress, sliding off the table. I looked at her and then back at Eren as he tied his pants.

"I'll just ... go," I said, walking past him without a word.

He grabbed my arm, pulling me back to him. He looked at Evinee, placing his politician mask on. "What is it?" he asked her.

"It's about the assignment you gave me. I've discovered something that affects the princess," Evinee said, nodding towards me.

"You can speak freely around her," Eren said.

Evinee hesitated before she walked towards us.

"I seduced Avalon Filarion, the queen's nephew, as you requested. He opened like a book. The queen has been slowly losing it for months now. Her brother is trying to hide it, but we've all seen her outbursts getting more violent and public. The stress of her position, her marriage, and not being able to produce an heir has sent her mad. The king hasn't visited her chambers in almost two decades."

"We assumed this already," said Eren.

"She has been secretly meeting with Houses Sollerum, Gyset, and Yositru for weeks, plotting against you and Genevieve. Her brother is trying to stay ahead of her schemes, but she is a loose cannon."

"My father will have her head," I swore.

"There's more." Evinee paused, looking at me. "Avalon told me that he overheard her admit to being the one that killed Princess Genevieve's mother. She took the king's form and visited her. When she had her guard down, the Queen used a benout insect on her. She didn't know about Genevieve, or I am sure she would have killed her as well."

"What is a benout insect?" I asked, looking at Eren.

He hesitated. "It's an insect that is inserted through the ear. It travels to the brain and eats the tissue until there is nothing left.

We haven't used them in centuries. It's a horrible way to go," he admitted, trailing his hand down my arm.

I felt the sting of losing my mother all over again. Not only had she been murdered, but she died painfully, even by dark alfar standards. My mind spun with what Evinee had discovered.

"Where is the queen now?" Eren asked.

"I don't know. No one has seen her in the past day," Evinee answered.

"My father needs to know this," I whispered.

"And we will tell him," said Eren, "but Gen, you must prepare yourself for an outcome you may not want. I know your father cared for your mother greatly, but it isn't a crime to kill a human. The council would never agree to sentence an alfar to death over this. Especially not their queen."

"There are other ways to kill an alfar without the permission of the council," I stated.

"Thank you, Evinee," said Eren. "Good work as always. If you find anything else, please come to us."

She nodded, looking at him longingly. She dropped her eyes and made her way out of the room.

He turned me towards him and raised my face to his. "We will have justice for your mother. I promise," he said, kissing me gently.

"You are the most dangerous alfar in the kingdom," I said, giving him a small smile.

"Now that you're in my bed and under my spell, I have no

competition."

I let a small chuckle escape, but my gaze fell away from him.

He ran his hands through my hair, pulling me in close. "You can talk to me," he whispered.

I paused, still trying to grasp what had happened to my mother. "She died because she loved my father. Because he loved her. He's never going to forgive himself for this," I said, feeling a tear run down my face. "How am I going to tell him his wife is the reason for her death?"

"You won't have to. I will," Eren said, lifting my chin. "We will do it together."

I nodded, a bit relieved. "We should probably tell him now, so when the queen makes a reappearance, we are prepared."

He nodded, taking my hand, and leading me to my father's chambers.

Eren told my father everything Evinee had discovered. I stood silent, unsure of his reaction. He refused to look at either of us. His face showed no sign of emotion. He didn't ask questions or react whatsoever. After Eren was done, the king thanked us and then we were dismissed. I stepped forward to go to him, but he stood, turning his back on me.

Eren and I went down into the city to check on the rest of his team. He led me towards the bottom of the cave where old halls and tunnels had been abandoned. There were no alfar in sight, and the area was barely lit. The place looked like it had been neglected for centuries.

"Where are we going?" I finally asked.

"My safe house," he said casually.

"You have a safe house?"

"I do."

"Any other secrets you want to let me in on?"

"We have at least another eight hundred years together. I have to keep you on your toes, princess."

I smiled, happy that I was the one he saw spending those centuries with. We stopped at a wall at the end of one of the tunnels. He waved his hand over the rock as a V and L interlocked inside of a circle. The marking glowed silver before a door appeared in the stone.

"This is amazing," I said.

He turned to smile at me. "Leave it to the twins," he said, grabbing my hands.

The door opened to reveal an extravagant floor plan with multiple rooms for science, weapons, dining, seating, and strategizing. The ceilings were tall, with rows of bright bulbs of light streaming across the surface.

Eren's family busied themselves around the room. The twins were in the lab. Zerrial inspected new weapons, and Firel sat at a table near the massive wall of books. Evinee and Leenia lounged on one of the couches near where Doria was reading. One by one, their eyes snapped up to us and they looked from Eren to me, hesitant and confused.

Evinee walked over to us while the others began to gather. "Eren, what are you doing?" she asked. "Why did you bring her here? No offense, princess."

"You've just compromised the space," added Doria.

Eren smiled at both of them and turned to the twins. "Voz, Oz, please make sure Genevieve can access the safe house," Eren instructed.

Evinee threw her hands in the air and walked away from us.

"So, what Firel told us this afternoon was true?" Leenia asked, winking at me. "You two have humped your way into a good place?"

Eren shot Firel a dirty look. "We've come to an understanding, yes," answered Eren.

"And what is this understanding?" asked Zerrial with a mischievous look. "Just so we're all clear."

Eren looked at me and smiled. "That she is mine," he said proudly.

The group looked at us for a moment, not saying a word, then all laughed hysterically.

Voz slapped Eren on the shoulder.

"*You* ... own the princess?" laughed Oz.

"Well, parts of her at least," added Eren.

I nudged him in the side with my elbow.

"Welcome to the family, princess," said Oz, pinching me on the chin. "We'll get you coded into the key lock as soon as we can."

I was taken aback by his physical contact. None of them had given me the time of day, even at the alehouse. Now that I was officially with Eren, it changed things. They trusted Eren and looked up to him, which meant they trusted his judgment. Zerrial came up to Eren and gave him a smile and nod. Eren smiled back. They silently communicated with each other in their own language. Firel approached, bashfully lowering his head to both of us.

"Sorry … for this morning," he said uncomfortably.

"Just don't make it a habit," Eren said, taking him by the shoulder. "Ev, have we found the queen yet?"

"Nope," answered Evinee. "I've scoured the entire castle. She is either in the city somewhere or has left the kingdom altogether."

"Why would she do that?" asked Doria. "She doesn't know we are on to her."

"She's crazy," commented Voz. "What do you expect?"

"We have some movement from house Gyset," added Zerrial.

They all took their seats around the round table. I stood next to Eren uncomfortably, realizing I was the outsider. He pulled me into his lap, tucking me against him as he lounged back in the chair. He held onto my hip tightly, trailing his fingers down the side of my arm.

"Alright, how do they plan to kill me this week?" asked Eren.

I looked at him in shock, but he was focused on Zerrial.

"During the next large-scale battle," Zerrial started, "They're trying to rally other houses to partake in a coup. They plan to make it look like an accident and say the creature was responsible."

"What proof do you have?" I asked.

"Nothing tangible," answered Zerrial. "I've been keeping tabs on house Gyset for five months. One of their chamber servants saw Yous Gyset meeting in his rooms with Beran Sollerum and Nal Yositru."

"And you trust this chamber servant?" I asked.

They looked at each other and chuckled.

"Genevieve, we have eyes and ears everywhere," explained Doria.

"We've been building this system for over a hundred and fifty years," Leenia confessed proudly. "We've gotten quite good at it, actually."

I looked at Eren. He smiled and shrugged.

"Most dangerous alfar at court," I whispered with a smile.

"Is that all I am, princess?" Lust and desire flickered behind his swirling silver eyes.

My heart quickened at the sight of him. I caught my breath as my cheeks blushed. I let out a small portion of my pheromones. He inhaled, closing his eyes, and letting out a small moan before his hand slid under the slit of my dress to my leg.

"Is it Jestu already?" Voz sarcastically asked.

Oz laughed at his brother. Eren pulled his attention away from me.

"So, what are we going to do about the houses?" asked Leenia.

"They each have their own separate armies that follow their command," continued Zerrial. "They would have enough people to surround Eren and take him down if we indeed go to battle again."

"We will," interrupted Eren. "We were just informed this morning that we are leaving for the light court in a week, to reinforce our alliance to prepare for battle. The king anticipates the rift will continue to open just as Narella threatened."

"I call light court chauffeur," yelled Evinee.

"You all will be coming with us," ordered Eren. "We didn't leave on good terms, as I am sure you can recall. We did steal Lysanthier's murderer." He pinched my side playfully. "Plus, I'm sure they're mocking our kingdom for allowing a lowborn bastard to sit on our throne. I don't expect this to be an easy trip."

My heart ached. I had never realized how much it affected him to hear people talk about his status. I could hear the shame and insecurity in his voice. I ran my hands through his hair for comfort.

"Yes! I call Gaelin," yelled Evinee. "If you don't mind, that is, princess."

"He's all yours," I said, uncomfortable.

"Any advice?" asked Evinee, leaning across the table. "Maybe we could meet up later and you can tell me what he likes. I am sure I can give you a few pointers about what makes Eren tick."

I felt a spike of rage and anger at the thought of them together.

She was goading me.

Eren's grip on my leg tightened. "Back to the houses," interrupted Eren, shooting Evinee a glare.

"I vote to kill them," suggested Doria.

"I second that vote," said Voz.

"It won't stop them from coming after Eren again," interrupted Zerrial. "We need a sign of force. Something they won't dare to challenge."

"Okay, let's just have Gen light their asses on fire," suggested Leenia. "That will shut them up."

"May I?" I asked with hesitation. They all looked at me for a moment in silence. Zerrial nodded his acceptance. "It can't come from me," I said, trying to think. "They need to fear Eren in order to respect him." I thought back to his advice to me when I first came to the dark court all those months ago.

"They do fear him," stated Leenia. "That's another reason why they're trying to remove him from the throne. They've watched him work and achieve everything he now possesses for the past hundred and fifty years. Now they believe he has reached too far."

I pondered for a moment. "Tell me about their heirs," I finally said. They looked at each other with confusion.

"Sollerum has two sons," started Oz. "Helor and Hashen. They seem to stay out of our way, for the most part. We see them at the gentleman's club often. They've never been hostile or rude to any of us."

"Gyset has a daughter," interrupted Voz, "Ophilia. She is a little over a hundred and twenty, but very experienced in the bedroom." His eyebrows rose up and down flirtatiously. "From what we have gathered, she despises her father. He ignores her for the most part."

"Then that leaves Soddram," said Leenia. "He and his father seem close, though Soddram is power-hungry. He is clever and good with a sword. He visits your cousin's bed almost every night."

"Every night?" I asked with astonishment. I turned back to Eren. "Guess you were replaced."

"A small mercy," he said, winking at me.

"What are you getting at, princess?" asked Doria.

I paused, thinking all the details over. "What if we got their heirs to betray them? We figure out what each of them wants and then deliver. We make allies out of the houses that currently want Eren dead. In exchange for giving them what they want, we make them sign blood contracts pledging their allegiance to Eren. Then they turn their houses against their fathers. We bring their treasonous acts to the court. Once we reveal their guilt, we have their heirs slit their throats in front of everyone. After, they will bow to Eren, and so will I," I said, turning to smile at him.

The room went silent.

"Damn, being killed by your own heir," mumbled Oz. "Brutal."

Firel smiled widely. "Everyone will fear Eren's mind and your power. They will have a front row seat as they watch Eren turn blood against blood. It's brilliant,"

Voz added, "Ophilia will be the easiest to turn. She will be happy to be rid of her father while taking her place as the head of the family."

Oz exhaled. "Helor and Hashen are going to be a challenge. I can't tell if they are just waiting to attack or if they truly have no ambitions."

"I can get Hashen to talk," admitted Doria.

Eren's face turned up into a smile. "I thought you ended that seven decades ago. You said you were scared of *feelings*."

"Oh, look who's talking, Erendrial Lyklor," Doria said with an attitude. "And no, I didn't end things, so I still have influence."

"That just leaves Soddram," added Evinee.

"Leave him to me," I said.

"Do you think that's wise?" commented Firel. "You were the wife he lost."

"I don't think I was the wife he wanted," I replied. "Out of all my suitors, he was the one who showed the least interest. And if what you say about him and my cousin is true, it's likely there is more to their involvement then even we know."

"Right ... now that all of that's settled, we should be getting ready for dinner," instructed Eren, standing and keeping me close to him. "Oh, where are we at with those new weapons?"

"Test runs are tomorrow," answered Voz smiling at Oz.

"My favorite day," said Leenia, smiling with glee.

"Can I attend?" I asked.

"It would be an honor," Oz replied, giving me a dramatic bow. Voz hit him, sending the twins into a fit of laughter.

"Also, Zerrial, I want you to start training Gen," instructed Eren, pulling me towards the door.

Zerrial bowed.

"What? But I already train with Varches," I said.

"You've seen how the beast fights," Eren said, pushing us to the door. "He is unmatched, and I will only have the best for my wife."

CHAPTER SEVENTEEN

Erendrial

T hat night at dinner, I danced with my wife. She laughed as I twirled and glided her across the dance floor. I had truly thought I would never see this version of her again, yet here she was, tucked into the safety of my arms. I hated that we had so many political matters to handle. All I wanted to do was worship her body for the next century, but we were royal and didn't have that luxury.

After dinner, we made our way back to her room and called for our ragamor. I wasn't thrilled that we were headed to the place that still haunted my nightmares, but I still believed Narella would align herself with us. Though, it disturbed me that she could manipulate Gen's visions, even if that meant we had a way of communicating with the god.

We landed near the dreadful cave. Poppies still lay at the base of the entrance, even though winter had come, and summer was on the horizon. The place must have been enchanted. I hadn't been able to look at the flowers since I had found Gen's body inside six months ago. She came up beside me, wrapping her arm around mine and leaning into me.

"We haven't talked about that yet," she said. "Lily told me you were the one that found me?"

I tore my eyes away from the cave, thinking about her body mutilated and half-eaten in the center of a burning pentagram. "I was," I said shortly. "Another time. We need to focus on Narella."

"Yes, you do," Narella's voice came from behind us.

We turned around to see the stunning blue-haired goddess leaning against a tree. She wore a blue flowing gown that contrasted her snow-white skin. "Glad you got my invitation, Princess Genevieve. Though, I don't remember asking you to bring guests."

"Where she goes, I go," I said.

"Yes, I've noticed." Narella snickered. "Oh, Otar, you can come out of hiding now."

Otar yelled out in frustration and anger as he came down from the mountain, cussing and tossing small rocks at nothing in particular.

"Controlling bitch," Otar spat, taking a place next to me.

"I've missed you too, you little hellion," crooned Narella. She puckered her lips and blew Otar a kiss. "I see you've replaced one master with another."

"If you try to hurt her, I will pull out your heart and eat it in front of you," threatened Otar with a growl.

"You've grown attached. How sweet," said Narella with surprise.

"You have no clue," I added.

"Why did you want to meet with me?" asked Gen.

Narella focused her eyes on Gen. She walked over slowly and extended her hand out to touch her face. Otar and I both stepped in front of her. "Calm down boys, I am not going to hurt your lady," Narella assured us, stepping back.

"Then what do you want?" I asked.

"You already know what I want, you clever boy. You figured it all out, without me having to say a word," answered Narella. She looked me up and down slowly, taking in my figure and the details of my face. She leaned around me and looked at Gen. "I can see the appeal. Got any more like these in that mountain of yours? I would love to have one of my own," she said, turning her eyes back to mine.

"Afraid he's a collector's item," replied Gen. "But back to what you say you want. Are you being held against your will, like Otar?"

Narella exhaled with a laugh. "My ... situation is similar, yes. I am unable to answer your questions due to some magical restrictions, but I am confident you both can find a way around that. I've been watching the two of you and I am impressed, to say the least."

"Alaric restrains your ability to speak about certain details of his operation," I said.

"But, if that's the case, then how are you here now?" asked Gen. "If he has that much control, wouldn't he be able to locate you and see that you're meeting with us?"

"My power allows me to break from his sight for ten minutes at a time. That was how I freed Otar's mind, returning his memories about Alaric. And how I helped you save your princess, twice," she emphasized.

"You were the one to free my mind?" asked Otar in shock.

"You were always one of my favorites," she said, winking at him. "But that means I only have about a minute left."

"What do you need from us?" asked Gen.

"I want you to destroy him. I want to be free," she said.

I had seen enough wild animals in captivity to recognize the one before me now. The desperation and pain of entrapment flickered behind her eyes.

"We are working on it," I said warily.

"Start getting creative with your questions. You need to focus on building your strength. The massive group of creatures I told you about is coming soon. He fears you, Genevieve. He is searching for a way to defend against you, and he will find it. But for now, you have the upper hand. I will reach out to you again when it is safe. Do as I have said and prepare yourselves," With that, Narella disappeared into the air.

"Can I have her hair ... once we kill her?" asked Otar.

"We're not going to kill her. She's telling the truth," said Gen.

"What makes you so sure?" I asked.

"The first time I met her, I saved her. She was testing me. She knew who I was, even then. The traps the light court set weren't designed to entrap gods. She could have gotten herself free, but she was waiting to see what I would do with her. I showed her she could trust me. She was looking for someone to save her. A way to set herself free," explained Gen.

"If we trust her, we're taking a huge risk," I pointed out.

"What other choice do we have?" asked Gen.

"We can kill her," suggested Otar. "We kill her and then I will suck the marrow from Alaric's bones as I roast the prick's fat over a fire and fashion rugs out of his hide."

Gen laughed at the creature.

"Are you really encouraging him?" I asked.

"What? I think he's cute," she said.

Otar turned to her and growled.

"And horrifying, and wicked, and violent, and powerful, and brilliant," she added with endearment in her eyes.

Otar smiled, nuzzling against her side.

I pulled her from him, but he yanked her back.

"If you are going to stick around this time, then learn to share," he snapped at me.

"Not a chance," I said, pulling her into me. *Sick little fuck.*

He growled.

Gen laughed again, pulling his head into her, and kissing him on the cheek. "Go kill some fairies for me. I will call when I need you," she said.

The creature laughed with delight before disappearing.

"Your relationship with that thing is disturbing," I noted.

"His name is Otar, and be nice. He has never hurt me or lied to me. He is very helpful and if he needs to cuddle occasionally, I don't mind."

"Just remember what he is."

"I don't really know what he is, but I know he is my friend. He is loyal and I think he even cares for me—as much as he knows how."

I shook my head. "This is a losing argument. Just promise me you will be careful," I said, pushing the hair back behind her ear.

"I promise. Now let's get back to the castle. Your room or mine tonight?"

I smiled at the eagerness in her eyes. "Your bed is bigger," I said, leaning down to kiss her.

We consumed each other that night. I had never been with someone that I desired so deeply. I couldn't get my fill, and I prayed to Azeer it would be like this forever. I took in every moment of our time together: her sounds, her smile, her scent. The way her mouth would grin and then form into an O just before she climaxed. I would never take her for granted. I had lost her once, and this was my second chance. My second chance to have everything I never knew I wanted.

We skipped breakfast and stayed in bed till lunch. I didn't care about our duties or responsibilities. All I cared about was pleasing my female, my princess, my wife. We finally pulled ourselves away from the bedroom and made our way down to the training arena where the twins were waiting for us to show off their new inventions.

Gen wore a loose, sheer dress revealing the shoulder that bore my imprint. All her dresses complemented the marking, bringing a sense of satisfaction I never knew I desired. Seeing my imprint on a female had never appealed to me until now. The marking fit her little body perfectly.

I pulled her in front of me, pushing my chest against her back as we walked through the halls to the arena. I traced my fingers over the dark lines, feeling myself harden while I pressed against her perfect, firm ass. She giggled, scrunching her shoulder as I tickled her. Dammit, I couldn't take it. That little giggle sent me over the edge.

I pushed her into a nearby hallway and took her up against the wall while court members passed by, oblivious to our presence. She looked out into the busy hall as I buried myself inside of her, making sure no one was watching. Once I hit the top of her, all her concerns and reservations disappeared. She began to moan. She sunk her teeth into my neck. I took her mouth with mine and quickened my pace until I pushed us both over the edge.

We straightened our attire, trying to make it seem as if nothing had happened, but the scent of our sex lingered all around us. She smiled up at me, pulling me in for another kiss.

"And to think," I whispered, holding her in my arms, "when you first arrived you looked down upon alfar who took their lovers in the hall. Hypocrite."

"That's before I had experienced the ambassador of pleasure. Honestly, I think I'd allow you to take me anywhere."

I laughed. "You'll regret that you said that."

She scrunched her little nose and shook her head. "No, I don't think I will."

I pulled her back into the hall as we made our way to the twins.

"Okay, now hold them firmly," said Voz, showing Gen his latest invention. "They got a bit of a kick to them,"

She held two crescent-shaped dark weapons with large blades that could cut through a piece of metal like parchment. Runes were carved into the surfaces just like the rest of the black weapons. They were close combat weapons, a sharp point at the end of each blade. Grooves etched into the curved body allowed the wielder to catch and disarm their opponents. They looked so large in Gen's small hands. She smiled, admiring the artistry.

"They aren't going to explode like the first models of your dark swords did, are they?" I asked, my arms crossed over my chest.

"No, smartass, they aren't going to explode. They're perfect," said Voz,

"Just like we designed them to be," added Oz.

"Now, these were designed to mimic a creature that we killed last year. It could send out massive waves of kinetic energy that slammed into you like a wall," said Voz.

"Leenia was also his inspiration. She's his muse," said Oz, batting his eyes at Voz.

Voz punched him in the gut. "Shut up, whore," Voz snapped at his brother, turning back to me. "They aren't only good for close combat, but when you spin them in the right sequence, the dark magic that feeds from you to the weapons acts as a net for the energy around you. When you have collected enough, you slam the blades into each other towards your target to release the energy. But remember, they have a kick."

"Got it. Slide, absorb, and slam," recited Gen with excitement.

"Right, now, follow me," Voz said. He began to spin and twirl the weapons around him like a choreographed dance. Gen watched closely. He did the motions slowly while she absorbed every movement. When he was done, she nodded with a smile and mimicked his movements, except at a faster pace. Voz and Oz started to panic, putting their hands out to stop her.

"No, no, not so fast, princess," said Oz.

Voz cut in. "The release is going to be—"

Gen brought the two weapons down in front of her towards the target. As the metal of the crescent blades clashed, a loud whine screamed from them, followed by a blast of pure green energy that sent Gen flying backwards through the air. The wall of energy expanded. When it hit the target, the wood evaporated into dust.

I rushed towards Gen, picking her up off the floor. She shook her head as she stumbled to her feet. The twins came rushing over to us, checking to see if we were okay. The whole gym turned in our direction, trying to figure out what had just happened.

"Are you okay?" I asked her, checking her over for any injuries.

"We're sorry," said Oz.

"We should have told you about the speed factor," said Voz.

She grinned at them. "That was freaking awesome!" she yelled, laughing with joy. "I want these. I want a pair. Can you make them for me? Please?"

The twins looked at each other and smiled. "Of course," they answered at the same time.

"You two are brilliant!" she squealed. "These are my new favorite weapons. I want to train with them as much as possible in the next week. Can you help me?"

"It would be our pleasure," they said in unison, followed by a small bow.

She turned to me. "You have to try these."

I smiled, running my hand down her back. "Adrenaline junky. I almost forget."

The rest of the day she trained with the crescent blades. Zerrial met us after he got back from a hunt and began training her properly. Even though she was fierce in a battle, I didn't trust Varches with her. He had been close to her cousin, Toreon. Though we had found no evidence he was involved in the attempt on her life, I wanted her to be safe, which meant keeping her within my inner circle.

We got dressed for dinner and made our way to the throne room. The king had not spoken to either of us since we had told him about the queen and Gen's mother. I could tell it was eating at Gen, but we both agreed to let him come to terms with the situation on his own. He was a private male, and I knew he would eventually open to her when he was ready.

We ate dinner together while we laughed and talked with Vena, Zerrial, and Lily. Icici sat quietly off to the side, observing like she had ever since her father and brother had been killed. A small part of me felt sorry for her. Her own brother and father had planned to kill her to install Toreon as heir to the throne.

The king retired to his rooms after dinner. I pulled my princess into my lap, teasing her to create that smile I'd do anything to see spread across her face. Besides Jestu, I usually kept my personal life to myself. I never showed affection to the females I was bedding in public, but she wasn't just any female. She was my life.

Doria came up beside me, bowing before she leaned into my ear. "The Sollerums have agreed to speak with you," Doria whispered. "Hashen wants to take the deal. We just need to make sure Helor is on board."

I nodded, turning back to Gen. She looked at me curiously. I kissed her head, running my hand down her beautiful black hair.

"I have to go make a deal," I said, winking at her.

She scrunched her nose and smirked, moving to her throne on the platform as was custom for the royals after dinner.

I made my way into the hall, following Doria to an empty meeting room. The Sollerum brothers were already waiting for me. I stepped in, feeling the weight of my mantle for the first time since I had been crowned prince. I unbuttoned my jacket and sat in a chair, folding my hands across my lap.

"Lords, what can I do for you this evening?" I asked them.

Hashen looked at Doria before shifting his attention to me. "We wanted to hear this supposed offer from your own lips, *Prince* Lyklor," said Helor.

"Why don't you both first tell me what you want?" I said mockingly. "What are your ambitions and goals in life?"

The brothers looked at each other and took a seat in front of me. Doria stood by my side at the head of the table.

"We each want a seat at your table when you take the throne," started Helor. "We also want the throne's treasury to run through our bank. We will handle all the crown's assets and dealings during your reign. We plan to prove ourselves. At the end of your reign, if you are pleased with the way we've handled your accounts, the deal that we make today will be transferred to our heirs."

I paused, taking into consideration what they were asking. It wasn't a lot. Their reward wasn't worth the death of their father, but who was I to weigh their options for them.

"Deal," I said.

They looked to one another, speaking that creepy, unspoken twin language I had seen Oz and Voz do many times before.

"Is there anything else, Lords?" I asked.

Hashen swallowed and tensed before looking at Doria. "There is one more thing, your majesty," said Hashen. He paused.

"I would like to get back to my wife, so what is your request?" I said, annoyed.

"I would like you to make an exception for a union between a High Lord and a lowborn," he requested.

I turned slowly, watching Doria's eyes widen with shock.

"I would like to be granted permission to marry Doria Felzborne at the time of our choosing," Hashen said, sitting taller than before. "I was hoping, considering your own situation, you would make an exception."

I took a heavy breath, acting like I was contemplating my answer.

There it was: the real reason they were agreeing to the deal. Their father would never allow him to marry a lowborn, especially one connected to me. Helor was going along with the deal so he could help his brother find happiness. Plus, their new stations and source of income and power wouldn't hurt.

"Please give Doria and me the room," I said to the brothers. "Wait outside. I will call you when I am ready."

They stood and nodded before leaving.

Doria collapsed into the chair next to me, her eyes flashing from side to side, reeling in shock.

"I assume you didn't know this was part of the deal?" I asked.

"No," she said frantically. "I would never use your situation to advance my own. My actions were solely focused on making sure you were safe."

I took her hand in mine. "You don't have to defend yourself. Not to me. Ever."

She grinned, turning her attention back to the table.

"Does he treat you well?"

She nodded. "I did try to get rid of him all those decades ago. I really did, but he wouldn't give up. He was the first male, besides you, that saw me for who I was. Not my past, or class, but the real me. The one I try to hide."

"And is this something you want? To marry him? I want you to know you have options. I would never broker a deal if it meant your unhappiness. You are my family. You come first," I said.

She gave a slight laugh. "I want this. I want him," she admitted softly.

I stood up, pulling her into me, holding her tightly. After all she had endured, the decades of abuse and torment, she had found her happiness. Just like I had. I pulled away and looked down at her.

"If he ever hurts you, I will personally skin him, understand?" I said, holding onto her.

She laughed with more emotion than I had ever seen her display. "You forget who you're talking to. You don't think I've already threatened him with the thousands of ways I could torture him? You taught me well, Eren."

I kissed her on the head, and she fetched the brothers. They came in and took their seats. I looked at both of them and smiled.

"I want you both to know that I want this arrangement between us to be real. I want to be an ally to you, and I hope in time you will feel the same. If you ever need anything, you may come to me freely. I would like to build something sustainable that can flourish between the three of us. Is this possible?" I asked.

"We would like nothing more, Your Highness," said Helor.

"Of course, Your Grace," said Hashen.

I turned to look at Hashen. "Understand that what you are asking for is precious to me in ways you cannot begin to understand. If you ever hurt her, I will destroy you. Are we clear?" I said, sharp threat lingering in the air.

"Perfectly, Your Grace," Hashen said, looking up to Doria with a smile.

"Then we have a deal," I replied, reaching for the parchment and quill.

We signed the contract and sealed our bond. Helor and I left the room while Doria and Hashen celebrated. We both smirked and nodded in respect to one another before we entered the throne room. This arrangement wasn't about power or my position. This arrangement was about our families' happiness.

Though that deal took an unexpected turn, I was happy to have one of the three contracts in place. I stood at the entrance of the throne room, looking into the crowd of dancing alfar and humans. They were laughing and gliding across the floor to Lily's beautiful voice. I moved my focus to my princess.

She sat on top of her throne, looking as exquisite as ever. Her attention was locked onto someone in the crowd. Her face was full of relief, pain, and surprise while she stared. I looked past the dancers to see a woman approaching her. She had long black curly hair and wore a plain dress. Her face was familiar in some way.

Gen stood from her throne, descending to the dance floor as she walked towards the stranger. Her face lit up with joy. Tears began to run down her cheeks. I looked at the familiar woman again. I had seen her face before; when the king shared his memory of his human lover with me. Gen's mother. Gen's *dead* mother.

No, this wasn't right. It couldn't be her. It had to be ... the queen. She was a shapeshifter. She knew what Gen's mother looked like. This was a way to get close to her to—

I looked at the woman's hands. An orange blade slid from the sleeve of her dress as Gen rushed towards her with joy. Before she could touch the queen, I misted and caught Gen in my arms, just as the queen reeled back and drove the ulyrium blade into my back.

I held onto Gen, looking down into her eyes as pain rushed through my body. The queen pulled the dagger free. I saw Zerrial, Leenia, and the twins tackle her to the ground as they slammed their powers into her. I held onto Gen, losing feeling in my legs.

Her eyes filled with tears. She cried out in pain, ushering me to the floor. I couldn't make out what she was saying. My vision went black. I felt my heart pumping harder, trying to keep me alive. My grip on her arms loosened and everything around me faded. The last thing I remembered was her calling my name.

Chapter Eighteen

Genevieve

"Eren?" I cried, holding onto his body as his weight forced me to lay him on the ground. "No, no, no. Please, stay with me. Eren?"

"No! No!" yelled my mother. "Get your hands off me. I demand you let me go." She struggled on the ground while Zerrial restrained her. Leenia shackled her with ulyrium cuffs. I looked back into Eren's face, watching as his breaths became shallow. His eyes began to fade. My body shook fiercely.

"Vena? Vena?" I yelled, searching the room for my cousin. She rushed over to me. I bent my head to his as the tears fell from my eyes.

"I'm here," said Vena, running her hands over his back to assess the damage.

"Please, stay with me," I whispered to him. "Please. We just found each other. You can't leave me. Not now."

The court surrounded us, but all I could focus on was him. I reached for his hand, squeezing it tightly, but there was no response. His arm was limp and showed no sign.

"I think I can save him," said Vena, reaching out to my shoulder.

"Let's move him to his room."

I nodded desperately.

The twins gently picked Eren up out of my arms and carried him from the throne room. I stood, swallowing my pain, then approached the woman who had appeared as my mother.

I knelt beside her, taking in the beautiful details of the face that I had prayed to see again for so many years. I felt nothing; my heart was cold. I touched my hand to her face as my flame roamed beneath my skin. She struggled as the heat burned her skin, leaving my handprint branded on the side of her cheek. She yelled with pain as she shook from side to side, frantically changing her features and coloring. When she finally calmed, the face of Queen Nora stared back at me. The court gasped in shock.

She smiled at me as her eyes widened.

"What would you like us to do with her, Your Majesty?" asked Zerrial.

"Take her to the dungeon, and tell my father what has occurred," I instructed, striding out of the throne room. "Inform me once he has decided what is to be done with her. I will be with the prince." As soon as I was out of the court's sight, I picked up my pace, rushing towards Eren's room.

Vena had him on his side while Evinee held his body in place. A black light billowed from Vena's hands as she ran them down Eren's back. He was still unresponsive. Evinee turned to me, her face stricken with fear and stained with tears. I went to his bed, taking his head into my lap while Vena worked.

An hour in, Eren finally responded with a deep and painful yell. Vena continued to heal the ulyrium wound. I held onto his arms while Evinee restrained his lower half. He fought us, reeling with pain from Vena's attempt to save his life.

Finally, twenty minutes later, Vena was finished. She looked exhausted; beads of sweat poured down her face. Eren had passed out again from the physical trauma. We rolled him onto his back gently.

"He is going to make it," informed Vena, standing from the bed. "I healed the internal bleeding and the torn tissue, but his body will need time to do the rest. He will most likely have a scar after he has healed, and some internal residual pain, but he will live."

Evinee snickered. "He isn't going to be happy about the scar."

I smiled at her. "No, but at least he'll be alive to complain about it," I replied. "How long will he be unconscious?" I asked Vena.

"A day or so. It was a fatal blow, and I did what I could, but the rest is up to him."

I reached for Vena, taking her hand in mine. "Thank you so much. I owe you a debt," I said, holding back my tears.

"That isn't necessary. I would do anything for you, Gen. I hope you know that," Vena said with a soft smile. She nodded at me before taking her leave.

Evinee stood from the bed, looking nervous and uncomfortable. "Will you ... will you inform me if his condition changes?" she asked.

"Of course," I replied.

She looked back at Eren for a long moment before leaving.

I turned back to him, curling my body around his. I held him as I buried my face into the hollow of his neck. My body began to shake while I cried fiercely. After a few long moments, I was able to regain control of myself. I kissed his cheek softly, running my hand down the side of his face.

"You stupid, stupid alfar. What were you thinking? You could have died," I whispered to him. I sat up to take his shoes off and pulled the covers over his body, making sure he was as comfortable as possible. I crawled back to his side, laying my head against his chest, listening to his heartbeat.

His family came in and out of the room throughout the night to check on him. I couldn't sleep and I didn't dare leave his side. I waited anxiously for him to open his eyes, but he never did.

The next morning, my father finally made an appearance in Eren's room. His face was long, and his eyes were heavy. I could tell he hadn't slept. He stood at the foot of Eren's bed, staring down at him.

"How is he?" my father asked.

"Alive, thanks to Vena," I replied.

"They tell me she intended to kill you, but Eren intervened at the last minute."

"He saved my life," I whispered, looking down at his perfect face.

"I'm eternally grateful to him," said my father.

"What will happen to the queen?"

He took a moment before he responded. "She is being inter-rogated. The court witnessed her attempt on your life, and she attacked the crowned prince. The council has decided that her penalty will be death."

I stood from the bed, walking over to his side. I took his hand in mine while his eyes remained fixed on Eren. "How are you handling all of this?" I asked softly.

He turned to me, eyes filled with pain. He ran his fingers gently down my face. "She killed the woman I loved. The mother of my child. If the council wasn't going to sentence her to death, her life would have still ended."

"Have you spoken with her?"

He dropped his eyes. "I have nothing to say to her. I brought this upon you and your mother. If I wouldn't have—" My father stopped himself, taking a quick breath in.

I hadn't seen him express any sort of pain in the time I had known him. He was always stoic and stone-faced. I tightened my hand around his, letting him know I was there for him.

"She loved you. I know she did," I whispered to him.

He took another deep breath, straightening his posture as he looked into my eyes and smiled. "You are so much like her," he said, glancing at Eren. "When Erendrial wakes, she will be sentenced to death in front of the court. If you need anything, please do not hesitate to ask." He kissed me softly on the head.

An hour later, Oz came to the room with a grin on his face.

"What is it?" I asked him.

"Ophilia Gyset. She's agreed to make the deal with Eren. As soon as he wakes, she will sign the contract," said Oz.

"That's good to hear. What does she want in return?"

"Nothing. Just to be the one to kill her father. Two out of three, which only leaves Soddram."

I nodded, remembering I had volunteered to secure that contract. "Speaking of, would you mind sitting with Eren? I don't want him to be alone, and I have a few alfar I need to pay a visit to."

"Of course."

It pained me to leave Eren, but I wanted him to wake to the remaining two contracts ready for him to sign, so he would have less people wanting him dead to worry about. I changed and cleaned myself up before making my way to Soddram's room. I knocked, then checked to see if anyone of importance noticed me. He opened the door, half dressed for the day. I smiled, peeking around the doorframe.

"Is this a bad time? I can come back," I said, looking for my cousin Icici.

"Of course not, Your Highness. Please, come in," he greeted me, smiling arrogantly and stepping back from the door. "To what do I owe the pleasure of this visit? Have you tired of your new husband already?" He smiled seductively, moving past me to gather his shirt.

"Actually, I have come to discuss a rather personal matter with you," I said flirtatiously. If this was how he wanted to play, I would oblige him. I gestured to his couch. "May I sit?"

"Of course," he replied, sitting next to me, barely leaving space between us. He stretched his arm around my shoulder, pulling himself closer. His eyes locked onto mine before he leaned forward. "What would you like to discuss?"

"I would like to know what your ambitions are, Soddram. I never got the chance to get to know you before the tournament, but I am all ears now."

He arched his brow. "I wish to only serve the crown," he said cautiously.

I held his gaze intently. "Soddram, I wish to speak freely with you. My sources inform me that you seek power. From what I have gathered, you are an influential leader, and you have a strong head on your shoulders. You are very valuable, and you could accomplish great things to further our kingdom, and your personal reputation and coffers, if that power were available to you."

He sat back seeming to search my face for answers. "I appreciate your high opinion of my abilities, but I am afraid I do not see how I can be useful to you now. What are you getting at, Genevieve?"

I took the risk. "How do you and your father get along?"

"He is my father. I respect him and look to him for advice and guidance."

"And, how old is your father?"

"A little over four hundred."

"That's a long time to wait to have your chance at making your mark. Even then, you will only get, what, two hundred years—if you're lucky—to be the head of your family?" I studied his face for signs I was hinting in the right direction. "What if I could offer you a place of power and influence with the backing of the crown *now*?"

"And how would I obtain this favor?" he asked guardedly.

"Simply take it. We have evidence that your father is plotting against the crown. His treason is going to come to light within the next few days. I would like to guarantee that the next head of House Yositru is truly loyal to the crown. In exchange, I am offering you my support and resources to accomplish your ambitions."

"What is the price?"

I lowered my voice, praying my plan was going to work. "When the time comes, you will slit your father's throat in front of the court, and then bow to the crowned prince, offering your full support and allegiance. In private, you will sign a blood contract with Erendrial outlining the details of your loyalty."

Soddram paused, looking to the floor while he chewed the offer over in his head. "And how do I know I will have *your* full support?"

"It will be stated in the contract, of course. As I said, this is a two-way trade. Whatever you need or want, I will do my best to secure for you, but your loyalty must be unwavering."

He took a n exaggerated breath and then looked at me, his dark eyes full of cautious hope. "I want another form of insurance in order to secure my position," he said.

I smiled, knowing exactly what was coming. "What did you have in mind?"

"I want to marry into the royal family. I also want the position of high councilmen over Erendrial's table when his time comes to reign."

"I will have to speak to my husband about the seat when he wakes. As far as a marriage, which cousin did you have in mind?"

"Icici. I also want you to sign a blood contract that you will not harm her or any children we have."

I paused, curious. "And why would I ever think to harm my own family?"

He huffed with amusement. "You've proven time and time again how easy it is for you to take a life. It's as if you were born and raised here all along. It comes naturally to you, princess. It's in your blood."

"Only if they commit treason. Is that not our law?" I asked.

"I insist on a blood contract between the two of you if I am to do what you ask."

I paused, studying the male closely. "Are you ... in love with my cousin?"

He chuckled. "I do not understand the concept of love, nor do I wish to, but your cousin and I work well together. I believe our unity through marriage could benefit both our houses."

I gave a slight nod. "I will speak with Icici. If she agrees to the marriage, I will agree to your terms."

He cocked a grin. I stood from the couch as he followed me to the door.

"When the details have been looked over, I will make contact. Until then, I expect you will keep this arrangement between us?"

"Of course, Princess Genevieve," he said with a bow.

"Soddram, if we are to work closely together from this point on, please call me Gen."

"Thank you ... Gen." He closed the space between us, leaning down to my face. "And if you ever get tired of Erendrial, I'd be happy to serve you in other ways." He pulled back with an entrancing smile.

"Thank you for the offer, but it won't be necessary." I exited his rooms and headed for Icici's. I took a deep breath, preparing myself for any outcome.

I got to her rooms and knocked. Her servant opened the door and bowed, allowing me to pass through. Icici was sitting at the table, eating her breakfast alone. Since the death of her father and brother, she only showed her face at court for dinner. Every other meal, she took alone. Her eyes locked on mine instantly. She placed her teacup on the saucer.

"Cousin, I wasn't expecting you," she said, gesturing to the chair across from her. "Would you like to join me for breakfast?"

"I'd love to," I replied, taking a seat.

The servant prepared a plate for me while Icici watched.

"How's Erendrial?" she asked calmly.

"He will recover. Thank you for asking. How have you been doing? I am sorry I haven't been able to check in. Courtly matters have kept my attention elsewhere."

"I'm fine. Thank you for inquiring over my well-being."

I smiled, and we ate in silence for the next ten minutes. Finally, she dropped her fork with a clang and allowed her well-mannered mask to fall away.

"What is it that you've come here for, Genevieve? I have done nothing to draw your attention, so you must want something."

I took a sip of tea and then looked at her calmly. "I have come to offer a marriage proposal to you."

Her face looked shocked. "Who?"

"Soddram Yositru has asked for your hand. I, of course, told him I would only approve if you agreed. If you don't, I will refuse his request."

She thought it over for a moment. "Why would you even give me the option? I must do whatever you command."

"Icici, we may have started off on the wrong foot, but I do not wish you any harm. I would never force you into a union you did not want."

"What do you get from this arrangement?" she asked.

"Soddram as an ally. He has also asked for the high councilman seat at Eren's table when our reign begins."

She paused, leaning back into her chair. "And he asked for my hand in marriage?"

"He did. He also requested that I sign a contract promising not to harm you or your children. I have agreed, if you agree to the marriage."

Her face turned to the side and her jaw clenched.

"Icici, I would like us to start over, if that is possible. If you agree to this, Soddram will be close to Eren and me. I would like to be able to rely on and trust you as well. This could be a good thing, for everyone," I said leaning into the table.

Her eyes met mine with a stern expression. "And why would you ever trust me? After what my father and brother did to you?"

"You aren't them. Plus, the contract you signed also proved your loyalty. I'd prefer not to rely on the contracts every time we speak. Instead, I'd like to build an actual foundation with you. You have many talents that can be helpful in political and courtly matters."

Her body relaxed slightly as she exhaled and crossed her arms. "I'm sorry for the way I treated you. And for throwing my relationship with Eren in your face. I saw there was something between you two from day one, and I was trying to hurt you."

"Thank you. I am also sorry for my actions. Though, I must

hand it to you, you get under my skin almost as much as Eren."

She smiled at me genuinely for the first time. She shrugged her shoulders. "What can I say, it's a gift."

"A gift we can use," I said, smiling back.

She looked at me and nodded her head. "I will do it. I will marry Soddram and I will take your offer. This way, we both can begin again, without fear and with a clean slate."

"I agree," I said, leaning back while I finished my tea. The third contract was secure. Eren was safe.

CHAPTER NINETEEN

After confirming the deal with Soddram, I had Firel draw up both contracts so they were ready for Eren when he woke. I met with my father and the council to prepare our negotiation tactics for our visit to the light court. We were informed that rift creatures had attacked the fairy hives the night previous. The minotaur ambassador had made contact reporting the same situation in their lands. The threat was spreading, and we would have to wage war on the creatures sooner rather than later.

After the meeting, I made my way back to Eren's room, praying he was awake. I entered the room and saw him sitting up in bed with his head against Evinee's. They were whispering, but I couldn't hear what they were saying. *Damn human ears.* Evinee shook her head before he pulled away from her. He held her face in his hands intimately while he spoke softly.

My heart sank. I didn't know exactly what I had walked in on, but I felt like the third wheel. Something was obviously going on between them, but I didn't have the nerve to ask. We were in such a good place. I didn't want to ruin it with my human expectations, even if the sight of them together was killing me. Eren caught sight of me and released Evinee's face gently. She turned around, her face lightly reddened.

"I can come back if—" I started to say, not knowing how to react in this situation.

"No," Evinee said, standing and moving towards the door. "I was just leaving."

The door shut behind her, leaving Eren and I alone. Everything in me demanded to know what was going on between the two of them, but I didn't know if I wanted the truth. I took a deep breath, moving towards the bed. He smiled as I slid next to him.

"How are you feeling?" I asked.

"Like I was just stabbed in the back with a ulyrium dagger. But hey, I'm alive, so I can't complain."

I dropped my eyes, trying to hide my insecurity. This wasn't the time to bring them to light. "Thank you for saving my life," I whispered.

"I think I am up by four, by the way. You have some catching up to do, princess."

I let a slight laugh escape. "I'm sorry I interrupted the two of you," I said without looking at him.

"We were finished. Though I do have to say, I was a little disappointed to wake up and find Evinee here instead of you. I thought you'd be at my bedside."

"I was all night. I just ... I was securing the last house. We have Soddram, along with Ophilia as well. They've agreed and are ready to sign the contract as soon as you are able."

"Look at you, my little politician," he said, pinching my chin between his fingers.

I closed my eyes, remembering the way he had looked while the life seeped from his body. "Eren, I don't know what I would have done if—" I said, but my emotions stumbled my words.

He leaned forward, pulling me into him. "I'm right here. I'm not going to leave you. I'm not going anywhere," he said, holding me while I cried.

"You could have died. If Vena hadn't gotten to you when she did … I don't know what I would have done. I just got you back."

He started laughing as he ran his hands through my hair.

I pulled away to look at him. "What's so funny?"

"The sex that good, is it?" he said smugly,

I smiled through my tears before hitting him in the shoulder. "Oh, shut up, you narcissistic asshole."

He grinned widely, pulling me back to him. "I don't want to leave you either, but I don't regret my choice. If I had to choose between your life or mine, I'd pick yours every time. There's no question."

I wrapped my arms firmly around him. "Let's stop almost dying, okay?"

"I would like nothing more." He turned my face up to his and kissed me softly. I melted under the feeling of him. He traced the lines of my face. "Ev told me the queen has been sentenced to death?"

"Yes. My father was just waiting for you to wake up. I suppose she will die this evening after dinner."

"But tonight is Jestu."

I laughed. "Always thinking about sex, aren't you?"

"Well, it is my favorite pastime," he whispered seductively, dragging his hand ever so slowly up my thigh. My body lit up from the contact. "Why don't we wait until tomorrow to kill the queen? We can sign the contracts in the morning with Soddram and Ophilia, and then have one large killing fest after dinner. Tonight, I just want to spend it with you."

"At Jestu, you mean?"

"It is our first as a real couple. I would like it to be a fond memory."

I smiled, kissing him on the chin. "Vena says physical activity isn't good for your wound."

Eren's face fell with devastation. "She lies. I feel wonderful. I could run the length of the kingdom if I wanted to. Don't listen to her. She doesn't know what she's talking about."

"Eren, you need to rest. You almost died."

He cupped my breast, kneading the soft tissue in the most delightful manner. "But I am alive. Shouldn't we celebrate that?" He kissed me again.

"If it's okay with you, I would just like to hold you for a bit. I just want to feel your arms around me," I said, still aching from the sting of almost losing him.

He looked down at me tenderly and nodded. "Of course, princess. Anything you need."

I curled up against him, relishing in his scent. His head nuzzled against mine while his arms held onto me like I was his lifeline.

We informed my father of what we had decided regarding the queen and what we had planned for the three traitors and the high houses. He agreed that we needed to show strength and that it was a smart maneuver.

After dinner, we made our way to Jestu. There was still only one throne on the high platform. Eren stood off to the side, waiting for me to sit. I pulled him to the chair and then sat on his lap. I was his queen, and he was my king. The alfar needed to see and respect him as such.

As the festivities began, I shifted uncomfortably while others engaged in their sexual explorations. Even though I had overcome my circumstances, it was still awkward to watch others engage in the act. I turned away, shielding my eyes from them. I heard Eren let a slight laugh escape as he nuzzled his nose into my ear.

"Getting any ideas for later?" he asked with a heavy voice.

"I ... it's still weird," I said, turning to look at him.

"It's a natural act. One you seem to enjoy very much, I might add."

"Yes, but not like this. I mean, I'm not judging, but I just—" I stopped, not knowing how to explain myself.

Eren shifted me in his lap to the side and took my face in his hands. He dragged his thumb across my lips slowly, parting them as I welcomed his taste. He leaned his mouth into my ear, biting at the lobe. "Close your eyes and relax. The next hour will only seem like a matter of minutes, I promise," he said, kissing me softly down my neck.

I obeyed, leaning into the feeling of his lips against my skin. His hand trailed across my jaw and down my chest until he reached the long slit in my dress. His fingers gently caressed the inside of my thighs, making my center throb with desire and need.

I took his mouth against mine, pressing my body firmly into his. He smiled, holding onto me as his hands explored my exposed skin. He pulled the strap of my dress down, kissing along my shoulder to the front of my chest. My breasts ached for his touch.

His fingers tauntingly slid up the length of my thigh until he reached my sex. I shifted, leaning harder against him while I opened my legs, inviting his skilled fingers.

Eren slid his middle finger over my seam and moaned. I was already wet from his affections. My heart began to pound out of my chest as my body heated. I arched my hips towards his hand, begging for him. Eren licked the side of my neck, swiping his finger over my slick opening, stopping just before he entered.

I groaned with frustration. The need for him to be inside of me was unbearable. "Please," I whimpered.

His lips moved back to my ear. "Please what, princess?"

"Please touch me ... I need more ... I need you inside of me ... please."

"Which part of me would you like inside of you?"

"Any part ... as long as it's you."

"Mmm, are you sure? In front of the court?"

I whimpered again, feeling out of my mind. Without thinking I took his hand and placed his fingers right where I needed them. They slid into me so perfectly and my entire body erupted from the pleasure.

I gasped at the sense of relief. I arched my head back, resting it on his shoulders while he moved his fingers inside of me, rubbing against my walls. I gently rocked my hips, wanting more ... no ... needing more.

"Naughty wife," he chuckled, removing his fingers. He grabbed my hips, turning me around to face him. I straddled my legs on either side while he slid his hand back under my dress, driving three fingers back into my throbbing sex.

My head fell back, reeling from the sensation while my body clenched around him. Eren slid his other hand to the back of my neck, kissing down my chest until his mouth hovered over the sheer fabric of my dress, taunting my nipple with his warm breath. I went to remove the dress completely, but he stopped me.

"You are mine, remember?" he said in a heavy and seductive voice.

"I haven't forgotten," I hissed in a husky tone.

"If you haven't noticed, I am a bit territorial, which means I don't want any other male to see what is mine. You're going to have to keep your clothes on a little while longer."

I let out a faint laugh pulling back to look at him. "That never stopped you from taking other females at Jestu in front of the court."

He touched the bottom of my traditional Jestu mask, drawing his thumb across my cheekbone. "They never mattered."

I looked into his beautiful silver eyes, the need to have him building inside of me. I pressed my lips against his firmly.

"Now," he whispered, moving his attention back to the three fingers that were buried inside of me, "relax and enjoy." I placed my hands on the throne's armrests, bracing myself while I moved up and down, sliding effortlessly against his long fingers.

The sounds coming from me were muted by the music that floated through the air. Everything around me faded as I focused on the pleasure only he was capable of giving me. The pressure inside of me began to build. As if Eren could sense my rising climax, his fingers began to pump harder and faster, driving to the very top with each thrust.

He placed his other hand on my back, bracing me while my body stiffened. Every inch of my skin was aware of him. Every place we touched, every pass of his lips, I savored.

My breathing became irregular. My grip on the chair tightened. I was coming undone. Then, my body exploded. I let go, roaring with pleasure as I came all over his fingers and lap. My pheromones released, intensifying my orgasm.

My body was no longer my own. I couldn't move. Eren pulled me closer to him, still moving his fingers inside of me, lengthening the pleasurable sensation while I shook and whimpered from the incredible feeling.

Finally, I was able to move my arms, holding onto him while I caught my breath. I pulled back, looking into his eyes. Eren's pupils were dilated, his jaw tense, and his chest heaved.

"Are you alright? Did I hurt you?" I whispered, feeling my cheeks blush.

"If I don't bury myself in you soon," he replied, tightening his grip on me to the point it almost hurt, "I am going to fucking kill something."

I laughed. He stood, pulling me through the crowd aggressively while we headed for the exit. "Screw the hour," he mumbled.

Apparently, Eren wasn't the only one my pheromones had affected. The crowd was ravenous, even more so than usually. I had never seen anything like it.

As soon as we got back to my rooms, I tore at his clothes, needing the feeling of his bare, silky skin against mine. He met my haste and ripped the dress from my body before picking me up and slamming me into the bed.

His tongue slid across the curves and planes of my body until we were tangled together. I closed my eyes, focusing on the feeling of our bodies gliding against one another. Everything around us faded, and I couldn't tell where I ended and he began. As our fingers laced together, he pulled his head up and looked into my eyes. He smiled, leaning into my neck and giving me everything he had.

The next morning, I woke in Eren's arms, our bodies intertwined. I could feel his warm breath on my forehead. I trailed my hands along his back, stopping at his new scar. My fingers traced the small, raised area that now adorned his perfect body. I felt him let out a long exhale.

"It's going to scar, isn't it?" he asked, leaning his head down into mine.

"Just a reminder that you almost died, that's all."

He laughed, opening his eyes heavily. "You don't mind?"

"Of course not. You're still perfect. Plus, I think scars are sexy."

"You've been around humans for too long. They've ruined your sense of beauty."

"Watch it, Lyklor. Remember, you're married to a half-breed. And your children will also have human blood running through them," I said playfully.

He pulled away, his face more serious than amused.

"What?" I asked.

"You ... you want to have more children?" he asked hesitantly.

I paused, taking a moment. "Do you?"

He ran his fingers through my hair. A small smile stretched across his face. "It won't replace her. Not a day goes by that I won't think about the child we lost, but yes. I never thought I'd say this, but if they have you as their mother, I want as many children as we can have."

I smiled at him, a deep happiness flaring inside of me. A hollow pit suddenly formed in my stomach. "The contract ..." I said, shame snuffing out my joy.

He shook his head. "I don't care about the contract. I already have everything I want," he said, kissing my head softly.

I pulled away again, looking into his eyes. "No one will ever know about the contract. Well, Levos knows, because it was his idea."

"Oh, it was now, was it? Little fucker," Eren grumbled, still smiling.

"But he won't say a word. I promise you. You will be king. You will have the power you fought so hard for. I won't stand in your way," I said.

"*We* will rule together, side by side, as equals. This is ours. Our kingdom, our court, our marriage ... our family." He pulled me against him, his words replaying in my mind. How he had changed. He no longer cared about the power he could obtain. There were more important things he desired, that he cared for. And I was one of them.

"I trust you, Eren," I whispered against his skin. I closed my eyes and fell asleep in the arms of my king.

Later that day, Eren and I met with Soddram and Ophilia separately to sign their contracts. Tonight, the court would have their entertainment. We met with the others down in the safe house before dinner to go over the plan. Evinee was quiet compared to her usual outgoing self. I still hadn't asked Eren about what I had walked in on, and I still didn't know if I wanted to know.

I tried pushing my jealousy and fear from my mind, but I couldn't look at the two of them without thinking the worst. I knew this would be something I would have to face eventually, but I didn't think it would be this soon. He cared for me, I told myself. He made me happy.

That night after dinner had concluded, my father instructed the guards to bring Queen Nora up from the dungeon. The court quieted while they brought her before us. She struggled against her restraints, screaming like a crazy person. Her hair was tangled, and her body was bloodied from the interrogation she had undergone.

Eren and I sat next to my father. Her throne had already been removed from the platform. Nora fell to the floor, crying and yelling while she looked up at my father for mercy. My father looked down upon her without a hint of emotion behind his eyes, then turned to the court.

"As many of you witnessed, Nora Filarion attempted to assassinate Princess Genevieve and succeeded in harming Prince Lyklor. The council has agreed that her actions are treasonous, and her sentence is death," said my father. The court nodded with their dark and hollow eyes.

The guard pulled out his ulyrium blade to take her head, but my father held out his hand. He stared at her for a long moment before approaching.

She looked up at him, tears streaming down her face. "I tried," cried Nora. "I tried to provide you with an heir. I tried to make you care for me, but instead, you turned to a filthy human. You chose her over me. I was your wife. I was your queen, yet you abandoned me."

"You killed an innocent woman because you couldn't restrain your jealousy?" asked my father.

"I killed her because you loved her," she said in a hateful tone. The court members looked to one another. My father's eyes stayed firmly on Nora's face. He bent down and whispered something into her ear before he pulled a small glass jar from his pocket. Inside, a black insect wriggled. He removed the lid from the jar and held it against Nora's ear. Nora struggled and fought, but eventually, the insect scurried inside. I turned to Eren.

"A benout insect. The same that she used to kill your mother," whispered Eren.

The king tossed the jar to the floor, turning from her and heading back to his throne. The court leaned forward, watching in awe while Nora scratched at the sides of her head, screaming in a panic.

Within seconds, Nora tore through her skin with her own nails, trying to get the insect out of her brain. Her body collapsed to the floor as her eyes rolled into the back of her head. Streams of blood ran from her nose and eyes. Her body flopped on the golden floor like a fish out of water. Sounds of pain and agony escaped her mouth as she fought for breath. Eventually, her body calmed. Her head fell to the side. The white of her eyes was streaked with blood as they stared towards us.

My father raised his hand to the guard to take her body away. Her brother and nephew stayed silent among the other court members, not daring to step out of line against us. The king turned towards me and nodded. I stood with a smile and looked for the next three victims that would die on the floor in front of me this night.

"Lord Beran Sollerum, Lord Nal Yositru, and Lord Yous Gyset, please come forward," I said with an unwavering voice. The three men stood hesitantly, looking at one another. They knew. Each bowed, gazing up at me with weary eyes.

"Princess Genevieve, how may we be of service?" asked Nal Yositru.

I smiled down at him, taking a step forward. "Lords, it has been brought to my attention that you three have been working with the queen, plotting to assassinate my husband, your future king, and myself during the next battle against the rift. Now, apparently I have not made the ramifications of such an act clear during my time as princess. If you take steps to harm the crown, your life will be forfeit."

"Your Grace, you are mistaken," said Gyset in a panicked tone. "We would never plot against you or the crowned prince."

I looked to Sollerum, whose face was unphased.

"Lord Sollerum, what do you have to say on the matter?" I asked.

He looked from me to Eren. "With all due respect, Your Majesty, you have allowed a serpent into your bed and onto our throne. He is not worthy of you, nor of the position of king," said Sollerum.

I turned to my husband and smiled.

Eren stepped forward. "Lord Sollerum," said Eren, pretending to be appalled, "I am offended by your perception of me. What have I done to earn your disrespect and ill will?"

"You are lowborn filth who fucked his way to power," answered Sollerum, spitting on the floor in front of Eren.

Eren took a moment to gather himself before looking at the court. "I have done what I had to, in order to earn my place among you. However, my actions have never gone against our king or our kingdom. It is an honor to serve Doonak, and I take my responsibilities and my position seriously. It is true, I was born lower class, but I have worked my way to where I am now because I believe in Doonak. Because I am confident that we are the strongest, most intelligent, and capable kingdom in this world.

"As your prince, as your king, I will support our kingdom and continue to expand our reach and our influence during Princess Genevieve's and my reign. I will not allow any threat to destroy what we have built, even if I must sacrifice my life in the process. I may not be the king you all imagined, but I am the king that you have. I will prove my worth to you, just as I have served this kingdom for the past one hundred and fifty years as its ambassador.

"It is time that we rise above our stations and positions. It is time that we stop looking at each other as competition and look to each other for support and guidance. There are things that attack our world daily that could end our way of life as we know it. Doonak is small in comparison to Urial, but we are far from weak. We need to band together now more than ever to solidify our power and our position among the other races, including the light alfar. But we *cannot* do this when our own court plots against its crown.

"Doonak needs to be unified. We need to stand as one body, of one soul, and of one mind. Those who oppose us will be cut down," said Eren, looking to the three heirs in the back of the room. They approached, each wearing a solemn face, taking their places behind their fathers. The lords looked back at their children in confusion.

"I bear no ill will towards any of the houses," continued Eren. "I wish to serve you to the best of my abilities. I wish to align myself with each of you to help support and create a stronger power to pass down to our children. To do that, the old ways must be forgotten, and we must embrace the enlightenment." Eren nodded. Ophilia, Soddram, and Hashen slit the throats of their fathers while Helor stood to his brother's side in support.

The four of them made their way in front of Eren and knelt before him. They each verbally pledged their allegiance and loyalty to Eren, while the court watched his army, influence and strength grow. I stepped in front of Eren and knelt before him with my head to the ground. The crowd behind me begin to whisper.

The true heir of Doonak never bowed to their spouse. They were always above them, but Eren was different. We were different. He was going to make an incredible king.

"I pledge my allegiance to Erendrial Valor Lyklor, future king of Doonak," I said with confidence. His black leather boots appeared in front of me. I felt his smooth fingers lift my chin. He assisted me to my feet, gazing upon me with love before kissing me in front of our kingdom. Eren then bowed in front of me, still holding my hand.

"I pledge my allegiance to Genevieve Drezmore, princess and future queen of Doonak." Eren kissed my hand and stood as we faced the four new lords and our court.

"Please stand, my friends," instructed Eren. They each stood, looking at us for instruction. "I look forward to working with you.

Thank you for your loyalty and support." Eren nodded as they took their seats at the head of their family tables.

My father sat silently, allowing all of this to occur without interfering. He knew Eren had to make a show of force. This was it. He had turned four heirs against their fathers. They had killed their own family members to prove their allegiance.

Eren signaled for a servant to bring us two glasses of wine. He handed me one and then brought his into the air as he held me close at his side.

"To the strong and powerful Kingdom of Doonak," he said.

"To Doonak," yelled the crowd, holding their glasses to Eren. We toasted, looking out into the sea of some of the most dangerous beings we would ever face, but Eren and I were unified. Together, we could unify this kingdom. Together, we would make it stronger. Together, we would rule.

Chapter Twenty

I t was the night before we were scheduled to leave for the light court. My stomach was in knots. I hadn't thought of that place in so long, and I had hoped never to return. I would be happy to see Levos and Gaelin, but I wished they were coming here instead ... to my home. The thought of that wretched place made me sick.

I pushed the memories from my mind as I sat at the seat in front of my vanity. I looked down at the small box I held in my hand and admired the jeweler's handiwork. I'd had a ring created for Eren that mirrored the one he gave me on our wedding day. The outer metal was silver, and the center contained a beautiful green ribbon of stone the same color as my eyes.

I smiled at the piece of art, imagining what it would look like on his finger. It was a very human thing to do, but since he had given me his ring at our wedding and repeated the human wedding vows to me, I wanted him to know I felt the same.

I knew he wanted and cared for me, but a part of me still doubted he could love. Even though Lily swore he did, he had yet to tell me, and I wasn't going to push to hear those words. I closed the box and slid it into my drawer just before he came into the room.

He leaned against the door, admiring me in the mirror. I turned to him with a flirtatious smile.

"Erendrial Lyklor, at a loss for words. Hell must be freezing over," I said, standing to my feet.

He laughed, approaching me slowly, looking me up and down. "You look stunning ... though, I *was* imagining you naked."

I hit him, trying to restrain my laughter. "You look very handsome too, husband. Are you ready for our last dinner among our own, before we must descend upon the horrid light court?"

"It won't be so horrid. Think of all the trouble we can get into while we're there. Voz and Oz are already making wagers about how many high ladies they are going to bed. I say you and I focus on how many times we can make the light queen explode." He wrapped his arms around my waist, pulling me closer towards him.

"I will win that wager," I said, taking in his sweet scent of oranges and whiskey.

"You're right ... you would win that one. How about I piss off Gaelin, and you take Daealla. Winner gets the other as a sex slave for a week."

"I'm already your sex slave, Erendrial Lyklor, and no. You leave Gaelin alone. He hasn't done anything wrong."

Eren rolled his eyes and exhaled. "Always so protective of that one. Ruining my fun. Speaking of, how do you think he will react seeing us together?"

I pulled away, trying not to think of the pain that would be written all over Gaelin's face. "Levos said he didn't speak to anyone for a week after the wedding, but the fact that we weren't getting along eased his pain a bit," I confessed.

Eren wrapped his arms around me from behind as he kissed my imprint. "And now that we are in a very … very good place … how fast do you think he is going to explode with jealousy and rage?" he whispered, kissing me along my neck.

I giggled at the feeling, turning around to face him. I exhaled, thinking about how we should handle the situation.

He bent down, trying to catch my eyes. "What's rolling around in that beautiful head of yours?"

"Should … should we maybe not flaunt our desire in front of him? Don't you think we should focus on a peaceful negotiation, since we need them to battle the creatures and the rift? Just until we come to an agreement on how to handle everything," I said.

Eren pulled away slowly. "You mean, you want to resume the facade that we aren't together? That I'm just the arrogant and manipulative lowborn that stole the crown?"

I could hear the hurt in his voice. I reached out, trying to reassure him. "I don't think that of you. You know I don't. I just … we need these negotiations to go smoothly. We all know how they both react when we're around. Our world is in danger, and we need an alliance with them if we are to push the creatures back."

He exhaled, thinking my words over. "I suppose we'll have to stay in different rooms during our time there as well. And I will have to tolerate his nightly visits to your chambers."

"Eren, I don't want him like that. You know I don't," I said, taking his face into my hands.

He removed my hands from his face, a mask descending to swallow his pride and pain. "You say that, but your actions don't," he replied in a low and heavy voice. He couldn't bring his eyes up to mine.

"Eren, I—"

"Come. We're going to be late for dinner," he said, extending his arm to me.

I took it, a weight in my chest pressing down against me. How could he think I would ever choose Gaelin over him? The ring would prove my devotion to him. I would give it to him tonight, so he had a piece of me before we went to the light court.

That night at dinner, I could tell he was fighting to hold in his real feelings. He smiled and held conversations with the others at our table, but he was raw. I reached for his hand, and he took it, but it was more a forced response than his normal adoring affection.

Halfway through our meal, two female alfar signaled for Eren's attention. I had seen them a few times in the city, but I had never made their acquaintance. Eren saw them and gave a faint smile before leaning into my ear.

"I'll meet you back in your room a little later. I have some business to attend to. Don't wait up," he whispered, kissing me on my cheek before going to them. Evinee strolled to his side, taking his arm with hers as the four of them conversed for a second before leaving the throne room.

I leaned across the table to Voz. "Who are those two females Eren just left with?" I asked.

He turned to catch a glimpse of them. "Oh, those are the two madams. They run the gentlemen's club in the city," answered Voz.

I felt the bile slowly rising in my throat. "And ... what business would Eren have with them?"

"Eren is one of their investors. He tries out the new product as it comes into the club. He also helps with their finances and operation. Evinee joined them a few decades back. She helps with the product as well."

I swallowed hard, trying to seem unfazed. "And by product you mean ..."

"The new human girls we acquire from The Frey."

I pulled away from the table, trying to retain any sense of composure I had left. He tried out the product, which meant he was going to the club to ... I closed my eyes, trying to bury the pain and jealousy consuming me. I stood, knowing I had to leave before I became an emotional mess.

"Thank you. Have a good night, Voz," I said, kissing my father on the cheek before I retired to my room.

I sat on my bed, torturing myself with images of his naked body and the bodies of all those new human girls. How many would he test out tonight? Would Evinee be one of them? Surely she would find a way. I pushed the thoughts out of my mind, moving to the bathroom to drown my feelings in the bathtub.

No matter how hard I tried, I couldn't stop obsessing. I sat at my vanity after dressing and ran the brush through my hair. I pulled open the drawer where the small box that contained his ring lay. I held it, looking down at the meaningless piece of metal.

I only wanted him. I only desired him. He was enough for me. Why wasn't I enough for him? I threw the box into the drawer and slammed it, covering my mouth. Tears began to fall from my face even though I fought them. I felt stupid and foolish. This was how things were here. I had to find a way to be okay with this—to look the other way when he chose to sleep with others.

A part of my heart broke. If I was to do this, if I was to be okay with this type of relationship, I had to change. I couldn't look at him or be with him like I was currently. That part of me had to die. I had to realized that I was never going to have him fully. I would have to tell him, and he would have to understand.

I went onto the balcony and looked up at the stars. I found my escape while my mind quieted and my heart went numb. I lost track of time as the cool summer breeze drifted past my face.

A pair of arms wrapped around my waist. He buried his head in my neck. I turned to see a dark head of hair.

"What are you still doing up?" Eren said with a smile. "I thought

I'd find you sound asleep in bed by now."

I forced a smile. "I couldn't sleep. I just have a lot on my mind," I replied, trying to sound normal.

He gave me that devilish grin I adored. He took my hands and began pulling me back into the room. "Why don't you join me for a bath while I distract that overactive mind of yours?"

I dug in my heels. "I already bathed, but thanks," I replied, looking away. He searched my eyes. He knew me. He could sense I was off.

"Then wait for me in bed, and I will make my bath quick," he said, kissing me softly on the lips.

I closed my eyes tightly as pain shot through me like a lightning bolt. I nodded. He turned and headed back into the room. I let out a few more tears once I was alone, commanding myself to stop acting like such an emotional human. I got into bed and waited for him, just as he instructed.

When he emerged, making his way over to me. He only wore his silk black night pants. His torso rippled with muscle. His wide shoulders and broad chest looked magnificent. His raven black hair still dripped with water. A smile stretched across my face, but quickly faded as I wondered how many women had enjoyed his body tonight.

He began to kiss me tenderly while his hands roamed under my gown. I closed my eyes, trying to focus on the contact instead of the pain inside. How did everyone else seem able to shut off their emotions and just enjoy sex, except for me? He kissed down my body, pulling the dress higher until his lips grazed my bare thighs. I leaned my head back against the pillow, trying to enjoy his mouth on my skin, but all I could think about was how many other bodies those lips had pleasured this evening.

How many other women had he kissed, or touched, or enjoyed? I exhaled deeply, forcing those thoughts from my head, but my body wouldn't comply. No matter what I did, I couldn't enjoy myself. I felt Eren push up and place himself next to me. I opened my eyes and turned to see his attention on my face while he rested his head on his propped elbow.

"Okay, what is the matter, princess?" he asked casually.

I looked away, trying to gather myself, then turned on my side to meet his gaze. "Eren, you make me so happy, and I want to be able to do the same for you," I started.

He smiled, arching his eyebrow towards me. "And what makes you think I am not happy?"

"It's not that ... I just ... this is all very new to me, and I am trying to adjust while mentally and emotionally preparing myself for this kind of relationship."

"And what *kind* of relationship are you referring to?"

I took a moment, gathering my confidence to say it out loud. "The type of relationship where I have to share you with others. So, I've made a list of boundaries that I am hoping will ease us both into this uncharted territory."

He paused, furrowing his brow.

"I don't expect you to only be with me, and I know I am going to have to get used to you having relations with other females. Like tonight, when you went to test out the new girls at the club. And with Evinee, and whoever else you choose, but for me to survive this, I need you to understand that I am going to have to change as well. I may ... I may not be able to be as free with you as I have been these past few weeks. I need to guard myself to make this work. I want you to be happy and I would never take your freedom away, but—" I stopped, tears welling in my eyes. I closed them tightly, holding them back.

"Gen—" he said, rubbing my face with his hand.

I inhaled, gathering myself. "I need to know that I am the most important person in your life. That my needs matter to you, and that you will respect me and what I ask of you moving forward." I opened my eyes to see his head shaking. I took a deep breath, trying to regain control.

"Princess, there is no question that you are the most important female in my life. And for the record," he said softly, scooting closer to me. "You are and will be the last person I ever choose to lay with."

My eyes snapped up to his. "What?"

"What did I promise you our first night together? I promised to make you happy. I knew when I made that promise that it meant only being with you, and I am very much okay with that. More than okay with that. I haven't been with anyone since the morning after the sacrifice."

My head was reeling. "But ... what about Evinee?" I asked.

"She has feelings for me. She came to me the day of our wedding and confessed those feeling, but I made it very clear who I wanted, and that person is you. She is still having a hard time with it, but I haven't touched her."

"So, you're okay with only being with me for the rest of your life?" I asked in astonishment.

He gave a faint laugh. "I am honored to stand by your side, to share your bed, and to build a life with you, for the rest of mine."

A cry of pure happiness and joy escaped me. I threw myself at him, taking his mouth with mine. I ravenously devoured him wholly ... completely ... entirely. I pulled away to catch my breath, pinning him underneath me.

"Say it," I demanded.

"Say what?"

"Say that your mine. Only mine."

"I'm yours, princess. Now and always."

I spent the next hour worshiping his body. After I had exhausted him, we lay in each other's arms, sated. He ran his fingers along my spine, kissing me softly. My head snapped up, remembering his present.

He fell back on the pillow. "What is it now?" he asked exasperatedly.

"I almost forgot. I have a something for you."

He pinned me to the bed and began kissing the side of my face. "I suppose I have another few rounds left in me."

I laughed, pushing him back. "Not that. Now, lay back and close your eyes."

He exhaled and did as I asked. I went to my vanity, pulling the small black box from the drawer before returning to the bed. I snapped the lid open and held my breath, then slid it onto his finger.

Holding his hand, I leaned into his ear and whispered, "with this ring, I take thee, Erendrial Valor Lyklor, to be my dashing husband. To have and to hold from this day forward. For better, for worse, for richer, for poorer. In sickness and in health, to love and to cherish from this day on. I give myself to you completely and take you as you are. Perfect in every way."

I pulled away slowly. He opened his eyes and looked down at the ring. His face was hard to read. There was no smile, no glint in his eyes. I waited patiently for a response, but time slowed while he fixated on the ring.

"I know it's a very human thing to do," I started to say, "but I wanted you to have something that reminded you of me. You don't have to wear it if you don't want to. I understand that things are diff—"

"I love you, Genevieve," he said softly.

The breath snagged in my lungs. "You ... you love me?"

"I thought I've made that quite obvious."

"I just ... I never expected you to say it. I thought you were incapable of love."

"I was. Until I met you. I tried fighting it. I tried running from it, denying it even, but if I am being honest, I think I've been in love with you since our first encounter at the light court in the hallway. You are the part of myself I've always been missing. That part I didn't know I was capable of accepting."

I looked at the male who had come into my life like a whirlwind and changed everything. The male who had taught me how to forgive, who helped me find my voice, and had protected my heart since the first moment we had met. This connection ... this love ... I didn't know it could exist.

"I love you too, Eren," I whispered.

I stood in my room, watching as Atalee finished packing my trunk. I didn't want to leave my home. I didn't want to go back to that torturous court, but I didn't have a choice. I had a job, and a mission that was bigger than myself or my fears. I was stronger now. I had faced what had happened to me and I had won.

Eren wrapped his arms around my waist from behind. I leaned into him. "You're going to be fine," he reassured, kissing the side of my head. "No one there is going to hurt you. And if they try, I will personally help Otar tear them limb from limb."

"Or I can just accidentally set a fire and burn the whole place to the ground, like Maleki did. I think he and I would have gotten along splendidly."

He laughed. "I think the Dark Flame would give you away, but if that is what you choose to do, I am sure we can swing it in our favor."

I turned to him, burying my nose into his chest. "Let's get this done so we can return home as quickly as possible."

"Agreed. Now, what mask should I wear while we are there? Overprotective husband? Arrogant whore? Sarcastic manipulator?"

I pulled away from him. "I'm sorry you have to wear a mask at all. It's just until we get them to agree. Then, I will talk to Gaelin. I promise."

He ran his hand down my neck, to my chest, and then the side of my waist. "How am I going to refrain from touching you?"

"Maybe you won't have to. I am your wife after all. Maybe you can wear the mask of the handsy sarcastic manipulator."

He smiled down at me. "Does that mean I get to touch you wherever I want?" he asked, leaning into me, tracing his fingers up my dress.

I lost my breath as the bundle of nerves in between my legs began to swell from the contact. "How do you do that?" I whispered in a gasping tone.

"I know what my wife likes." He kissed me just as his family came barging through the door. He dropped his hand, exhaling in frustration. Lily was with them. Voz and Oz chuckled at us while the others acted like they didn't see anything.

"Everything is ready," reported Leenia.

"Good, we should get going then. The faster we leave the faster, we can return," said Eren, winking at me.

I walked to Lily and took her into my arms. "I'm going to miss you," I said to her.

"Actually, I am going with you," she said.

"What? No, I would never bring you to that place."

"I tried talking her out of it, but she insisted," added Zerrial.

"I will be safe with all of you there, and I am just another human. I will blend in," said Lily.

"Lily, Urial is not like Doonak. They don't treat humans the same there. If anything happened to you, I—"

"She will be safe," Zerrial said firmly.

"Yeah, plus, if they mess with me, I'll just have my sister unleash the Dark Flame on their asses," Lily said, wrapping her arms around Zerrial as she smiled.

I laughed at her, shaking my head. "Did you just say 'asses'?" I asked.

She shrugged. "What? I am not the same innocent little lamb I was back in The Frey. You're not the only who has changed, dear sister," Lily said, winking at me.

I looked at Zerrial sternly.

"She will be safe, Princess Genevieve. I swear it on my life," he reassured me.

I looked back at Lily and gave her a slight nod. "Don't go anywhere without one of us, understood?" I asked her.

"Got it," she said, beaming with excitement.

I turned back to Eren as we headed for the main gate. We each called our ragamors and took off into the sky, towards the palace that had been my prison for far too long.

CHAPTER TWENTY-ONE

W e landed in a clearing in front of a crowd of light alfar waiting to witness our magnificent beasts. I didn't know which they were more afraid of, our ragamors, or us. I thought back to the first time I had seen Eren and the dark court. I had felt so afraid, yet in awe. How strong and authoritative they had appeared. I wondered if the light alfar looked at me with the same entrancing perception. Especially since I had died and come back with the Dark Flame, our greatest weapon.

Eren dismounted Eeri without turning to look at me. He usually came to help me off Tarsyrth, but his mask was firmly in place. My heart felt heavy at what I had asked of him, but it would only be until we got them to agree on peaceful terms.

We walked towards Gaelin, Daealla, and Levos with our court following behind. I wore a black silk dress that held my body tightly. It exposed the fullness of my breasts and some of my abdomen. Two high slits traveled up my legs while the length of the dress fluttered in the wind behind me. My imprint was on display; even though I had to act like Eren wasn't the love of my life, I wore it proudly.

I kept my eyes facing forward, not looking at any of the city alfar we passed on our way to the castle gate. My gold crown adorned my black curls that flowed loosely in the wind. Each step Eren took rippled with arrogance, his golden crown reflecting the sunlight. We appeared just as intimidating and dangerous as they feared. Even Lily looked fierce in a black and gold gown. The rest of our family wore black leather that revealed far more skin than customary in the light court.

Gaelin's face lit up as we approached. I gave him a half-smile and nod before addressing them. "Queen Daealla, King Atros, we are honored to be welcomed into your palace," I greeted evenly.

"Princess Genevieve, Prince Lyklor," replied Daealla coldly, "we are humbled that you accepted our invitation. We look forward to working together to eliminate the threat that is sweeping through our lands."

"Speaking of, when might we begin negotiations?" asked Eren smugly. "The less time I have to spend here, the better."

Daealla smiled widely, her eyes twitching with annoyance.

"Tomorrow," Gaelin intervened, "we will discuss plans and strategies. But tonight, my wife would like us all to dine together … in peace." He gave Daealla a warning glance.

"Fantastic," replied Eren. "I can't wait to see what human entertainment you have waiting for us."

Daealla narrowed her eyes as she looked behind us at our court.

Her eyes locked on one individual ... Lily. "Are our human servants not able enough for you? Is that why you brought your own?" asked Daealla.

"She isn't a servant," I said with bite.

Daealla peered at Lily again, approaching her. Zerrial stood close, unmoving.

"Right," Daealla said with a grin. "This must be the little human girl that you fought so triumphantly for." The light queen assessed Zerrial from head to two. "Looks like she's found herself a bed to keep warm in. You will entertain us tonight with song. If I remember correctly, you have a lovely voice ... for a human, that is." Daealla turned away, walking into her castle without another word. We followed while I fought to keep from ripping out her perfect blonde hair.

The castle was just as I remembered. Human servants lined the halls, looking miserable and broken. The building itself was magnificent, with tall ceilings and archways that gleamed with gold details. Artwork and tapestries lined the halls. The light court members lounged lazily on couches in seating areas scattered throughout the great hall.

Daealla led us into a private meeting room where lunch had been served. She signaled to a servant girl to show our court to their rooms. Only Levos and Firel followed us into the room, along with Gaelin and Daealla. We sat around the table staring at each other while the servants prepared our plates and poured wine.

Gaelin hadn't taken his eyes off me. Eren sat to my left, acting as if he didn't notice. We all began eating, waiting for the other party to begin a conversation.

"How's the heir making going, Daealla? Any news?" asked Eren arrogantly.

Daealla almost choked on her food, reaching for her wine. Eren sat back and smiled. "That is none of your business, Lyklor," Daealla said, appalled by his inquiry.

Eren leaned forward, popping a grape into his mouth. "If Gaelin here is having problems, I'd be happy to show him how it's done. That is, if you don't mind me warming your wife's bed, King Atros," Eren said, turning his eyes to Gaelin.

Gaelin didn't seem fazed, which wasn't surprising, since he had no love for Daealla.

"Not at all, Erendrial," Gaelin said without flinching. "As long as I get the same opportunity with your wife. It's only fair, don't you think?"

Eren remained stoic, except for the small clench in his jaw that I had learned was his tell. He sat back, looking at Daealla once more. "Looks like this visit to the light court is going to be one for the books. Don't you think, *wife*?" Eren said, not looking at me.

"How are your lands?" I asked, trying to defuse the situation. "Have the creatures attacked any other races who occupy Urial?"

"The nymphs have reported seeing a few creatures on their land, but they haven't had any interactions with them," answered

Gaelin. "The dryads who live deep in the woods have reported members of their race missing. So have the mermaids. They have decided that to remain safe, it's best for their race to stay deep beneath the water until the threat has passed. We haven't had contact from them since."

"Have the creatures only attacked when the mermaids are in their human form?" asked Firel.

"Yes," answered Levos, "but that doesn't mean they are opposed to water. I believe they are harder to find for the creatures who aren't adept at hunting in water."

"We're hoping that your Dark Flame will act as a deterrent for the creatures, now that you are here," said Daealla.

"They know I have the gift, and yet Alaric still sends them through the rifts," I pointed out.

"Well, from what I hear, it is quite the gift," Daealla said in a taunting voice as she bit into a piece of fruit. "I suppose dying was the best thing that could have happened to you, if you came back with that little souvenir. Makes everything you had to go through worth it, don't you think?"

I plastered on a smile, refraining from showing her exactly what my power could do to her pretty little face. Gods, I prayed for the day when I would kill her.

"My gift is a blessing from Azeer that I am humbled to wield," I replied, standing. "Excuse me, I need some fresh air." I made my way to the balcony, cursing under my breath the entire way. A few moments passed before Gaelin appeared next to me. I looked back at the table to see Eren and Daealla flirting next to one another. Oh, I would kill her for sure.

"Are you okay?" he asked in his deep, tenor voice.

"How do you put up with her? She is a disgusting and foul creature," I said, turning away from them.

"I could ask you the same thing about Lyklor," he said with a smirk.

My stomach turned.

"Is he … is he kind to you?"

"Does he force himself on me, you mean?"

Gaelin stood in silence, waiting for me to respond.

"No, he doesn't," I answered softly. "He's useful, when he wants to be."

"I've wanted to visit you so many times since the last time I saw you. How are you after everything?"

"I've learned to adapt, just like before. There were a few rough patches, but I made it through. And, as your wife so graciously pointed out, I didn't return empty-handed. I've learned to control my power, and I continue to train which only makes me stronger."

"That's good. I am glad to hear it. I'm just sorry you got stuck with that lowborn after everything. I still can't believe your father allowed him to enter the tournament. What was he thinking?"

I laughed to myself. My father was thinking that Eren was the only male that would lay his life down for me. Because he truly loved me. My father knew it, and he wanted me to be happy. Thinking back on how fiercely Eren fought for me in the tournament just made me love him more.

"Rules are rules," I said without a flicker of emotion.

I felt Gaelin's hand stroke the side of my face. His eyes scanned my body with desire. "You make a beautiful royal," he said endearingly.

I gave him a small grin. "It's just a dress, Gaelin."

He shook his head. "No. It's your power. The authority you demand when you enter a room. I should have known who you were the first time I laid eyes on you. It's always been there, but now, you wear it with elegance and pride," he said, taking a step closer to me, his other hand moving to my waist. "For what it's worth, I am so proud of you." He went to lean his head into mine, when a hand appeared out of nowhere, pushing Gaelin back.

"Now," said Eren, moving next to me, "I know my wife outshines yours on all fronts, but really Gaelin? You could only refrain from touching her for ten minutes? And you call us wild animals."

"Can I help you with something, Lyklor?" asked Gaelin, his pale face reddening as his temper flared.

"Yes, you can," Eren replied, pulling me into him from behind territorially. "You can refrain from touching what is mine."

"She isn't yours," growled Gaelin.

"Oh, but she is," Eren replied with a cocky grin. "See this?" He said, tracing my imprint with his fingers. My body lit up at his touch. "This marks her as mine. She is the only female that will ever have it, because she *is* mine. My imprint, my female."

I looked back into the room to see if Levos or Firel could help, but they were all gone.

"We have an entire castle of warm bodies you can have. Just leave her alone," demanded Gaelin, taking a step towards us.

"Well, thank you for the offer. Why don't you have a colorful buffet sent to my room after dinner? But for now, I think my wife will do just fine," Eren said, matching Gaelin's dominating stance.

I moved in between them, placing a hand on Gaelin's chest. He took a deep breath at the contact. "Gaelin, I am fine, really," I assured him.

He looked down at me, his face softening. "If you need anything, I am here," Gaelin said. I nodded, trying to hold back the shame on my face. He signaled for the servant in the corner. "Show Princess Genevieve and Lyklor to their *separate* rooms." Gaelin left as the servant bowed.

I looked at Eren, but he refused to meet my gaze. I knew this was eating him alive, but we had to remain strong.

We followed the servant to my room first, where my trunk was waiting for me. The servant took Eren down the hall and he disappeared into his separate room. I sat on the bed, trying to gather my thoughts when Eren came bursting through the door without warning. He slammed it shut and rushed towards me, taking me into his arm as we toppled onto the bed. He kissed me with such passion and possessiveness I fought to breathe.

"Say it," he demanded, pulling away from me only for a moment.

"I'm yours. Only yours," I said in between his kisses. I tore at his shirt as he lifted the length of my dress. I reached for his pants, needing to assure him of my love. Our fingers laced with one another as a knock sounded at the door. Levos stepped in, immediately looking away while we straightened ourselves out.

"I'm so sorry. I didn't mean to interrupt," said Levos, waiting until it was safe to turn around.

"Well, you did," snapped Eren, tying his pants closed. He turned back towards me. "Have I told you how much I hate this court today?"

I laughed at him, pulling the straps of my dress back onto my shoulders. "Be nice," I replied.

He rolled his eyes as Levos turned back towards us and smiled.

"Fine, I'll give you two a minute," Eren said, turning me to face him. "But this means you owe me double later." He leaned down and kissed me gently on my lips before leaving the room.

After the door shut, Levos came towards me, a curious expression on his face. "Did I just rescue you from Lyklor or was I truly interrupting?" he asked. I couldn't help but blush as I sat on the edge of the bed and fell backward. He joined me.

"I'll leave you to interpret what you saw on your own," I turned, smiling at him.

He laughed, cradling his head on his elbow. "It's been a few weeks since we last spoke. What in Odin's name have I missed?"

I walked over to my chest, pulling a piece of paper from one of the side pockets. I handed it to Levos before I lay back on the bed. He looked at the picture carefully, not saying a word for a few moments.

"Is this ... is this your daughter?" he finally asked.

"Eren saw the image I had of her in my head during the tournament. He's drawn dozens of portraits of her," I said with a heavy heart. Besides Lily and Vena, Levos was the only other person I had willingly told about the baby. I had broken down the night before the wedding and divulged everything.

"Who knew Lyklor was so talented? She's beautiful Gen, truly beautiful." He reached over and embraced me while I held back the tears at the thought of the little girl I'd never know. "Now, about Lyklor ... "

I laughed, rubbing my hands down my face. "After the night I presented the contract, he wouldn't speak to me. I was too prideful to see his silence as anything more than another manipulation. The next month when he was supposed to visit my chambers for, you know, he didn't show up. I was speaking with Lily about him when she completely lost it on me. She even punched me!"

He laughed hysterically. "I think your human sister has spent too much time in the dark court for her own good."

"She told me how much Eren was suffering, all he did for me, and how after he learned about the baby, he was wrecked and ended up crying in her arms. She used the projection sphere to show me memories of him when I was dead. I realized I was being completely unfair to him. So, I began to work to fix it. It took a while, but eventually, he caved and now things are great. They're wonderful, in fact," I said, warmth spreading in my chest.

"So, all that back at lunch was a show?" asked Levos.

"I thought it best that we don't flaunt our happiness in Gaelin's face before negotiations begin."

Levos ran his hands through his shining white hair. "I'm still worried about you. I don't want to see you get hurt again, and he's ... he isn't known for his self-control, if you know what I mean."

"It's different with us, really," I said, still smiling at the thought of Eren.

Levos looked at me for a long moment, tilting his head to the side. "You're in love with him, aren't you?"

"And if I said yes, would that be so awful?"

"I just ... I don't see him being the one to give you what you want, or need. Unless your moral system has completely changed and you're okay with sharing your husband with half the court."

"We're in a monogamous relationship. He hasn't been with anyone but me since the sacrifice to Azeer, and he promises I'm all he wants."

"Erendrial Lyklor is in a monogamous relationship? Loki must be playing a trick."

I felt a little stupid trying to defend myself to Levos. It was still hard for me to wrap my mind around too, but last night, Eren seemed to be telling the truth. He had never lied to me before. Why would he start now?

"Is it so hard to believe that I would be enough for him?" I asked, feeling my cheeks heat.

"No, that's not what I am saying. I just ... I knew he loved you months ago, but it seems that you've completed changed him."

"What do you mean you knew months ago?"

Levos exhaled heavily. "The night we found your body. He was leading the party. When Gaelin tried to step near you, he snapped. He wouldn't let anyone touch you. He covered your mutilated body and held you for minutes. It was evident he loved you. Then, back at your court, he wasn't himself. He was a complete mess. In all my years of knowing Erendrial Lyklor, I had never experienced a falter in his façade, until your incident."

"Why didn't you tell me?" I asked him.

"I wanted to, but you had made up your mind about him at that point. I wasn't going to belittle your experiences with the demons. If he reminded you of what they had done, I thought it best to just ignore him. I figured he would move on eventually, but I was sorely wrong. I about lost it when he volunteered for the tournament that night. He hasn't told you any of this?"

"We avoid *that* topic as best as we can," I said.

"Well, if you are truly happy, then I am happy for you. You

deserve it more than anyone I know." He smiled at me, running his hand down the side of my face.

"I am, I really am," I whispered, still reeling with happiness.

"Gaelin is not going to take this well," Levos said, falling back on the bed.

"I know, but he is going to have to accept it." Just as I fell back next to Levos, a sharp bolt of lightning sprung up my back to the base of my skull. I saw Narella leaning forward, whispering to me by the large spring where I had first seen the kelpie with Gaelin. The vision ended as I sprung forward, panting for breath.

"What is it? Are you okay?" Levos asked.

I sat up, feeling a bit lightheaded. "I'm fine. I um, I need to handle something. Will you relay a message to Eren for me? Tell him I went out, but not to worry because I brought backup."

Levos looked at me curiously. "Keeping secrets from me, sweet Gen? After all we've been through this past year?"

"Please, Levos."

"Alright, alright, but you owe me."

"I did bring Vena to court just for you."

Levos smiled and headed to the door. "I noticed. Though, it's not the same here as it is in your court. If they found out I was with her, they'd excommunicate me from court."

"That's ridiculous. You should be able to be with whomever you choose."

"A conversation for another time. Whatever you're up to, just promise me you'll be careful."

"Aren't I always?" He looked at me with a stern expression. "Alright, I promise."

I called Otar as soon as Levos left. He appeared next to me, mouth and teeth full of blood. "Yes, my wicked one?"

"Where in the hell did you just come from?"

"Dismembering a creature I came across in your lands. I left its dead body at your gates." Otar looked around the room and then spat over and over again. "Why in the fuck are you back here in this filthy prison? Are we here to kill the stupid queen?"

I laughed. "No, not yet, but when that day comes, you can have her."

"Always generous you are, wicked one."

"I need to meet with Narella again. She called for me through a vision. Will you come with me?"

"Will it be just me and you?" he asked with a smile.

"Yes. Eren has to stay behind. It will look too suspicious if we both disappear."

"Excellent, let's leave now," said Otar, rushing to the balcony.

"Does that mean you'll finally ride Tarsyrth with me?"

"Fucks no! They are ugly, monstrous beasts. I will never touch one, never."

"Fine, just follow us then. Don't stop until you reach me."

"As you wish."

CHAPTER
TWENTY-TWO

"Where is your pretty prince, Genevieve?" asked Narella. Otar flashed to my side.

"I don't have much time. What is it you need?" I asked.

"A new development. Alaric plans to open war on this world in less than a year's time. Fate has brought you to the light court because this is where he plans to hit first. He will open the portals for an extended time, allowing hordes of creatures through. I will be forced to call forth the creatures that roam this land to attack your forces. I have no control, you must understand."

"What should we do?" I asked.

"Hold them off for as long as possible while you build your forces. Your power alone will be able to slow them down." Narella grimaced and strained her neck up and to the side. "He is beckoning me. I must go," she said, disappearing.

"Well, that wasn't any fun," snapped Otar. "I didn't even get to threaten her!"

"Sounds like you are going to do plenty of killing soon enough. Keep guard around Doonak and report to me if there is an increase of creatures."

"I can do that," said Otar, flashing his sharp teeth before he disappeared.

I made my way back to my room and prepared for dinner. I dressed in the proper dark court fashion of dramatic makeup and a revealing dress. The diamond crown sat on top of my dark hair. I looked down at my left hand, admiring my wedding ring.

When I entered the light throne room, I took a deep breath and readied myself. Memories of the king flashed through my head. His smile, his smell, his voice. The feeling of my hand smashed underneath Filo's hammer. How my skin had smelled while Daealla burned the Lysanthier sigil into my chest. The screams of light alfar on the night Otar had, at my command, torn this place to shreds.

A cruel and wicked grin crept across my face. I let it all go and walked with pride to my seat.

Eren was conversing with a few high ladies. His charm was turned all the way up while they batted their eyelashes at him and laughed at his jokes. One of them caressed his forearm. I forced myself to turn away before I incinerated her ass on the spot. Gods, I couldn't wait until this was over.

I took a seat across from Gaelin as the servants began to bring out the first course. Gaelin smiled at me. Desire flickered behind his eyes while he took in my appearance.

"How was your afternoon?" he asked.

"Uneventful. And yours?"

"I came looking for you before dinner, but you weren't in your rooms."

"I went for a ride on my ragamor. Being back here is ... more challenging than I expected," I lied.

"I hope all of your memories aren't bad," he said with an insinuating smile. "Maybe tonight I could stop by your rooms so we could talk."

I swallowed hard, not knowing what to say. As if he heard my mental plea for help, Eren appeared. He took his seat next to me while Daealla took hers beside Gaelin. Eren ran the back of his hand down my arm.

"Good evening, everyone. What have I missed?" Eren asked, turning from me to Gaelin.

"Making plans for this evening's entertainment?" Gaelin asked him, indicating the three high ladies.

"It's always good to have options." Eren smiled back at him.

We began to dine, and Eren looked at me for answers about my outing. I smiled and nodded, letting him know I'd fill him in later.

The light court had some theatrical play for entertainment that nearly put me to sleep. How in Azeer's name had I ever thought this place entrancing? The dark court was so much more seductive and alluring. I laughed at myself. Oh, how my morals and expectations had changed in the past year.

After dinner, boring music played throughout the room. A few alfar stood to dance, which was unusual. When Daealla's father had ruled, there was no dancing after dinner. That only happened at our court.

Daealla stood, looking to Eren. "Prince Lyklor, would you care to dance?" she asked, extending her hand to him. Without looking at me, he stood and kissed her hand a little too long for my liking. A flicker of jealousy and annoyance rushed through every nerve in my body. My hands and arms began to warm. I looked down to see my flame flicker to life. I snuffed it out quickly before anyone could notice.

"It would be my honor, Your Majesty," Eren said with a smile.

Gaelin looked to me and shrugged. I nodded my acceptance and we moved to the dance floor. He wrapped his arm around my waist, pulling me in tighter than I cared for. I could feel his longing gaze on my face while we glided across the floor to the slow and mundane music.

"You never answered my question about my visit to your rooms this evening," he whispered softly.

I looked back at him and forced a smile. "Gaelin, I'm married," I said, not knowing how else to respond.

"Only on paper. It doesn't have to stand in our way. I meant what I said before I left your court last time. We can make this work. I will fight for you, whatever it takes. After almost losing you, I've realized I want nothing more than to be with you. To make you happy."

"I'm the heir of Doonak. This could never be more than a casual acquaintance."

"We can make each other happy. I can make you happy, if you give me the chance."

I looked up at him, the guilt of my deception heavy in my heart. "Gaelin, we can't. I'm sorry, but—" Eren pulled on my arm as he spun Daealla into my place.

"My turn," Eren said, attempting to remove me from Gaelin's grip. Gaelin let go of Daealla and pulled me back to him.

"I don't think so," growled Gaelin.

Eren stepped forward, accepting his challenge. "King Atros, you forget your place. This is *my* wife, which means I get to have her whenever I want. Especially when it inconveniences you. Now, please remove your hands from her, or I will be forced to resort to less comfortable methods of removing your hand."

I tried to hide my smile. I never realized how enticing it was to hear him threaten others. Gaelin reluctantly let me go as Eren swept me into his arms and over to the other side of the dance floor.

"Thank you," I whispered.

He smiled down at me. "Oh, I didn't do that for you. I did it for me. Guess what offer the queen just made us? She suggested we all share each other."

A laugh fell out of me so loudly, I had to cough to play it off. "She did what?"

"Oh, yes. Apparently, I am that good. She told me all the things she wanted to do to me and wanted me to do to her. If I didn't know better, I would say she was dark alfar."

I smiled at him while his face grimaced with disgust. "Well, you will have a free bed tonight. Might as well fill it," I said tauntingly.

"I'll find my way to yours, don't you worry," he said, running his hand down the side of my breast to my hip. I exhaled with relief, my pheromones slipping past my control. He inhaled with a low moan. "Princess, would you like me to take you right here? I will, if you give me permission, but if not, I suggest you reel that back in. You're getting strong and it's harder to control myself." He pulled me closer to him and I could feel the hardness already rising under his pants.

"Sorry, I just miss you," I said, getting a handle on my power.

"I'll take care of your needs, don't you worry. Now, about our mutual friend. What did she have to say?"

"Alaric is going to wage war on this world within the year. She believes fate has brought us here. They're going to attack Urial first. She said we need to build our forces while we hold off the oncoming waves of creatures. She will be forced to control the ones already roaming free in the lands, but she has no control of her actions."

"Well, it looks like we're going to war."

"On the plus side, I will get to try out my new crescent blades," I said with a smile.

Daealla made her way over to us as the music came to an end.

"Princess Genevieve, I bid you a good evening. I am retiring for the night." She turned her gaze to Eren. "Prince Lyklor, my offer still stands if you change your mind. And I very much hope you do," she said, placing a hand on his chest.

Without thinking, I pushed it off in irritation.

She looked at me in shock and then gave a low laugh. "You're a dark alfar, learn to share," she hissed, walking out of the throne room.

Eren looked down at me and smiled. "Who's territorial now?" he whispered.

"I will kill both of you," I said through my teeth.

He took my chin between his fingers and rubbed his nose against mine. "I already told you: you will never have to worry about that. Now, let's go back to the table and act like respectable royals for a few minutes longer so we can get the hell out of here," he said, dropping his hands from me.

I followed him back to the table while Gaelin watched the two of us closely. I went to take a seat in my chair, but before I could, Eren pulled me onto his lap, running a hand up my thigh under my dress. He rubbed his nose against my neck before turning to Gaelin.

"You are not in the dark court, Lyklor," snapped Gaelin, jealousy consuming his expression.

"Dear Gaelin, *we are* the dark court. The party goes wherever we go," Eren said, stroking his hand down my arm.

"What are you doing?" I whispered.

"You said I could wear the handsy mask. Well, here is it," Eren said, nipping at my ear. The scent of oranges and whiskey filled the air. Unable to control myself, I leaned back against him, taking in the scent, letting it turn my body to putty.

"So, you have to use your power to get her to sleep with you. How respectable," said Gaelin, leaning into the table.

"I don't have to, but she does enjoy the scent. Don't you, wife?"

I couldn't respond. My body was lighting up from his power and the feeling of his skin against mine. I didn't know what he was doing. This wasn't a part of the plan, but I didn't care. I just didn't want him to stop.

"You're pathetic. You're only doing this to get a rise out of me," said Gaelin, sitting back in his chair.

"Am I? Or do I just enjoy the feeling of *my* wife?" Eren said, running his hand down my neck. I turned and smiled at him, unable to control myself. He reached down, taking my left hand in his as he laced our fingers together.

"What are those?" Gaelin demanded, sitting up straighter.

"Wedding rings, you idiot," Eren said, not taking his eyes from mine. "They're our commitment to one another. You're familiar with the symbolism in The Frey, aren't you Gaelin? Since my wife is half-human, I had one made for her to represent our union. In return, she had one made for me. Adorable, aren't they?"

I turned to Gaelin; his face tensed while he absorbed Eren's words.

"You're lying," whispered Gaelin.

"Not about this," Eren said, finally looking at Gaelin. "Never to her. My promise is real, and so is hers."

Gaelin's face flashed from pain, to shock, and then to a look I had never witnessed before. He sat back with a smile, appraising us both.

"Since you offered to compare notes," began Gaelin, "how does it feel to know I was buried in your wife first? To know that my seed swam through her body before she ever knew you? To know that her mouth ... the mouth that you now kiss ... was around my cock?"

Eren's body stiffened and his grip on me tightened. His face remained calm, but his jaw tensed as he tilted his head towards Gaelin. "I'd suggest, for your own safety, that you forget any images of my wife," said Eren.

"Doesn't surprise me you're okay having my seconds," Gaelin said. "You are a lowborn, after all. Eating our scraps is something your kind gets used to."

I snapped out of Eren's powers. "Gaelin!" I said furiously.

He looked at me with mild disgust. "You seemed to enjoy me that first night I took your maidenhood. Though, it could have been just another way to manipulate me, since that seems to be what you are good at. Come to think of it, you both deserve each other. You're one and the same," Gaelin spat.

I could hear the pain in his voice. I couldn't defend myself, because everything he said was true. I had manipulated him, over and over again, until I got him to move the way I needed.

"Refrain from insulting my wife. You are treading a line that you will regret crossing," Eren said.

"I hate to break it to you, Lyklor, but I've already ridden and crossed every line with your lovely wife. And she moaned my name the entire time. Mm, I remember the way her little body quivered underneath mine," Gaelin said.

Eren let out a light laugh, dropping his eyes. He pushed me up and placed me in my chair before he casually walked over to Gaelin. Gaelin stood, face-to-face with Eren. The court readied themselves for their evening entertainment.

Zerrial and the others stood, preparing to attack if necessary. I rushed forward, putting myself between the two of them. As I placed a hand on both Eren and Gaelin, Gaelin pushed me with enough force that I went stumbling to the ground.

"Do not ever touch me again, you whore," Gaelin yelled, more hatred in his eyes than I had ever seen.

Eren's hands flew up in front of him. Gaelin dropped to his knees, holding his head while he screamed. Leenia helped me from the floor while our family surrounded us.

"Do not ever think to touch my wife again, nor call her anything other than her name! Am I clear, *king*?" Eren yelled.

Gaelin grunted and roared as he brought a hand forward.

Thorned vines twirled up Eren's legs, slashing the fabric of his black suit while they held him in place, severing his connection to his power. I never realized how strong Gaelin's will was until that moment.

Gaelin smiled and approached Eren. Zerrial and the others took a step forward towards Eren. Gaelin reached for the sword in his belt that I knew was made of ulyrium.

I raised my hands, calling on my dark magic. My fire ate through the vines that restrained Eren in seconds. Wild, lashing flames blazed from me into a circular barrier around Gaelin, Eren, and myself, protecting those on the outside. Zerrial tossed me his sword, and I slammed the hilt into the side of Gaelin's head.

Light court guards surrounded Eren and I instantly. My power billowed from me, anger raging freely beneath my skin. How dare he think to threaten what is mine? Gaelin shook his head as I reached down and picked him up by the neck. My power gave me a strength I had never experienced before, but all I could think about was destroying Gaelin. Dark flames licked around me while my grip on his neck tightened. Gaelin looked down at me in disbelief. I threw him forward, absorbing my power. I took a deep breath, calming the violent storm inside of me while smoke and ash sizzled around us.

"Let me make myself clear, Gaelin Atros," I said, tilting my chin sharply to crack my neck, as I had witnessed Otar do so often. "Erendrial Lyklor is my husband ... and my future king. He is the only male I have *ever* chosen for myself. He is the only one I have and will ever want. If you ever think to disrespect him or me again, I will burn this whole fucking castle to the ground. I will destroy anything you hope to build, and I will take away everything that means anything to you. You will never speak of me in that vulgar manner again, and you will never lift a hand to harm my husband, or I will dissolve our treaty, and you will become my enemy. Do I make myself clear?"

Gaelin stood and signaled to the guards to put their weapons away. He walked over to me slowly until we were face-to-face. He took a moment to study me.

"He has destroyed you," he said with a heavy heart. "The Genevieve I knew and loved is gone."

"Thank Azeer for that," I said, turning away from him to face Eren.

Eren looked at me with pride and smiled, offering me his hand. I grinned back, taking my husband's hand as we sauntered out of the throne room. Once clear of the guards, Eren nodded to the others that it was okay to go back to their rooms. We continued in silence until we were safely behind my bedroom doors.

"What was that about?" I said with aggression. "I thought we weren't trying to piss off Gaelin until after the arrangements were decided upon."

"How much did you expect me to take, Genevieve? I heard him propositioning you on the dance floor. When were you going to tell me he had offered this deal to you? What—the two of you would meet each month to have your dalliance, without either court noticing?" Eren said, running his hand through his hair, trying to cool his temper.

"It was never going to happen. I told him that. Do you really think I would ever let him touch me?"

He turned to me; his eyes heavy with worry. "Honestly, before tonight I did, but—" he stopped and let out a laugh of relief. "Not after the performance you just gave."

I smiled, wrapping my arms around his neck. "You know, the definition of a monogamous relationship means both parties are committed. On top of that, what female would ever choose him over the great Erendrial Lyklor?"

"The only female I care about is this one right here," he said, leaning down into my face.

"Then you have nothing to worry about."

He kissed down the side of my face as I leaned back, allowing him full access to my neck.

"I've never had a female claim me the way you just did in front of everyone. It was sexy as fuck."

I chuckled, pulling my head back. "Now, enough talking. Let the oranges and whiskey free and take me against every surface in this room."

His eyebrow arched. "Just this room? Or is the hallway a possibility too?"

"I don't care, just take me," I said, not wanting to wait a minute longer. I took his mouth with mine. We spent the rest of the night making love to each other until I was unable to move.

CHAPTER
TWENTY-THREE

Erendrial

"Firel, pay attention and call out anything you see," I said, walking towards the meeting chambers with Zerrial and Fi flanking either side. "Zerrial, interject when needed as we plan our strategy.

"After last night, I don't see this going well," grumbled Zerrial.

"What are they going to do? Refuse our help? They need us," said Fi.

"Doesn't mean they're going to make this easy," Zerrial replied.

"When has the light court ever made anything easy?" I added. They both laughed softly as we approached the double doors.

Levos and Gen were waiting off to the side. Levos gave me a small nod before kissing Gen on the cheek and entering the war room. She smiled suggestively at me while she scanned me from head to toe.

Her presence demanded attention. She was dressed in black lace that revealed some of my favorite parts. Diamonds adorned her shoulders and trailed down her arms. Her makeup was subtle, yet complimentary, with a red lip that drew attention to the lush, elegant lines of that mouth I loved to watch take in certain parts of me. Fuck, it was hard to focus around her.

"You three are late," she greeted us playfully. "What mischief have you caused?"

"Us? Never," I said, leaning down to kiss her.

"Shall we?" she whispered.

"After you, princess," I said. She took my hand as Zerrial and Firel opened the doors.

Daealla, Gaelin, and Levos sat on one side of the table with a light alfar I didn't recognize. Four chairs were set across from them. I pulled out the chair for Gen, and leaned in to kiss her cheek before I took my place at her side. The light court members watched our every move. I sat, leaning back against the large wooden chair, lacing my fingers casually.

"Before we begin," started Daealla, "I would like to address the attack on my husband last night after I retired. Your actions and threats are unacceptable, and another attack will not be tolerated, regardless of the threat we face. You should thank Odin I didn't throw you and your court out directly after the incident."

"Your king," spat Zerrial, "threw our princess to the ground. He initiated the attack. How did you expect us to respond, *Your Majesty*?"

"From what my witnesses have told me, your princess slipped on her own dress. King Atros did not touch her," replied Daealla.

Zerrial stood from the table in a threatening stance, growling under his breath. He looked directly at Gaelin with hatred. "Is this how the light king conducts himself?" roared Zerrial. "Allowing his wife to fight his battles for him. Take responsibility where it is due, you jealous—"

I held my hand up to silence him before he could lash out further, forcing a smile across my mask. "Our apologies, Queen Daealla, King Atros. Last night was unacceptable on all accounts. Now, if you would grant me permission to speak, some information has come to light that we'd like to share." I nodded at Fi to take the floor. He sat up with more confidence than I had seen him ever portray. His lessons were paying off.

"The rift will open in less than a year for a long period, allowing creatures to come through by the hordes," reported Firel. "The roaming creatures that live within the forest will also be called to fight."

"And how did you come across this information?" asked Gaelin in a monotone voice.

"The *how* is not your concern," snapped Firel with a smirk. "We are certain the portal will be opening somewhere in your lands. We have already informed our court to send reinforcements as soon as possible. They will camp outside your city limits until we are—"

Daealla held up her hand to stop Firel. She took a second to gather her thoughts. "Princess Genevieve," she started, "this is not the time to be keeping secrets from your allies. Especially something that could save lives and give us the upper hand in this battle."

"I can assure you that our informant's information is reliable, but we have not found a way to locate the rift openings consistently," Gen replied.

"You are to inform us immediately next time you get a lead this important, and before you call more of your warriors to set foot on my land. Is that clear?" Daealla said forcefully.

"We did not mean any offense, Queen Daealla," I replied.

"I find that very unlikely, Prince Lyklor," Daealla said, standing to leave. "My king and I will discuss military strategies to combat the upcoming attack. Until then, refrain from anymore ... outbursts in my court." She set her eyes on Gen and me, then Gaelin. Gaelin did not return the glare.

I stood, extending my hand to Gen. We took our leave, returning to her rooms. My trunks had been moved in the night before. The ruse was over, and I couldn't have been happier about it.

Gen fell onto the bed, letting out a breath. "We got nowhere in that meeting," she said, running her hands over her face.

Firel stepped into the room, taking a seat at the small round table in the corner. I could tell he was deep in thought. That beautiful brain of his was spinning away, trying to find a solution to our ever-growing pest problem.

"That was a pointless waste of time," said Gen. "We got nothing accomplished."

"I know, princess," I replied, running a hand through her hair. "As usual, the majority of the work is going to fall to us."

Firel sat up slowly with a twinkle of brilliance lighting behind his eyes.

"Fi, what is it?" I asked.

"Our forces," he started. "They aren't going to be enough."

"Yes, thank you so much for stating the obvious," I said, pouring myself a thumb of whisky.

"The others. We need the others," he said, jumping to his feet, beginning to pace back and forward.

Gen sat up. "What others?" she asked quickly.

"The fae," he started. "We need the other races. All of them, matter of fact. This is not only our fight. They risk losing everything to Alaric and his horde of monsters. They will fight. They must."

I smiled widely. Why hadn't I thought of this? My decision to name him as my next ambassador had not been wasted.

"You really think they will all work together?" asked Gen. "The light and the dark court, and all the fae from *every* race?"

"It's the only way," Fi replied. "Every race, every territory, every court is being attacked. The only lands that have yet to be touched are the humans. This is no longer about what court you stand in support of. This is about survival, and unless we all band together now, these creatures are going to pick us all apart until there is no one left to stand and fight."

I looked from Fi to Gen, waiting for the information to settle in her mind. I knew what our next steps would be, but I wanted her to have time to get to that conclusion on her own.

"We have to go to Levos," she replied.

I smiled with pride. "Just what I was thinking, beautiful," I said, leaning down to kiss her on the head. "We will go to Levos and have him present this idea to the royals as if it were his own. That way, there will be less pushback and our fun little banter fest won't be necessary."

"Fi," I said, "send Leenia, Doria, and the twins to meet with the incubi, imps, and the draugr. Tell them to bring gifts for each of them. The rest of our group will go to the fairies and dwarfs."

Firel turned to look at me. "Dwarfs? But the dark court hasn't had contact with them for over five hundred years. We don't even know where they are. How do you expect to find them?"

I winked at Gen as she approached my side. "Would you like to tell him?" I asked her.

"Well," she started, "fate has smiled upon us. Otar found them last week by mistake. They killed him for spying on them, but he knows what mountain they have migrated to. It sounds like a long hike, but not impossible."

"Thank Azeer," Fi said, placing his hands on the edge of the chair, letting his head drop. "We are going to need all the help we can get, and the dwarf race are brutal and fierce. If they agree, this could be a true game changer. I can't wait to see their mountain city and compare it to our own."

"Actually," I said, moving closer to him. "I have another task for you this time. A task only your brain can accomplish."

Fi straightened, coming to attention. "I'm listening," he said intensely.

"Narella, the goddess," I explained. "She is being controlled by Alaric. We need to set her free. We don't know how he is keeping her controlled, or what type of magic he might be using. We do know that she has some control over the beasts using the rune symbol we've discovered on so many. Maybe if we can release her, she will help us in return."

"How do you know she will switch sides?" asked Firel.

"We don't," Gen interjected. "But we can only hope. She seems to be a fair and just god. I believe she will help, even if only to enact her revenge on Alaric."

"I will be honored to serve the house of Doonak," Fi responded with a small bow. "I will need everything you know about Narella to place her origin or find a reference in our archives. I will return home as soon as I have the information."

"Fantastic," I said, standing. "I will fill you in when Gen goes to speak with Levos. Princess, please find your sister as well. She will be returning with Firel to make sure she remains safe."

"Good idea," Gen said with a sweet smile. She rose on her toes, kissing me before she exited the room.

After filling him in, Firel wished me luck before I went to

find Zerrial and Evinee. The fairies shouldn't be too much of a problem, but the dwarfs ... they were another story. I had never negotiated with their race before. This would be a learning curve for sure.

Evinee came around a corner, two light alfar on either arm. Her smile was brilliant, and her laugh bellowed through the halls of the kingdom. She spotted me and I nodded for her to follow. She gave me a pouty face before bidding the two light alfar good day.

"This better be good, Lyklor," she snapped, slamming the door behind her.

"Do I ever disappoint?" I replied.

She side-eyed me, leaning on one hip and turning on her sassy, playful demeanor. "Do you really want me to answer that?"

"Ouch. Getting to the point, I need you to come with Gen and me to negotiate with a few races."

She rolled her eyes, falling into a seat at the table. "And what are we negotiating this time? Sounds more like a job for Fi than me."

"He has his hands full. We are going to ask the different races of our court to join in the fight against Alaric."

"Ha," she barked out a laugh. "Good luck with that. Sounds like a waste of my time."

Evinee had been bitter ever since Gen and I had made up. I knew she was hurting because of the feelings she claimed to have towards me, but I couldn't help her. She had made her intentions very clear before my wedding and then after a few different times, but I had to be honest with myself. Evinee was an amazing female, but she wasn't Gen. It wouldn't have been fair ... to either of us.

"Ev, I need you on this. We're going to the fairies. You know how much they love you," I spoke softly.

She smirked. "Of course, they do. What's not to love? Honestly, I think I was born to the wrong race. I hope I come back as a fairy in the next life."

"Most likely the hive ruler," I said with a little laugh, "But that's beside the point."

Evinee giggled, looking up to me with those beautiful violet eyes. The humor faded into hurt. "Is there any way you can do this one without me?" she whispered.

I knelt beside her chair, taking her hand in mine. "Ev, you are one of my dearest friends. If I didn't need you on this, you know I wouldn't ask."

She chewed on her bottom lip, refusing to make eye contact with me. "Who else do we need to convince to join the cause?" she asked in a sarcastic tone.

"Oh, you know. Just the dwarfs. Doria and the others have the other races covered."

She sat up quickly, leaning towards me. "Wait a minute. What do you mean, dwarfs? When in the hell did you find the time to track those pains in the asses down? And why was I not the first person you told?"

"Well, I didn't exactly find them. Otar got killed by one last week and told us what mountain they've been residing in."

She sat back, rolling her eyes. "Of course, the princess's creature found them," she huffed, running her hands through her thick black hair. "Fine, I'll go. Only because of the dwarfs though. I've never seen them, so I'm intrigued. Takes a lot to get me going these days."

I smiled at her, standing to my feet. "Thank you, Ev. Really."

She pushed herself out of the chair, tilting her chin from side to side. "Yeah, yeah. When do we leave and who else is coming with us?"

"As soon as we can. It will be you, Zerrial, myself and Gen."

"Yay. One big happy family. I'll go find Zerrial. Someone's going to have to pry him away from his human pet."

"I wouldn't let him hear you call Lily that, if I were you."

She turned around, her face stone-cold. "Do I look like I give a damn? Just remind me to stay the hell away from The Frey. That place is contaminated with *love*, and *feelings*," she said, making a puking face as we headed towards the door.

"Ev, the day some male wins your heart, I will institute a new holiday just to commemorate the impossible feat."

"Oh, stop being a smart-ass Eren," she said, nailing me in the chest with the back of her fist.

CHAPTER TWENTY-FOUR

Evinee

The wind whipped and slashed against my face as I kept my distance from the happy couple. Erendrial Lyklor, in love. Azeer, it still felt like some cruel, sick joke. Gen represented everything he detested. Commitment, innocence, monogamy ... ugh, the thought made me taste bile in my mouth.

We used to make fun of the humans for their outlook on relationships and family. Now, he was running straight for the life he once mocked. I couldn't understand it. If I was honest, I was jealous. I had never expected a monogamous relationship with Eren, but I truly thought we were each other's destiny. Now, because of her, I was forced to rewrite my ending, and I hated change.

After this mission was over, I needed to take a step back from our merry little clan. I had given everything to Eren and his cause: my skills, my body, and my heart ... and for what? For him to go and fall in love with a half-human. Anyone who knew me was aware I didn't enjoy sharing the spotlight. That's why I appreciated Leenia and Doria. They knew their places. We each had a role to play, and we each did so perfectly. Now, with the addition of the *princess* to our family, she was standing in my damn light.

I leaned down against Pasiese, my ragamor, drawing my hands down her purple, iridescent scales. At least the fairies would be a nice distraction. Eren was smart to bring me. Out of all of us, I knew them the best. Pyra and I went way back into our youth. We got in trouble anytime we were together. Month-long, scandalous parties that we'd needed another month to recover from. We used to sneak onto other races territories, causing mischief anywhere we went. And then there was Phasis. Azeer, he was absolutely delicious in bed.

At least this trip wouldn't be completely a waste of my time. I'd have some fun in the fairy court and then investigate the dwarf city. I'd just keep my distance from the others. After the politics were settled, maybe I'd spend some time exploring my own desires and ambitions. I had followed alongside Eren and his path for so long, I didn't know what I wanted for myself anymore. Where did I belong? Did I have a purpose, or was I just a pretty face that could lure men to bed?

After a two-hour flight, we finally landed on top of the royal hive. The land around the area was barren, with little foliage or tree coverage. The ground was covered in dead shrubs and straw, just as the fairies liked it. At the center of the clearing was an eight-by-eight-foot hole which led deep beneath the ground into the center of their kingdom.

"They live ... in there?" asked Gen dubiously.

Eren laughed. "Yes, princess. What did you think you'd find? A castle? It is called a hive for a reason."

"Are there more exits then just this one?" Gen asked.

"Nope," Eren answered. "That's what makes their kingdom so deadly. Once you're inside, there's no getting out unless they allow you to leave."

I walked over to the two of them, standing on the other side of Zerrial. "They aren't going to be happy we just showed up without an invitation," I said, crossing my arms.

"And that's why we brought your beautiful face, Ev," Eren replied, winking in my direction. My heart leaped at the action, but I quickly turned away, forcing the feeling down.

Behind us, the straw snapped and shifted as horse hooves sounded in the near distance. I turned and was met by a white steed. A tall, white-haired alfar dismounted, walking in our direction. His shimmering yellow eyes caught the rays of sunlight. His white linen shirt hugged tightly to his lean and well-toned body.

Levos Atros.

I turned to Eren, flailing my arms in aggravation and frustration. "Are you kidding me? What in the hell is he doing here?"

"He's here for ... negotiation purposes," Eren mumbled.

"What do you mean, *negotiation purposes*?" I spat, throwing air quotes around the word. "The fairies despise the light court, let alone the Atros cousin. Is your plan to get him killed? Because that's exactly what's going to happen if he sets foot inside that hive."

Gen looked to Eren, worry for her beloved Levos written on her face.

"No one is going to be dying today. There is no need for worry," Eren replied, caressing his hand down Gen's arm to comfort her. I was going to be sick.

Levos approached our little huddle with a sly smirk on his face. "What are we all yelling about over here? It can't be fairy negotiations, since they are missing from this little equation," he said, scanning each of us. I folded my arms over my chest and rolled my eyes. I needed to kill something, and it might just be this fair-haired prick.

Bang. Boom. Bam. The ground shook as a dozen fairy soldiers slammed into the surface, surrounding us. Their black ionight spears pointed towards us as they crouched, ready to attack.

Eren pushed Gen behind him subtly, careful not to appear threatened. He looked around the group of fairies and then held his arms wide in a dramatic gesture. "Now this ... is what I call a welcome party," he said, plastering on the mask of ambassador.

"You do not have an invitation, *Your Majesties*," one of the soldiers hissed, clicking his teeth together.

"You're not welcome, without permission," another snapped, taking a step towards us.

"Now, now, I thought we were all friends," Eren said.

Smack. One of the soldiers slammed the length of his ionight spear into the back of Levos's head, sending him to his knees.

"Not this light piece of shit," a guard said, standing over Levos. The guard chattered his teeth together, baring glorious sets of sharp razors.

"Or, have you brought us a treat, my lord?"

"Oh yes, a treat indeed."

Another guard sniffed the air around Levos. "Ah," the guard gasped, inhaling deeply. "Atros blood."

"Mm," a second guard approached. "Yes, I can smell the light king, yet this one ... smells sweeter."

"That's enough," Gen demanded, stepping in front of Levos. The guards returned to their positions in the circle. "We've come to speak with King Phasis and Queen Pyra. Are one of you capable of informing them we have arrived, or is that beneath your abilities?" Swirling flames, black as night, played through her fingers like snakes coiling around her hands.

"Ah, fine. Fine!" One of the guards yelled, taking off into the air and diving into the hive.

Gen helped Levos to his feet while he rubbed the back of his head.

"Well, on the bright side," Levos started, "I've finally found someone that prefers me to my cousin, I suppose. Even if it is for ... consumption purposes."

Gen smiled, elbowing him in his ribs. "Oh, shut up. I'm not

going to let anything eat you."

I stepped towards them. "Why are you here?" I asked bluntly.

Levos looked down at me. Even for alfar standards, he was ridiculously tall.

"I'm assuming they don't teach manners at the dark court," he said, tilting his head towards me as if he were assessing my worth.

"Oh, I'm plenty polite, just not when it comes to those who don't have much worth," I snapped back at him.

Levos made a pouty face, placing his hand over his heart. "Oh, the dark court whore hurt my feelings. I'm crushed," he mocked me.

My blood began to boil, my vision going red.

"Well, this is off to a fantastic start," added Eren.

Levos didn't see my fist flying through the air until it made contact with his face, slamming so hard he stumbled back a few steps.

"Don't you presume to know anything about me, you light alfar piece of shit!" I yelled, stalking away before I was tempted to take my dark sword and sever his precious little head from his shoulders.

"Well," Levos said behind me. "Glad to see you have another talent besides spreading your legs for anyone that looks at you twice."

My hand found the hilt of my blade. I pulled it from the sheath, swinging the sword directly at Levos's neck. He jumped back, my blade missing him by only an inch. I took another step, bringing my sword up for another attack, but a strong pair of arms reached around my waist, lifting me up and away from him.

"Let go!" I screamed. Zerrial held me firmly against him while I thrashed and kicked, trying to get free. The fairies around me began to snicker and chatter their teeth as encouragement to continue.

I took a few breaths, my heart racing. Zerrial's grip lightened gradually before he returned my feet to the ground. Levos smoothed out his jacket, never taking his eyes off me. Eren walked casually over to Levos. My future king looked at me, then back at Levos, then slammed his fist right into the light alfar's face, sending Levos to the ground.

Eren bent down next to him, dusting his pants off. "If you ever," Eren said, loud enough for me to hear, "speak to Evinee or anyone in my family like that again, I don't care who your friends are or what family you are related to. I will personally feed you to the fairies myself. Are we clear?"

The fairies around him started to yelp and flutter their wings with excitement, knocking their weapons against their armor in approval. Levos nodded at Eren, wiping the blood from his mouth. Genevieve stood silently. Her face was wrecked with worry.

Eren stood, extending his hand to Levos. Levos accepted the gesture, dusting himself off as he regained his balance.

"Now," Eren said, allowing the smile to return to his face. "I believe an apology is in order. Wouldn't you agree, Ambassador Atros?"

Levos's face strained as he turned to me. "I am sorry for any disrespect I have shown you," he said shortly.

Eren folded his hands behind his back. "Evinee darling, what do we say?"

I shook Zerrial's remaining grip from my shoulders and turned my back to the both of them. "Go screw yourself, Atros," I replied, moving closer to the edge of the circle. I swore I could hear him let out a little laugh.

The sound of buzzing wings echoed from the mouth of the cave just before a swarm of fairies shot from the ground. Phasis and Pyra landed in the center of the circle nearest to us, while the rest took position around the existing perimeter.

Phasis walked gracefully towards Eren, taking note of his travel companions. His dark chocolate eyes found mine. He nodded in my direction with his devious smile before returning his attention to Eren and Gen. "Prince Lyklor, Princess Genevieve. Have I told you how utterly appalled I was not to be invited to your nuptials? And here I thought we had become fast friends."

"Of course we are, King Phasis," Eren replied. "Unfortunately, the wedding was a bit rushed due to my bride's eagerness to claim me all to herself. A bit impatient, this one is."

Gen knocked her elbow into him before smiling proudly.

Phasis laughed, looking between the two. "Well, in order to

make up for the complete disregard of my feelings, I must request that I be named the … godfather of your first born." Phasis turned to Gen. "Isn't that what you call it in your Christian faith?"

Gen rose her eyebrow. "Yes, I believe it is. But as I am the living embodiment of Azeer's power, it's safe to say the Christian god is not the one I revere."

Phasis let out a deep laugh, showing all his teeth as he tilted his head to the sky. "Have I ever told you how pleased I am that my people didn't eat you that first night across the border? Thank the heaven's the *King Fucker*," Phasis stopped, clearing his throat, "I mean, King Atros, chose another human to give up to my hungry soldiers. You have become quite the source of entertainment." Phasis's eyes filled with hunger while he lowered his head, studying Gen's face.

Out of the corner of my eye, I saw Pyra's tall, lean figure circling Levos. She picked up a strand of his hair and sniffed. Levos stood completely still, no emotion appearing on his face. She moved in front of him, running her hand down his chest to his abdomen. As she got to his pant line, she let a small smile of satisfaction slip before he grabbed her hand, stopping her from exploring further. She snatched her arm back, letting out a little growl before angling her head towards her brother and Eren.

"Why did you bring one of *them* to our hive?" she demanded, turning her attention back to Levos, examining him from head to toe.

"And, might I add," said Phasis, "you've come without a proper invitation." He clicked his tongue in disappointment. "Bad alfar."

"We mean no disrespect," Eren began. "Time is of the essence, and we must speak in private now."

Phasis's wings flapped aggressively as he moved into Eren's face, baring his teeth. "You are in my court now, *prince*. Mine. You do not have authority to demand anything of me or my time. Do I make myself clear?" Phasis roared.

Eren didn't budge. The two males stared each other down, waiting for the other to submit. I rolled my eyes, stepping forward.

"Isn't he rude, Phasis?" I said playfully, moving to his side. "I have tried training this one for the last century, but nothing I do seems to work. His manners are appalling." Phasis looked to me, his eyes softening as he regained his composure. "Maybe you can teach me a thing or two about how to make those around you submit," I said softly, running a hand down his bicep while I gazed up into his eyes. He looked at my hand and then smiled, releasing any tension he had.

Phasis laughed, taking my hand and bringing it to his mouth, kissing my skin softly. "My sweet Evinee ... if memory recalls, you are the teacher in our relationship, not I," Phasis whispered.

I bit the side of my lip, allowing him to see it. "King Phasis, always the flirt. Time hasn't changed you a bit. And thank Azeer for that."

Phasis exhaled. He took a moment, deciding how to proceed.

He held my gaze, but spoke to Eren.

"I will let you and your companions stay one evening. We shall dine and enjoy each other's company," he ordered, looking me up and down slowly. "Then, in the morning, you will have your meeting, Lyklor. After that," he said harshly, snapping his head in Eren's direction. "You will leave and not return without a proper invitation. Am I clear?"

Eren bowed slowly, ever the vision of grace. "Perfectly, King Phasis."

Pyra came up behind me, sliding her hand down my back before kissing me softly on my cheek. "Hello, old friend," she whispered, making sure I was the only one that could hear. She turned her gaze slightly to Eren and Gen. "It appears we have some catching up to do." Her soft, cold tongue ran a line up my check.

I turned to her, leaning my forehead into hers. "You have no idea," I replied, letting out a small sigh of relief.

"Come," said Phasis. "We will get your sleeping arrangements settled and then, we shall feast." Phasis pulled me into his arms, smashing my soft body against his firm torso. With one powerful thrust, he flew us into the air, diving deep into the hive. I looked back to see Eren and the others following closely behind in the arms of the fairy soldiers.

The smell of earth and moisture filled my nostrils. Phasis nuzzled his nose into my neck while we flew through the dark tunnels. "Mm, you're lucky I have a soft spot for you, or your little tribe would have been dead."

I laughed, hitting him playfully in the shoulder. "I might not have been disappointed if you took out a few of them."

His teeth bit softly on my earlobe. "Wicked little siren," he whispered.

My heart leaped with panic. I looked back at the others. They were too far to have heard a thing. "Phasis," I whispered.

He chuckled. "Don't worry my friend, your secret is safe with me. Always."

CHAPTER TWENTY-FIVE

P hasis led us deep into the hive where we landed in the center of a commons area. The room was large and circular. The ground was covered in an extravagant mosaic pattern that radiated from the center. The walls were lines with tree roots and vines. Beautiful floral blooms stretched open in a spectrum of color along the walls, creating the most beautiful scenery while releasing the most delicious fragrance. Carved into the walls were four hallways that led back into private bedrooms.

"I presume these sleeping arrangements will suit your needs?" asked Phasis.

Eren nodded. Gen circled around the area, taking in the details. "This is amazing," she said softly.

Phasis chuckled. "What did you expect?" he asked.

"I just mean," she said, turning to face him. "It's so extravagant. Truly. I had no idea your palace was created with such detail and natural beauty."

"Well, I don't recall you ever asking to come visit our little court," Phasis said, moving towards her. "Though our ways might seem ... barbaric to some, there is much to appreciate." His eyes scanned Gen's face and he licked his lips slowly. He reached out a hand, sliding his finger down her bare arm, cocking his head to the side like a predator.

Eren stepped in between the two of them. "Thank you, King Phasis," Eren said, wrapping his arm around Gen, pulling her into his side. "Your hospitality will not be forgotten."

Phasis clicked his tongue in annoyance, grimacing at Eren. "You're welcome, Prince Lyklor. I would arrange nothing but the best for my favorite alfar. Dinner will begin in two hours. Rest and get settled. I can assure you: you will need it."

Levos shifted his weight to the side, catching Phasis's attention. The fairy snapped his head towards Levos and snarled, then turned back to Eren. "I presume you will keep a leash on that thing," he hissed, pointing to Levos.

"Of course, Your Grace," replied Eren. "Leash is firmly attached."

Phasis sprang his wings out to the side, flying towards Levos and slamming him into the wall. He held Levos by the neck, baring his teeth and growling. "No snooping," Phasis spat. "If we find you unattended at any point, you will be the entertainment for the evening. Are we clear?"

Pyra came to her king's side, placing a hand on his shoulder. "Sweet brother," she whispered. "I think the light one has been beaten enough for one day. Might we work on showing him our best selves, so he has something enlightening to report back to his court?"

Phasis slowly removed his arm from Levos's throat. Levos remained glued to the wall. I chuckled, enjoying the show. As Phasis moved away, Pyra reached out and ran a finger down Levos's face. A low moan left her lips before she followed her brother to the entrance.

"We will see you all at dinner," Pyra said softly with a small bow before she exited, leaving the five of us in the commons room.

Gen rushed to Levos, checking to make sure he wasn't too badly injured. Zerrial moved to a couch, shaking his head, fighting to hide his smile. Eren began to check each room to make sure the areas were secure and didn't hide any threats.

"Well, that was fun," I said, taking a seat across from Zerrial. "Ya know, I might just ask to transfer to their court. I am finding more and more to like about them with each encounter." I shot a glace towards Levos, who had finally removed himself from the wall.

Zerrial laughed. "They would probably accept you, no questions asked."

"Wouldn't you?" I replied, gesturing to my body.

Zerrial shook his head with a smile. "I'm not touching that comment."

I threw a pillow at his head. "Don't worry Z, I won't tell your human," I whispered with a wink. Eren came out of the last room as Gen and Levos joined us in the seating area.

"Phasis wouldn't seem to mind adding you to his collection," Levos had the gall to say.

I stared at him for a brief moment, calming myself before I engaged. "And ... is that a problem?"

"Not at all. More of a solution, I would say," Levos replied in a sarcastic tone, tilting his head towards me with a snide smile.

"Levos, enough," Gen whispered.

I exhaled in frustration. "It's okay, princess," I replied. "Let the pissant speak. All he is doing is showing how ignorant he truly is."

"And how so?" Levos replied.

"Because, once again, you are making inaccurate assumptions about a court you know absolutely nothing about. You light alfar are all the same: thinking that you are better than the rest of us because you are too narcissistic to get to know another way of life besides your own."

Levos scoffed. "And what, pray tell, would interest me about a flesh-eating race of creatures who act on animalistic instincts rather than using the small brains the gods gifted them with?"

I was going to murder this male in his sleep. He seemed to notice, because he let out a small laugh as his eyes met mine. I looked to Eren. He tilted his head, signaling to me he wasn't going to get involved.

I let out another deep breath, calming my murderous intent. "Not that it would matter to you," I said in a low tone, "but the fairies do have many redeeming qualities. For instance, it is against their law to kill one of their own. Something *we* as a race do not abide by," I said, looking in Gen's direction. She held her head high, meeting my gaze.

"When a male courts a female in their culture, they spend an entire year devoted to her and her needs. The female has exactly one year to fall in love ... and yes, I said in love, with the male. By the end of said year, if the chosen female does not accept the marriage proposal, the male forfeits his life. Once a male proclaims his intent towards a female, a bond is created. If the female does not accept the bond, it physically kills him.

"A marriage is for life. Though they may venture outside of the marital bed, they are truly bonded in every way. I have watched bonded couples fight harder and more fiercely for their significant others, let alone their children. This race values children over all else. They are coveted and protected. That, I am confident, is not equal in the light court," I said, narrowing my eyes at Levos before I continued.

"And have you ever seen their gardens and lands?" I asked. "They are the most luxurious and lush landscapes you will ever lay eyes on. They tend to the ground and planet with more passion and care than even the light court possesses. In return, the planet has provided these intricate hives they now call home. Those are only a few things that make their race unique and special, but you wouldn't know, because you've never asked."

Levos nodded, arching one eyebrow into the air. "And what

purpose does the flesh-eating and torturous part of their court serve in the grander scheme of things?" he asked.

"Everything must eat," I answered. "Just because they prefer a diet that you deem unacceptable does not mean it is wrong. Everything is designed for a balance and a purpose. You once thought the dark court barbaric, did you not?" I asked Levos.

He stared back, clenching his jaw.

"And have we not disproven all the false rumors?" I continued when he refused to speak. "In fact, now looking behind the curtain, wouldn't you agree that your court's treatment of the humans is more inhumane than our own? Take the princess, for instance." I gestured to Gen. "Your court broke her. Ours healed and rehabilitated her. Everything in life has a cycle and a purpose. Until you remove those light alfar blinders, you will never see the beauty of our world and the cycle of life. Now, if you'll excuse me, I am going to use the next two hours to get some peace and quiet," I said, standing to my feet and turning towards one of the rooms.

Eren followed until we were safely behind a closed door. "What you said about the fairies was very poetic," he said, leaning against the door.

"You know me, poetry is in my blood," I replied, tossing the pillows to the side as I pulled back the sheets.

"Are you okay, after everything today?" he asked.

"I'm resilient. But next time, I'd appreciate a little heads up about additions to our traveling party."

He laughed, moving towards me. "It was a last-minute adjustment. When Gen told Levos about the dwarfs, he insisted on coming. I am sure he will try to persuade them to join the light court territories, but you and I both know that will never happen."

"Ha, right. If Levos thinks the fairies are bad, just wait until he meets a dwarf. Half-wit," I said, crawling into the cool damp sheets. "Thank you for sticking up for me today. You didn't have to, and I am sure punching Levos didn't sit well with your princess."

"*Our* princess," he clarified.

I rolled my eyes, pulling the sheets over my legs.

"And of course, I stuck up for you. No one calls you a tramp and gets away with it."

I let a small smile escape my lips.

Eren bent down his head, trying to catch my eyes. "Hey, what is it? What's wrong?"

"Do you ever get ... exhausted, playing your role? I mean, I know we all must appear as one thing when we're really another, but ... but sometimes, I just want to give up. I just want to run away where no one knows me, so I can start over."

Eren grabbed my hand, squeezing it tightly. "I understand completely. I used to have the same feelings before all of this. Hearing the rumors of what people thought of me and how I slept my way through the courts. Never being appreciated or respected for everything I gave for this kingdom and for our race. I felt looked over and unappreciated. Sometimes, I would ask myself what the point was in all of it. And then I met Gen. My masks, my ambitions, all of it no longer mattered. She made me feel safe and loved me for who I was."

I chewed on my bottom lip, forcing my eyes to his. "You were loved for exactly who you were long before Genevieve entered into the picture," I whispered.

He gave me a smile that had pity written all over it. "Yes, I was, and so are you. What I am trying to say is that all of this, all these feelings and worries, will pass someday. I can't say when or how, but you will get everything your heart desires, Evinee. And I will be by your side, helping you forge that path, just like you were for me for all those decades." He leaned down and kissed me softly on the head. "Get some sleep. I'll see you in a couple of hours."

As he left the room, I buried my face into the pillow, fighting the tears that welled behind my eyes. I was determined to have my own life. To find my own purpose. He was right in those things. But I would never have everything I wanted. I would never have him.

CHAPTER
TWENTY-SIX

*S*mack! *The side of my face swelled with pain.*

"I told you not to speak with any male, you stupid bitch. You are a poison and blemish to my blood line. You are lucky you serve a purpose, or I would have disposed of you as the law requires."

The toe of his boot slammed into the side of my ribs. I tasted copper in my mouth as blood saturated my tongue. He leaned down next to me, removing a strand of hair from my face. "The next time I give you an order, you follow it. Your life depends on your cooperation. The moment I no longer have a use for you is the moment your life ends. Am I clear?" he whispered.

I swallowed a few times, my throat beginning to swell. "Yes, father," I replied.

I jolted awake, rushing to the toilet to alleviate the contents of my stomach. I sat back against the cold wall, taking a few deep breaths. I ran my hands across my face, trying to calm my frantic heart.

"Dammit, Evinee," I said out loud. "Get your shit together."

I stood up, going to the sink to wash my face and then mouth.

I had only been asleep an hour. Better than most nights, but not what my body needed. I peered into the mirror, taking in my violet eyes—her eyes ... my mother's. I exhaled, still shivering from the fear I had felt in my nightmare.

Looking at my reflection, I gradually released the hold on my power, allowing the facade to fall away from my appearance. I closed my eyes, the cool breeze of my magic washing over me. The smell of salt and sea engulfed my senses as it passed across my face, tangling its fingers through the strands of hair. Finally, the weight fell away. I cautiously opened my eyes and stared back at the real me ... the me without my mask.

My facial features were recognizable, but shockingly different. My eyes had dark circles underneath them from the lack of sleep. My cheek bones were sharp, adding to my sunken cheeks. My hair wasn't as full and appeared a duller shade of black. My body was thin and frail from a lack of nutrition. I only ate when absolutely necessary. My normal diet consisted of wine and more wine.

I ran my hands down my unfamiliar form. My body looked sick. My clothing hung over my depleted husk, drawing attention to my sharp shoulders and knobby knees.

I didn't often reveal my true self. It was easier to fake a desirable form than to actually work on my issues. Though I still had the same features, the picture I projected gave the illusion I was a happy and confident female—not someone still haunted by childhood trauma.

I took a deep breath, closing my eyes and focusing on the mask everyone knew and desired. I felt the blue and purple swirls of my magic begin in my fingertips, coiling around my arms before spreading across my body. When I opened my eyes, my full figure and soft face had returned. I went to the wardrobe and picked out a deep eggplant-colored dress that hugged my desirable form and elevated my breasts.

I stood before the mirror, examining my appearance. I pushed the memories from my nightmare out of my head and practiced a few smiles and seductive facial expressions.

"Time to conquer another court, Evinee," I whispered.

In the commons area, everything was silent. They were all still asleep. I ascended the staircase into a busy hallway. Fairies passed me by and nodded in my direction. I always felt welcome here: sometimes more so than the dark court. Here, I fit ... I made sense. Back home, I was misunderstood and undervalued, just like the fairies.

In the main throne room, I found Pyra leaning up against a table, speaking with a few other fairies. She spotted me as soon as I crossed the threshold. She quickly ended the interaction and beelined towards me.

"Finally!" she said, wrapping an arm around my waist, ushering me towards a back room behind the thrones. "I've been waiting anxiously to hear all about your drama. Also," she said, stopping to hit me in the arm.

"Owe," I yelped. "What in the hell was that for?"

"I've written you once a week for the past four months and you have yet to reply. How do you think that makes me feel?" she said, closing her chocolate brown eyes and flicking her bright red hair over a shoulder. I loved the fairies, but they were extremely sensitive creatures.

"Py, I am sorry," I said, reaching for her and turning her to face me. "We've been so busy with court politics and the rift. I've barely had time to do anything for myself."

"Liar," she spat, chattering her teeth in annoyance. "I know you don't sleep. You had plenty of time to reply to my letters. Yes, you did."

I smiled, taking her into my arms, hugging her tightly. "I'm sorry. I have learned my lesson and will never go more than a week without replying to your correspondence. Deal?" Her arms wrapped around my body.

"Fine, but I will hold you to this bargain, yes, I will."

"I'd expect nothing less." I pulled away, taking her slender, pale face in as she finally let a small grin slip.

"Now, get to the good stuff," she said, sprawling on a red velvet couch. "What happened with Lyklor?"

I rolled my eyes, falling onto the cushion next to her. "Well, I made a play for him. Was vulnerable, like we discussed. I told him everything. And then he rejected me for the princess."

Pyra made a spitting noise, sitting up forcefully. "Ah, I don't understand your kind. With all you two have been through ... what you two mean to each other. ... the sex! And he wouldn't even consider it?"

"Nope. He is completely head over heels for Genevieve. And honestly ... even though it hurts like hell, I do want him to be happy. That's what matters in the end."

"Bah, don't talk like that. Maturity doesn't suit you."

I laughed, hitting her in the shoulder with a pillow. "Excuse me, I think I am handling this whole situation with grace, thank you very much."

She ignored me, looking at the wall. I knew she was deep in thought. Her body straightened. "What if ... what if we remove the princess? Eren would hurt, but then you could heal him."

I looked around the room, making sure the door was still closed, and we were alone. "Pyra, don't talk like that. After what Gen has been through, if you even think about harming her, King Drezmore would destroy this place."

"Ah, let him try. We could make it look like an accident. She wouldn't see it coming."

"No," I said bluntly. "I don't wish her anymore harm. Eren has made his choice, and I must live with it. I have to move on and learn how to be happy for my friend."

Pyra took my hand in hers, nuzzling my neck with her head. "You will find your mate, my sister. He is out there, just waiting for you to conquer him."

"Honestly, I am tired of conquering males, and females, for that matter. It would be nice to have someone fight for me as hard as I've fought for those in my life. To know, without a doubt, I am the only one they want. Without worrying if it's because of what's inside of me. My power, that is," I admitted.

Pyra grabbed my cheeks abruptly, turning my face towards hers. "Do not think like this. Your gifts, your abilities, are from the goddess Persephone herself. You are unique: there are so few like your kind. You are beautiful and entrancing, just as you were made to be. When your mate comes for you, they will see the true you and won't be able to stay away. You will lure them with this. Not with your power ... but with your heart," she said, placing her hand over my chest. "Nothing else."

Tears pricked behind my eyes as I leaned my forehead into hers. "Thank you, sister. I love you," I whispered.

Pyra ran her long, pale fingers through my hair. "And I love you. Always, I will love you," she said, kissing me softly on the lips.

"You two are starting without me, I see," Phasis's voice startled us both. I turned to see him leaning against the doorway. "Usually, I prefer to be the center of attention, but for the two of you, I am willing to share the spotlight."

"Ah, brother." Pyra stood, making her way over to her husband. "No worries, no worries at all. Wasn't that type of kiss." She fluttered in the air, kissing him on the cheek.

"Well, if you two are done, the rest of your friends," Phasis said, nodding towards me, "are waiting to be fed. Shall we proceed to the merry festivities?"

"How about the three of us call it a night and head to your rooms instead?" I suggested, approaching them. They both wrapped an arm around me while we stood in a huddle.

"I adore the way your brain works." Phasis clicked his teeth, his wings rattling behind him with excitement.

"Oh, oh," Pyra said, clapping her hands together. "May I make a request?"

Phasis nuzzled her nose with his as he looked upon her with love and admiration. I almost forgot they were brother and sister sometimes because of the undying love they had for one another. Incest wasn't permitted among the alfar, but their race didn't have the same social standards ours did. They were happy. Their kingdom was thriving. Who was I to judge?

"Anything for you, my little sprite," replied Phasis.

"May we bring the light one? He smells so sweet, and his yellow eyes are so entrancing," said Pyra, licking her lips.

"You mean Levos?" I asked.

"Mm, yes, Leee-vossssss," she said, exaggerating the letters in his name. "I want him, I want him, yes I do."

"If he's invited," I said, "I'm out."

"Oh, Evie," she said with a pleading face. "Don't ruin my fun. I just want to take a bite. Please. One ... little ... bite."

"If he lets you sink your teeth into him, by all means, don't let me stop you. But I am not getting physical with that judgmental, hypocritical, closed-minded asshole."

Phasis chuckled, drawing the two of us into him. "We would never force something on you that you are not comfortable with, dear Evinee. And little sprite," he said, looking to Pyra. "If it is a bite you want, it is a bite you will get." He leaned down and kissed her on the head while she beamed with excitement.

"Don't say anymore," I said. A game was now in play between the two of them, with Levos's flesh as the reward. "I don't want to have any part in this. Eren would have my head."

"And a very pretty head it is," replied Phasis, kissing me.

The door cracked open behind us. Phasis and Pyra snapped their heads towards the intrusion, baring their teeth as they growled.

Eren walked through casually, taking in the sight of the three of us huddled. He arched his eyebrow, placing his hands in his pockets before smirking. "And here I thought dessert was going to be served after the main course," Eren said.

"Are you spying on me, *prince*?" growled Phasis.

"Not at all," he replied. "I was simply looking for the restroom. Oops, my mistake."

Phasis dropped his arms from around us, heading towards the door. "Come. We eat," he said, brushing past Eren. Pyra followed, stopping in front of Eren, slamming him back against the door frame.

"Ungrateful bitch," she hissed before exiting.

Eren straightened himself, looking towards me. "And what in the hell was that for?" he asked.

I walked towards the door and shrugged. "I don't know how her mind works. Who knows?"

He fell in step beside me as we made our way to the dining tables. "Uh, you and I both know that is a lie. You, out of everyone, know best how both those twisted little minds work. A little too well, if you ask me."

"Jealous much?" I asked, winking at him.

"I've had Pyra once already, remember. And though it was an ... experience, let me say, I admire you for braving both of them at the same time."

"Oh, stop assuming you know what is between the three of us. Because you don't. I don't talk about what happens in my bed. You know that."

"Yes, I am aware. Even after a century, you still haven't told me about the fairy twins. But I am all ears, whenever you feel like divulging your adventures."

I knocked him into a wall and smiled slightly He laughed, giving me a quick side hug before we made our way to the table with the others.

Gen, Zerrial, and Levos were waiting for us as we approached the head table, which was shaped like a horseshoe. Phasis and Pyra took seats in the middle. Pyra signaled to me to take the chair next to her. Eren, Gen, and Zerrial sat on the other side of Phasis, which left Levos next to me.

He approached my right side and nodded, then took his seat. I turned to Pyra. She was beaming while she drummed her fingers on the table, eyes locked onto Levos. As the food trays began to circle the room, Pyra never took her eyes from her prey. Levos made a point to look anywhere but in her direction. If only he knew her intent. I took a bite of fruit and then brought my napkin to my mouth to hide my amusement.

Levos finally dropped his fork to the plate and turned to meet Pyra's gaze. "Is there something I can help you with, Queen Pyra?" he asked.

I sat back, taking my wine glass with me. "Should have just left it alone," I whispered, taking a deep drink.

"Oh, there are many things you can help me with," she replied, leaning across me towards him. "Actually, I've been making a mental list of all the things you could do for me, and I could do to you, as I've sat here just now, yes I have."

Levos looked taken aback. "And why, might I ask, are you interested in me?" he whispered.

"What do you mean, *why*? Have you seen yourself? You are most handsome, yes you are. I dare say, more beautiful than your king cousin."

Levos nodded, focusing on his wine glass. "Well, thank you, Queen Pyra. I am flattered," he said, taking a drink.

"And here we go," I mumbled into my glass.

"May I have you then?" she asked.

"Though I am humbled by your offer, I'm afraid I would only be a disappointment," Levos said, more kindly than I had heard him sound since he had been at our court.

"Nonsense. I insist. I must have you," she hissed.

Levos looked at me, presumably for help, but I shrugged. It was a death sentence to get between Pyra and her sexual ambitions.

"Thank you for the offer, but I am going to have to decline," he said, returning his attention to his food.

"Ah!" Pyra screamed, slamming her hands onto the table. "Not fair, not fair, not fair!" she spat. Phasis was in the middle of a conversation with Eren and Gen, but managed to slide a hand to his wife, rubbing her leg softly. Her wings fluttered at the contact. She nuzzled into his side, turning away from Levos.

I moved my food around my plate, looking out into the fairy court. The large domed room was filled with underground trees and flowers that bloomed along the walls. An unexplainable light source illuminated the entire room. The floor was made of beautiful black stone that had gray veins stretching throughout the design. All the attendants were in high spirits. Fairies flew throughout the room, laughing and dancing, on the ground and in the air.

"This isn't what I had in mind," Levos commented quietly.

Without looking at him, I replied, "Which part?"

"Their court. I was expecting hanging bodies and torture chambers. Instead—"

A group of young fairies ran past us, laughing and fluttering off the ground as they played tag. One ran into his mother's arms, and she swept the child up, kissing him profusely.

"—that," he said with astonishment.

I smiled, watching the group of young fae. "Yes, come to think of it," I replied, "I've never seen any light court children within the palace when we've visited your court. Only in the streets."

"They're kept isolated, in the nursery, until they're eighteen."

"Why would you want to keep something so joyous hidden?" I asked.

He shrugged. "Not my call. That's just how it's always been."

"Well, the fairies have a different mindset when it comes to their young. They believe their children are the most precious and valued gift. When a female fairy is with child, there is only a forty percent chance that she and the child will survive the birth. Complications due to their anatomy often result in a dead child or mother ... very often both.

"When a birth is successful, the hive throws a massive celebration to welcome the new member into their kingdom. I've never seen anything like it. The love they have for their young ... it's beautiful."

"Do you want kids?" he asked.

I about spit out my drink. "A bit personal, isn't it?"

Another shrug. "It's just a question."

I placed my cup on the table, circling the bottom of the glass with my finger. "I'm too fucked up to be a mother," I finally replied.

"Aren't we all," he whispered, shooting the rest of the liquor in his glass.

"Ambassador Atros," said Phasis.

"Yes, Your Highness," Levos replied.

"Come. I must show you some more of our kingdom," insisted Phasis as he and Pyra stood. Pyra's grin was wide with anticipation. Levos stood and nodded to the two of them. As they left the table, I couldn't help but giggle, coughing to cover it up. Pyra was going to get her bite of flesh alright.

Eren looked across at me and arched an eyebrow before looking in Levos's direction. "What is it?" he asked.

I shrugged, bringing my wine to my mouth. "I don't know what you mean."

Eren took the seat next to me, leaning in closely so only I could hear. "Is our friend Levos in danger?"

"Nah," I said. "He'll be just fine."

"Evinee," Eren said, taking a quick look back to Gen.

"Oh, Eren," I said. "They won't risk starting a war with the light court over its ambassador. Not when we are dealing with the rift. Calm down. He will be returned to you. He just might ... be missing ... parts."

"And what is that supposed to mean?"

"Pyra was very taken with him. She asked very nicely to have him, but he refused her. You know how sensitive fairies are when they are refused."

"Dammit, Evinee," Eren said, running his hand through his hair.

"He's a big boy. He can handle himself." I finished my fifth glass of wine.

Eren's gaze drifted to my plate. "You haven't eaten."

"I took a bite. Not very hungry."

"When was the last time you had a whole meal?"

I shrugged, not knowing the answer myself.

"Have the nightmares returned?" he whispered. I didn't answer. Eren ran his hand down my arm. "I am here for you, always."

"No Eren, you're not," I snapped, feeling the tether on my self-control finally give. "You have a life now, and someone you need to take care of, which doesn't leave much room for me." I settled myself, taking a deep breath. I noticed Gen's eyes shifting away from Zerrial, focusing on us.

"Ev—"

"No, I am sorry. That wasn't fair. I am happy for you Eren, really, but I am on my own and I need to figure this out by myself."

"That's not true. You have all of us, your family."

"What I go through, what I am, none of you can truly understand. And that's not for a lack of trying, I know, I just ... I need time away. By myself, for a bit, okay? Just focus on your duties and the princess. I'll be fine," I said, pushing away from the table, heading for the exit. He didn't follow or call after me. A part of me was glad, another part ached.

For the next four hours, I drowned myself at one of the fairy bars. No one bothered or even spoke to me. It was glorious. Alone at last. I thought about what I wanted out of life. Where I wanted to go and who I wanted to be.

I was tired: of playing games, of being someone I wasn't. And I was tired of people assuming they knew me. No one knew who I really was ... not even Eren. It was time for a change.

I made my way back to our commons area. The fireplace within the circular room was still blazing. I stumbled into the large, open space, using the wall for support. Yup, I was drunk. I'd sleep a little more tonight because of it.

Hiss. A sound came from one of the couches off to the side. I looked over lazily to find Levos sitting alone. His shirt was off, and his sun-kissed skin shimmered in the firelight. A large, open wound bled from the back of his shoulder blade. He brought a bloody piece of cloth to it, dabbing the opening gently. I took a step towards him. His head snapped in my direction as he stood defensively.

My eyes trailed down his long, bare torso and arms, admiring the lean muscle that was tragically hidden by his clothes most of the time. His pants hung low on his hips, revealing a perfect V that led to his more masculine parts. His hair hung down loosely, no longer tied back away from his face. His expression was stern.

"This is why you were laughing," he said. "Before I left, you were giggling. You knew what she was going to try."

I stumbled my way towards him. "I learned a long time ago not to stand between Pyra and what she wants. Especially if it's sex."

He looked away from me.

"So do tell," I continued, "how was it?"

His head tilted back. "I did not sleep with that … with the fairy queen. She might have gotten a bite in, but that was all she got her lips around. Thank Thor," he said, sitting back on the couch.

I laughed, bending down to look at the wound. He leaned away, as if appalled by my presence. I straightened.

"May I … take a look at your wound?" I asked.

He studied me for a moment and then nodded. I leaned down, placing my hands gently on either side of his mangled flesh. The bite mark was deep. She somehow managed to take an inch and a half of meat from his shoulder muscle. He hissed at my touch.

I sat in front of him, taking the rag out of the bloodied bowl of water. I made a circling gesture with my wrist, summoning the salve I had for wounds from my room. Blue and purple smoke appeared around my fingers before the container appeared in my palm. Levos studied the action.

"What's your power again?" he asked.

My inhibitions were lowered, thanks to the five bottles of wine and ambrosia shots I had ingested on my own. "Bone spurs and shielding are my unique gifts. Everyone in the dark court can summon objects, though. You should know that."

"Yes, but they usually just appear. They aren't accompanied by a colorful smoke show."

"Look, do you want my help or not? I'm not in the mood to play twenty questions," I said flatly.

He smirked at me and nodded. "Yes, Evinee, your help would be greatly appreciated."

"Okay then, turn around and shut up."

He did as I asked, wincing every time I ran my hand across the wound. His skin was soft and felt like velvet. I couldn't deny I was enjoying this, maybe a little too much.

"All done," I announced. He turned around to face me. I placed the jar in his hand. "Here, use this twice a day. Fairy bites take a little longer to heal because of their saliva, but it should be gone in a few days. Can't say you won't have a scar afterwards, though. She got you pretty good."

"Really? I hadn't noticed," he mumbled sarcastically.

I laughed, standing. "You would have been better off sleeping with her. She wouldn't have taken such a big chunk."

"Duly noted. Next time, accept the fairy's invitation to bed me."

I shook my head, turning away from him, stumbling towards my room.

"Evinee," he called out.

I turned, trying to keep upright as the alcohol rushed to my head. "Yes, Ambassador Atros?"

"I'm sorry ... about what I said to you earlier today. Truly."

"Ah, I've been called worse. A part of the mask, I guess," I slurred.

"Your mask?" He tiled his head, seeming intrigued.

"Levos, if you can't tell, I am very intoxicated. If you wouldn't mind, I am going to bed. Good night."

"Good night, Evinee," I heard him whisper before I shut my door. I crashed into the bed, allowing the alcohol to rock me to sleep.

CHAPTER
TWENTY-SEVEN

I woke to the rattling of teeth. I ran my hands over my face. My head was still spinning. It wasn't often I over drank like that, but yesterday had been especially hard for whatever reason. I just needed to forget and let go of myself for a bit. On a positive note, I hadn't dreamed during the night.

A warm finger ran down my chest, to my abdomen, and then over my sensitive parts between my legs. "Wakey, wakey, my little lush," whispered a husky voice. The hand began to rub on the outside of my dress, making my bundle of nerves swell. I let out a sensual moan, pressing my hips up into the feeling. The voice laughed. A nip on my earlobe jarred me awake.

I sat straight up, reaching for my ear. "Owe," I yelled, turning to see Phasis lounging next to me. He placed his hands behind his head.

"Well, good morning to you too," Phasis said, flashing his teeth in a wide grin.

"What in the hell was that?" I asked, knocking him in the leg.

He laughed, sitting up as he stroked his hand down my arm. "I couldn't help myself," he said, nuzzling his nose against me. "I've always loved the way your little body responds to me. And how you smell when you free yourself. And ... you haven't sung for me in forever. I do miss that little talent of yours."

I gave him a small smile. "I'll make you a deal."

He sat up, clapping his hands together, his wings rustling. "I'm listening."

"If you promise to agree to Eren's terms today, I will sing for you, sweet Phasis."

"Blah, not fair, not fair at all. I do not mix politics with pleasure. You know this, Evie."

"Oh, come on," I said, holding onto his arm, making a pouty face. "I promise it will be to your liking. You will get to kill things. You love to kill things."

"Kill? What things will I get to kill?" he asked with excitement.

"I can't say more, but I would never make you agree to something if it was going to hurt you or Pyra. You know this."

He pondered over the deal for a moment before exhaling. "Fine, fine, but right after the meeting, you sing."

My stomach turned at the thought. "Of course," I agreed, leaning into kiss him on the cheek. A knock came at the door. I rolled my eyes, falling back into the bed. "I'm not ready to be social today."

"Oh, my little one, do you want me to get rid of them? I can do that, yes, I can."

I laughed, looking up at Phasis. "Maybe. Depends on who is behind the door." I sat up, fixing my dress. "Come in," I announced.

Gen's head appeared. Her hair was pinned off her neck, her beautiful crystal crown adorning her dark bundle of curls. She looked at me and then at Phasis. "Oh," she said. "I'm sorry, I didn't mean to interrupt."

Phasis sat up, his smile elongating across his face. "Oh, you are not interrupting. In fact, you are right on time for dessert." He licked his lips, looking from me to Gen.

I laughed, knocking him in the arm. "You're relentless," I whispered. He winked. "What can I help you with, princess?"

"I was hoping to speak with you alone for a moment," she replied, leaving the door open behind her.

I shrugged at Phasis. "Sorry my friend, it's not going to happen today. Maybe in a century, when she tires of Eren," I said.

He chuckled, his head rocking from side to side as he rose from the bed. He leaned down and kissed me gently before walking towards Gen. "You're missing out, little half-breed. My tongue can do things your husband's physically can't," he said against her ear.

She took a step back, seeming appalled by his comment. I couldn't help but laugh.

"I'll make sure to relay that to Eren," she replied.

"Oh, please do," he winked at her and then shut the door behind him.

I rose from the bed and went to the wardrobe to find something clean to wear. Pants and a shirt today, for sure. I wasn't in the mood to look fancy. "I have to jump in the bath," I announced to Gen. "What is it you need?"

"Eren's been worried about you the past few days. I just wanted to come see how you were, or if you needed anything," she replied.

"Eren's a mother hen. No need to worry about me. But thank you. I appreciate the thought."

"I just want you to know that I am here too, if you ever need to talk. You know, girl to girl."

I turned towards her slowly, taking in the female that had been chosen over me. "Thank you, but I have friends for that."

"I know, I'm just hoping maybe, we could become friends as well. Since we share the same family and court."

"Thank you for the offer, but my friend card is currently full. If there is a vacancy anytime in the next millennia, I will let you know."

Her face fell in defeat. "I understand. I just wanted you to have the option, if ever ..." she said, turning towards the door. Dammit, what the hell was I doing?

"Princess," I called after her. She turned around. "Look, I appreciate the gesture, I just can't be that way with you right now. I know you are aware of Eren's and my history. I'm still trying to unravel my feelings with all ... *that*. So, for now, I just want to keep my distance. It's nothing personal. In fact, I admire the shit out of you, with all you've overcome. But to get personal, I'm just not capable of that. Not right now."

She nodded with a small smile. "Thank you for explaining. And I get it. I hope in time things get better for you. For what it's worth, he loves you very much."

"I know he does; I just need some space right now. Just to figure my life out and what happens next."

"I can respect that," she said.

I turned back to the wardrobe. When I heard the lock click, I exhaled in relief. Thank Azeer that was over.

I bathed and went to the commons to meet up with the rest of the group. Zerrial looked like a lost dog, staring aimlessly in the fireplace. I went over and knelt beside him.

"How you doing, buddy?" I asked.

"I can't wait to get the fuck out of here," he grumbled.

"Oh, come now, they aren't that bad," I replied.

"It's not that. It's just ..." he paused, running a hand through his hair.

"Hey, you can talk to me," I said softly. "You know that. About anything."

He huffed. "I know you think I am an idiot for being with a human, because of how weak and fragile they are; but I'm worried, Ev. How am I supposed to protect her while still doing my job? While fighting whatever is out there? And I know Fi is watching over her back at court, but there are dangers there as well."

"First, you're not an idiot. If this past year has shown me anything, you dumbasses can't seem to help who you fall in love with."

Zerrial laughed, shaking his head.

"Second, you aren't alone. We are all here. If you love her and claim her as your own, then we all claim her. She has all of us to protect her. No matter where the threat comes from. Fi maybe quiet, but he is far from harmless. Remember when he and Doria got into that debate about which high lord would attempt to overthrow King Drezmore about fifty years ago?"

We both started laughing at that fond memory.

"He leveled the whole fucking forest," he said, still laughing.

"Exactly. Now think what he would do if anyone attempted to lay a finger on sweet little Lilian."

He paused, nodding in agreement. "You're right. I just can't think straight when she's not with me. When I can't physically see her."

"You'll be with her soon enough. In the meantime, I know Eren will need you the most with the dwarfs. You are one hell of an intimidating figure. With all those rippling muscles I so often admire."

He smirked, gently nudging his fist against my jaw. "Thank you, Ev. You always know just the thing to say."

I shrugged. "What can I say? One of my many gifts."

Levos was the last to exit his room. We all turned in his direction. "What?" he asked. "Did I oversleep?"

Fairy servants entered the room, carrying platters of breakfast dishes. They lined the table off to the side of the room and nodded before leaving.

"Shall we?" Eren said, gesturing to the food. We all sat at the round table and filled our plates. Levos sat next to me, with Gen on his other side.

"What's the plan for today?" asked Zerrial, stuffing his face.

"Flatter them, flirt with them, appease them. The usual," said Eren.

"You won't have to go overboard," I said, pouring myself a glass of white wine.

Eren paused mid-bite. "Evinee, what did you do?" he asked.

"I made a deal with Phasis. He'll give you what you want."

"What was the deal?" asked Gen. "Did it have to do with what I saw this mo—" she stopped, looking around the table at the others. I rolled my eyes, shaking my head in frustration. It took everything I had not to toss my glass at her perfectly crowned little head.

I could feel the judgment begin to silently pour out from the others. The court whore was at it again.

"What happened this morning?" asked Levos, chewing on a baked pastry.

I slammed my fork into the plate. "The deal doesn't matter. It affects none of you. Is it not good enough that I secured what we came here to do? Without help from any of you, might I add," I snapped, standing from my seat, throwing my napkin on the table. I stormed towards the exit.

"Evinee," I heard Eren call after me, but I didn't stop until I found a quiet room and an unopened bottle of wine.

"And what do we get out of this?" asked Pyra, sitting next to Phasis. The five of us sat across the table as negotiations began. I didn't say a damn word the entire time. I couldn't wait to be rid of my companions.

"Your Majesties," said Gen. "None of us get anything more than keeping our lands and protecting our kingdoms. If they destroy our kingdoms, they will come for you next. Your court is next in line for its size, resources, and abilities."

Pyra chattered her teeth, appearing annoyed. "I want ten humans a month," she snapped.

"Absolutely not," replied Levos.

Pyra angled her head towards him, flashing her bright white teeth. She launched herself across the table, stopping only a few inches from his face. To his testament, he didn't flinch.

"I was not talking to you, you light prude," she snapped. Her nose wiggled as she sniffed around him. A low, sensual moan came from her while she licked the side of his face. She returned her eyes to his, examining his reaction.

"The humans are not a bargaining chip," Levos said firmly.

Pyra slammed her hands into the table, making a whining noise.

"The choice is simple, really," Eren butted in. "Either we combine our forces and fight as a united front, reducing casualties in the process, or they pick us off court by court until there is nothing left. The choice is entirely up to you."

Phasis drummed his fingers on the table. He looked at me for a moment and grinned. "Fine, Prince Lyklor. We will join forces with you and the light fucks and any other race that will fight for the same cause. This treaty will hold ONLY until the rift is permanently closed and all the beasties are put in the ground. Then, we shall go about our courtly business as usual."

"We are grateful for your assistance," Eren said, smiling with what I could tell was relief. He slid his eyes to me. I looked back at the table. Eren pulled out the paperwork and slid it across to King Phasis. They both slit their hands and signed the document before mixing their blood together to seal the deal.

"You will stay two nights more," Phasis insisted. "Now that we must fight together, there is planning to be done."

Eren nodded. "I agree. I sent a message to my other companions this morning for an update on who has agreed to help us. We should have a response by tomorrow morning."

"And what of the light court?" asked Phasis, turning his attention to Levos. "Will your territories fight in the war?"

"I have also sent a messenger," answered Levos. "I am confident our allies will rally around this cause."

"Fan-fucking-tastic," commented Phasis. He stood from his chair abruptly, walking around the table. He grabbed my arm, pulling me up out of the chair as he continued for the door. Another hand grabbed my opposite arm, pulling me back. Phasis felt the tension, turning around aggressively.

"Where are you taking her?" asked Levos, still holding onto me.

Phasis stepped up to Levos, chest to chest, pushing him so hard the alfar slammed into the table, releasing his hold on me.

"None of your fucking business. She is mine. All mine. Do not touch," the fairy king snapped, turning back to the door, pulling me with him.

Phasis relaxed his grip as we headed for his rooms. "Sorry about the aggressive grab," he said with a devious smile.

"Did I complain?" I asked.

He chuckled, sliding his hand down my back. "You never complain. That's why I like you. You're always up for anything. Easy."

"Yes, I am easy. Everyone knows it," I replied, rolling my eyes.

Phasis looked puzzled.

"What is it?" I asked.

"Why did the light ambassador grab you?"

"Psh, you got me? He probably thinks you are going to eat me for lunch."

Phasis chuckled. "That can be arranged, pretty one. Ah, here we are," he said, pushing the double doors open.

His rooms were just as I remembered. An oversized bed full of furs and plush pillows. A black velvet couch and two matching chairs. Black leather straps hung from the ceiling, used for more experimental sexual endeavors. Lush rugs covered the floor and beautiful dark blue flowers bloomed along the walls.

"Now," Phasis said, shutting the door behind us. "Time for my song, little siren."

"Go lay on the bed and get comfortable. Any form I should take in particular?" I asked.

"Mm, the dark princess. Yes, she will do," he said, laying back against his pillow.

I felt sick. The thought of wearing her face—the face Eren truly loved. I exhaled, now regretting my decision to make this bargain. *It will only be a few moments*, I told myself. I closed my eyes, holding Gen's image in my mind. Once I had a firm grip on it, I allowed my magic to flow over me. The smell of the sea and sunshine filled the room as swirls of purple and blue fog consumed me. When the transformation was complete, I opened my eyes and peered down at Phasis. His wicked grin was stretched wide across his face.

"Happy?" I asked.

He clapped his hands together, his teeth chattered in excitement. "Yes, I like very much, yes I do," he said.

"Lay back and close your eyes," I whispered, leaning over him seductively.

The monster underneath my skin began to shift. The animalistic desire to kill, especially males, was overbearing, sometimes impossible to sate. When I was younger, the siren part of me took control often. During sexual experiences, I hadn't been able to stop myself. By the time I was twenty-two, I had killed thirty-eight males and nine females. Not intentionally, but still, I was responsible. That guilt ate at me and sent me to the darkest place I had ever been.

My canines began to elongate as my pupils dilated. The smell of Phasis's testosterone was delicious. I took a deep breath, closed my eyes and opened my mouth, allowing the song of the sea to flow throw me.

The melody was transcendent and tranquil. The sound came deep from within, and Azeer, did it feel good. It was as if I had a ball of tension and pressure trapped deep in my chest. When my song began to flow, the ecstasy I felt was just as powerful for me as it was for my victim. Probably why it had taken me so long to control the murderous aspect of my power.

I leaned down as purple and blue magic drifted from between my lips. I kissed Phasis softly, sending my magic into him, targeting his nucleus accumbens, the part of the brain that controlled pleasure. I pulled away, cutting off the song.

Phasis eyes were fluttering back in his head. A relaxed grin spread across his cheeks. His body was twitching from the impact of my power. Azeer, I wanted to sink my teeth into his throat and rip out his jugular. My nails elongated into thin black talons. My body trembled ... I was losing control.

I stumbled away from him, grabbing at my head while I shook, trying to snap myself out of it. I knocked into a wall, turning to see myself in the mirror. Gen's face stared back at me. My breath caught in my chest. I gazed at her for a few moments, feeling the heaviness in my heart. I hung my head, changing back to my normal form. I looked back at Phasis, watching while his body quivered from my pleasure.

My gift was unique. I created sound frequencies that released endorphins in the brain of my victims, while blocking other pathways. Depending on how I wanted to affect them, I could change my frequency as I sang. I could make them fall in love with me, turn into my slave, or make them trust me fully to extract information from them. I could also render them brain-dead or paralyze them for as long as I wanted. There was a reason the sirens were almost extinct. Other races feared them, with good reason.

I walked out of Phasis's room, drained and pissed off at the same time. I wanted to kill something. I *needed* to kill something. And fuck something. And tear something apart. My teeth ached. My gums throbbed, desperate to sink my fangs deep inside of someone. My vision became tunneled. I could hear my heart pounding as my pulse went ballistic.

I stumbled into fairies along the way, trying to stay close to the wall. I kept my eyes down to avoid looking at anyone. My skin felt like it was on fire. This happened every time I used my power, but today was especially volatile. Maybe it was due to my mental and emotional state, with Eren and my nightmares. My control was slipping, and I needed to get somewhere isolated, fast.

I staggered down the hallway to our shared commons area, praying to whatever god listened that no one was there. My ears were humming so loud it made my eyes vibrate, casting a blinding haze over my vision. I tried to focus, scanning the room. One head turned around from the couch as I tripped into the table, knocking the vase of flowers to the ground. I closed my eyes, panting heavily, trying to regain control of myself.

Levos stood, turning slowly towards me. "Evinee, are you alright?" he asked in a deep voice.

I moaned at the sound of his voice, fighting the urge to look upon his tall, lean body. I had never noticed how sensual and delectable his voice was, and Azeer, his smell. Now, with my senses heightened, I could smell the sweet caramel scent mixed with the warmth that he radiated. I took another breath, licking my lips as I noted tones of vanilla. Mm, I bet he tasted good too. Maybe just a quick little—*no*!

I pulled myself towards my room, making it down the short corridor. I could hear his boots circle the couch, heading in my direction. I managed to open the door, sliding in before slamming it shut. My entire body shuddered with need and desire. A bath. Yes, a cold bath would help. I had made it halfway across the room when I heard the door latch click.

Fuck! I screamed in my head. I turned around predatorially. Levos closed the door behind him, and paused.

"Are you okay?" he asked, assessing me.

"You need to go," I growled, baring my teeth.

He took a few steps towards me. "Did he hurt you? Let me help," he said. His words flowed over my skin like a silk sheet. I closed my eyes and extended my neck into the sky, bathing in the tenor of his voice. When I opened my lids, his brilliant golden eyes were peering down at me. I examined every inch of his face. Pyra was right, he was magnificent.

And that smell ... warm vanilla and caramel. I could taste it. I inhaled, my chest rising to barely brush against him. I stumbled back from the contact. He lunged, grabbing my arms to steady me.

That was all it took.

One moment, I was looking up into his eyes, and the next ... I had smashed him against the wall, taking his mouth with mine. My tongue lashed between his lips, savoring his sweet taste. My hands scoured his body, relishing every ripple of his perfectly muscled physique.

His hand tightened around my waist, while the other fisted my hair, yanking my head back before he began devouring my neck. Azeer, I was coming undone. Warmth began to spread between my legs. I needed him—inside of me. Now.

I pulled him from the wall, needing to be closer, needing to taste more. We knocked over the table, sending all the glass to the floor, shattering it into a million shards. But he didn't stop. I could smell his desire. I could feel it. I pressed my body against his, feeling his hardness fighting against his pants, wanting to be released.

He slammed me into the mirror hanging from the wall. The glass splintered, small pieces tearing at my shirt. His mouth engulfed mine. His hand slid down my neck and over my full chest. His fingers lingered there as he let out a deep moan that sent me trembling. We knocked over the small table and a statue on a pedestal. I tangled my hands through his beautiful white hair, pulling his head back and sinking my teeth into his neck.

"Fuck, Evinee," he gasped.

I pulled back, realizing what I had done. I looked at him for a moment, tasting his blood that now stained my lips. Shaking my head in shame, I whispered, "I'm so—"

I didn't manage to get the words out before he ploughed me into the wall, knocking a picture off the wall. We twisted and turned, consuming each other while we destroyed everything in our path. He felt so good. Better than anything I had ever had. And he wanted me. I hadn't used my power on him, but he still wanted me.

We were so taken with each other that I didn't notice the others enter my room until I felt a strong pair of arms pull me from Levos. I fought against the restraint, trying to get back to him. I needed him. I wanted him so badly my entire body screamed.

"Evinee!" I heard Eren's voice. He sounded far away.

Levos took a step back as Gen turned him to look at her, checking his neck where I had bitten down. She looked at the state of my room, holding onto Levos firmly.

"Evinee, that's enough!" Eren roared again. I steadied in his arms. My breathing was rapid. I could still feel my heart pounding out of my chest.

"What are you doing?" Levos demanded, pulling away from Gen and looking at Eren. "Get out, now!" he snapped, taking a step towards me. The demand and desire in his voice charged my need. I pulled away from Eren's grasp, fighting to get to him.

"Levos, leave now!" Eren ordered. "Gen, get him out!"

Levos looked at me and then at Eren, seeming confused. Gen pulled Levos towards the door, and they left the room. Eren threw me to the bed, pinning me there while I thrashed underneath him.

"Let me go!" I whined, twisting and turning.

"Evinee, look at me. Look at me now," he demanded.

"Get off!" I screamed, refusing to open my eyes. I licked my lips again. Azeer, his taste. I had never had someone so delicious. I was going mad!

A warm citrus scent wafted in the air. It was comforting, but not as delightful as the way Levos smelled. Eren was using his powers on me.

"No ... stop," I whispered, feeling the calming effects of his gift.

"Don't fight it," he said gently, loosening his grasp. "You need to relax. Calm yourself. Take deep breaths."

I listened, breathing in deeply until my heart stopped raging and my canines receded back into my gum.

"There you go, that's it," he encouraged. He finally got off me and sat on the edge of the bed. He ran his hands over his face, taking in a deep breath.

I pulled myself up, shame and horror colliding into me as I came back to my senses. Tears began to fall silently from my eyes. "What have I done?" I whispered, bringing my fingers to my lips. Levos's warm, sweet blood stained my skin.

Eren wrapped his arms around me, pulling me into him. "Shh, you're okay. Everyone is okay, that's what matters."

"I haven't lost control like that in ... decades, Eren. Not since—" I looked up at him but stopped myself as memories flooded back to my mind. Not since I had been with him the first time.

"It happens, Ev. It's to be expected. We all snap at some point." We sat in silence, while he rubbed my arms in a comforting manner.

I shook my head. I was humiliated. "I'm never going to be able to show my face in the light court again," I said.

Eren started chuckling, shaking his head. "Levos didn't appear to mind your attentions. In fact, I think he was enjoying himself."

I elbowed him hard in his ribs.

"Owe," he yelped, as we both laughed.

"Azeer, what in the hell was I thinking? With the ambassador of the light court for heaven's sake?"

"Your power is effective. Irresistible, in fact. He didn't stand a chance." I stared at the floor, pursing my lips.

"What is it?" he asked.

"I ... I didn't use my power on him. I didn't sing for him, I mean. In fact, I told him to leave when he came in, but he wouldn't."

"And the bite mark on his neck?"

I shrugged. "It seemed to ... excite him."

Eren paused, then burst into a fit of laughter, falling back onto the bed. "Holy fuck! Levos Atros is a freak in bed. I should have known. It's always the quiet do-gooders that are the craziest." He turned, propping his head up with his elbow. "So, little Atros desires the beautiful Evinee from the dark court. And the plot thickens."

"Is that so hard to believe?" I asked, turning towards him.

"Of course, not. I just find his behavior towards you when we arrived interesting. I thought he was repulsed by you. Instead, he was just flirting, like some schoolboy."

"Azeer, what the hell is wrong with me." I said, falling back into the bed and covering my face with my hands.

Eren pulled my hands back. "Nothing is wrong with you, Ev. You are perfect just the way you are."

I smiled up at him. "Ugh," I gasped. "What am I going to tell everyone? How am I going to explain this?"

"If you don't want to talk about it, then don't. It's your business, no one else's."

"Right, like Gen is going to let this go."

He shrugged. "I'm not going to tell her. This is your life and your secret."

I laughed. "You know what's funny? Gen and I share a lot more in common than I care to admit, being a half-breed myself and all. You apparently have a type."

He chuckled. "What do you mean? Beautiful, brilliant females with lush black hair? I see nothing wrong with that."

"You're intolerable," I groaned, pushing myself up.

"Irresistible is more like it, but I'll take the compliment."

I smiled at him, looking at the state of my room. "It's a damn war zone in here."

"I've seen war end cleaner than this place. What caused you to lose control? Was it Levos's dashing looks?" His eyebrows bounced up and down.

"He's easy on the eyes, but no. The deal I made with Phasis. He wanted me to sing for him. So, I did. I unleashed my power, and I wasn't in the best head space. My monster took over and wanted what it wanted. I was able to make it down here without touching anyone, but then Levos came to check on me. I fell back and when he reached out and grabbed me, I lost it. He smelled and tasted so good, I couldn't help but get as much of him as—" I turned to see Eren looking up at me with taunting eyes.

"Oh, please continue," he said sarcastically. "I am enjoying this immensely."

"Shut up," I said, smacking him with a pillow. He laughed, ripping the pillow from me, and burying it underneath him.

"You could have at least killed him for me. It would have been so nice to be down one Atros."

"Always thinking of yourself, aren't you."

His mouth gaped open. "I don't know if I am more hurt or offended by that comment. *Me,* narcissistic? Never."

"Alright, alright. Maybe not completely selfish, but selfish enough. Now, if you are done taunting me, I'd like to try and sleep. That took a lot out of me."

"Fine, fine, kick me out. I see how it is." He pushed himself off my bed and bent over, kissing me on my head softly.

"Will you do me a favor?" I asked. "Make sure Levos is okay."

"Dear Evinee, are we developing a liking for young Atros? First, you want to murder him, then you want to bed him. Now, you are concerned about him?"

"My statement remains. Intolerable."

He chuckled. "Yes, yes, I will make sure the young light alfar is alright. Get some rest," he said, turning and taking his leave.

CHAPTER TWENTY-EIGHT

I woke up feeling like I had been hit by a boulder. My head was pounding, and my body was still shaky. It was dinner time. Everyone would already be in the main hall.

I chose a tight, formfitting red dress that hung off my shoulders. I pinned my hair up on top of my head, leaving a small piece of purple curling slightly down the right side of my face.

I left my room, still putting on my earrings. As I entered the commons area, I spotted Levos in a chair along the wall. He stood as I approached. I looked around for anyone to save me, but we were alone.

"Everyone else is at dinner, I presume?" I asked.

He nodded. "Eren threatened to drag me to the hall by my hair, but Gen somehow convinced him to let me stay so we could talk. I never thought I'd see the day that Erendrial Lyklor was muzzled, yet here we are."

I smirked, looking down at my hands as I began to fidget.

"How's your neck?" I asked.

"Already healed, no need to fuss. Now, my shoulder, on the

other hand, still hurts like a bitch."

A laugh slipped from between my lips. My eyes rose to meet his. My breath caught in my chest at the sight of his shimmering golden irises. The moments we had spent together rushed through my mind. How our hands had explored each other. I pushed the thoughts out of my head.

"Right, we should probably join the others," I said, moving towards the exit.

He caught my hand gently as I passed. "Evinee, we need to talk about what happened earlier today," he said softly.

I readied myself, turning to face him. "What is it you wish to discuss?"

He studied my face. "What are you?" he asked bluntly.

I took a step back. "What do you mean, 'what am I'? I'm a dark alfar, just like the others." I said without hesitation.

He smiled, closing the space between us with one step. He folded his hands behind his back. "I may be young and not as experienced in some areas, but I excel at reading. Studying history about our world. In particular ... other races."

I swallowed hard.

"My intellect and observation skills have earned me the position I currently hold, though others believe it is because of my relation to the king. Based on your behavior, your appearance, and a few little things I remember so fondly about our ... dance earlier today, I have my suspicions, but there's one small problem. If I am correct, that means our records have been wrong for millennia. Both the light and dark court archives believe your race to be extinct."

He was close enough that I could taste his scent. He peered down at me, his expression calm. "Even though you owe me nothing," he whispered. "I would like you to tell me what you are and where you came from."

I looked up at him, not knowing what to say. I could kill him, that would be easier. Yesterday, I wouldn't have hesitated. I would have enjoyed it. But now, since I had felt him, tasted him, all I wanted was to consume him entirely. I wanted to know what every part of his body tasted like. I craved to hear the sounds he would make. To watch his face while I rode him to completion. To feel his cum drip down my body. I wanted him … every … single … drop.

He reached out slowly, wrapping his hand around my arm. "I know you have no reason to, but you *can* trust me. Gen is proof of that. I believe many of our laws are barbaric, and believe it or not, I admire King Drezmore for changing that one specific rule."

"It's not that simple, Levos. If you know what I am, then you know there's a price on my head: not just for being a half-breed, but also for being *what* I am."

His eyes widened as I confirmed his suspicions. "A siren. You're a siren."

I dropped my head, not able to say it.

"How? The courts called for a genocide of your kind over a thousand years ago. How are you here now?"

"The dark court. When they use to experiment on other races. The crossbreeding projects. My father was a dark alfar. My mother, a siren of course. Instead of killing me when I was born, my father thought to weaponize his ... *experiment*. He would use me for his own political gain. Thankfully, I appeared more like an alfar physically, but when my powers are unleashed ... sometimes I can't control myself."

"You were born from an experiment?" he asked.

"Yes. Even after the dark king at the time abolished the experiments, there was a small group of alfar who continued the project in secret. My mother had been a prisoner for nearly five hundred years. Once I was born, my father had her killed. She had served her purpose."

"And who is your father?"

"Orfias Duprev. He died a hundred and fifty years ago."

"He was a scientist, right?" Levos asked.

I was startled. "You know of him?" I replied, panic rising, along with the anxiety that controlled most of my life.

"I remember reading about him. His experiments and findings were amazing, though brutal at times. He was the head of the initial interracial experiment sector, IES, correct?"

"Okay, it's freaking me out how knowledgeable you are about my father."

"Evinee, it's my job to know everything about the dark court. It doesn't mean I agree with how your father conducted his business. But, if I remember correctly, your mother is listed as Sophia Duprev, his legal wife. A dark alfar who came from a high house. She willingly raised you?"

I scoffed. "No, she barely looked at me. He threatened her to keep her mouth shut about my biology, and she agreed, but that doesn't mean she had anything to do with me. She never had children, so there was no need to destroy me and risk the wrath of my father."

"And how did you end up in Lyklor's crew?"

"That story is complicated and one I am not willing to revisit," I said firmly.

His hands rose defensively. "I'm sorry, I didn't mean to push. I appreciate your honesty with me. You don't have to trust me, but you are. That goes a long way in my book."

"Well, I figured I owed you something after I attempted to rip your jugular out. Sorry about that."

He laughed, rubbing his hand over the spot where my mouth had been. "Yea, that was unexpected. Not completely unenjoyable though, if I'm being honest."

I blushed, dropping my eyes away from his.

"Is that normal ... the biting?" he asked.

I exhaled, crossing my arms over my chest. "We're not going to make it to dinner with all the questions rolling through that head of yours, are we?"

"It's not every day I get to meet a member of an extinct race. My curiosity is getting the best of me."

I chuckled, going over to the servant's rope, pulling it once. A female fairy fluttered down the hallway. "Yes, Lady Duprev, how can I be of assistance?" she asked in a high-pitched voice.

"We'll be dining in here this evening. Would you please fetch a few bottles of wine and some food for Ambassador Levos and me?" I asked her.

"Of course, Lady Duprev," she said with a sharp smile. She growled at Levos before leaving.

"Either they want to bed me," Levos said, "or kill me. I don't know if I should be flattered or afraid for my life."

I laughed as we took our seats around a small table. "Yes, you appear to have that effect on most. Yesterday, I wanted to kill you, then this afternoon I tried ... you know," I said, still feeling embarrassed.

"Yes, about that," he said. "When you came into the commons area, you were ... different. What caused that?"

"That had to do with the deal I made with Phasis," I started, as the fairy servant appeared with food and wine. I waited for her to leave.

"Did you ... did you sleep with him?" he asked, hesitantly. "Is that how your power works?"

"It can work like that, but no, I did not sleep with Phasis today. He wanted me to sing for him. My song ... my power can do many things to the neurowaves in the brain. It can soothe someone, make them fall in love with me or under my power, or kill them instantly.

"I have never killed anyone that way, just so we're clear. It takes a lot of power and control to do that. I can only use a little bit of my power at a time. It takes its toll on me. That's probably why I lost control today. It's like a muscle: if I don't use it, it weakens. But the more I use it, the stronger I get."

"So, why not use it more? Train with it?"

"Many reasons. One, if I was ever caught, they would kill me. Two, I don't want to hurt anyone with this curse. Three, when I lose control, it's hard to come back. Eren's power helps, but what if he's not around? I could hurt someone. And most importantly, if I am being honest, a part of me is scared to explore deeper than I already have."

"What happens if you lose control?"

I paused, thinking back to the innocent males I had killed in my earlier years. "Those around me die," I admitted. "The siren inside of me takes hold. If I am not in my right mind, or in a good head space, my emotions take over and give way to the desires of the siren. The creature desires to kill. To sink its teeth into someone. To rip them to shreds. It's my natural instinct to try and kill the lover I have sung to or lay with. I don't fully understand it, but it's a bitch to control."

"So, why am I still alive?" he asked.

"I could have killed you. A part of me wanted to. I could feel my song creeping up my throat, but you tasted too good. And the way you felt. I didn't want to stop what we were doing."

He laughed lightly, shaking his head. "Well, the feeling was mutual, if that makes this," he said, gesturing between us, "any easier. Even the biting part, surprisingly."

I took a deep drink of the wine.

"Why were you off your game?" he asked.

I paused, not wanting to dive too deep. "I've been having some nightmares, and then ... Eren," I admitted.

"You don't have to say anymore," he said, taking a bite of his food.

I turned my focus towards him. "You know? I'm starting to feel a little freaked out. You know an awful lot about me and my life."

He chuckled. "As I've told you before, it's my job to know. And as far as you and Eren, I don't know the details, but Gen has told me enough for me to put the pieces together."

"I'm adjusting. I just need time," I said, trying not to seem pathetic.

"No need to explain," he said, winking at me.

I thought for a moment. My reckless actions not only affected Levos, but someone else I cared for.

"Oh, Azeer. Vena," I said, running my hand across my face. "She is going to be so hurt when you tell her what I did."

He took a deep drink of his wine this time. "Vena and I aren't exclusive. We're just ... talking. No need to worry her about nothing."

"Nothing! I basically raped you without your consent. How is that nothing?"

"Evinee, let me make this clear." He leaned in close, brushing the loose strand of hair from my face. "I was a *very* willing participant in whatever that was this afternoon. You didn't rape me and you had my consent and more. I wanted to murder Lyklor for interfering."

I was surprised by his directness and physical contact. This wasn't the same male I had dealt with yesterday.

"What," he said, leaning back. "You look surprised."

"I am," I admitted. "Did you not *just* yesterday call me a useless slut who was only good for one thing?"

"I apologized for that already."

"Yes, you did. And then within twelve hours, you want to bed me? Talk about sending mixed signals." I took another drink of wine, reaching for a new bottle.

"My particular sense of humor isn't for everyone."

"Yea, I would say insults are not a way to win a females heart."

"Are you ready for another question?" He arched his brow, swirling his wine in his glass.

"If I must," I said.

"What do your powers consist of? From the siren side, that is?"

"Physical and mental manipulation, as I've already explained. My physical attributes I suppose: sharp teeth, nails, oh, and I physically turn into a siren in water, if I choose. I can also change my physical appearance, like a shapeshifter."

He looked me up and down. "Show me," he demanded.

I laughed. "Bossy much?"

"Oh, come on. If you do it, we'll call the little biting thing even."

"I thought you said you enjoyed that?"

"I did. But I know you feel guilty about hurting me, so I am playing my hand."

"You're awful."

"Only in the most pleasant way," he said, holding his bottom lip between his teeth. I couldn't help but focus on that lip, fantasizing about his teeth and how they would feel around my clit.

I concentrated, closing my eyes and imagining him: his face, the details of his figure, the colors that made up his hair, and those brilliant eyes. The cold magic swept over me as the smell of sea water engulfed my nostrils. I heard his chair scratch against the floor. I opened my eyes to see him looking back at me, astonished.

"Happy now?" my mouth said, but in his voice.

"Oh, Thor, this is amazing. I mean, I knew the dark queen had this kind of gift, but I never got to see it in person. The detail, it's ... it's amazing. You can even change the tone of your voice? Incredible."

I arched my eyebrow, running my hand up his leg. "Wanna take *you* for a test drive?"

He flinched away from me. I let out a deep, gut-wrenching laugh.

"Not in the slightest," he said, joining me in laughter. I closed my eyes, still laughing, and shifted back to my normal form. The cloud of blue and purple magic dissipated around me.

"I wish you could have seen your face. It was so worth it," I said, still gasping for air. My stomach hurt I was laughing so hard.

"I'm glad you got amusement out of this little experiment," he said. He steadied himself, looking at me with a softer gaze.

"What?" I asked.

"Is this," he said, gesturing to my body, "your true form?"

"It's my biological form, yes. Why? Is there something wrong with it?"

He sat quietly, not answering my question while he studied my face.

"Okay, stop doing that. Why did you ask that?" I demanded.

"I thought maybe you had created this form from pieces of females you encountered."

"And why would you think that?"

"Because you're the most perfectly assembled female I've ever seen," he said, leaning into me with a flirtatious smile.

My mouth gaped open. I shut it, realizing I was beginning to let my mask slip. He wasn't serious. I felt the warmth go to my cheeks as I fought it. The silence was killing me. Not knowing what to do, I plucked a grape from the platter and threw it at him. He caught it without flinching and popped it in his mouth.

"Mm," he said, chewing slowly. "Are you a mind reader as well?

Because I was just thinking about how good a grape sounded right about now."

"You are a shameless flirt, you know that? Completely awful. Probably one of the worst I've encountered in my long life. And that includes Phasis, if that puts things into perspective."

He sat back, laughing at me. "And how long of a life span are we talking?"

"You first," I said, folding my arms over my chest.

"I'm ninety-nine years old. One hundred in the fall. Now you."

"Azeer, you're a baby," I said, bringing the wine to my lips.

"Oh, come on. Your turn."

"I'm ... I'm three hundred and four. Three hundred and five in the winter," I admitted.

"Damn. You look pretty good for your age."

"Oh, shut up," I said, reaching for the bottle.

"Do you not eat?" he asked.

I looked back at him with confusion.

"I noticed you maybe take a bite or two, but you don't eat a full meal. I didn't know if sirens ate something different."

"No, I can eat normal food. And I do eat when I need to. I just ... I don't really have an appetite most of the time."

"Why is that?"

"That's a long story, and one I'm also not willing to share," I said softly.

"I understand."

"Alright, that's all I am going to tell you. Enough about me. Tell me something about you. It's only fair," I said, folding my legs underneath me, preparing for a story. "What's it like being cousin of King Fucker?"

He laughed, shaking his head. "Gods, I love that nickname." His smile faded as his face went stern. "Don't tell him I said that."

I threw my hand over my heart. "Blood oath's honor." I winked.

"Well, my father and Gaelin's father were in the military together. They were raised by a very stern father figure, so in return, they were hard on us. When I came along, Gaelin was already about a hundred and fifty. He basically raised me. He looked after me and made sure I had everything I needed.

"He noticed my skill in history and my love for books right away. He made sure I had the appropriate tutors and resources to have a happy life. He protected me when my father expressed his disappointment. I wasn't a born warrior like the rest of our family. Don't get me wrong, I can kill almost anything—thanks to the endless years of training I was forced to endure—but I wanted to explore. I wanted to learn about the races, about our world, and others. Which obviously has come in handy with our current situation.

"In the light court, I was basically invisible until Gaelin became king and appointed me ambassador. Now, everyone kisses my ass, trying to gain my favor. Can't say it's all bad. I get to travel between courts. And I take the opportunity to piss off Lyklor anytime I can."

I chuckled. "Yes, I am sure he appreciates that." I leaned forward. "Don't tell him I told you, but when he found out you were the new ambassador of the light, he was pissed. He told us he had to start actually thinking about negotiations with your court. If you ask me, that's as good of a compliment as you're going to get from him."

"Hey, I may not be a fan of his, but he is one smart and tricky fucker, I'll give him that. If he was born in the light court, I would have wanted to be tutored by him. He's that good."

"Yes, he is. Sometimes too good," I felt my heart tug slightly as my face fell.

"I'm sorry. I shouldn't have brought him up," he said sincerely.

"No, it's fine. Really. He's a part of my family. Even though we're in a weird place, I know we'll always be there for each other. And regardless of my own situation, I am happy for him and Gen. They have fought so hard. One can only hope to have an equal like that someday. Someone who would go to the ends of the world to be reunited with their soulmate. Someone who would fight through anything ... even death."

My words felt heavy. I did want that. Someone to completely rely on. It would be nice to share the burden of this life with another. To know they would stop at nothing to find me. Just to love me.

"Yes, their entire relationship has made me rethink my perception of Lyklor. Gen is happy. That's all that matters. That she's alive and that she's happy," he said, twirling his glass of wine on the table.

"Have you … ever been in love?" I asked, trying to move away from the topic of Gen and Eren.

He smirked, with a slight nod.

"I'm sorry. If you don't want to talk about it. I shouldn't have—"

"It's fine. It's in the past. I fell in love. She was in danger. So, I sent her away to safety. End of story."

"That was a very honorable thing to do," I whispered, knowing it was a subject I shouldn't have approached.

"Thank you. I appreciate the sentiment."

I paused, trying to think of a way to lighten the conversation. Flirting: I was good at that. "So, you're only ninety-nine and you kiss like that, huh? Must have had a lot of experience in that department. That was some Jestu action this afternoon."

He started laughing. Thank Azeer.

"I don't know if my limited experience can compare to yours, but—"

"Hey," I said, kicking him in the leg. "What in the hell is that supposed to mean, my 'experience'?"

"Well, with you being a siren, and from what I've heard about the great Evinee Duprev—"

"And here I thought you were smarter than to believe rumors,"

I said, arching one eyebrow.

He smirked, tilting his head forward. "You mean to tell me that all these elaborate stories I have heard from hundreds of males across the fae lands are fabricated?"

I raised my brows, taking a deep drink.

"You've got to be shitting me," he said, laughing under his breath. "How?"

"Well, first of all, as I have already told you, it is extremely hard not to kill a person, especially a male, during intercourse. So I try to refrain from getting to that point at all costs. I pride myself on not being a murderous siren. And with my powers, I can construct elaborate images and stories in the brain, making my target crave more. Making them believe we were together, even though I only ever kiss them."

"So, your power isn't activated without a kiss?" he asked.

"Correct."

"So, you haven't slept with thousands of males and females?"

"Also correct."

He leaned forward with his wine in hand. He hung his head low. "Gods, Evinee. I feel terrible about what I said to you yesterday. No wonder you wanted to kill me."

"I'm used to it. Our entire family must wear masks to get shit done. I am the whore. Eren is the selfish throne climber. Zerrial is the big heartless brute, even though he has the biggest heart out of all of us. Doria is the brutal psychopath, even though she's a lover.

Leenia is the warrior princess, yet she'd rather be behind a canvas with a palette of paint. The only true ones in the group are the mad genius twins." I laughed, thinking of them.

"No wonder why Gen chose to follow this path. You're all ... astounding," he said. "Don't tell Gaelin I said that either. He would cut off my balls for giving anyone in the dark court a compliment."

"Don't worry. I am hoping we agree that everything we've discussed this evening stays here and isn't used against one another. Not everyone knows about me," I admitted.

"Who does?" he asked.

"Well, you. Eren of course. King Drezmore. Pyra and Phasis."

He looked at me in shock. "That's it? The rest of your chosen family doesn't know about you?"

I shook my head. "When my father died, I burned all my medical records and my mother's medical records. Everyone who knew of me is ... is dead. My secret is safe. It's not that I don't trust my family. It's just ... I didn't want to put them in danger. I don't want to burden them with another secret. The only reason I told you was because of today. There were things I couldn't lie my way out of, so I spoke with Eren and just figured I'd come clean. Believe it or not, I think he believes you to be honorable, or something like that."

He smirked, looking to his wine glass. "Full of surprises that one."

"So, does that mean you agree to keep my secret? You won't tell anyone in the light or dark courts?"

He looked at me for a moment, then scanned the room.

"Hold that thought," he said, rushing to his room. A few moments later he came back, holding a quill and piece of parchment. He began to write with haste. I watched him, knowing what he was going to propose: a blood oath. Finally, he put the quill down and handed me the piece of parchment.

"Here," he said proudly. "I insist you read it first."

I took the piece of paper from him, fighting the smile on my face. It read:

I, Levos Theryian Atros, swear to never reveal the secrets of Evinee Duprev now and forever regarding any personal, physical, mental, or biological information. If I reveal her secrets in any form of communication, whether it be written or verbal, I will become her male servant and slave, pleasing her every hour of every day until my heart ceases to beat. If that does not please Evinee, I will be forced to cut off my own testicles and serve them to her in whatever manner that pleases the lady.

I couldn't help but laugh. He watched my expressions.

"I think we need to add some details about what the male servant's duties will be. I just want everything to be as clear as possible, so I know what I am getting out of you," I said, laughing over my own words.

He snickered, snatching the parchment from me. "Attention to detail. Another attribute to like about you."

"Oh, I was unaware you were making a list about little old me."

"I do this with every person I meet. Don't let it go to your head ... Now, about the details of my indentured servitude. What shall we include?"

"Hm, how about, all laundry cleaned and put away."

"Check."

"Full body massages whenever I want."

"Definitely including that."

"Armor and weapons cleaned and shined."

"Of course."

"You will scrub my back when I wash, and all those hard-to-reach places."

"Mm, I like how you think. Got it."

"And of course, at least three orgasms a day," I said, biting down on my lower lip. The thought of his mouth on me made my body warm.

He stopped, raising his eyes to mine. "Ya, know," he whispered, looking over his shoulder. "I might break this damn contract just so I can fulfill these duties immediately."

I dissolved into another laughing fit.

"No, I am serious," he continued, chuckling along with me. "This is far more pleasing than being the light court's ambassador. Better yet—" he said, standing and going over to the servant's cord. He pulled it once, standing tall and proud. "I am going to break the damn contract right now so I can take you in the room and begin my duties."

The servant appeared instantly while we both were roaring. "Yes, what can I get you," she said in her high-pitched voice.

"Wine," Levos said, in between laughing. "More wine."

"Right away," she responded, leaving the room.

Levos took out a knife from his belt, slicing his hand and signing the contract. He handed me the knife and I did the same. He held out his hand towards me. I placed my wound over his, feeling the contract snap into place. When I went to pull away, he tightened his grip, slowly placing his soft lips to the back of my hand, keeping his eyes on mine. He pressed a kiss against my skin, leaving his lips there a few seconds longer than normal.

"You can trust me, Evinee," he whispered on top of my hand.

"I know," I replied without hesitation.

He smiled at my response. The servant dropped off the bottle of wine and then left. He refilled our glasses, looking at me with alluring eyes.

"So, would you like a test run of what you will be stuck with if I break the contract, or are you confident that my ninety-nine years of experience has taught me enough to please a siren?" he asked.

"Confident now, are we?"

"I am. But I am also teachable. And I would very much like it if you would teach me."

"You are absolutely awful."

"Yes, you've said that about a thousand times tonight." We both giggled, leaning towards each other. I couldn't remember the last time I laughed this hard. I was truly enjoying myself, with Levos Atros, of all alfar. Conversation was easy with him. And for whatever reason I *did* trust him.

"There you two are," Eren said as he, Gen, and Zerrial descended the hallway. "We were waiting for you all evening. Phasis and Pyra were not pleased by your absences. You will be hearing about it tomorrow, I am sure."

I waved my hand in the air. "They'll be fine," I said, taking another sip of wine.

"You might," said Levos, "but I won't, if Pyra has anything to say about it," he said, laughing and gesturing to his shoulder. We both roared.

"Well, you … you are delicious. I can't … I can't blame her," I said, gasping for air in between each word.

"What?" Gen asked, approaching Levos's side, reaching for his shirt. "What do you—" she stopped in horror as she pulled the fabric back, revealing Pyra's handiwork. "Oh, my gods. She took a bite out of you. I am going to kill that fairy bitch."

Levos swatted her hand away. "I'm fine. Really. I'm apparently very edible," he said, winking at me. I chuckled, shaking my head. I could feel Eren's eyes assessing the situation.

"What is happening here?" Eren asked, looking between Levos and me. "Because whatever it is, I don't like it, nor do I approve."

Levos stood, taking one of Eren's hands and bringing it to his chest.

"Don't worry brother, I know you secretly love me. It's okay. I know you admire me, and I, you. Mutual respect," he slurred, looking at me with a smile. Eren pulled his hand back.

"Did you just call me, *brother*?" Eren spat, turning his attention to me. "What in the hell have you two been gossiping about?"

"Too many things," Levos said. "I can't tell you half of them, because then I would become an indentured servant." We both fell into a fit of laughter. Eren and Gen glanced at each other with confusion.

"I'm going to bed," stated Zerrial.

Levos rolled up the contract casually, making sure not to draw attention to the document. Eren noticed the paper and glared at me suspiciously. Levos looked from Gen to Eren.

"Did anything happen at dinner we should know about?" Levos asked.

"No. Everything was surprisingly mild," replied Gen, still assessing us both.

"Good to hear," replied Levos. "Now, if you would be so kind, would you please give us a moment alone?" he asked Gen and Eren.

Eren furrowed his brow. "Ev, I'd like to speak to you when the two of you are through."

"Of course," I answered.

They went back to their bedroom, shutting the door behind

them. Levos grinned widely at me. He knelt on one knee, taking my hands into his.

"What are you doing?" I asked, giggling to myself.

"Tonight was ... unexpected, to say the least. I haven't had this much fun with a female ever. With you, this is easy. All of it."

"I agree," I said.

"I want you, Evinee. I want you tonight. May I visit your room?" he asked.

My smile faded from my face as I pulled my hands away from his. "No," I said plainly. His smile evaporated, replaced with confusion.

"I'm ... I'm sorry. I must have misread all of this," he said, pushing himself up of the ground.

"No, Levos, you didn't misread anything. Tonight was wonderful, but you know what happens if I ... if I engage in intercourse. The risk we would be taking. And right now, with everything being held together by a thin thread, I can't risk killing the ambassador of the light court."

"I trust you, Evinee."

"That's sweet, but I don't trust myself. I ... I actually like you. Azeer, I can't believe those words just came out of my mouth, but I couldn't live with myself if I hurt you."

"You aren't going to hurt me. I can handle myself, I promise," he said, leaning towards me. His hand grazed down the side of my cheek, sliding to my chest and stopping right before the curve of my breasts. My breath quickened. I felt the warmth pool between my legs and erupt as I leaned into his touch. *Treacherous body*, I thought to myself.

"I ... I can't," I managed to get out.

"You know what I can't do," he said. "I can't get the memory of how you felt out of my head. How your body felt against mine when I slammed you into the wall. How your neck tasted in my mouth. How euphoric it was to have your teeth bite into my skin. I can't get the sound of your moan out of my head. I need to hear it again, Evinee. Please ... please don't deny me," he said, leaning into my lips.

I felt the brush of his bottom lip and knew if I didn't pull away in that moment, I would be the end of him. I placed my hands against his chest, putting distance between us.

"I can't, Levos. I want to, but I can't. I am sorry. I hope you understand."

He pulled away with disappointment, looking away from me.

"I really did enjoy tonight," I added, trying to lighten the blow. "I can't remember the last time I laughed like that."

"Good," he said, taking his wine glass back in his hand. "I'm glad we were able to clear the air."

"Me too. I hope this is the beginning of ... a friendship," I said.

He stood up. "If a friendship is what you wish, then a friendship is what you will have," he whispered, leaning down and kissing me on the cheek, allowing his lips to linger. He pulled away, remaining face to face. "But know, I will always want more." He drew his thumb across my bottom lip, then brought it to his own lips, placing it in his mouth before he pulled away and retired to his room.

I took a few deep breaths, calming the ever-growing need between my legs. Azeer, I did want him. I wanted him so badly I almost gave in. But the sensible part of me was right. I couldn't risk it. I was unhinged at the moment.

I knocked on Eren's door. A moment passed before he slipped out, taking me by the arm and leading me into my room. He slammed the door behind us, turning to me with worry in his eyes. "What was that?" he demanded. "What game are you playing with Levos Atros?"

I shook my head. "Nothing. I am not playing any game," I admitted.

"So, what? You two are best friends all the sudden? I don't like this, Ev. I don't trust him."

"Well, I do," I snapped. I paused, taken aback by my own admission.

Eren took a moment, assessing me. "Are you insane? He is Gaelin's cousin. Loyal to the light court."

"And? How does that affect me?"

"Evinee, stop and think. He could use your secrets in a heartbeat to further his ambitions?"

"And what do you know of his ambitions, Eren? Have you even

had a conversation with him? Do you know anything about him, besides the fact that he's Gaelin's cousin?" I waited for a moment. "No, I didn't think so. Your princess trusts him. Why shouldn't I?"

"Ev, you're not thinking clearly. You're hurting and looking for someone to fill a void—"

I whipped around towards him, pointing my finger in his face. "Do not presume what I am feeling or how I cope with situations, Eren. Tonight was nothing more than two alfar enjoying each other's company. It had nothing to do with you, or Gen, or this impending war. I deserve moments of happiness. Even if they are with someone from the light court," I spat in rage.

He took a few moments, pondering my words.

"I don't care," he said bluntly. "You are forbidden to continue any type of relationship with Levos Atros. Am I clear?"

"The fuck you are," I said, in disbelief. "No male is going to tell me how to live my life. Am I clear?" I snapped back at him.

"He is too much of a liability to this family and to our court. This is for your own good, Evinee. I am sorry, but you will end the relationship immediately," he said, and left my room in haste.

I took the new vase the servants had placed in my room and threw it at the door after him. There was no way in hell I was going to let anyone tell me how to live my life—especially Eren Lyklor.

CHAPTER TWENTY-NINE

The next morning was spent going over battle strategies and fortifications for different parts of our land. We received correspondence from both the dark and light court. Leenia and the others managed to secure the draugr and imps, thus far. They were on their way to the incubi. The light court was in the process of securing most of their allies, but I knew, even with the numbers, we would be lucky to make it out alive. Eren wrote back to Leenia, asking her to meet up with us when they were done negotiating.

I kept quiet the entire time, deep in thought. There had to be something more we could do. I sorted through everything we knew about our enemy: the creatures, the gods, the rift—*that was it.* Excitement sent adrenaline rushing through me, but I managed to remain calm. I felt a pair of eyes on me ... Levos.

He furrowed his brow. I mouthed *later* before returning my attention to Phasis and Eren. I caught Pyra assessing the two of us from across the table. She arched an eyebrow with a wicked smile as her gaze settled deeply upon me.

When the meeting was done, I excused myself, making a beeline to my room. Before I made it to the commons, I was picked up without warning and carried up into the higher levels of the hive.

I looked behind me to see Pyra's striking face smiling back. "You've been keeping secrets, little friend," she hissed against my ear.

"Pyra, we literally just spoke yesterday. What could have happened between then and now?" I asked as we flew in a zigzagging pattern.

She took a deep sniff along my neck. "I smell the light one on you and I demand details," she snapped, slamming us both into the ground outside the doors to her room. She grabbed my arm, pulling me inside. "Tell me, was he good?" she asked eagerly, only inches from my face.

I laughed. "Pyra darling, I didn't sleep with Levos. I swear on our friendship, that did not happen."

She stomped her foot in aggravation. "Then why do you smell of him?"

"Well, I may not have slept with him, but I may have ... bit him," I admitted.

Her wings twitched while her eyes widened. "You tasted him too," she said, her smile reappearing.

I chuckled. "Yea, it wasn't intentional. I lost control after using my song on Phasis yesterday and Levos happened to be in the wrong place at the wrong time."

"Mm, I see. And how did he ... reciprocate your little love bite?"

I paused, biting on the bottom of my lip while the images and feelings of his desire sent my skin erupting in gooseflesh. "He ... he wasn't opposed."

Her mouth fell open. "You lucky bitch," she said, falling onto her bed.

I laughed, crawling in next to her. "Believe me, I was just as surprised as you at his reaction, and my own, for that matter."

"Oh, found something we like, did we?" she asked, drawing a finger down my arm.

"I might have," I laughed at myself. "Azeer, Levos Atros. The universe has an odd sense of humor."

She nodded. "I can agree to that, but I can also attest to how absolutely delicious that alfar is."

"You aren't lying about that. But even so, Eren has forbid me to continue any type of relation with him," I confessed.

She straightened instantly. "Excuse me? He did what?"

"Yea. He walked in on Levos and I having a conversation last night—that's why we missed dinner—and he saw the interaction between us and then Eren forbid me from even having a friendship with him."

"The nerve of that selfish, narcissistic male. I want to rip his balls out through his mouth for even attempting to tell you how to conduct your personal relationships. After everything he's done to you."

"Well, he can bark orders all he want," I said. "I am in charge of my own life. When my father died, I swore I would never let another dictate how I conducted my life. That includes Erendrial Lyklor."

"Jealous prick," she spat.

I shrugged. "I don't think he's jealous, but I don't believe he trusts Levos."

"And you do?" she asked.

I paused before nodding. "I do. Some part of me just ... just feels so drawn to him. Like I already know him better than myself."

Her eyes widened. "Do you think it could be the siren bond?" she asked frantically.

Azeer, I had forgotten all about that. The siren bond was a myth. I didn't have anything concrete to back it up, but the legend supposedly stated that a single male came along once in a siren's life. He would have to forfeit his life, and then be reborn.

There were benefits to the bond. The two would share one mind. They could communicate without uttering a word. The male would be able to breathe underwater, and the siren would gain the strength of the male she was bonded to. That was all I knew from the books I had found on my kind in the library back at the dark court.

"Evie," Pyra said, jarring me out of my thoughts.

I shook my head. "It's a myth, Pyra. I am not willing to risk my life just to test a theory."

"But imagine if it is true," she said, scooting closer to me. "Imagine having the love you crave. The strength and power you've always wanted."

I stood from the bed, not wanting to talk about this any longer. "It's a nice dream, but eventually, everyone has to wake from their dreams." I leaned down and kissed her on the cheek. "I have to go handle some business, but I will find you later, okay?"

She nodded, standing, wrapping her arms around me before I could protest. "Remember, only you have the power to make your dreams come true."

I pulled away, putting my forehead to hers before heading for the door. I made my way back to the commons area of our rooms to find the four of them in a huddle. They all turned to me as I approached.

"Did I miss a meeting?" I asked.

"Pack your things," Eren said. "We're leaving."

"What? Why?" I asked.

Eren went to his room, shutting the door. Gen approached me. "I had a vision. The nymphs are going to be attacked by a horde of some hominoid creatures. We've sent word to the others to meet us there and we've sent a warning to the nymphs. Let's pray it gets there in time."

I nodded, heading to my room to pack my things.

We bid Phasis and Pyra farewell. They stayed behind to rally their troops for the upcoming war. We would travel to the nymph's lands, which thankfully weren't too far from the fairies.

We called our ragamors down into the clearing. As they landed, Levos stood off to the side, staring in awe. Pasiese slammed down, her purple scales catching the light of the setting sun. She nuzzled her head into me while I embraced the dragon-like creature. I looked back at Levos while he assessed the two of us.

"Want to say hello?" I asked him.

"Can I?" he replied. "I mean, it isn't going to eat me or anything?"

I chuckled. "No, she isn't going to eat you. Unless I tell her to, that is."

He smiled, cautiously approaching. He reached out his hand and waited for her to come to him. Pasiese looked at me and I nodded in approval. She slowly bowed her head, allowing his hand to skim the surface of her scales. He grinned, taking another step forward.

"She's beautiful," he whispered. Pasiese let out a low whine of approval.

"She apparently liked that compliment," I told him.

"She can understand me?"

"Sort of. She and I are bonded. So, she can sense what I am feeling, and we talk through our emotions. What I hear, feel, and see, she can also."

"Amazing. I must admit, I am slightly jealous of your court. All the different gifts and the ragamor as a bonus."

I laughed. "Let me guess: don't tell Gaelin you said that?"

"You got it," he said with a wink.

I looked at Pasiese and then back to Levos. "Do you want to ride with us to the nymph's lands?" I offered.

"Really?"

"I don't see why not. We don't want to be waiting around for you to arrive on your horse, now do we?"

"Smart-ass," he mumbled with a smile.

"Fantastic. You're going to have to hold on tight. If you fall off, I am not responsible, just so we're clear."

"I would expect nothing less, Evinee."

We climbed onto Pasiese as she stomped, preparing herself for takeoff. Levos locked his arms around my waist and leaned into my back. I slashed both of my palms, sliding them into the slits underneath Pasiese's shoulder blades.

Eren appeared, mounted on Eeri. "And what do you think you're doing, Ambassador Atros?" he asked, clearly pissed.

"Hitching a ride, it would appear," replied Levos. I snickered, impressed by Levos's lack of fear where Eren was concerned.

"I think your horse would be a better mode of transportation," Eren said.

Before the bantering continued, I pushed Pasiese forward, readying for takeoff. I sent my power through the bond, urging her to take flight. She fanned out her wings, causing gusts of dirt to fly up around us. "See you there," I said to Eren before we shot into the sky.

Levos's grip tightened as my thighs locked around Pasiese's scaled back. We reached a high altitude before she steadied her glide. The clouds whipped around us as the colors of the sunset bounced throughout the small droplets of precipitation.

"This is ..." Levos whispered, trailing off in thought.

"I know, right? The most peaceful and beautiful thing you will ever see."

"I am one hundred percent jealous now," he said, loosening his grip as he sat up straighter, taking in our breathtaking surroundings.

"So, are you ready to do some negotiating with the nymphs, since they're aligned with the light court?" I asked.

"They're easy. They will most likely be even more negotiable since you all are flying to help them defend whatever attack is heading their way. They won't be too thrilled to work with the fairies, but once they see the contract, I can't see it being much of an issue. Speaking of the impending war, what was that little epiphany you had back at the meeting this afternoon?"

I exhaled. "Well, it's going to sound crazy, but I've been thinking on ways we can beef up the groups of races that have agreed to fight with us. Besides the fairies and the draugr, most races aren't very confrontational. We need warriors, not farmers."

"Yes. You sound surprisingly a lot like the first king of the dark throne. Planning to make another bargain with a god, are we?" he laughed, but when I didn't, he stopped, looking at me intensely.

"Oh, do tell," he said, leaning in towards me.

"It doesn't really have to do with gods; maybe demigods, if we're lucky." I paused, chewing over how to make this work. "Since Alaric is getting his forces from different worlds, through the rifts, why shouldn't we? I'm going to propose to Eren that a team and I go through the rift to recruit other beings to help fight this war. Since Alaric has been pulling creatures from all over the universe and timelines, I am sure there are a few creatures who want revenge on him or to get their companions back."

"Evinee ... that's brilliant," he said. Not the response I was expecting, but one I appreciated.

"Really?" I asked. "You think so?"

"Absolutely. You're right about not having the strength in abilities, fighters, or numbers. Even with those we're recruiting from our lands. This could turn the tide, and Alaric wouldn't see it coming. The only issue is the rift requires a sacrifice to be opened. And how do we get back?"

"Yes, I've thought about that. I know it's awful to think of asking anyone to sacrifice themselves, but I thought we'd go about it the same way we do during our sacrifice to Azeer every winter. Finding those who are willing, old, and sick. Eren can take away their pain. I don't know of another way to make it work."

"Light court isn't going to like that little detail."

"It's the only chance we have."

Levos said nothing for a moment as the blanket of darkness

stretched across the sky, allowing the stars to lead the way. "Why aren't you involved in the more political side of your court? You're brilliant."

I hid my smile. "My mask, remember? I need to appear as a sex object. Most males wouldn't open up to me if they believed I had an actual brain between my ears. This way, I have a hidden weapon that I can manipulate to my advantage without them ever expecting."

He leaned down, pressing his chest against my back. His lips brushed against the tip of my ear. My entire body lit up from the sensation. "Beautiful, brilliant, with a side of wicked," he whispered.

"I serve my purpose," I replied.

"But you could be so much more."

I shrugged. "I am happy to help make our court a better place and to keep my family safe."

"You're a good alfar, Evinee. I hope you see that."

I paused, thinking of all those innocent males I had killed during my life. Levos was entranced by my pretty shell, but I knew better ... I wasn't good.

I was a monster.

CHAPTER THIRTY

Genevieve

We landed in a field of lilac and sage. The smells were fresh and overwhelming in a comforting way. Even though the shadow of the night still hung over the sky, the nymph lands were extraordinary. Their settlement was in a heavily treed area deep within the forest. On the other side of the tree line, I could see the sparkling shimmer of a beautiful lake that was fed by the fresh spring water from the mountain peak.

The nymphs' homes were built within and through the trees. Their entire community was connected by bridges and ropes hung from branch to branch. Only natural materials were used in constructing their buildings. Fresh patches of gardens and farming fields were spread throughout the clearings. It was like I had stepped into paradise.

"What do you think, princess?" I heard Eren's rich voice from behind me. He leaned down and nuzzled his nose into the curve of my neck, wrapping his arms around my waist.

"I'm just glad we got here in time to try to save all of this," I answered. "Who would want to destroy such a beautiful place?"

"Mindless monsters. Thanks to you, they'll have to get through us first," he said, leaning around to kiss me.

I ran my hand down his arm before he pulled away, looking to the sky. Zerrial had landed with us, but Evinee and Levos were still nowhere to be found.

"I wish you would tell me what is going on?" I whispered. "I could help."

He ran his hand through his hair, exhaling. "I've already explained. It's not my story to tell. I just ... I know Evinee. Better than she knows herself sometimes. She can make reckless decisions and sometimes she is unpredictable, which I absolutely despise, because then I don't know where her crazy, brilliant mind has fluttered off to when I am not watching. Usually self-destruction, mayhem, and chaos. And ... because of everything recently, she's shut me out. I don't know what she's up to, which means I can't protect her from herself." He looked defeated. It was killing me.

I turned to face him, wrapped my arms around his waist. "Hey, you are a good friend. And you can't be responsible for everyone all the time. She is grown. She is going to make her own decisions, regardless of your opinions or meddling. I don't like the idea of her with Levos any more than you do. She's not good for him," I said honestly without thinking.

Eren stiffened, looking down at me. "And what is that supposed to mean? You think Levos could do better than Evinee?" he asked in a defensive tone.

"I don't mean to offend you, but come on, Eren. The madam of the dark court and innocent Levos? Doesn't quite fit. She'd break his heart as soon as he handed it over. I know him, and I know what he expects out of a relationship."

Eren pulled away. I could tell his temper was flaring. "And I know Evinee. In ways you do not," he spat.

"Oh, yes. Please, rub it in my face about how *intimately* you know Evinee," I shot back.

"That's not what I meant Genevieve and you know it."

Zerrial found an interesting tree to look at, not daring to get involved.

I threw my hands out to my sides. "Then tell me why I should expect anything more from her. I've heard the stories. I've seen her in action. I am fully aware of all her lovely attributes. She is using Levos, to whatever advantage she can swing, and I will not stand by and let that happen," I yelled.

"She is using him? Are you kidding me right now? He is the enemy. He is the one who works for the opposing court. Evinee is loyal and trustworthy. How can you not see how he is using *her* to his advantage?" he roared.

"Levos is not the enemy. I trust him with my life."

"Well, I don't. He is Gaelin Atros's cousin and right-hand man. Or are your feelings for Gaelin clouding your judgement, as always?"

I huffed in annoyance. "Here we go again. When are you going to get over your jealousy issues? I married you, not him, remember?"

"I am not the only one with jealousy issues here, princess. You can't accept my past with Evinee, even though it's been over longer than you've been alive."

"Easy for you to say. You don't have to stare Gaelin in the face every day, like I do with her. I see the way you protect her. The way you comfort her."

"Yes, and I always will. She is a part of my family. She is my oldest friend and when she needs me, I will be there. Just like I would for anyone in our family. It doesn't mean I want anything else from the relationship. I am in love with you, as I have proven time and time again."

A ragamor slammed into the ground near us while we faced off. We didn't flinch or even break eye contact. Eren and I had never fought like this before, but I wasn't backing down.

"I see the fighting has already begun," Evinee said from behind me as she strolled our way. "Zerrial, what did we miss?"

Zerrial didn't respond, focusing on something off in the distance.

Levos approached, looking from Eren to me. He gently placed a hand on my back. "Gen, everything alright?"

I snapped my head in his direction. "Of course, why wouldn't it be."

"Where were you two?" asked Eren, turning his eyes to Evinee.

"Scenic route," she replied in a sultry voice, before she sauntered by him towards the village.

Eren grumbled and headed after her. Zerrial followed, leaving Levos and me behind.

"Hey," he said, turning me towards him. "What was that all about?"

"Evinee," I said with bite.

"Popular, that one, isn't she?" he replied, trying to be playful.

"A little too popular for my liking."

He laughed. "You are aware that Lyklor is head over heels for you. You have nothing to worry about."

"He's not the one I am worried about, Levos," I said, turning towards him.

He furrowed his brow, cocking his head to the side. "And why are you worried about me? Does Evinee still plan on killing me? Because I am pretty sure letting me slide off Pasiese would have been an easy way to accomplish that."

"What do you see in her?" I asked bluntly.

He smirked. "Are you blind?"

I shook my head. "No, I am fully aware of her physical attraction. It's her other ... *skills* I'm concerned about."

"Dear Genevieve, I am touched that you feel the need to protect me, but I can look out for myself."

"Why Levos? She is nothing like Madison. And what about Vena? She must be more to your liking than Evinee."

Levos's face went stern, his stare intense and intimidating.

"Madison is gone," he said in an icy tone. "And as far as Vena and I are concerned, that is none of your business. Who I choose to spend my time with is not regulated by you. I know you are speaking out of concern, but you and Eren both need to stay the hell out of this. Am I clear?"

I nodded, feeling a bit foolish. "I'm sorry Levos. I didn't mean to offend you."

"You didn't, but I wanted to make myself clear on the matter. And for the record, Evinee turned me down."

"What? She turned *you* down?" I shook my head, astonished.

"She isn't who you think she is. Out of all people, I wouldn't have expected you to judge someone before getting to know them."

"I know her plenty, thank you."

"No, you don't," he said plainly, walking towards the others.

I followed him, embarrassment heating my cheeks. How did Levos think he knew Evinee better than I did in just three days? Was that little conversation we walked in on the other night especially life-changing? Or was she manipulating him, as I expected?

As we approached the base of the nymph village, I could feel the tension rolling off our group. A semicircle of nymphs stood in front of us. I recognized Haeza, the nymph ambassador, from when she had visited the light court. She stood beside a green-haired female who wore a crown made from twigs and crystals. The female had deep brown skin with large doe eyes. and long green lashes Her lips were full and the color of cherries. Her body was covered in a thin linen fabric, hinting at her more private parts.

Eren nodded to her, the rest of us followed. "Queen Hashian, thank you for receiving us," Eren started.

Queen Hashian's expression remained cold and unwelcoming. She did not reply.

Levos approached the queen. Her face gave way to a small smile as she extended her hand. He took it and pressed his lips against the top of her skin. Her other hand rose, stroking the length of his white-silver hair with her long, slender fingers.

"Queen Hashian," Levos said, standing upright. "Thank you for receiving us on such short notice."

"Interesting company you now keep, Ambassador Atros," she replied, scanning the lot of us.

"Desperate times call for desperate measures," Levos said.

She grunted. "Yes, we received your warning. We have scouts patrolling but we haven't discovered anything out of the ordinary."

"We are here to assist you in any way you need," Eren said.

Hashian walked past Levos until she faced Eren. She assessed him from head to toe and scoffed. "I do not require your assistance, nor want it. We've heard of your current ... *rise* in station. Apparently, the dark court will allow anything to sit on its corrupt throne," she hissed, turning towards me, "won't they?"

My magic rose in response to my anger, and I fought to keep the Dark Flame from bursting through from my skin. I turned to

Eren; his face remained the perfect vision of coolness.

"And who are you exactly referring to?" I asked. "Let me be clear." I moved in front of her so we were now face to face. "I will not be spoken to in such a disrespectful manner, nor will I allow anyone to speak to my husband that way. Erendrial Lyklor deserves everything he has accomplished. If you have the gall to question the inner workings of me or my court again, I will cancel the reinforcements currently on their way and leave you to be picked off by whatever creature comes crawling through that rift. Am I clear?"

She did not smile or flinch. Without a word, she turned around and made her way back to Haeza. She leaned down to her ambassador, whispering in her ear before taking her leave. The other nymphs followed behind her as Haeza came towards us. Eren grabbed my hand and squeezed it, giving me a small smile.

"Well, that went splendidly," Levos said, running his hand through his hair.

"Never a dull moment," Evinee added.

Zerrial grunted. "I want to kill her for speaking to the two of you in that manner."

"Wouldn't solve anything right now," Eren replied. "And we'd be down in numbers. Remember the goal."

"Alfar," Haeza spoke confidently towards us. "Please follow me to your lodgings." She turned around, heading back towards the village in the trees. At the base of their settlement, three small tents were set up on the ground. Nothing special or grand about them: they reminded me of the tent I had slept in when I first arrived in the fae lands. Only a sleeping roll and pillow were inside.

"You've got to be kidding me," Evinee said.

"Is there a problem?" Haeza asked.

"No," Eren intervened. "The lodgings are fine, thank you."

Haeza nodded to Eren before turning towards Levos. "Ambassador Levos, please follow me to your lodgings."

Levos stood in place. Haeza turned back, noting he wasn't following.

"I will stay here with my companions. Thank you, Ambassador Haeza," Levos said, moving towards the tent Zerrial stood by.

"As you wish," she said, taking a winding staircase up into the trees.

"The nerve of these nymphs," Evinee complained. "After we offered to help them. And to treat our royals in such a way. Even when they visit our court, they are treated with the utmost respect and given finer accommodations than these pieces of shit."

"Hopefully, we're not here very long," Zerrial said. "We need to get to the mountain to deal with the dwarfs."

He was right. The faster we dealt with this threat, the faster we could secure more allies. "Otar," I called. A few seconds passed before he appeared next to me.

"Yes, wicked, lovely one," he said in his usual whiny voice. "Finally done with those fairy pests I see. Thank the gods!" He stopped, sniffing the air around him, looking towards the houses in the trees. His eyes got wide as his smile grew. "Nymphs. You've brought me nymphs. Sexual little balls of deliciousness," he yelped in excitement, clapping and bouncing from foot to foot.

"No, Otar," I said. "Do not interfere with any of the nymphs. Is that clear?"

"Ahh!" he screamed, stomping his feet. "Not fair, not fair, not fair. First, you say no killing the fairies. Now, no touching nymphs."

"But there will be killing," I said, reaching for his shoulder. "Very soon."

His face lit up with excitement. "I am listening," he replied.

"There are creatures coming through the rifts that will attack this land soon," I said, kneeling to him. "I need you to do a patrol. The nymphs said they're already on it, but I only trust you."

He licked my face as he played with my hair between his fingers. "As you wish, wicked one." He pulled away and disappeared.

"I don't think I'll ever get used to that thing," Evinee commented with a look of disgust.

"Now that we have someone patrolling," Eren said to us all. "Let's try and get some rest. The others should be here by morning."

They all nodded, disappearing into their tents without another word. Eren went into our small tent first. I followed, exhausted from our fight and the lack of rest I so desperately needed. He pulled out my bed roll, placing it close to his. He readied his own bed before sitting down on the floor and taking off his boots. I sat by the opening, observing him.

"Do you plan on watching me sleep," he asked, "or are you going to come and join me?"

I smirked, kicking off my boots and crawling in besides him. He pulled me closer. I buried my nose in the center of his chest, taking in his smell.

"I'm sorry," I whispered against his shirt.

"Me too, princess."

"I hate fighting with you."

"That, we have in common. Though, you are quite sexy when you get adamant like that. I almost forgot."

I laughed, knocking my fist against his chest. "You're lucky you're so damn cute, you know that?"

"My looks are my most powerful weapon. They allowed me to conquer you, didn't they?" he said, stroking his hand down my side. He cupped my bottom, pulling my body in closer.

"Oh, is that what happened? You conquered me?" I whispered.

A low growl rattled in his throat. "Hm, I dare say, you've been my most rewarding quest yet." He leaned down, biting my bottom lip while his tongue slid across the sensitive skin.

I wrapped my arms around him, sliding my hands down his firm, muscular back. A low moan of pleasure escaped me.

"Azeer, that sound," he whispered against my lips. "I love that

I am responsible for you making that little noise." His hands continued to explore my body.

I began to undo his pants, needing to feel his body inside of me. Against me. I heard him chuckle lightly. I pulled away, looking up at him. "Is something funny?" I asked.

He smiled, flashing those beautiful bright teeth. "Someone is impatient tonight."

"I can stop if you prefer to sleep," I replied.

He chuckled, nuzzling his nose against my face. "Now, now, I didn't say that. Though, we should be resting, but I find that I'm incapable of that when you are next to me." He took my mouth, moving his lips slowly this time. I relaxed against him, his power washing over me. His fingers undid each button of my blouse too slowly.

"I need you," I pleaded to him.

"I know, princess," he said, before making all my dreams and desires come true.

CHAPTER THIRTY-ONE

Evinee

"**C**ome here, little one. Don't be afraid," said Lord Baldern. I stood by the door, praying to Azeer my father would come back for me. No amount of training was going to be enough to prepare me for this. I was sixteen. My powers were barely out of the toddler stage, and I didn't know how to control myself. This was a bad idea, but my father wouldn't listen. He needed Baldern to fund the hunt to find other creatures for the IES to experiment on. Baldern would agree to the sum my father had asked for, if he gifted my virginity to him. Little did the lord know what I was capable of.

Baldern patted the bed. "I don't bite ... much," he said.

Sick fuck, I thought to myself. I moved towards him hesitantly, wishing someone would come for me—would save me. I had to control my powers. If I lost it and killed him, my father would beat me senseless. If I tried using them and failed, Baldern would figure out what I was and turn me in. This had to go perfectly. I had no choice.

"Yes, my lord," I said in a meek voice. "How can I be of service?"

A grin spread across his face. "Undress," he demanded.

My breath caught, but I did what I was asked. I slid the straps of my dress off my shoulders, letting the fabric pool at my feet, leaving me completely bare. I was trembling with fear, fighting to hold my tears back. Without another thought, he grabbed me, slamming me into the mattress.

"No!" I screamed, jerking upright. I was drenched in sweat as I pushed the covers off my legs. "Dammit," I yelled, feeling sick and nauseous. I wiped my brow just as a deep cry filled the air. It sounded like—

"Levos!" I screamed, scrambling to my feet, pushing the flaps of the tent open.

I exited just in time to see some humanoid creatures pull Levos into the lake. Levos went under. Zerrial came flying out of his tent, dark blades ready. Eren and Gen followed, looking around.

"What happened?" asked Gen frantically.

"Levos," Zerrial said. "Those things came into our tent. I managed to kill one, but the other two took Levos.

"Where did they take him?" asked Gen, panic stretched across her face.

"The water," I said, knowing what I was going to have to do. "Wake the nymphs. They're here," I ordered, heading towards the lake. I began to take my clothes off, preparing for the dive.

"Evinee, wait," Eren demanded, but I didn't listen.

I could hear him screaming after me, but I didn't care. I picked up my pace, stripping the last article of clothing from my body. My feet hit the warm water before I dove straight in headfirst. The inviting water filled every pore. I allowed my body to adjust, bracing myself for the most painful part of the transformation. I inhaled a deep gulp of water, feeling the burning erupt in my lungs.

My body began to thrash back and forward, fighting the metamorphosis. By the second breath, a wave of relief flowed through me as my body pulled oxygen from the water. My legs melded together, forming a solid fin and tail. Spikes sprouted down my back, stretching along the length of my tail. Webs of skin formed in between each finger. My teeth elongated as small slits of gills opened along my neck. My eyes adjusted to the lack of light and were now able to see as clearly as I did on land. My long claws were the last part to change: the weapons I would need to save Levos.

I calmed myself, searching the surrounding water for any sign of the creatures. I spotted legs kicking frantically at the mouth of a cave. I took off towards the movement, whipping my tail ferociously, cutting through the water like an arrow. My eyes adjusted to the darkness the deeper I dove. I had to get to Levos fast, before he ran out of air.

I got to the entrance of the cave and two spears came flying at me. I dodged the first and caught the second, twirled, and threw it back towards the monster, nailing it in the chest. I saw Levos, weighed down with a net and rocks in the center of the cave.

I rushed towards him but was pulled back by another creature. Without a second though I turned, slicing, biting, and shredding through him, sending bloody bits of flesh and body parts floating throughout the cave.

I removed the weights; Levos lay unresponsive. I pressed my mouth to his, using my lungs to filter the oxygen out of the water. I forced the air into his lungs and he breathed in deeply, choking. He opened his eyes, looking at me for a moment in fear. He scurried away, reaching for his throat, needing more oxygen. I put my hands up in a surrendering motion, pointing to my mouth and then his. His eyes widened, realizing who I was. I approached him slowly, placing my lips to his once more. He breathed in shallowly at first and then deeper, realizing it was safe.

Once he was able to stay conscious, he held onto me while we exited the cave. Hundreds of the creatures were emerging from a small rift I could see open at the bottom of the lake. As we swam to the surface, they attacked. I gave Levos another breath of air before the fight began. I ran through them, sending bone spurs into their fragile bodies. The ones that dared to get too close ended up dismembered. Levos called on his power, blasting the creatures back and restraining them with vines that erupted from the bed of the lake.

Once we had a clear path to land, I took it, grabbing ahold of Levos and swimming towards the surface. As we broke through the skin of the water, Levos took a deep breath, gasping for air, expelling the water from his lungs. I held onto him, pushing us towards the shore.

"Are you okay?" I asked.

He nodded, still choking. He examined my face and my form.

"Stop staring or I'm going to let go," I said.

"Sorry, I can't help it. You're magnificent."

"Most males would say terrifying, but thank you." On the shore, the battle had reached the surface. Leenia and the others flew in from the sky, landing just in time as their ragamors tore into the creatures. Powers of nature, darkness, and fire consumed the surface of the lake.

I got Levos to the beach, turning back towards the hordes that continued to pour from the rift.

He looked at me, shaking his head. "You can't take them all on your own."

"No, but I can stop a lot of them from reaching the surface."

"Evinee, no," he said, reaching his hand out towards me. "Fight with us, on land. We'll watch out for each other."

"Go, Levos," I said, and dived back underneath the water.

Dozens of them flooded into our world. The rift shimmered with magic. I called on my gifts, manipulating the water around me into a force of power towards the swarms, sending them tumbling back across the lake. I slashed my tail at those near me, using my claws to sever their necks from their shoulders. I swam faster than I ever had, sinking my teeth into them while my claws ripped their flesh open. Bone spears flew through the water, landing in their chests and heads. Body after body floated to the surface, dead.

I heard it coming before I could see or shield from it ... then ... I felt it. A long metal spear protruded from my abdomen. My blood floated in the water around me. I pulled it free, turning just in time to spike the creature who attempted to attack. The monster was hairless. Its skin was covered in a mucus-like texture. It had large, insect-like black eyes, no nose, and a small set of little teeth scattered in its mouth. Long, lean, muscular limbs and webbed feet and hands allowed the creature to move seamlessly throughout the water.

I pulled the spear from it, and the lifeless corpse floated to the top with its comrades. I continued to fight, even though I could feel myself weakening from the loss of blood. The wound wasn't healing. Something was wrong. I shredded the creatures apart until nothing living remained in the lake but me.

My body heated as I reached the surface. My heart slowed. Even though I had a fever, my body felt cold. My fin couldn't take me any further. I saw the others on land, fighting off the last of them. I managed to pull myself up on the shore. Zerrial turned towards me, locking his eyes with mine. I reached for him, pain of my transformation beginning to take hold. I yelled out in agony.

Zerrial rushed me, his dark sword high, aiming to attack. I couldn't say or do anything to prevent it. As his footsteps quickened, I closed my eyes, readying myself for the end.

Suddenly, Zerrial collapsed into the ground, holding his head in pain. My vision began to flicker. I saw a pair of black boots. Eren appeared, turning me over gently. My breathing was rapid. I could move my hand to the wound on my abdomen, but I couldn't say anything. Another yell of pain escaped my lips while my fin split into two, allowing my legs to form. My bones snapped back into place. My teeth retracted, along with my claws. I gasped for breath, but no relief came. I siphoned just enough of my power to make sure my physical facade did not falter. The last thing I remembered was feeling the warm sand under my naked body.

Chapter Thirty-Two

I woke in a warm hut. My head was spinning. A large animal hide was draped over my body. I was still naked underneath and covered in sweat I pulled back the blanket, looking down at my wound. Small green veins of what I presumed was poison sprouted from the opening. A patch of herbs sat on top of the slit. I winced, laying my head back against the pillow.

Footsteps approached and Eren's face appeared. He sat down on the stool next to me with a small smile on his face, pushing the hair from my sticky forehead.

"Poison?" I asked in a raspy voice.

He nodded, bringing a cup of water to my lips. I took small sips until I began choking. He sat me up, sliding another pillow under my head. I looked around the quiet wooden hut. The fresh breeze flapped against the curtains that hung in the open windows. Fresh herbs and greenery hung from the ceiling, and small flames flickered from candles placed along the wall.

"They upgraded my lodging arrangements, I see," I said.

Eren laughed. "Yes, they've suddenly changed their opinions of us. Looks like we'll be staying in comfort from now on."

I nodded. "How long was I out?"

"Only ten hours. Not your longest."

"How many saw?" I asked, afraid to know the answer.

He licked his lips, placing his elbows on his knees. "Only our family. I made sure of it."

I exhaled.

"They have questions, Ev," he said softly.

"I'm sure they do." I ran my hand over the soft animal fur. "Is Levos okay?"

Eren scoffed, shaking his head. "I want to make it perfectly clear that I value your life over his. The next time that idiot goes and gets himself kidnapped, you do not risk your life. Yours is worth ten times over his."

I waited for a moment, chewing on the bottom of my lip. "Well … I disagree."

He chuckled. "Of course, you do. The light prick is fine. He owes you a life debt."

"He kept my secret; I saved his life. I think we're even."

"More than even," Eren said, taking a glass of whiskey from the nightstand and sipping it. "By the way, you were a complete badass today. You tore through at least a hundred of those things all on your own. Probably more. There were so many random body parts floating in the lake we couldn't tell which ones they belong to. Needless to say, I don't think the nymphs will be bathing in that lake anytime soon."

I laughed, and the pain in my abdomen stabbed at me. I grabbed at the wound and hissed.

Eren lunged forward, placing a hand on me. "Are you alright?"

"Yes, it just hurts. How long till I heal?"

"We're unsure. We got it to stop spreading, but their healer has never seen this type of poison before. Time will tell."

"Fantastic. Can you get me my clothes please?" I asked.

"And where do you think you're going?"

"Well, I would like to not remain naked, for one. But two, I want to get the questioning out of the way from everyone who saw. I just want to be done with it and move on."

"There's no rush. They will understand that you need time."

"I know, but I just want it over. Now please, will you stop arguing and do one thing I ask?"

"Bossy," he hissed.

"Pain," I replied.

He placed a thin green dress on the bed and then took his leave. I managed to pull the dress over my shoulders, even though my wound protested and stung the entire time. Once I was finished, I sat at the edge of the bed, waiting for my family. A few minutes later they all entered, assessing me one-by-one.

For the better part of two centuries, I had kept this from them. They had shared some of their deepest and darkest parts of themselves, and I had chosen to hide who I truly was.

Gen was nowhere to be found. Levos came in last, leaning against the wall as the door shut behind him. I stared at them ... my family ... five pairs of eyes staring back at me. I didn't know where to begin. I began to fiddle with my fingers.

"I ... I'm sorry I—" I managed to get out, before Leenia came crashing into me. She wrapped her arms around my bruised form.

"I'm so glad you're okay," said Leenia. "You had us worried."

"Uh," piped in Voz. "Can we talk about all the bodies she left in her murderous wake? Awesome!"

"Imagine," added Oz, "if we had a whole army of Evinees. We would bring this world to its knees."

I laughed as tears streamed down my face. "You guys aren't ... aren't mad at me?"

"Why would we be?" asked Doria.

"Eren explained everything," said Zerrial. "At least, the part about you wanting to lessen our load of harbored secrets."

"But, as I have explained many times before," said Eren, "we are the masters of secrets. What's one more?" He shrugged, winking at me.

"You can always tell us anything," reassured Leenia, stroking my hair. "Biology doesn't define you. If that was the case, we'd all be royally fucked. No pun intended, Lyklor." They all began laughing, nodding in agreement.

"Thank you all for understanding," I whispered.

Zerrial came and knelt next to me. He took my hand and kissed the side of my cheek. "No more secrets," he said.

I nodded in agreement. My family formed a circle, wrapping their arms around each other.

"Now that we have all the mushy shit out of the way," said Oz, "can we talk about those glorious teeth of yours?"

"And the spikes," added Voz. "Magnificent."

"The singing," Oz gasped. "We must hear the singing."

I laughed, wiping the tears from my face.

"She is not something to experiment on, Telgarie brothers," snapped Eren, always the protector.

"Of course," nodded Oz, bowing dramatically towards Eren.

Voz followed. "Whatever you say, my liege. Please, accept our humble apology."

"Don't worry about it," I said, winking at them. "I'll sing for you sometime. I'll make you both fall in love with me."

Voz dropped to his knees with a flourish, placing his hands over his heart. "Aren't we already?" he said passionately.

Doria pushed him over. "Shut up, idiot," she said, shaking her head.

"We should let you get some rest," Leenia said, ushering the others towards the door. "We'll see you in the morning, since it looks like we'll be staying a few more nights."

I looked to Eren. "Why?" I asked. "We need to be getting to the mountain."

"We will get there," Eren explained, "but right now, we need to focus on getting you better. We've also agreed to stay for their summer solstice celebration tomorrow evening. Look at it as a trust-building exercise."

Doria huffed. "Right. More like them groveling because they would all be dead without us."

"Now Doria," said Eren, "try looking on the positive side of things. Aren't you supposed to be a radiating ball of joy with your impending nuptials on the horizon?"

"Eren," she snapped back. "Do you really think 'radiating ball of joy' fits my personality?"

He laughed. "It does when Hashen is in the room."

Lightning cracked outside the hut as Doria's fists clenched.

"Funny," Voz commented. "I didn't think it was going to rain."

"Nor I, brother," added Oz.

"Oh, would the two of you shut up!" said Doria.

"Alright, alright, that's enough," demanded Zerrial. "All of you out."

Leenia squeeze my hand one more time before taking her leave.

I looked towards Eren. "Does Gen have questions?" I asked.

He shrugged. "We'll talk about that later. Right now, you focus on resting." He bent down and kissed my head. Eren nodded at Levos, who was still posted at the door, then hesitated. I could tell he was debating if he should leave us alone. He looked back at me, his hand on the doorknob and gave me a small smile before taking his leave.

Levos finally pulled away from the door, walking casually to me. He took a seat on the edge of the bed.

"Well," he started, "if I didn't think you were amazing before … damn, talk about exceeding expectations."

I laughed, covering my face. "That wasn't exactly how I wanted you seeing me in that form for the first time."

"What was missing? A home-cooked meal and a romantic place setting?"

"Well," I replied dryly, "you were the one who had to go and get themselves kidnapped in the middle of the night."

"I am telling you: these creatures can't keep their hands off me."

I chuckled, aware of my aching stomach. I felt his knuckles along the side of my cheek. I closed my eyes, leaning into the contact. He took my chin between his fingers, turning my face towards him.

"I owe you my life," he said seriously. "Thank you Evinee … truly."

I smiled, not knowing what to say. He dropped his hands from my face, standing from the bed. He offered his arm for support while I inched myself back into the mattress. He covered me with the blanket and fluffed my pillows.

"Need anything before I go?" he asked, moving a piece of hair from my face.

"I'm good. Thanks."

He nodded, moving towards the door. "Oh," he said, "tomorrow, we're telling Eren and Gen about your idea with the rift. After watching how the nymphs fought today, you were right. We need warriors, or we're all dead."

"Glad you see it my way," I said playfully.

He smirked, opening the door slowly. "Good night, my little *minnow*."

My eyes bore into him. "Do not. Call. Me. That," I demanded.

He chuckled. "I kind of like it. It's cute, don't you think?"

"No."

"Whatever you say ... minnow."

I threw Eren's whiskey glass so hard, my wound burned from the action. Levos shut the door just in time, causing the glass to shatter on the surface. I could hear his deep laugh even with the door between us. I let out a frustrated sigh before dropping my head back down on the pillow.

A burning sensation from the poison pulled me from sleep. I managed to swing my legs over the edge of the bed, planting my feet firmly on the ground. I stood slowly, feeling a little lightheaded. I walked to the mirror, pulling my dress up to my wound and removed the bandage. The green veins were receding, but the skin around the area remained raised. The injury was healing, just at a slower rate than normal.

I soaked myself in the stone bathtub in the washroom, removing the smells of the lake from my body and hair. From the wardrobe I took out a short flimsy white dress. I stared at the thin piece of clothing, detesting the lack of color. I wasn't sure I had ever worn white before. It had a low neck and cuffed sleeves that hung off my shoulders. Assorted fragrances were spread across the dresser in the corner. I found one that smelled like sage and fresh rain and placed a few droplets under my jawline and on either wrist.

I let my hair dry naturally, soft waves forming around my face. My purple streaks were still visible. I ran my hands over my figure, feeling the hunger inside of me grow. I couldn't remember the last time I ate a full meal. The transformation yesterday had taken a lot out of me. If I didn't replenish, I would begin to lose hold on my magic and this healthy appearance I portrayed.

The door clicked open behind me. I turned, surprised to see Gen standing in the doorway. "May I come in?" she asked.

"Of course, princess," I said, turning to face her.

She closed the door, trailing her eyes across me slowly before moving further into the room. "You look well," she added.

"I'm feeling better. Minor pain from the wound, but it is fading."

"Good," she said, moving closer towards me. She examined my face, taking her time. "A siren, huh? A half-breed."

I nodded.

"My other half is just a lowly human," she said, approaching the table and two chairs that were to the side of the room. I followed her. "At least your other half is something interesting."

I let a small laugh escape. "I wouldn't go that far. More like a liability," I replied.

She smiled as we sat. "A liability? You think so?"

I shrugged. "If I lose control, yes."

"And how often do you lose control? Was the situation back at the fairy court between you and Levos the outcome of you 'losing control'?"

I paused. "What are you getting at, princess?" I asked.

She exhaled, leaning towards me. "Regardless of what Eren says, Levos is a good male. An honest male. He deserves happiness and security. Someone who is ... stable. Those are things you cannot give him. You said so yourself, you are a liability. I need you to stay away from him. I need him to remain safe."

"And what makes you think I would ever hurt Levos?" I asked.

"I spend a lot of time reading. Something Levos and I have in common. I don't presume to know much about your kind, but I do know that the other races viewed your species enough of a threat that they worked together to eradicate your ancestors. That tells me you are a risk. To get to the point: I don't want you involved with my friend."

My breath quickened with anger. "What are you trying to say, princess? That I should be put down because I am a threat? Something you can't control?"

She sat back in her chair calmly, keeping her eyes on me. Dark flames began to twirl around her fingers.

"I'm saying, if you give me a reason to question or doubt your ability to control your wilder side, I won't hesitate to protect those that I love. And for the record, everything is controllable. You just have to find the right leash."

My vision narrowed and my teeth and nails elongated. I jumped to my feet, knocking the table across the room, shattering it against the wall. She rose, readying to attack.

"Those who *you* love?" I sneered. "How dare you come into my family and threaten me! Acting as if you know what is in their best interest."

"You are unpredictable and a danger to everyone you come in contact with," she barked.

I took a step forward, ready to remove her head from her shoulders when the door flew open. Levos barged in, followed by Eren. Both males froze, staring at the two of us.

"What in the hell is going on?" asked Levos.

Gen and I didn't take our eyes from one another. Eren placed a hand on each of our shoulders.

"I don't know what has transpired, but we all need to take a breath before one of us does something we're going to regret," he said.

"You want to know what happened, Eren?" I said, still grinding my teeth. "Your *wife* threatened to put me down like some wild animal if I stepped out of line."

Eren turned to Gen. "You did what?" he asked.

She took a step back. "She doesn't have control over her siren half. She is a danger to everyone around her," she stated.

Levos walked over to the three of us, eyes locked onto Gen. "Please tell me," Levos started, "you did not just threaten to kill the female who saved my life and the nymph territories a few hours ago. Who risked her own life for an alfar male who serves the opposing court. Who acted selflessly without a single regard for her own well-being."

Gen rolled her eyes. "Oh, come on Levos. You're under her spell," she said, folding her arms over her chest. "For all we know, she could have seduced you and sung her little song and now you're defending her because you've lost all control."

Levos huffed, taking a moment. "I've never been more disappointed to call you my friend than I am right now, Genevieve. You are completely out of line and blinded by your own insecurities."

"This has nothing to do with me and everything to do with—" Gen started to say, but Levos cut her off.

"The fact that you don't realize where this hatred is coming from speaks volumes," Levos spat. "How do you expect to run a kingdom when you can't even separate your personal feelings from the truth in a situation? Do you plan to rule like Queen Daealla?"

He paused, letting the words sink in.

"I was just looking out for you," she replied in a softer tone.

"For the last time, I do not need, nor do I want, your help," Levos said, reaching for my hand, pulling us from the room.

We headed down the stairs and into a small dining area. Attendants went from table to table taking orders. I could smell fresh soup and warm tea. My mouth watered from the overload of senses as we took a seat against an open window. I could tell Levos was still fuming as he sat across from me, not making eye contact.

A waitress stopped by. I ordered myself tea and some food. Levos didn't say a word. I ordered him the same. I didn't know what to say to him. I wasn't usually in the business of meddling in other people's relationships, but I was the cause of this mess, and I didn't know how to act.

"Want to talk about it?" I asked.

He wrapped his hands around his warm cup of tea, leaning back into his chair. "I don't know if the power has gone to her head, or she did indeed come back different, but the Gen I knew would never have threatened someone's life based off of assumptions about their biology."

"I think there's more to it than that, Levos. I think there's an element of jealousy about Eren and I, and she obviously can't stand the thought of you and me," I replied.

"There is no you and me," he answered.

"Yes, but even a friendship. She sees me as competition. Eren and I had a relationship long before her, and now you and I are forming one. I am encroaching on the two most important males in her life."

"I still can't believe she actually threatened to put you down."

"She basically told me the sirens deserved what they got. Don't get me wrong, I wasn't obviously alive when the genocide happened, but from what I've been told, the sirens kept to themselves. They just wanted to be left alone."

"Where did you get your information?" he asked.

"When my father died, I helped the other creatures in his lab escape. There was a mermaid that shared a tank with my mother. She told me about her and what she was like. She also gave me a small purple gem I keep hidden back in the dark court. It is the only thing I have of my mother's."

Levos reached across the table, taking my hand. "I'm sorry you never got to know her."

I smiled. "Thank you." The food arrived: a large bowl of vegetable soup with a loaf of bread. My stomach growled with anticipation as I dug in. Levos sat across the table, staring at me. I paused, wiping my mouth. "Is there something wrong with yours?" I asked.

"Not at all. I just think this is the first time I've seen you eat all week."

"The transitioning. It takes a lot out of me. If I don't get my strength up, I lose control of my power and my real—" I stopped, swallowing the food in my mouth, diverting my eyes.

"Your real what?" he asked, leaning towards me.

I didn't answer.

"More secrets, huh?"

I ignored him, turning my attention back to my food. "So … are you going to go talk to Gen?" I asked, changing the subject.

He shook his head. "I think I'll let Lyklor take care of her. I can't imagine he's very happy with her threatening his closest friend."

I shrugged, taking another spoonful of soup. As if they heard us calling, Eren and Gen appeared in the doorway of the café. I straightened, locking my eyes on them. Levos turned, spotting them and then grunted in aggravation. They walked over to us. Eren took two chairs from another table and slid them over to the edge of ours. I scooted around closer to Levos while they took their seats. Levos stared at Gen, not taking his eyes off her. I looked to Eren for guidance. He gave me a small smile and winked.

"I think the four of us need to talk," started Eren. "Since we don't need to traumatize the nymphs any more than they already are, I would suggest everyone keep their tempers and gifts in check. Can we all do that?"

I nodded and so did Levos and Gen.

"Good. Now, I am just going to pull the thorn out here and dive right in, so we can all have a merry summer solstice." Eren paused, looking from me to Gen. "You two are the most important females in my life. I care about you both. I love you both. Gen is my wife, and she will always come first. But, princess," he said, turning towards her, "when I feel you are out of line or heading down the wrong path, I will always challenge you, because that is how we grow stronger, together and separately."

Eren paused, shifting his focus to me. "Evinee," he said, "you and I have been through hell and back at least a dozen times during our life together. I trust no one more than I trust you. I feel protective over you, as I know you do me. I will always be there for you, no matter what. With that being said, we are all aware of your and my past relations. I am sorry if I have ever caused you pain, but from conversations you and I have had, I also know that you understand where my heart is, and I know you want me to be happy, just as I do you."

Eren shifted his focus to Levos. He stared at him, narrowing his eyes before he spoke. "I am not blind," Eren said. "I know there is something between the two of you. Whatever it is, I want you to know right now, you do not deserve her. But if she chooses to trust you or continue the relationship, that is her choice, and hers alone. I won't stand in the way of her happiness. Both females seem to trust you. I do not. But I will do a better job of trying to understand you and not base my opinion off who your relatives are. But I promise you, if you ever take our secrets or our court's information and weaponize it against us, I will not hesitate to kill you. Are we clear?"

"Perfectly," Levos said without hesitation.

Eren nodded, patting Levos on the back. "Now," Eren said, standing to his feet. "I think we should let the females talk for a bit. Join me for a drink, will you?"

Levos stood, looking between the two of us. "I'll be right outside," Levos whispered nodding to me. I smiled, bring the tea up to my lips.

Gen sat across the table, staring out the window past me. Once they left, I placed my teacup down, readying for a fight.

"Now that our keeper is gone, what other threats would you like to toss my way?" I asked.

Her jaw tightened as she turned her eyes to me. "I'm sorry for threatening to kill you," she replied.

"Ha, like you could," I mumbled, bringing the tea back up to my lips.

"Evinee, I'm … I'm insecure at times, about Eren and I," she admitted.

I didn't say a word.

"I wasn't raised like the rest of you," she continued. "I still can't understand how monogamy is not important to you."

"Hasn't Eren already promised you monogamy?" I asked.

"Yes, but … but what happens in one hundred years when he gets bored, or wants something different? I am worried that I won't be enough for the extent of our lives together. And then there's you. Not only are you drop dead gorgeous, and you have this ability to flirt the pants off anyone you come in contact with, you're a freaking siren. Some extinct, mythological creature, whose sole purpose is to seduce men."

I shrugged, "I mean, that's not my sole purpose but—"

"And on top of that, the fact that you and Eren have been intimate just throws me. He still cares so much about you and the two of you are so much alike. Gods, if I was him, I would have chosen you," she exhaled, sitting back in the chair.

"Gen," I said softly, leaning towards her, "there was never a choice. He fell in love with you. Real love. A kind of love I didn't know existed. And yes, we are a lot alike, but we probably would have ended up killing each other along the way. He needed someone like you. With feelings and with a heart. Someone who can combat the darkness inside of him. In the end, all I care about is that he is happy and safe. If you do that for him, then you and I have no qualm."

She processed the information for a few moments. "What about Levos?" she asked. "How does he fit into your life?"

"I like him," I admitted, "more than I thought I was capable of. He is kind and trustworthy. But I would never put him in danger. I am in control of my powers for the most part, but if I am physical with someone, it gets harder not to kill them. The animal inside me wants to take over and do what I was designed to do. Believe it or not, most of the men who have claimed to have visited my bed haven't. It's all an illusion. A mask I wear, just like Eren's."

She chuckled. "You all are full of surprises," she said.

"Coming from the half-breed who came back from death," I pointed out.

We laughed together for the first time.

"I am sorry," she said, "for all those hateful things I said."

"Let's start over," I suggested. "You keep Eren happy and alive, and I will make sure I don't kill little Levos. Deal?" I extended my hand to her, and she took it as we shook in agreement.

"Now," she said, standing from her chair, "I am ready for a fae summer solstice party. Tomorrow officially marks a year I've been in these lands. Crazy to think how so much has changed in that short amount of time."

I stood, heading towards the door. "Tell me about it." I paused, looking at her.

She furrowed her brow. "What is it?"

"On the grounds of our new friendship, I need your support with something that Eren isn't going to like," I confessed.

"Eren, it's a good idea and you know it," I said.

Eren paused, looking from me to Gen while he paced in front of the table where we sat in the tree house.

"And you're in agreement? The two of you are best friends all of the sudden?" he snapped.

"I'm not saying it is going to be an easy task," Gen answered. "But this is a good idea. Even with the entire force of the fae continent, we don't stand a chance against Alaric and his forces. We do not know for sure if we'll be able to free Narella in time to help. Evinee is more than capable to lead this mission. We will gather a team that will assist her through the rift."

"I'm going," Eren demanded. "If you insist on marching yourself into a death trap, I'm going with you."

"Eren, you can't," I said. "You're going to be our future king. You're needed here, to run this side of the war. Your life matters."

"So does yours," he replied in a low voice.

"Hey," I said, standing and making my way over to him. "Are you really doubting my abilities to sway someone to our side? After all these years of watching me master my craft, you still doubt me?"

He huffed. "No, I don't doubt you, but I'm ... I'm frightened for you. We don't know what is on the other side of those rifts. No one has ever traveled across from our world."

"I'll be fine. I'll do my best to come back in one piece. And hopefully I will come back with more reinforcements."

Eren ran his hand through his hair. "You're taking Leenia," he demanded. "She's the best warrior we have."

I nodded in agreement. "I was thinking Voz and Oz as well, if you could spare them. I am sure they will be excited to explore different worlds and creatures. Plus, they could assist with getting back home."

"Of course," Eren said.

Gen stood and walked to us, taking both our hands. "This is going to work," she said, looking hopeful. "Everyone is going to come home."

Eren's eyes were heavy with worry. He pulled both of us in, holding onto us tight.

"Go get the others, Evinee," Eren said, letting me go. "We will inform them of the plan."

I nodded, leaving the small hut to gather our family.

"Hell yes!" yelled Voz and Oz in unison.

"Why didn't we think of this?" asked Voz.

"Right," replied Oz. "Evinee is catching up to us in the brains department. We must up our game."

"Would you two stop it?" snapped Doria. "This is not a joking matter. This is a suicide mission. I do not agree. My vote is no."

I looked back at Levos sitting in the corner of the room, trying to stay out of the way.

"I agree," added Zerrial. "This is too much of a risk. And we aren't even sure if you'll able to recruit anything, let alone get home."

"Oh, we've got that handled," Voz said, looking to his brother.

"Yes, perfectly under control," added Oz.

"What are you two getting at?" asked Eren.

The twins giggled, moving into the center of our circle. "We've been studying the rifts ever since Gen's mad uncle found a way to open it himself," said Voz.

"Yes," added Oz. "We've been obsessed with it for months. But we couldn't find a way to open the damn things without the blood sacrifice the recipe calls for."

"But thanks to Ambassador Levos," Voz said, nodding in his direction. "We've solved the last piece of the puzzle." Levos nodded back with a small smile.

"How?" asked Gen.

"We've created a machine," started Oz, "that works as an anchor between worlds."

"We took the fueling concept from our dark weapons design, thanks to Ambassador Levos's keen observations," continued Voz. "We used our blood and the ambassador's blood to create a fueling system that pulls the magic from both, opening a small, door-sized portal into different realms."

"But how can you be certain which realm you will be opening the door to?" Gen asked.

"That is our only unknown variable," Voz said with a wince.

"But no matter what world the portal sends us to," added Oz, "we will be able to get home, thanks to our signal beacons."

"We will travel with one," explained Voz, "and we will keep the other safe within the kingdom."

"When we are ready to come home," said Oz, "the beacon here will act as a bridge to ours, creating a direct anchor for the portal to attach to."

"You two are brilliant," Gen said, in awe.

They shrugged. "We can't take credit for this one," said Voz.

"Besides the dark magic fueling system," added Oz, "the rest of the system was the ambassador's idea."

We all turned to look at Levos. He acted as if he didn't notice.

"This is still too unpredictable," Doria said.

"Family vote it is," Eren said. "All in favor of going into the rift in search of recruits, say aye."

"Aye," said Voz, Oz, Gen, Leenia, and myself.

"All opposed, say nay," Eren said.

"Nay," said Doria and Zerrial.

"Looks like the four of you are going into the rift," said Eren.

"The five of us, you mean," added Levos, standing to his feet.

"No," I said plainly.

He strolled next to me with a hurt look on his face. "What, you can risk your life to save our world, but I can't? Plus, the light king and queen insist I attend. The data we would collect from this little trip is priceless."

I felt him graze his knuckles down the length of my back without anyone noticing. I elbowed him in the ribs, causing him to grunt. I smiled to myself with satisfaction.

"Well, it's settled," said Eren. "The five of you will leave tomorrow after the festivities this evening. Tonight, we will spend together."

"Hopefully, it won't be the last," added Doria, her voice laced with worry.

We all stood in silence, looking at each other. The room felt heavy.

"It won't be. It can't," whispered Leenia.

"We've been through too much together this past century for this to be the end," I added.

Voz laughed. "Like the time we robbed the crown's coffers," he said. We all began to laugh at the memory. "Sorry, princess."

"No need to apologize to me," she replied, smiling.

"Or the time we let the draugr into Icici's birthday celebration she had been planning for a year," said Oz.

"She was so pissed," Doria, giggled.

"Her face was priceless," Zerrial added.

Another moment passed as we all settled down.

"Remember when Eren became ambassador?" asked Leenia.

We all nodded, remembering the emotions of that moment. The pride each of us felt. Through his success, we had all elevated ourselves.

"That's when everything changed," I said, looking to Eren. "For the better."

"We all made that happen," Eren whispered.

"Without each other," Leenia pointed out, "who knows where we all would have ended up?"

"Probably dead," said Voz.

"Definitely dead," said Zerrial.

"Without a doubt," added Doria.

"This isn't the end," I said, taking a more serious tone. "We will be successful in this mission. And when we return, we will have a party that will outshine any other we've had to date."

"Promise," Doria said. "Promise you all are coming home."

The four of us nodded.

Doria turned her attention to Levos. "You too, ambassador of the light. Against my better judgment, you've grown on me."

He smiled at her, bowing slightly. "I will do my best to return in one piece. Though, with my current track record, I can't promise something isn't going to try and eat me along the way."

We roared.

"Pyra wasn't to your liking?" asked Gen.

"I can still feel her teeth, even though the wound has healed for the most part," answered Levos. "I don't know if I'll ever recovery fully."

"Alright," interrupted Eren. "Enough talk about eating little

Atros. I'm going to be sick."

"Alright, alright," I said. "If I remember correctly, the nymphs promised us free food, alcohol, and entertainment. After almost dying twenty-four hours ago, I am ready to live."

"And this is why you're my favorite," Voz said, heading towards the door.

"Always have been, always will be," Oz added, following him out.

I turned for the door as Levos placed his arm around me, leaning down to whisper. "Looks like we're going on a little adventure together, minnow," he said.

I threw his hand off my shoulder. "I should have let you drown," I replied.

He laughed. "Don't lie to yourself. You and I both know you'd have missed me."

I rolled my eyes as we all headed to the party.

CHAPTER THIRTY-THREE

That night, we drank and partied like it would be our last. I hadn't been separated from my family since we had all come together as one. I stopped myself from thinking about how much I would miss them and how worried I was about leaving. The faster I accomplished our objective, the faster we would be reunited.

Though the nymphs couldn't fight worth shit, they knew how to throw a party. Brilliant light shows stretched across the sky while ribbons and streamers fluttered through the air. Their food was delicious, and the wine flowed freely the entire evening. The music was transcendent as we all bounced and moved to the lively compositions. Even Zerrial joined in.

Gen and I swung each other around, laughing and smiling while the wine and ambrosia took us on a trip. I decided she wasn't too bad. She knew how to let go and have fun, which was always something I appreciated in an alfar. The nymphs around us began to get handsy as they celebrated the longest day of the year. Clothes began to come off and groups of them moved deeper into the woods.

Levos appeared, sliding his arms around me, his body swaying in sync with mine.

"You look like you're enjoying yourself," he said, resting his head against my hair.

I laced my fingers with his, enjoying the feeling of him so close. "Mm, you're going to get yourself killed, little Atros," I said, turning around to face him. I slid my hands up his chest until I wrapped my arms around his neck.

"Planning on taking another bite out of me?" he asked, a soft smile on his face as he leaned down until our noses touched.

"Azeer, I want to," I whispered. The feeling of his body against mine was almost too much.

Levos slid his hand through my hair, grabbing a handful, pulling my head back. His golden eyes flickered in the moonlight. His expression was soft and relaxed while his eyes traveled around my face. "I'm not afraid of you," he said softly.

"You should be," I whispered, taking in a breath. His caramel fragrance made my mouth water.

He leaned down, brushing his soft, full lips against mine. A small whine escaped me. Levos chuckled against my lips.

"Stop fighting, and let me make you happy," he said, pressing the sweetest kiss to my mouth.

He pulled away. I peered up into his eyes.

"I don't know how to be ..." I swallowed my pride. "... happy," I admitted.

His hand stroked the side of my face, tracing down my neck intimately. "Well, I'd love to try, if you'd give me the honor."

I moved his hand from my face, kissing it softly before stepping away. "We need to focus right now," I said. "We can't afford any distraction."

He ran his hands over his face, exhaling. "You're right, I know you are," he said. "I just ... I've never wanted another this badly before," he admitted, laughing a bit. "I'm sorry, you're right. I am going to take this mission seriously, I promise. No distractions."

I laughed, taking a step towards him. "Thank you for understanding," I whispered, kissing him gently on the cheek.

I turned away, heading to my hut. In the morning, we would leave, embarking on an impossible mission.

"Ready!" yelled the twins at the same time.

I looked back at Eren, not knowing what to say. I opened my mouth, but he shook his head.

"Don't say it," he said, not able to make eye contact with me. "Don't say goodbye. This isn't goodbye."

I smiled, taking a step towards him. "Think of it as a vacation from my overly emotional crazy ass," I offered, pushing him gently.

"It's going to be quite boring without you," he replied.

"Of course it will be. I expect you all to be miserable and bored without me."

"I promise," he said. He held out his arms and I raced into them. He squeezed me tight. "Please be careful."

"I will, I promise," I pulled away from him with tears in my eyes.

"Okay," Doria said, carrying bundles of bags alongside her. "These provisions should last you all about two weeks. Hopefully you won't be gone longer than that, but if you are, you're on your own for food. I added a water filter in each pack along with a fire starter kit, bed rolls, and some essentials."

I walked over to her. "Thank you," I said. "I know you aren't for this plan, but I appreciate your support and attention to detail when it comes to the survival sacks."

"Well," she replied, "trying to prevent you all from dying early on, at least. It's the least I can do." I rushed her, wrapping my arms around her small frame.

"Thank you, sister," I whispered.

"Please be safe," she said, pulling away. "And I swear, if you or any of the others get killed, I'll bring you all back and torture the shit out of you."

I laughed, grabbing a pack. "It's a promise."

Gen was behind me. She shrugged awkwardly. I wrapped her up in my arms, pulling her in.

"Take care of him for me, will you?" I said, nodding towards Eren.

"Always," she replied. "And you do the same for Levos."

"Deal."

Zerrial was next, giving me a huge bear hug as only he could.

The twins were setting up the device. Levos joined them, slicing his hand and filling one side of their cylinder. Voz filled the other.

"Ready to make history?" Oz asked, turning towards me as Leenia joined my side.

"We're fucking crazy," Leenia commented, a dazed look on her face. We all laughed.

"Would we be us if we weren't crazy?" I asked.

"We'd be fucking alive, I know that."

I bumped her shoulder and we both laughed, stepping up to the males.

"Let's get this shit over with," said Leenia.

"Here goes nothing," said Voz. He flipped the switch and turned a dial as the energy surged through the machine. A loud zap shot through the air, a metallic black and purple static door appearing in front of us. It vibrated, pulling the energy from the blood the males had provided.

Oz went to Eren, handing him the other beacon we would need to return home. Once we were all together, we loaded up our packs and weapons, looking at each other.

"Well," said Oz, "here goes nothing." He stepped through the rift, disappearing into thin air. Voz followed, then Leenia. I took one last look back at the rest of my family. They smiled, trying to hide their worry. I turned forward, looking at Levos.

He winked at me. "After you, little minnow," he said.

I took a deep breath, stepping through the portal.

My body felt like it was being pulled apart at every joint. Electricity shot through me as I closed my eyes, locking my jaw to prevent a scream of pain from escaping. I held onto my bag and my weapons tightly, knowing they would be my saving grace. Finally, warm air flooded my lungs as I fell through the air.

Bam! My body hit the ground with a powerful force. I felt bruised and heavy, fighting to push myself up from the floor. I clenched my palms, feeling the warm grit of hot sand underneath them. I coughed, forcing myself up. We were in the middle of a desert. Orange and red sand surrounded us. Mounds of the crap created a dull and treacherous landscape. I looked around, finding Leenia and the twins gathering their stuff as they struggled to stand to their feet.

Bam! Levos slammed down next to me, moaning as he wiped

the sand from his face. "Shit," he grumbled.

"Right?" I turned to Voz and Oz. "You assholes didn't warn us about that part," I pushed myself up to stand, feeling as if I was being pulled back to the ground.

Voz came over, dragging his feet through the sand. "It appears," he said, huffing, "that gravity works a little differently here."

"No shit," commented Leenia.

We pulled ourselves to our feet, looking out into the vast landscape of nothingness. Sand cut against my cheeks as three suns bore down upon us. The land was barren, without vegetation or wildlife. So foreign from our home. I took a deep breath, choosing a direction randomly, praying to Azeer we would find what we had come so far for.

And so, our journey began.

Acknowledgments

This book hit differently than any other I've written to date. Incorporating new points of view and characters into this story really changed my perspective on life and myself. As an author, I believe each character embodies a part of that authors soul and very being. Having to divide yourself into multiple parts; pulling from challenging experiences while cohesively stringing a story together was challenging yet so rewarding in the end.

As I progress in my writing journey, I continue to find myself changing alongside my characters. The growth and power that these books hold and represent in my life is why I write.

As always, I want to thank my wonderful, supportive husband for everything he continues to do to support me. My friends, for picking up my books and pushing me to write faster so they can discover what happens next. My business partner Sarah, for being the soul I didn't know my life had been missing.

Thank you to my readers, for loving my books as much as I do. You are another reason why I write. Thank you for the support and the motivation to continue on. I love each of you.

ABOUT THE AUTHOR

Jessica Ann Disciacca, an Italian American from Kansas City, Missouri, holds a Master's in Educational Leadership from Northwest Missouri State University (2023). Graduating in 2015 from Park University with a diverse Bachelor's degree, she now pursues a career in educational administration while teaching.

Beyond her professional life, Jessica is an avid artist and writer, finding solace in family moments. Her lifelong passion for literature and storytelling led her to debut as an author with "Awakening the Dark Throne."

facebook.com/authorjessicaanndisciacca
instagram.com/authorjessicaanndisciacca
JessicaAnnDisciacca.com